Pra...
You Made...

"I love this novel. It has a wonde... put it down and was sorry whe...
—Eliza Clark, author of *What You Need*

"A cross between *Four Weddings and a Funeral* and *Hannah and Her Sisters*....Goodman has crafted exceedingly believable, multidimensional characters and strikes just the right tone between poignancy and melodrama."
—*Quill & Quire*

"Brimming with strong characters, sharp dialogue, and good-natured humor about human nature, *You Made Me Love You* is a sheer delight to read. It will leave you smiling and wishing for more."
—Diane Schoemperlen, author of *In the Language of Love*

"The strength of Goodman's storytelling skills, and her sure touch with the canny observation and the revelatory bits of business, elevate the material beyond the disposable beach or airplane book to make for an engaging and satisfying read....Textured, resonant domestic novels are alive and well, and *You Made Me Love You* is an enjoyable and well-crafted Canadian addition to that genre."
—*The Globe and Mail*

"Readers who are Jewish and have sisters may get a special kick from this novel, the story of three Jewish sisters raised in Toronto. But its humor and insights into family life also give it a broader appeal."
—*The Gazette* (Montreal)

"Many will relate to the pull between pleasing your well-meaning parents and trying to live your own life. Goodman captures this dilemma amazingly well."
—*National Post*

Written by today's freshest new talents and selected by New American Library, NAL Accent novels touch on subjects close to a woman's heart, from friendship to family to finding our place in the world. The Conversation Guides included in each book are intended to enrich the individual reading experience, as well as encourage us to explore these topics together—because books, and life, are meant for sharing.

Visit us online at www.penguin.com.

Also by Joanna Goodman

Belle of the Bayou

you made me love you

joanna goodman

FICTION FOR THE WAY WE LIVE

NAL Accent
Published by New American Library, a division of
Penguin Group (USA) Inc., 375 Hudson Street,
New York, New York 10014, USA
Penguin Group (Canada), 90 Eglinton Avenue East, Suite 700, Toronto,
Ontario M4P 2Y3, Canada (a division of Pearson Penguin Canada Inc.)
Penguin Books Ltd., 80 Strand, London WC2R 0RL, England
Penguin Ireland, 25 St. Stephen's Green, Dublin 2,
Ireland (a division of Penguin Books Ltd.)
Penguin Group (Australia), 250 Camberwell Road, Camberwell, Victoria 3124,
Australia (a division of Pearson Australia Group Pty. Ltd.)
Penguin Books India Pvt. Ltd., 11 Community Centre, Panchsheel Park,
New Delhi - 110 017, India
Penguin Group (NZ), cnr Airborne and Rosedale Roads, Albany,
Auckland 1310, New Zealand (a division of Pearson New Zealand Ltd.)
Penguin Books (South Africa) (Pty.) Ltd., 24 Sturdee Avenue,
Rosebank, Johannesburg 2196, South Africa

Penguin Books Ltd., Registered Offices:
80 Strand, London WC2R 0RL, England

Published by NAL Accent, an imprint of New American Library,
a division of Penguin Group (USA) Inc. Previously published in a
Penguin Group (Canada) edition.

First NAL Accent Printing, August 2006
10 9 8 7 6 5 4 3 2 1

Copyright © Joanna Goodman, 2005
Conversation Guide copyright © Penguin Group (USA) Inc., 2006
All rights reserved

FICTION FOR THE WAY WE LIVE
REGISTERED TRADEMARK—MARCA REGISTRADA

Library of Congress Cataloging-in-Publication Data

Goodman, Joanna, 1969–
You made me love you/Joanna Goodman.
p. cm.
Includes conversation guide.
ISBN 0-451-21853-1
1. Sisters—Fiction. 2. Jewish families—Fiction. 3. Man-woman relationships—Fiction.
I. Title.
PR9199.4.G6658Y68 2006
813'.6—dc22   2005058093

Printed in the United States of America

For Miguel

Estelle

*M*ake it in Hollywood.

Estelle Zarr wrote that down over a year ago in her manifestation journal. She read somewhere that writing down the purpose of one's life is a proactive way of manifesting it—the idea being that putting it on paper is a way of sending it out into the universe in a more permanent, affirmative way. Making it in Hollywood might seem rather hollow and misguided to some; but Estelle also read somewhere (probably in the same book) that *anything is possible*. (She's supposed to say that to herself every morning when she wakes up, and every night before she goes to sleep: *Anything is possible*.) She's dreamed of directing movies since the day her mother took her to see *Lies My Father Told Me*. That was her first movie in a theater and although she was only five at the time, bold ambition lodged itself in her psyche.

She is wise enough and cynical enough to know it is a dangerous ambition. But she didn't choose it. It chose her.

Now, as she gazes triumphantly at that entry in her journal, she notices with some dismay that she accidentally wrote down *Make it in Hollywound*. Nevertheless, she is most definitely on track to achieving her bold ambition. She's in the right field, anyway. Her current job editing movie trailers at a second-rate postproduction company may not be as prestigious as working for a production company like Eye Candy Post or doing postproduction on feature films, but it's a hell of an improvement over being a wingless psychic angel at Kasha's Psychic Hotline, which was her first job in L.A.

The wingless angels weren't even "accredited psychics." All they were allowed to do was read horoscopes over the phone. Estelle has no psychic ability whatsoever. She got the job because she lied and said she'd had a near-death experience when she was nine. She wrote on the application that she'd been struck by lightning. Not true. Kasha herself probably was not psychic either, but she had this frantic pink hair and a dazed, abstract personality that lent her credibility. (Her real name was Elspeth Mauer.) The job was demeaning and mind-numbing. The wingless angels couldn't even make outgoing personal calls; Kasha presided over the phone records with the calculated precision of an SS officer. Thankfully, Just-A-Trim came along, as did freelance commercial work at a company called Splice, rescuing Estelle from the world of telemarketing and catapulting her into the film industry.

"What's that?" Sally Hicks asks, poking her head into Estelle's editing suite.

Estelle shoves her journal into her knapsack. "My manifestation journal."

"Your what?"

"When I was working at the psychic hotline, I wrote down my number one ambition. A few weeks later I got this job."

"Editing B-movie trailers is your number one ambition?"

"It's a start."

Sally nods. She's almost sixty. She's been "in the industry" for more than thirty years, has watched the technology evolve from sync blocks, uprights, and flatbeds to Media Composer. Back in the day, Sally used to use a Steenbeck. She still claims a good editor should know both ways, digital and traditional, but Estelle manages just fine with digital. In fact, knowing the Avid software as well as she does is what got her most of her editing jobs.

Sally is satisfied editing trailers and commercials, the occasional lame WB sitcom. (Just-A-Trim doesn't exactly have a stellar client list.) Technically Sally's work is flawless, but she's not very creative or ambitious. She has no misgivings, though—none of the usual delusions. A rarity for L.A. Maybe it's because she's always lived here, but she's immune to that prosaic Hollywood dream that first attracted Estelle. Sally's just happy earning a living, maintaining her condo in the Valley, and entertaining her many friends, most of whom are musicians and—Sally's term—"fags." As long as she can throw swish parties, she says, she's got nothing to complain about. Not that she's critical of Estelle's ambitions; they just make her weary.

"Any feedback on J-Date yet?" Sally asks her. Sally is four foot eleven with dyed red hair. She always wears green.

"None. Not even a single e-mail."

"Be patient."

"I should have put 'toned and shapely' instead of 'medium frame,' but I wanted to be honest."

"Huh?"

"You're given a choice of adjectives to describe your body style," Estelle explains. "I chose 'medium frame.' Everyone knows that's just a euphemism for plump."

"You're not plump."

"I'm not thin."

"By whose standards?"

Estelle shrugs. "J-Date's, I guess."

J-Date is the largest Jewish singles network on the Internet. Estelle registered six weeks ago, hoping to meet

Mr. Right without having to set foot outside her apartment. Now that her career is almost in order, it's time to focus on the other entry in her manifestation journal: meet Jewish men. The search is not going very well. She's sure her failure to hook up with anyone has to do with the picture she supplied, a picture taken when she was on vacation in Santa Barbara. She was tanned and blonder than usual—it was the best snapshot she could find—but cameras don't lie.

"I think you're brave," Sally says. "Putting yourself out there like that."

"What's brave about looking for a husband on the Internet?" Estelle asks.

"Looking for a husband is brave, period."

Estelle smiles gratefully. She resumes her work, reading through Astrid's paper edit for the *Taxi to Tijuana* trailer. Astrid Blansky is the postproduction supervisor. She conceptualizes all the trailers and commercials, writes the voiceovers and paper edits, then rides the editors mercilessly until they manage to re-create her arrogant, inflexible vision.

Now Estelle starts assembling her shots and then splicing them into the time line. She clicks on her "Sex" bin and starts viewing the clips. With a movie as low-budget as *Taxi to Tijuana,* the trailer needs all the sex scenes she can find. The premise is moronic. It's a romantic comedy in which a woman—the busty, dim-witted Sheila—hails a cab in downtown L.A. and begs the driver to take her to Tijuana. It turns out she murdered her boyfriend and is on the lam. Dano, the cabdriver, is enchanted with Sheila and obliges. They fall in love on the road and hilarious antics ensue. There are virtually no redeeming qualities to the picture.

Enter Estelle, whose job it is to make the film look enticing, funny, and worth eight bucks. No small task, but she has a knack for making the most hideous movie look promising, or taking the blandest trailer and infusing it with edgy artistry. Which is why she endures her job at Just-A-Trim. She knows Avid editors are in demand. She's just biding her time, slowly building a reputation. She's already edited a couple of music videos for friends of friends and, a few months ago, she edited a documentary called *The Key Party,* about couples who swing. There may also be an indie film in the works, if her neighbor, Peri, lands the director of photography job and can give her a recommendation. Connections are vital in L.A. She even got a call from the creators of Bubble Video last month. They'd just sold the rights for Bubble Video to Channel 4 in the U.K. and wanted her to fly out to London to teach them how to edit the show on Avid. The gig fell through, but what matters is they called *her*.

She is close to where she wanted to be at thirty-six. Of course, her childhood imaginings included a husband and children, but times are different now. Her generation has bumped marriage age up by about a decade. (Except Jessie, who was married and pregnant by twenty-two, which, Estelle thinks, is more of a Jewish, not a generational, thing.) Still, Estelle is now pushing the boundaries of even *her* generation's marriage age. Don't think that doesn't nag at her (by way of her mother's voice) day in and day out. Luckily, most of her L.A. friends are still single. What matters to them is where they're at in their careers. In that context, she can hold her head up fairly high. She hasn't exactly achieved great success yet, but she's *here* at least, in L.A. That's something.

Now she selects a few clips from the bin and puts together a short montage of sex scenes: necking in the backseat of the cab, Dano's hand moving up Sheila's thigh, a hint of breast, just enough to tantalize. Then she clicks on the "Funny Scene" bin and starts cutting that one into the time line. She plays it back. It's the one scene that may generate a chuckle, only because it's penis humor. If you ask her, it's a blatant rip-off of *Grease:* the scene where Sandy slams the car door on Danny's balls at the drive-in.

There's a knock on her door. Estelle glances up from her source monitor to find Astrid standing in the doorway, waving a DVD. "I got some feedback on the *Storm Watch 2004* trailer," she says.

Estelle gets up and follows Astrid into her office. Astrid presses play on the DVD player. "First of all," she says, snapping a wad of green gum, "get rid of the lion. It doesn't belong in the trailer."

"It's one of the few nice shots—"

"The producer wants the lion out." She fast-forwards several seconds. "Then over here, you've got a jump cut, see?"

"Right."

"And there should be a scene of the two leads kissing. There's that kiss in the gondola, remember? Right before the avalanche? That should be in there."

Estelle nods.

"And it's too long. You're over five minutes. It feels like a short film."

"I'll clean it up after I finish cutting *Taxi to Tijuana*."

"Do it now. Okay?"

Estelle takes the DVD and leaves. She stops in Sally's editing suite, then Ruby's, then Luca's, rounding them up for a smoke break and a session of Astrid-bashing. Estelle is the Pied Piper of Just-A-Trim; throughout the day, they will all come to her at some point—the sound designer, the dialogue editor, the other picture editors. They come for a joke, a story, technical advice, gossip. She is admired and appreciated, not just because she is a tech wizard, but for her wit and imagination. She fills a room.

"Fucking Astrid," she complains. "I'll never finish *Taxi to Tijuana* before I leave for Toronto."

"You're going home?"

"My parents already sent me the plane ticket." She inhales deeply from her cigarette. "I can't get out of it. The Life Network is airing an *Intimate Canadian Life Story* on my father. He wants us all to be there and watch it together."

"What is it?"

"It's like an A&E *Biography.*"

"Your dad's famous?"

Estelle nods blandly. "He's a singer. He had a show in the sixties."

"Would we know him?"

"It was a Canadian show."

"That's something," Sally says, sounding impressed.

"So my mother's lined me up with another one of her blind dates," Estelle tells them. "For my first night back. This one's supposed to be very successful. He has his own company."

Sally puts out her cigarette. "Listen, kiddo," she says, "I can lay down your music and Foley, if that helps."

"It totally would. Thanks."

Sally winks and turns to go back inside.

"Now," says Estelle, "I've just got to lose thirty pounds by Thursday."

At the end of another long day, Estelle starts gathering up her things. She's bleary-eyed and a little delirious from having spent too many hours in the cab with Sheila and Dano. She decides to check her e-mails before clearing out of the suite.

Elliot, her assistant editor, arrives while she's launching Outlook Express. Poor, eager Elliot works the five-to-two-A.M. shift—Estelle's old job.

"I'm finished logging the mattress commercial," he tells her.

"Then you can redigitize everything in my 'Taxi Scene' bin."

He nods obligingly.

"Also, can you output an EDL of reel two?"

"No problem."

She kisses his cheek. "Thank you, sweetie."

She stares at the monitor in disbelief as her new e-mails come up. She blinks. Aside from the usual junk mail, there's one message: J-Date access code 45681. Screen name: Ronnie.

Her first bite.

Jessie

*J*essie Jaffe glances out the kitchen window and gasps. She drops her glass of iced tea on the linoleum, smashing it. The tea splatters everywhere, blotting her new suit with beige stains. She bangs on the window and, thinking they will hear her, screams through the glass, "GET OFF THE GRASS! GET OFF THE GRASS!"

Neither of them looks up. She flings open the back door and hurls herself at them on the lawn. "Get off the grass!" she shrieks. "I told you about the grass!"

They both look up at her, startled. "But, Mom—"

"They sprayed!" she rails. "They *sprayed!* I told you not to go *near* the grass!"

She scoops Ilana into her arms and drags Levi by the arm back inside the house. "Levi, I told you a million times to keep your sister away from the grass after they spray."

"But they sprayed yesterday!" he protests.

"That's not long enough! Those are dangerous chemicals they spray on the lawn, Levi. Remember, we talked about this?"

He nods morosely.

"What did I tell you would happen if you played on the grass?"

"Cancer."

"That's right."

"Cancer," Ilana repeats.

"I'm going to put you in a bath," Jessie says.

"Aw, Mom—"

Ilana starts to cry. "Baths are for before bed!" she wails.

"Baths are to *wash chemicals off* children who don't listen."

She takes them upstairs and into the bathroom, where they strip and hand over their offending clothes. The clothes go directly into the hamper. Later, they will be bleached. She runs the water and fills the tub with about three inches of water, never higher than Ilana's belly button. She's not in the mood for this today. She's already frazzled about having to spend an entire weekend with her parents. It's not them so much as Gladys. She hates that Gladys Gold will be there—is *always* there—celebrating with them, impinging. Gladys with her high-pitched voice and the way she's always saying to Jessie's father, "*Remember* this, *Milty*? *Remember* that?"

She plunks the kids in the tub and starts scrubbing Ilana's face and hands with the loofah.

"Mom, what does our last name mean?" Levi asks her.

"I don't think it means anything."

"Kyla Kirshbaum's last name means 'cherry tree' and Jordan Birnbaum's name means 'pear tree.' What does ours mean?"

"I don't know what Jaffe means," Jessie admits. "But I know that your first name means 'joined.'"

"Joined to what?"

"Just joined."

"To what?"

Jessie sighs. "To God," she says impatiently.

"What does Ilana mean?"

"Tree."

"And what about Daddy's name? What does Allan mean?"

"Allan means 'never does laundry,'" she mutters, then proceeds to scrub them until their pale skin is raw.

"How come th' other kids can play on the grass?" Ilana asks.

Jessie wraps a bath sheet around her daughter and rubs her back affectionately. "Because their mommies don't love them as much as I love you."

Satisfied, Ilana buries her nose in Jessie's neck. Levi looks less convinced.

She settles them down in front of the TV and pops in an Olsen twins video. Then she goes into the bathroom and slumps against the sink. She takes two aspirin and stares at her weary face in the mirror.

She is twenty-nine. Keeping her children out of danger is taking its toll; she feels fifty. She keeps expecting to peer into the mirror and see gray hair, a bent posture. The other day Ilana innocently pointed out that there were stripes around her eyes. Jessie laughed at first, not understanding. Then Ilana traced her fingers along Jessie's crow's-feet. "Stripes!" she declared.

Not yet thirty and she's already got wrinkles. Allan tried to reassure her in his own aloof, misguided way; he bought her a book called *Aging Gracefully: Embrace the Wrinkles!*

She called Lilly and wept. "I feel so old, Mom."

"You're still a baby," Lilly said. "A *baby*. You're only in your twenties."

"Not for long."

"I had a crisis at twenty-nine too."

"This isn't a crisis. I'm just old."

Allan once mentioned having another baby to get her mind off her stripes. He said if she's got enough time for so much introspection and self-pity, they could surely squeeze in a third kid. She wasn't sure if he was serious, but he never brought it up again. Regardless, he doesn't understand how exhausted she is between the two they've got now and her job. He thinks her company runs itself; that any career other than being a doctor is inferior, invalid. Never mind that he has become a diet guru rather than a healer. As long as he's got the M.D. tacked onto the end of his name, he can be as smug as he likes.

She rubs her temples. Her head is killing her. She was on her cell phone for hours today, probably sending waves of radiation directly into her skull. God only knows what kind of damage she's inflicting with that thing. She's got the Motorola StarTAC 130, which has the lowest SAR rating based on the cell-phone radiation chart she downloaded off the Internet. But still, who knows?

She goes back down to the kitchen and, ignoring the tea and broken glass on the floor, she pulls the phone book out of the pantry.

"Mom?" Levi cries out.

"Stay out of the kitchen!" she yells. "There's broken glass! Don't come anywhere near here!"

She finds the number for Motorola. Another phone call, just to be sure.

"Mom?" From out in the living room.

"Levi, I said don't come near the kitchen until all the broken pieces are gone!"

She hears herself yelling and the sound of her own voice fills her with dread. Allan calls her a screamer, begs her not to yell so much around the house. She tries. God, she tries. But there's always something. She sees them flinch every time she raises her voice and it makes her want to grovel for forgiveness and undo the damage she's causing. And yet if she catches Ilana playing with the dirty change in her wallet or if Levi sneaks a burger instead of a Filet-o-Fish or a salad at a McDonald's birthday party, she explodes. (He knows he's forbidden to eat red meat, but can she trust him when she's not there?) She puts all her energy into protecting them—from germs and bacteria, mishaps, pesticides, strangers, and now an alarming new crop of diseases like mad cow, SARS, and West Nile. If she can't watch them every minute of the day, she can at least put the fear of God in them. How else do you teach children to be careful?

Estelle says she's going to turn them into petrified, neurotic adults. How easy to pass judgment when one is childless and self-indulgent, erratic. Estelle has no concept of what it means to be a parent, to hold two precious lives in your inadequate hands. Estelle can't even quit smoking, let alone run an entire family. Overseeing the lives of a four- and a six-year-old is a formidable operation. It's easy for Estelle to criticize from the safe confines of her frivolous life in L.A. Even Allan is impervious to the demands of motherhood. He may call her a "screamer," but without her relentless supervision, their babies might not survive a single day. Who else would have pulled them out of nursery and junior kindergarten when SARS broke out? Or when the Iraq war started?

Fear and freedom are parallel lines; they never meet. They can never be experienced together. The problem is, she has not figured out how to cross over, not even temporarily. The gap between them is so vast and insurmountable. Freedom is absolute oblivion. It is all the things that are out of her realm of possibility: roller coasters at Canada's Wonderland, bare feet on grass, a conversation with a stranger, a spontaneous trip, a deep, undisturbed sleep.

"Mom?" Levi steps tentatively into the kitchen.

"Levi!"

"I have socks on."

Jessie hoists Levi off the floor and sets him down on the table. She examines the bottoms of his feet. "You think glass can't go through a sock?"

He shrugs.

"Do you do it on purpose, Lee?"

"What?"

"If I say don't come into the kitchen, why do you?"

"Because I have to ask you something."

"But you can see the broken glass everywhere. Can't your question wait two minutes?"

He rolls up his sleeve and shoves his arm at her. "Is this cancer?"

She examines his arm. There's a burgeoning rash on his skin, probably from all her scrubbing. Her heart cracks. She pulls him into her arms. "Of course not, Levi," she soothes. "It's just a little rash from where I scrubbed you. I guess I scrubbed too hard." She strokes his damp black hair.

"Are you sure?" he whimpers.

She nods, feeling guilty. Bad mother, bad mother. Maybe she *is* creating little worrywarts, perfect replicas of herself. And both of her damaged children will be on display this weekend for her two judgmental sisters to observe and critique with sanctimony.

Erica

*P*rofessor Van der Heyden sets his chalk down with much satisfaction and steps away from the blackboard. Scribbled there behind him are the words

> *Interior Monologue = places reader in character's HEAD. Expression of unexpressed thoughts. Description vs I.M. Dialogue vs I.M. Perils of overuse!!*

"And now the celebrated epiphany passage from *A Portrait of the Artist* ..."

He opens his book—an old burgundy hardcover from his personal collection—and begins to read in a booming, melodramatic voice. "'Her image had passed into his soul forever and no word had broken the holy silence of his ecstasy. . . .'"

He pauses for a moment and scans the classroom, a vain attempt to gauge the interest level of his students. Professor Van der Heyden is one of those self-important teachers who isn't satisfied with just teaching; he wants to enchant and mesmerize. He wants to perform! The more Erica knows about him, the more she finds his classroom demeanor absurd. He doesn't need to entertain. He's a brilliant writer, a legend. He's written nine novels (two of them nominated for National Book Awards) and three collections of short stories. He's a regular contributor to *The New Yorker* and a reviewer for *The New York Times Book Review,* and he's only forty-six.

His reputation is plenty enchanting without him needing to grandstand.

Erica thinks his shtick is also an attempt to be the resident heartthrob of Columbia's creative writing community. He seems to want to portray himself as a sexually viable yet unattainable literary genius, and he accomplishes this by exploiting both his charisma and his students' blind worship. He's witty, he's opinionated, and he's attractive in a hapless sort of way—but he knows it. Still, that he manages to be in possession of both a buff body and a brilliant literary mind does add to his mystique, self-conscious and overcultivated though it may be.

But that's just Erica's opinion, which today, admittedly, is rather cynical. She's not in the mood for James Joyce or for Professor Van der Heyden's antics; she's got other, more pressing things on her mind, like having to go home for the weekend.

Her father sent her the plane ticket, so she couldn't get out of it. It's supposed to be a happy occasion—a family reunion, among other things—but she's decided to tell them her news anyway. She knows it will shatter any possibility for a peaceful visit, but that's never stopped her before.

"'Her eyes had called him and his soul had leaped at the call!'" Professor Van der Heyden continues. And then he rather indiscreetly gazes across the room at Erica. She glares back at him, seething. She notices the faintest smile forming on his lips—for a moment she thinks he's going to wink at her—and then he resumes reading. "'To live, to err, to fall, to triumph, to re-create life out of life!'" he thunders. All of a sudden he slaps the book shut and stares wildly into the class.

"Now *that* my friends, is an interior monologue!"

*   *   *

*E*rica is what's known as a Creative Writing Nondegree Student. In other words, she wasn't accepted into the Master of Fine Arts Writing Program and so she audits these writing workshops for no credit. Paul is the one who encouraged her to apply to Columbia's MFA program in the first place. When she didn't get accepted, it was his idea for her to attend the workshops anyway; he thought it would be a good place for her to "polish her diamond."

The goal is to spend one year writing, and then reapply to the MFA. He thinks with his help, and the help of the other professors—all of them brilliant authors in their own right—she has an excellent chance of getting accepted next year. He says the only reason she wasn't accepted the first time is that her pieces are still "rough." The bones are there, he assures her. What she needs is practice; she needs fine-tuning. It's not her fault she's a late bloomer. Up until very recently, she thought she was going to be a photographer. She moved to New York to do the one-year certificate program at the International Center of Photography, which included a photo-journalism course, but realized midway through that she was a technical dyslexic. Although she felt she had a good eye and that creatively she was a natural, the technical side of photography—lighting, developing, loading the film into the camera—held her back artistically. The light meter was her nemesis, and she couldn't manage to produce a single picture that wasn't grainy. Her shots were either underexposed or overexposed, if they were even exposed at all. A successful roll was when an image emerged on the negative. (Her standards for success deteriorated as the year wore on.)

After the photography course, which she came very close

to completing, she signed up for a level-one class at the Upright Citizens Brigade and tried her hand at improv. Creatively, she has always felt as though she's bursting at the seams. Something inside her is screaming to get out and she figured if it couldn't come out of her camera, maybe she could let it out onstage. For although there has been some question as to what *sort* of artist she is, the fact that she *is* an artist is something she herself has never questioned.

When she was a child of five or six, she wanted to grow up to be rain. Grown-ups were always asking her that question. *What do you want to be when you grow up, dear?*

"Rain," Erica would answer decisively. And the grown-ups always laughed.

It was Jessie who told her one day, in the most belittling voice, that it was impossible to grow up to be rain. Erica was crushed. She resented Jessie for having wrecked her plans, and also for lacking imagination.

And then Gramma Dorothy said she thought Erica would grow up to be a poet. She said Erica had an artist's soul. Erica has never forgotten that, especially because it came from her grandmother.

It was during her stint at the UCB Theater that Erica happened to read a book called *Breedy's Will,* which blew her mind. It was about an adopted woman who sued her natural half aunt for a mammoth inheritance; it was scathing and funny and the characters—especially the women—were tenderly rendered and utterly memorable. It was Dickensian in its ambition. And although it might have been a compelling family saga in the most mainstream, *Oprah* sense of the genre, the superb (though somewhat dense) writing, which never wavered, and the highbrow subject matter (estate laws, domestic relations amendments, et cetera) elevated it just beyond the grubby clutches of the masses, so that it never found its way onto the bestseller list. In short, it astounded Erica. When she heard that the author was going to be signing books at the Barnes & Noble on Fifth, she headed straight down there. And when she saw how cute he was, she asked him out.

Paul is terrifyingly clever and accomplished, but just insecure enough to make him accessible. (Otherwise, she never would have been able to ask him out.) He's got a complex about his teeth, for one thing. The left front tooth slightly overlaps the right one, which makes him feel "trailer-parkish," presumably because he couldn't afford braces as a teenager. He's also got a nerd complex, the clinging residue from his high school years. Even though he really is quite handsome now, no amount of literary success or weight lifting can erase the post-traumatic stress of having egg sandwiches smeared in his face regularly for five years. (Something he tearfully confessed to Erica one night over a bottle of wine.)

And in return for taking care of him, both emotionally and around the house, he nurtures her creativity; he reads all her poems and encourages her to send them out to the literary magazines. He buys her journals so she can write (or "stream," as he calls it) every morning. He compiles reading lists for her. He critiques her short stories and poems without ever diminishing her. He takes charge of her writing; he guides her and provides structure so she can be prolific. And of course, he supports her financially, so that the writing is possible.

Her current dilemma is about this upcoming weekend: her parents don't know about Paul. They don't know that a) her lover is forty-six years old, b) that he's not Jewish, and c) that she's living with him. All three circumstances are sure to offend them. Not that her path up till this point has ever pleased them. Her adolescence was turbulent. Her parents claim she's lacked direction from as far back as they can remember. (*Is it possible to already be floundering in kindergarten?* her father once joked.) Her pattern has generally been characterized by a sudden, all-consuming latching on to something or someone. She has latched on to styles: mod, 1988; grunge, 1992; rave, 1997; and these days, aspiring literati. She has latched on to people: friends, lovers, mentors. She has latched on to substances: pot, acid, alcohol, cigarettes. But most of all, she has latched on to what her father has dubbed her "passion du jour." These have included (in no particular order) poetry, painting, sculpture, writing, photography, drama, backup singing for a local ska band, cake-decorating, and collage-making.

Estelle calls her Zelig—but is it her fault she can't seem to settle on one singular outlet for her creativity? It's easy for her sisters; Jessie's got no artistic talent whatsoever and Estelle excels in only one area. So what to some might be perceived as "floundering"—her father's favorite word— Erica thinks is really just an unwillingness to limit herself.

*A*fter the workshop, during which Professor Van der Heyden spent the better part of three hours dissecting someone's short story about a rabbi forced to choose between his love for an Islamic fundamentalist and the rabbinate (he called it prosaic, unimaginative, and stolid), Erica grabs her notebook and rushes out of the classroom.

Professor Van der Heyden follows her into the corridor. "Erica?"

"I'm late," she says, hurrying out of Lewisohn Hall.

He walks beside her for a couple of blocks, not saying

anything. Students are spilling onto Broadway from Columbia, Barnard, and the Manhattan School of Music. Erica and Professor Van der Heyden continue along past 112th, where still more students, these from Bank Street College, are filling the streets. The hilly enclave of churches and schools in Morningside Heights makes the entire neighborhood feel like one giant campus—serene and secluded, an oasis for the city's religious, artistic, and intellectual elite. And in the fall, with everything tinted red and orange as it is today, it's all the more captivating; this is the way New York is meant to look. It makes Erica feel safe and privileged and slightly removed from the seedier parts of the city. She loves living here, loves being part of a community that is sustained on ambition and talent and the pursuit of excellence, a community that thrives on achieving.

"What did you think of that short story?" he asks her.

"You were hard on her."

"Come on. She was pandering to the headlines. An Islamic fundamentalist and a rabbi?"

"Calling it 'stolid' was a bit much," Erica says. "It was better than anything *I've* written."

"Your pieces might be raw, but they're not maudlin."

She hates it when he calls her stories "pieces." It makes them sound unfinished, inconsequential, as though they don't merit being called stories.

"Will you call me when you get to Toronto?" he asks her.

She shrugs.

"Were you going to say good-bye?" he asks. "Or are you punishing me?"

"I'm late for my flight. Don't take it personally."

"Erica, come on. I know why you're doing this—"

"You should come with me, then," she sulks.

"They don't even know I exist. I really don't think it's

appropriate for me to just show up uninvited and announce that we're living together."

"You think I feel like telling them by myself?"

"They're *your* parents."

"I want you to be there when I tell them. I want you to meet them."

"Next time. I promise." They turn onto 108th Street and he stops her. "Don't go away angry."

She doesn't want to go away angry. She wants him to hold her right there on the street; but she also wants her way.

She looks up at him. "I want you to come."

He smiles. (God, those beautiful white teeth. She even loves the way they overlap.) She reaches over and runs a hand through his hair, which is thick and soft and mostly gray. The only trace left of blond is in his beard. He's always reminded her of an older, more bookish Tim Robbins. His credentials don't hurt either.

"I really am late," she says, her tone softening.

They walk to the end of the block and turn onto Riverside Drive, at which point they arrive directly in front of their apartment building, a prewar neoclassical that was converted to co-ops in the early seventies. The limestone façade, which is decorated with cornices and balconies, overlooks Riverside Park. Erica still can't get over it; every time she sets foot inside the lobby, she feels like a Fitzgerald character or some Upper West Side socialite who summers in the Hamptons. (In fact, Paul has mentioned spending a weekend in Sag Harbor this July.)

They ride the elevator up to the fourteenth floor, holding hands and nuzzling each other's necks. Paul's five-room apartment—which he now shares with Erica—is a prodigious step up from her former hovel in the East Village. It's got high ceilings, plasterwork moldings, walnut paneling, dark parquet floors, and a gasp-worthy view of both the park and the Hudson River. In light of the real-estate horror stories she's heard from countless New York neophytes, she has no idea what she did to deserve to live in such a palace (although sleeping with a successful author does come to mind).

"Are you packed?" he asks her, dumping his keys on the antique mahogany secretary in the foyer.

"I threw some things on the bed this morning—"

"Love," he says. "Don't worry. Your parents will be fine about this."

"You don't know Lilly and Milton."

He pulls her into his arms. "How bad can it be?" he asks naively.

"Put it this way," Erica says. "When I told my mother I wasn't graduating from college, she covered all the mirrors in our house."

"What for?"

"It's a custom when someone dies."

"But I'm a famous author," he reminds her, sounding slightly wounded. "Won't that impress them?"

"There's a 'Van' in your last name," she says, taking his hand and kissing it to console him. "Trust me. That'll over-shadow all your good points."

Estelle

"You're wearing *that?* Pants from the army?"

"They're cargo pants. Everyone's wearing cargo pants."

Gramma Dorothy looks her up and down. "What do you need all those pockets for?"

Lilly comes out of the kitchen then. "You're not wearing those awful pants tonight, are you?" She touches the fabric and grimaces.

"She says they're cargo pants," Dorothy explains.

"Are you going on a date or to boot camp?" Lilly asks.

"Muh, please."

"They make you look frumpy. You don't need all those bulky pockets on your thighs, Bean. Don't you have some nice slacks?"

"Slacks?"

"And the black sweater makes you look so somber. But if that's the impression you want to make on Yossel—"

"Yossel?" Estelle shrieks. "Who did you set me up with? The fiddler on the roof?"

"He's very successful."

In the end, despite her showy protest, Estelle skulks back into her room and takes off the cargo pants and black sweater, cursing her mother's victory.

*   *   *

*H*aving changed into something a lot more elegant, Estelle was hoping Yossel Schvok would take her to Jump or Canoe, or one of those chichi downtown restaurants where they put baskets of homemade flatbreads with hummus on the table. He's supposed to be successful. He's supposed to be a real big shot, that's what Lilly promised. Instead, they're at Lick's sitting in a vinyl booth with squeeze bottles of ketchup and mustard. She should have kept the cargo pants on.

"You ever play Tropico?" he asks, looking up from his menu.

"What's that?"

"It's a computer game. You know, it's like SimCity? You have to build your own island, right? You're *el presidente* and you control this island and you have to make it successful. . . ."

She's already gone. She checked out of the date about the time he showed up at her parents' place. Her first thought was: he's George Costanza. His shirt was half untucked and he was wearing those chinos with pleats in front, from Eddie Bauer or something. She hates chinos. It's the telltale sign of indifference to style. He's stocky and sloppy and he's got two black earmuffs of hair with nothing on top.

The waitress comes along to take their orders and Yossel tells her he wants spaghetti, but instead of the salad, he wants french fries on the side at no extra charge.

"The spaghetti comes with a salad," she says. "Fries are extra."

"So instead of the salad, you'll give me french fries."

"Fries are more expensive than salad. I'll have to charge you."

"That's ridiculous. Why should potatoes cost more than lettuce?"

"The special includes a side salad," she tells him. "I can't just give you a free order of fries."

"What difference does it make to you if I have fries or salad? What are we debating here?"

"It's not part of the special," she says wearily. "Salad is."

"All right," he says. "Charge me for the fries, but make sure you deduct the cost of a salad from my bill."

"Are you serious?"

"It's the principle," he says.

Estelle is secretly plotting the execution of her mother. She's praying for her cell phone to ring, anything to get out of this. It's still early. She can still hook up with some old Ryerson friends and go out.

"My mother tells me you're an entrepreneur," she says, scrambling to make conversation.

"I have my own business."

"Doing what?"

"You ever eat hot dogs or pepperoni?"

"I guess so."

"Well, I manufacture the plastic casings for sausages. All kinds of sausages. Name the wiener, it's probably my casing."

She stares at him, dumbfounded, not sure where to go from here. A few years ago she was watching a documentary on PBS where they actually interviewed a poultry historian. Until this moment, she thought poultry historian had to be the most obscure career in existence.

But that coveted title has now been usurped by sausage-casing manufacturer.

What she can't believe is the quality of the dating pool her parents are culling from; she can't believe that this neb represents their best hopes for her.

Erica

She grabs her suitcase and heads out of the baggage claim. She takes a breath, knowing they'll start in on her right away. *Have you found a job yet? Have you met someone? Have you been to the Holocaust Museum yet? When are you moving back to Toronto?* (In other words, when will you be giving up and coming back home with your tail between your legs *again?*)

She spots them in the arrivals area, planted front and center of the crowd, waving frenetically and bellowing out her name in a reception worthy of the Iranian hostages. "Erica! Over here, darling! Here we are!"

As if she could miss them. They hardly blend inconspicuously into the crowd; he's barely five-foot-three with a shock of curly salt-and-pepper hair (his pride and joy), wearing a leather jacket and cowboy boots with sweatpants. Her mother is always well turned-out; maybe too well turned-out for an airport. Her hair is dyed several shades lighter than its natural blond and looks a bit like spun sugar. She's wearing an electric-blue pashmina shawl draped across one shoulder and a pair of sunglasses perched on her head.

Milton smothers Erica with kisses, then grabs her suitcase.

"You look so young, Muh," she says.

"Laser surgery," Lilly confides, beaming. "I feel forty again."

"How's our baby?" Milton asks, tousling her hair.

"A little tired."

"I hope you're hungry," Lilly says, caressing Erica's cheek. They head out of Pearson and into the indoor lot where Milton's Mercedes is parked.

"You sit in the front," Lilly says.

"No, Mom. I'll get in the back. It's fine."

Lilly smiles, looking relieved. "Estelle was quick to take the front seat," she murmurs reproachfully. "Do you see how different they are, Milty?"

"Estelle thinks she's a princess."

"Milt," Lilly says, "get in the right lane. Don't get on the 401! Get on the 427 so we can take the Gardiner!"

"Why don't you get out and take the 427 and let me drive where I want?"

*T*heir condo on Front Street is a far cry from the mansion where Erica grew up. Their old place was a fortress at the corner of Old Forest Hill and Russell Hill roads, a four-story, redbrick Georgian enclosed by a wrought-iron gate, with a front yard that resembled an English countryside estate. It had a heated circular driveway, leaded-glass bay windows, and it overlooked a ravine. Lilly had a fountain put in and a sprawling English garden that she tended to compulsively. The old place was Lilly's statement, a testament to her wealth and good taste. It was designed from the top of its cathedral ceilings right down to its broadloomed basement to entertain and impress.

But these days, Lilly and Milton both prefer condo living for a number of reasons—low maintenance, less space to rattle around in, a swimming pool on the ninth floor, a doorman to greet them and keep them safe, and an indoor parking garage to ensure shovel-free winters. There's also the St. Lawrence Market across the street and the HotHouse Café buffet downstairs, which they attend faithfully every Sunday morning.

Dorothy looks up from the book she's reading. Her round blue eyes brighten at the sight of her youngest granddaughter. "The last of the *yentas* is home!" she exclaims. She rises to her feet, using the sofa for leverage, and holds out her arms. "Come here!"

Erica goes over to her and they embrace. "You're shrinking," Erica remarks, patting her grandmother's puffy silver curls.

Dorothy laughs, revealing that famous Cynamon overbite. Old age has a way of diminishing beauty that only a rare few can defy, but Dorothy, despite her stooped posture and arthritic hands, has the sort of exquisite face that time has gracefully preserved. Her skin is heavily wrinkled—the result of having almost no body fat—and most of her bottom teeth are false, but up close, her fine Polish features have held up.

"What're you reading?" Erica asks her. Ever since she met Paul, she likes to know what everyone is reading. As he says, it tells you all you need to know about a person.

Dorothy looks at the cover of her book, as if she can't remember what it is since she put it aside three seconds ago. *"An Unfinished Woman."*

"I've never heard of it," Erica admits, silently admonishing herself for her ignorance.

"Hellman," Dorothy says matter-of-factly. "Lillian Hellman. When are you moving back home? I miss you."

"I like New York," Erica responds, stung.

"It's such a hard city," Dorothy laments. "It'll change you, if you stay long enough. You're better off here—"

"Where's Estelle?" Erica asks, interrupting.

"On a blind date," Milton says. "Your mother fixed her up with Hildi Schvok's son."

"Guess what I'm making tomorrow night for supper?" Lilly interjects. "My famous Cornflake Catalina Chicken."

Erica forces a smile. While Lilly may be the spitting image of her mother in all ways physical, culinary flair is not something she inherited from Gramma Dorothy. Or maybe it was an outright rebellion; she's always refused to use her mother's old recipes. Instead, she's created her own, with a little help from Kraft. Lilly's two favorite ingredients are garlic powder and any kind of Kraft sauce she can get her hands on—salad dressing or jam or mayonnaise. For instance, chicken is rolled in cornflakes, smothered in Catalina dressing, and then baked; meat loaf is smothered in peppercorn ranch and then baked; meatballs are drowned in a sauce of ketchup and plum jelly; even her spaghetti sauce has a "secret" ingredient: nonfat Italian-style dressing, in lieu of olive oil.

"Milty, don't forget to pick up the chickens tomorrow," Lilly says.

"It's all under control."

"I want grain-fed, remember. You have to be so careful these days," she warns him. "Oy, with the bacteria and the diseases. You make sure they don't have the bird flu, Milton."

"These aren't just ordinary chickens I'm getting," Milton boasts. "I'm getting them from Ungerman!"

"Who's Ungerman?"

"Ungerman's got the best, healthiest chickens in Toronto. And I'm getting them for *free*."

"For free?" Erica echoes, alarmed. She knows there must be some complex scheme involved, probably an elaborate bartering system. "How?"

"Ungerman's mother-in-law needs a new valve on her washing machine. I'm going to replace it, in exchange for the chickens."

"You're not a plumber," Dorothy points out. "How can you change a valve? You don't even know what a valve looks like."

"That's the beauty," Milton gushes. "My plumber, Gino, is going to do it as a favor to me."

"A favor for *what?*"

"For singing at his daughter's wedding in June."

"Why don't you just *pay* for the chickens, Dad?"

Milton looks offended. "Pay for them? Why?"

"Why should he pay for them, darling?" Lilly asks. "Grain-fed chickens are very expensive."

"Because Toronto isn't a Turkish bazaar."

Milton shrugs. "Says who?"

*E*rica passes the rest of the evening waiting for a window of opportunity to tell them about her new living arrangement. She knows with Lilly there will be a scene. She wants it over with so she can relax the rest of the weekend. At least her grandmother can be counted on for support, if for no other reason than her own past.

"So you're taking a class," Lilly chirps. "A class about what, darling?"

"It's a writing workshop."

"I always said you had a poet's sensibility," Dorothy tells her.

"So there's no credit?" Lilly says.

"No, but it's a great opportunity for me to fine-tune my craft."

"But it doesn't *count* for anything?"

"I'm putting together a portfolio, which should help me to get accepted into the MFA next fall—"

"Any husband potential at Columbia?"

"That's not why I'm there."

"Still. You're twenty-eight. You should be thinking about it. It's good to get marriage over with and out of the way. Like brushing your teeth in the morning. Then you don't have to think about it anymore."

"You can stop worrying," Erica says, emboldened. "I'm seeing someone."

Lilly's face brightens. "What does he do?"

"He's a writer. A very successful writer." She looks over at her grandmother, hoping for some sign of allegiance. "He's written nine novels and he's a reviewer for the—"

"Nine novels?" Milton says. "How old is he?"

"Forty-six."

Lilly gasps. The color drains from her rouged cheeks.

"He's my professor," Erica explains.

"You're dating your professor?"

"Actually, I'm living with him," she blurts. "I moved out of my place on Avenue A and I'm living with Paul now. It's a beautiful apartment on the Upper West Side, very safe—"

"What do you mean 'living with him'?" Lilly shrieks.

"What's his last name?" Milton asks, as if this matters somehow.

"Van der Heyden."

"Van der Heyden?" they all cry. *"Van der Heyden?"*

"What is he? A German?"

"It's Dutch—he's a writer," Erica adds, looking beseechingly at her grandmother again, hoping to elicit some shred of sympathy or recognition—maybe even a little pride. *Help me!* she silently begs. But Dorothy appears to be as baffled as Lilly and Milton.

"Don't make her an accomplice," Lilly says icily. "Your grandmother may have had some poems published, but that doesn't mean she wants you living with your professor any more than we do—"

"Lilly," Dorothy says, "don't speak for me."

Lilly starts pacing. She throws her head back and looks up at the ceiling. "My daughter is living with her middle-aged professor!" she announces incredulously. (She has this habit of addressing God in her moments of indignation and crisis, usually informing Him of her misfortune in bitter, angry tones; as though He doesn't know what's going on until she tells Him.)

Erica suddenly remembers Paul's parting words—*How bad can it be?*—and she wants to call him up and give him shit for making her do this alone.

"And you're not working?" Milton asks. "He supports you?"

"Just while I'm developing my portfolio."

Lilly lets out a small whimper; she seems to be moving through the five stages of Jewish mother-grief, her expression morphing from bliss to shock to denial to outrage and finally settling on the one Erica likes to call "shattered dreams."

Lilly

*L*illy turns around when Estelle stumbles into the kitchen for breakfast. The rest of them are already eating lunch. "I heard you come in at three in the morning," Lilly remarks.

"I went out with friends."

"What about Yossel?"

"Yossel manufactures sausage wrappers for a living," Estelle responds. Erica laughs. "What the hell did you think we'd have in common, Muh?"

"He has a good sense of humor."

"Just don't ever set me up again, I don't care if the guy owns his own airplane."

"I found a pack of cigarettes in your jacket pocket," Lilly says.

"You went through my pockets?"

"I was hanging up your jacket. You left it in a heap on my floor before you passed out on the couch."

Estelle ignores her and hugs Erica.

"You look great, Bean," Erica says.

Bean has been Estelle's nickname since the girls were old enough to speak. It's a derivative of Jelly Bean, which eventually mutated into Estelly Bean, and finally, just Bean. A long time ago, all the girls went by nicknames. Erica was Tick because she was so tiny, and Jessie was called . . . Lilly can't even remember. Jessie was never a "nickname" girl anyway; anything other than her own name always seemed too playful, too light. Estelle's is the only one that stuck.

"Do you want leftover roast beef?" Lilly asks Estelle. "Or I've got tabouleh from Pusateri's." She starts pulling everything out. Little packages wrapped in tinfoil. "And there's some cold chicken I think might still be good. Here's a *knish*—"

Estelle sits down at the table. "Are there any bagels?"

"Are there any bagels," Lilly repeats, exasperated. "Have you ever known me not to have bagels? In the freezer."

"I'll have two," she says. "Toasted with butter and cream cheese."

"Butter and cream cheese?" Lilly moans, pulling a bag of St. Urbain bagels out of the freezer. "Why don't I just spread them right on your rear end?"

"I want to hear all about L.A.," Erica says. "Have you edited any features yet?"

"Not yet. But a friend of mine might be DOPing an indie film and he's trying to get me on board."

"An Indian film?" Lilly says.

"Indie, Muh. *Indie.*"

Lilly plunks the toasted bagels on the table in front of Estelle. "The butter and cream cheese are in the fridge," she says. She'll toast Estelle's bread but she won't put the offending condiments *on the table*. "There's also marmalade," she suggests. "Why don't you have marmalade instead?"

Estelle sighs.

"Erica is living with her forty-six-year-old professor," Lilly tells Estelle. "Did you know?"

She watches Estelle's face very carefully for clues of prior knowledge, but Estelle seems genuinely surprised. She turns to her little sister. "You moved in with your professor?"

"He wasn't my professor when I moved in with him. I'm just auditing his course."

"Is this the writer you mentioned?"

"Yeah. He . . . he looks like Tim Robbins."

Lilly pounces. "You knew she was dating him?"

"She told me she was seeing a writer. . . ."

"Did you know he was old?"

"He's *not* old!" Erica fires. "He's forty-six, not eighty-six."

"So you quit the newsstand?" Estelle asks. "He supports you now?"

Erica used to sell newspapers in the lobby of the Paramount Hotel, before she became a kept woman. "Just while I work on my portfolio. I'm sort of on a . . . you know, a literary hiatus. I'm just doing a ton of writing and reading. Paul compiled a reading list for me—"

"You've got a reading list?" Lilly cuts in. "That's what you do for a living? You *read?*"

"I'm reading the classics," Erica says defensively. "It's to help with my writing. Paul says a writer has to read the classics."

Lilly bites her lip. She holds back. It's only the first day and she doesn't want to get off on the wrong foot.

Erica is watching her. So is Estelle. They're waiting. They're all waiting and watching each other.

"*L*evi means joined," Levi announces at the supper table.

"And Ilana means tree!" Ilana exclaims. She says "twee," which makes it all the more charming.

Everyone loves the way Ilana talks, but Jessie worries that in two years it will be a full-blown speech impediment, not so cute anymore. But then Jessie worries about everything.

Lilly wonders where it comes from.

"What does Zarr mean?" Levi asks. "Zadie, do you know what Zarr means?"

Milton chews on a mouthful of chicken.

"It's his latest obsession . . ." Jessie explains. "What names mean."

"Our real name is Zarritsky," Milton tells his grandson. "But I don't know what it means."

"How come you changed it?" Levi asks.

They all know he shortened his last name from Zarritsky because it was too Jewish for the kind of fame he was after back then. What he says to Levi is, "I never could remember how to spell it."

Everyone laughs.

"Pass the chicken," Lilly says.

"What time is your show on?" Allan asks Milton.

"Eight." He checks his watch.

Lilly thinks he seems preoccupied. He's not his boisterous self tonight. He's been subdued ever since he went to pick up the chickens.

"Can I have margarine on my bread?" Levi asks.

"What do you need margarine for?" Jessie says. "The bread is much yummier without it." She takes a bite of her roll. "Mmm. Delicious. Margarine doesn't even taste good."

"Don't use reversible psychology on me," he says dryly.

Jessie sighs. "You can't have any margarine because it's full of trans fats. You know what they do to our bodies."

"Speaking of bodies," Allan says. "Estelle, if you want to talk to me about my book later, I'd be happy to go over it with you. I think you might really benefit from my green tea diet."

Estelle looks up from her plate of Cornflake Catalina Chicken.

"Oh, what a good idea," Lilly says. "I have a copy of it on my bedside table."

"It's number two on the national bestseller list," Allan boasts.

Erica rolls her eyes. Allan obviously isn't her idea of a real writer. She probably frowns on commercial bestsellers.

"You're not the only famous person in the family, Milt," Allan says cheerily.

Milton smiles wanly and pushes his half-finished plate aside. He absently starts humming the old Edie Gorme and Steve Lawrence duet "This Could Be the Start of Something Big." Lilly hates that song, she always did. Even when Milt sings it.

Milton's got a voice like satin. By twenty-one, he had cut his first record—a tremendous success by Canadian standards. Not long after that, he landed a job hosting a TV show on the CBC. It was called *The Young Entertainers Showcase*. That's where he met Lilly.

It was the late sixties. Lilly was eighteen years old; she'd left Montreal to "make it" in Toronto. She got the job on *The Young Entertainers Showcase* because she could think fast and keep her cool. She had to audition in front of the CBC brass. It was a dry run. Live. The orch was in a separate room and only the conductor could hear her singing because he had on a set of headphones. She had chosen to sing "This Could Be the Start of Something Big." She was so nervous she came in two full bars behind the orchestra. But she kept on singing as though nothing was wrong and the conductor managed to catch up to her. In the end, they finished on the same note.

After it was over, she ran into the dressing room, hid behind the wardrobe, and cried like a baby. The director found her and told her she'd got the part.

"But I screwed up!" she sobbed.

"And no one in the audience knew it," he told her. "You did the right thing, kiddo. You kept right on singing. That's exactly what we need." He patted her back. "Now *you* need a new name. Cynamon is too . . ."

"Too what?"

"Too burlesque."

No one could believe it was her real name. They thought it had to be made up. They finally settled on Lilly Peters. Peters was a good Canadian name. It wouldn't offend anyone. (Except her father, who thought all of *his* contributions were being erased from her new life.) But the name Peters worked well alongside Milton Zarr; although once they became famous, no one used their last names. It was always Milton and Lilly.

Milton was this short, obnoxious kid. He had a big mouth and he was cocky. He knew he had talent. People called him Duddy Kravitz. But when he opened his mouth to sing "I'll Never Smile Again," Lilly fell madly in love with him. She was pregnant by the middle of the second season. The show was a ratings hit, but a pregnant hostess would not have gone over well with viewers. Not in 1966. She married Milton and the long and short of it is, her career went swirling down the drain. He stayed on the show with a new cohost, Gladys Gold. The CBC's replacement of Lilly was seamless. Everyone said Gladys had a stronger voice and bigger boobs.

Lilly's dance with fame had lasted only eighteen months. She never even got to record an album. She adored her baby, Estelle, but the oblivion that followed was not sweet or cherished. She had always envisioned a lifetime of accolades and attention. Her parents were intellectuals and they mostly kept to themselves. Her father had been in a union her whole life;

he was serious and political-minded. Her mother, a poet of some renown, was a fanatic about education and always had her nose in a book. She wanted Lilly to get a degree. She wanted Lilly to pursue something nobler than television.

But Lilly had only ever dreamed of a life filled with parties, music, excess, and adoration. She'd never shared her mother's interest in literature or poetry or the pursuit of knowledge. She remembers her mother's reaction when she announced she'd got the job on TV. Dorothy was horrified; she just broke down sobbing and pleading. "What do you want to be on the TV for, where everyone will know your face and recognize you?"

"That's the whole point. I *want* people to recognize me."

Dorothy kept shaking her head. She was disappointed, angry. "I forbid it! You want all the world should know your business? Besides, TV is full of idiots."

"Then I guess I'm an idiot," Lilly said, hurt. "I want to be famous. I'm tired of you holding me back—"

"How can an education hold you back?"

"I want more than that."

"More than an education?" Dorothy gasped. She didn't understand her daughter at all. She didn't *know* her; they were strangers.

From the day she started on that TV show, Dorothy made Lilly feel like it was a crass and worthless career; that it lacked merit. And yet it earned her money (unlike her mother's career as a poet). It got her recognized on the street. And while Dorothy had had several volumes of poetry published in Canada before Lilly was born, very few people knew her name.

But in the end, for all their bickering, both Lilly and her mother followed the very same path: they both gave up promising artistic careers to have a family. As it turned out, Lilly would only have the fame and the parties and the money vicariously, through her husband's celebrated career. (And in all fairness to Milty, he *did* provide them to excess.) Still, to Lilly it was never the same as attaining them for herself.

These days Lilly keeps busy working part-time at a fancy linen shop on Mount Pleasant, and volunteering at the Jewish Community Center on Bloor. She's a stellar salesperson and a competent volunteer, but it's nothing like what she once imagined for herself.

"Where's Gladys tonight?" Jessie asks her father. "I thought she'd be here."

"Gladys isn't feeling well."

There's something in his voice. Lilly looks over at him, tries to read his face. It's the first she's hearing about Gladys not feeling well. All he told her this afternoon was that Gladys couldn't make it. Lilly didn't pursue it. She is just relieved Gladys isn't here.

"How come you're so quiet, Dad?" Jessie again.

"He must be nervous about the show," Erica says.

"Daddy? Nervous about his life story airing on TV? *Please*."

"It's almost time," Milton says flatly. "We should go watch."

It still strikes Lilly as ridiculous, the idea of Milton having his biography on TV. It's amazing the way even the most mundane life—not that Milton's has been especially mundane—can be shaped into a gripping hour of entertainment. Why should anyone care about Milton Zarr's story anyway? And yet A&E's *Biography* has proved over and over again that the life of Vincent Price, for instance, is as compelling and dramatic as that of the most influential historical figures. The same can be said about Jacqueline Susann or Tom Selleck—or even the founder of Wendy's. (Lilly actually watched that episode, riveted!) Millionaires, movie stars, gangsters, child actors, authors, royals, game-show hosts. *Any* person's life merits its own show these days, especially when condensed into an hour and narrated by some maudlin announcer with a deep, soothing voice. Who says her husband's life is any less noteworthy than Princess Diana's?

To the rest of Canadians, he is a star. A national treasure. He has achieved something coveted and fleeting: fame. Even national fame, which crosses no borders and is often dismissed, is both a triumph and a rarity, bestowed only upon society's most charismatic and talented.

To Lilly, Milton Zarr is just the man she wakes up next to every morning, the same one she has lived with, and been annoyed by, her whole adult life. Up there on the TV screen, in Pamela Wallin's hands, he will somehow become a more important man than the one who leaves his used dental floss on the sink every night. His life story will take on a grander, fictional quality. There will be the insinuation that he was destined for greatness (in hindsight, aren't all famous people?). He will be portrayed as someone who was chosen, someone in possession of special, mysterious gifts.

Lilly glances over at him, feeling a little proud and a little envious. If things had unfolded differently, she might have had her own Intimate Life Portrait.

Milton

Milton Zarritsky was born in Montreal in 1944. He grew up an only child on the Main until his family moved to Côte-Saint-Luc when he was fifteen. His father, Moishe, worked in the *shmata* business, at a shirt factory. Every day, he came home with armloads of white cardboard from the inside of shirts. Milton's mother, Frommie, kept and hoarded these cardboards for her grand-children. Whenever Erica, Jessie, and Estelle came over, Gramma Frommie doled out the cardboards for drawing. It was always a hit. They would sit quietly and color for hours—really the only time they were all still and cooperative at the same time. For years, it was the fresh white card-boards that *made* them want to visit their grandparents.

Milton never finished high school. He was restless, rambunctious, and lacked concentration skills. His father called him a shit disturber and his mother called him an *arumloifer,* which meant "street urchin" in Yiddish. They mistook his failure in school for a lack of ambition, and it worried them. If he couldn't be a doctor, they wanted him to succeed in business. But Milton would not be guided or contained. He wanted to sing.

Thankfully, he had a magical voice. Within months of abandoning his education, he moved to Toronto and started singing in nightclubs. Not long after that, he cut his first album. It happened fairy-tale style: someone important heard him sing and offered him a Canadian record deal. When he sliced the "itsky" off his last name he really took off.

Milton Zarr went on to record two more albums and headline in hundreds of nightclubs across Canada. (Canadians wanted their very own Sinatra, and Milty enthusiastically aspired to live up to the comparison.) Then he got his own show, which is where he met his future wife. *The Young Entertainers Showcase* was a smash with young Canadians; a whole new generation was coming up. Milty and Lilly clearly had chemistry, which eventually resulted in a child, Estelle Rachel Zarr. By the time their baby was born, Milton and Lilly were married, and Lilly was off the show.

It was Lilly's departure that paved the way for the swooping entrance of Gladys Gold, who, critics concurred, had a stronger voice than Lilly. In fact, the ratings on the show soared when Gladys arrived. Gladys and Milty also had chemistry, which they managed to sustain on the air for eleven seasons.

The seventies were a renaissance for Milton, both personally and professionally. On the home front, he had three beautiful daughters and a devoted wife. His career was soaring. He was flush.

And then tragedy. His parents were killed in a car accident the same year his TV show got canceled. They were coming home from a movie—*The Goodbye Girl*—when a woman in a station wagon ran a red light. At their *shivah,* Milton reflected on how he hadn't seen them since Passover, his last visit to Montreal. He was sick with guilt. But beyond the initial grief, he kept thinking that it was such a peculiar thing to have happened to him—losing both his parents in one shot like that. Nothing in his life up until that moment could have forewarned or prepared him for such a monumental loss. He had always viewed himself as someone blessed: an untouchable. Death had never afflicted his world. Nothing bad ever had. The car accident that took his parents' lives was an anomaly, drastic and incomprehensible. In its aftermath, he was incredulous.

Milton was now in his mid-thirties. He had three children under age ten, no parents, and no job. It was Gladys Gold's idea to continue their partnership and start up Crooners; against her soon-to-be ex-husband's wishes, she and Milton wrote and sang hundreds of commercial jingles for TV and radio. Milton always said it was Lucky Strike that paid for his home in Forest Hill.

In 1990 Gladys and Milton opened a restaurant, also called Crooners, on King Street. And then Crooners 2, in Mississauga. The food was mediocre but people lined up to hear Gladys and Milty belt out oldies by the piano. Money kept rolling in. Whatever they did together was a gold mine. They were invincible; their chemistry endured over three decades.

The Crooners restaurants closed down in the early nineties and Milton retired from writing and singing commercial jingles. Occasionally he still sings in nightclubs, for special occasions. And he thinks he'll do another album someday, but not for a while. He's a grandfather now, which is his priority. Being with family comes first nowadays.

And that's his life, a full hour's worth. Even he feels impressed by it, having watched it play itself out on the TV screen as though it were someone else's life. But there's sadness, too, and an overwhelming feeling that it's all over now, that his hour—in more ways than one—is just about up. He's retired, his voice isn't what it used to be, he's a grandfather . . . *what's left?*

"What's wrong, Daddy?" Jessie asks him.

Her voice startles him. He looks over at her, noticing the rest of them for the first time since the show started. He touches his cheek; it's wet. He's been crying.

"He's feeling old," Lilly says, her voice bleached of compassion.

Erica goes over to him and puts her arm around him. "Don't get sentimental, Dad. Your life's not over just because the show is."

He looks up with a runny nose and wet eyes. He shakes his head. "It's been so good," he sobs. "Too good. I've been blessed."

"Then why are you crying?"

"He's feeling nostalgic," Lilly says. There's an edge in her voice.

Milton shakes his head and then buries his face in his youngest daughter's shoulder. He doesn't want them to see this. He feels foolish.

"Daddy, what is it?" Erica asks him.

"My Gladys is dying," he blurts. "I found out this morning. She has cancer in her pancreas."

He saw out of the corner of his eye that Lilly's lips tightened when he said "*My* Gladys." But he doesn't care anymore. He doesn't even care that Jessie is getting up and walking out of the room. He hears the door close. None of it matters anymore: the arguing, the pretending, the guilt. *Gladys is dying.* That's all that matters now. In the end, the others will still be there. They'll forgive.

Estelle

*R*onnie—or J-Date access code 45681—has a bob haircut, which is the first bad sign. In his J-Date picture, he had on a baseball cap, so she couldn't tell. As far as she's concerned, the man-bob—a worse offense than the man ponytail—hasn't been in since '93. And she isn't crazy about his name either, which is a tongue twister. Ronnie Weinroch, Wonnie Weinroch, Wonnie Weinwock. Still, upon arriving at her favorite place, the Rose Café on Venice Boulevard, for their first date, she manages to coax herself out of her immediate disenchantment. He can't be any worse than the sausage king.

"What's your favorite band?" he asks her.

"Hole," she says.

He looks disappointed.

"What about you?"

"Savage Garden."

Estelle chokes back a gag. It's true that you can tell everything you need to know about someone by the music they listen to.

"You don't like Savage Garden?"

She lets out a diminishing laugh. "I think they're the modern-day equivalent of Air Supply."

"Oh." He shrugs. "I don't mind Air Supply. I love ballads."

"So, you're a writer?" she says, eagerly shifting the subject. "Screenplays? TV?"

"TV. Actually, I'm still trying to break in—"

"Who isn't?"

"I have an agent, though."

Estelle perks up. "That's something."

"I wrote a couple of specs for *Boy Meets World,* which my agent thinks are pretty good. He's circulating them around the networks. Hopefully I can get on a midseason replacement in January."

"It's like a lottery, you know."

"Someone's got to make it," Ronnie counters.

"You'll probably have to start out as a story editor," Estelle tells him. She feels vicious.

"As long as I get in, that's fine."

"Who's your agent with?"

"He's independent."

"Oh," she responds, feeling sullen. It's the curly hair. It's Savage Garden. It's the piece of avocado between his teeth. It's her looming singleness.

"So what have you edited lately?" he asks her. "Anything I'd know?"

She rattles off the last few gigs on her résumé. "Do you know Howard Empey?" she asks him. "I edited his last documentary, *Line-Up.* And now I'm working on the trailer for *Taxi to Tijuana.* But I'm hoping to edit an indie soon. . . ."

He's nodding benignly as her voice trails off. She looks down at her plate.

"Listen," he says, checking his watch. "I've got to take my dog to the vet."

She looks up at him, stunned.

"But finish your salad. Please."

* * *

*H*e drops her off in West Hollywood, not quite at her door, but close enough on Santa Monica Boulevard to walk. Her apartment is on North Larabee, in a gated complex called Mediterranean Village, a place as charming as the name suggests. She was prepared to take the first place she saw— a one-bedroom dive on Pico—but her parents insisted on paying the difference for her to live in a "safe" building. She can't complain. She's got a small one-bedroom apartment with a patio that overlooks the swimming pool and a yard that is shrouded with palm trees. Her parents deposit $500 U.S. into her account every month and she pays the rest, only $800. She sometimes feels a little embarrassed that her parents still support her, but most of the time she just feels deep relief. She loves her neighborhood, which is within walking distance of West Hollywood Park, Sunset Boulevard (home of numerous well-known bars she rarely visits), and Melrose, in case she ever loses enough weight to go shopping there.

Back at her apartment, she grates a brick of Monterey Jack and dumps it over a tray of tortilla chips. After the Ronnie debacle, she is in search of numbness. Her drug of choice is cheese. Being the only fatso in a family of slender women has been an ongoing humiliation. Erica and Jessie both resemble Meryl Streep in *Sophie's Choice*—angular and exquisite. Estelle is more the Bette Midler type. She paved the way for them by getting all the bad genes. Growing up, her parents never let up on her. She never could please them. For starters, they wanted her to be prettier. They always said she was heartbreakingly "Jewish-looking." The Russian peasant of the family. Big-boned and stocky. In a family of slim, blond, blue-eyed females, all descended from the delicately beautiful Polish women on Gramma Dorothy's side, Estelle was unfortunate enough to have inherited her father's coarse features—the broad mouth, the small bulging eyes, the prominent nose with (in her opinion) giant, curling nostrils. She has a good clear complexion, but other than that, not much else to boast about—not even blond hair. The one time she tried to lighten her naturally pale brown hair, it turned the color of an orange Popsicle.

Her parents have so much vested in her appearance; they act as though it was *their* responsibility to create something of a higher standard. If she fails, they fail. During her teen years, usually on her birthday, she got offers for a nose job, caps for her front teeth, summer at a fat camp. She always refused. They thought she was ungrateful, spoiled. She was a stain on their perfect image.

They also complain that she demands too much attention. But growing up, she had to *earn* that attention. Unlike her younger sisters, it never came naturally. It did not come from having a pretty face and golden hair, from batting her lashes or smiling coyly. Erica was a master at using her sweetness to manipulate and draw people in. Jessie's modus operandi was to follow the rules; she never strayed. Perfect Jessie always had praise heaped on her. She earned praise for getting good grades, a scholarship to U of T, a degree, a career (superfluous; overkill!), a husband, two children, and even for getting her figure back right after the births. Milton and Lilly have always been bloated with pride over Jessie. And although Erica hasn't quite managed to dazzle them yet, at least she's always looked good and had boyfriends, and that's half the battle with the Zarrs. Besides, being the baby, Erica gets extra leeway. Estelle, on the other hand, has had to use her personality and her perseverance to get attention. In the Zarr household, these are not qualities that earn respect. Zero points for *chutzpah*. Her fearlessness has always gone unnoticed.

Money. Success. Artistic talent. Beauty. Marriage. These are the things that earn respect in her family. Anything that impresses; anything that provides good fodder for boasting and reflects well on Lilly and Milton. Estelle can't hide behind any of those things. She never could. She can only hide behind the pierce in her brow, the dozen or so earrings in her ears, the streaks of pink dye in her hair, all of which are meant to be declarations of her irreverence. In school they called her Estelle Bi-zarr. She likes to think these things are a testament to her uniqueness, her unwillingness to conform to her family's standards of acceptability, but really, they're just distractions.

Her Toronto friends wonder how her self-esteem stays intact in Hollywood around all those beautiful blond actresses, in the heartland of superficiality. *Try growing up in my family,* she always retaliates. Hollywood is easier than going home. It's not just Milton's and Lilly's disapproving glances or their disparaging remarks about how she's turned out. It's her sisters, too. It's the way she is constantly being compared to them, assessed against their credentials. *(Why is Erica so slim and you're so stocky? Are you bingeing secretly? Why can't you meet a nice man like Allan?)* They even got the good names! Lovely, three-syllable names that dance off the lips and connote femininity. *Erica. Jessica.* But Estelle is an old *yenta*'s name. Estelle is your Bubby's bridge partner or the neighbor at your great-aunt's condo in Florida.

The microwave beeps and she removes her nachos. She devours them one by one, barely tasting them. This dark mood always descends on her after a visit home. It's Lilly, it's them, it's the way they all look at her. It's the way Ronnie looked at her on their date—with that veil of disappointment. Maybe even a touch of repulsion or embarrassment. It is the look that echoes the belittling, begrudging voice inside her.

The phone rings.

"Estelle? It's Peri."

Peri is her neighbor upstairs. He wants to be a director. He's twenty-four and is a prolific, frenzied L.A. prodigy. He spends his days scribbling screenplays, pitching them, going to screenwriting workshops, directing music videos (two of which have been in heavy rotation on VH1), and was even first assistant camera on Vince Fields's last movie, which sadly got negative reviews on the festival circuit and went straight to video. He has a million connections and, by sheer perseverance alone, deserves to make it. He is the real deal, definitely the closest thing Estelle's come to a Hollywood success story. At night, he bartends at Gate on La Cienega.

"I'm going to D.P. Russell Hirsch's next movie!" he tells her.

"Oh my God!" Estelle bellows, feeling bleak with envy. "Congratulations."

Russell Hirsch had a moderate hit at Sundance in '96 but his follow-up movie tanked. He's got a name at least. Estelle can feel tears burning her eyes. She's happy for Peri—but why do the breaks always happen to other people?

"You've got to get your demo reel together, Estelle. Russell wants to see it."

"What?"

"No more than five minutes, okay? And make it outstanding. I've been bragging about you."

As she hangs up the phone she takes a deep breath. She

already knows which trailers and which music video she's going to put in her reel. The hard part will be keeping it under five minutes. But she's an editor. That's what she does. Her mind is whirling. She dumps the remains of her nachos into the trash and lets out a primal, jubilant scream. Then she thinks, *Fuck you, Wonnie Weinwoch!*

Erica

*E*rica pulls a book from one of the shelves in their library and turns to Paul. "Is this one good?" she asks him.

He reluctantly looks up from his desk. "Hmm?"

"This book. Is it good?"

"It's D. H. Lawrence," he snips irritably.

"I can see that. Is it *good?*"

"Of course it's 'good.'" He takes off his bifocals. "Why aren't you writing?" he asks her.

She shrugs. Her journal is facedown on the coffee table; the screen saver is flashing on her laptop. She's supposed to be working on a new short story, the idea for which came to her during one of her morning "streaming" sessions. ("Streaming" is what Paul calls free-form writing, an exercise he practices every morning for one hour, religiously.)

"I'm taking a break," she tells him.

"But you only started twenty minutes ago."

"I'm not really in the mood right now. I can't focus."

"Being in the mood to write is a luxury a writer can't afford. You have to just do it."

"I don't work that way."

"Well, could you go in another room, then? Because *I'm* working."

"I just asked you if this was a good book," she mutters. "I wasn't exactly harassing you."

Paul sighs. "I'm sorry," he says. "It's just . . . I guess I'm disappointed that you're not taking your writing seriously."

"Maybe if you take a look at what I've written so far, I'll know if I'm going in the right direction. My problem is, I don't really have too much confidence yet."

Paul stares at his computer screen, where his latest book review for the *Times* awaits completion. "I have a deadline," he says in a pained voice.

"You just said you were disappointed in me for not taking my writing seriously," she reminds him.

"Can't you take your writing seriously without me having to hold your hand?"

"Never mind."

"I mean, I do this for a living, Erica."

"What's that supposed to mean?" Erica says, miffed.

"This isn't a hobby for me."

Stung, Erica shoves the D. H. Lawrence book back in the shelf and rushes out of the library.

"I didn't mean it like that!" he calls after her.

She slams the door on her way out of the apartment.

*A*rtists are temperamental; she knows that. She's dated them before. Her last boyfriend was a gifted but insecure photographer who plummeted regularly into paralyzing depressions over his perceived lack of talent. He would go months without picking up his camera—he called it photographer's block—which inevitably made him more depressed.

Paul is less predictable. From one moment to the next, she's never sure if she's going to get the gentle mentor or the irritable author who's got deadlines and pressure and the weight of the literary world on his tweed-clad shoulders. Just last week she asked him to read over her latest story for their next workshop. They were both reading anyway, he in his leather club chair and she sprawled on the couch. He looked up from his book—Ayn Rand's *The Virtue of Selfishness*—and said, "Pardon?"

"Can you read my excerpt for the workshop?" she repeated. "I haven't written the ending yet, but maybe if you looked at it . . ."

"Now?" he whined, sounding extremely imposed upon.

"You're reading anyway."

"I'm reading *this*." He held up his pretentious Ayn Rand book. "I can't always be your professor, Erica. It's Sunday morning. Can't we just be companions? Lovers? Can't I just read my book without having to be your mentor?"

"You're obviously learning a lot from that book," she muttered.

But then an hour later, he came to find her—she was sulking in the Jacuzzi tub—and he read her story and wrote all kinds of helpful and encouraging comments in the margins. "I didn't mean to be derogatory," he told her, as he peeled off his clothes. "I'm still getting used to this, you know."

Meaning he hadn't lived with someone since his last serious relationship, almost ten years ago. He got in the tub with her and they discussed her story some more and then they made love and he seemed perfectly content to be her mentor again.

She can live with his sporadic flare-ups of selfishness. She can even understand how sometimes he just doesn't feel like reading her mediocre "pieces." He reads enough crap in his workshops that he's entitled to read Ayn Rand if he wants to. What she's having trouble with is deciphering his agenda.

One minute, he's nagging her to write in her journal, the next, he's jumping down her throat because she's disrupted him or asked for some help. How can she know what he wants when he keeps sending mixed signals? She wants to be prolific and improve her writing skills and read every book on his suggested reading list; she wants to prove she is genuinely enthusiastic about becoming a writer. And then out of the blue, he turns around and snidely belittles all her efforts. *This isn't a hobby for me.*

The way he said it made her feel like she was sixteen again. In his voice she could hear her father's accusatory tone. She could hear the same derision, the same edge of mockery, the same utter lack of faith. Her parents have always made her feel foolish for never having staked her claim on one particular career or interest or even on an enduring identity. She is the family flake; her choices are always wrong, she never finishes anything. That's how they see her life up until now. *She* prefers to view her past as a journey; a journey toward finding her true calling, her passion. Whether anyone else knows it or not, she is an artist. She is merely in pursuit of the right outlet. Is it so wrong to *not* want to wind up working in an office for the rest of your life? Is it wrong to want to figure out what the hell your purpose on earth is?

Unfortunately, her parents have neither the patience nor the belief in her to suspend judgment. They never did. They want tangible results. They want success in the most literal sense of the word. (And P.S., they do not define success as a noncredited writing workshop, even though Erica feels she is finally zeroing in on her true passion and perhaps her one real artistic talent, no doubt inherited from her beloved grandmother. But how to convince *them* this one is legitimate?)

Even in high school, they made no bones about their relentless disappointment in her. Why was she so inconsistent? Why didn't she try harder? Why did she always coast? Why didn't she "get involved" anymore? What about yearbook? Volleyball? School play? Why couldn't she be friends with the overachievers and the more well-rounded girls the way she had been in junior high?

The high school she went to in those years was Branksome Hall. She'd been popular back in junior high, always surrounded by clusters of adoring friends. Teachers loved her, and her sweetness was rewarded with good grades, encouraging remarks, titles. She was the seventh-grade class president and the games captain in gym. All was going well.

And then in her first year of high school, she met Tiala McQueen. Tiala was a beautiful loner. She was a year older than Erica and seemed like a good entry point into a more interesting, more adventurous life. They rode the bus home together every day. Tiala always sat alone with her Walkman on. She was self-sufficient; she didn't need any friends around her, giggling and gossiping and doing the usual embarrassing things teenage girls did on a bus. She wasn't ashamed to be alone. She was beyond that. Erica knew just by looking at her that she had another life somewhere outside Branksome, a life that was much more important and probably contained . . . men. She had an air of indifference, which impressed Erica. She also looked down on popularity, which was at odds with the normal private-school mentality; popularity was something one strove for, chased after, battled to achieve. But Tiala wasn't interested in any kind of status—not with a bunch of high school girls anyway. So Erica's credentials meant nothing to her.

One day on the bus, Erica dared to speak to her. "What are you listening to?" she asked.

Tiala looked peeved by the disturbance. She glanced over at Erica with a mixture of surprise and disdain. Maybe no one from school had ever talked to her before. "New Order," she said, without taking off her headphones.

"Age of Consent?"

Tiala nodded and that was it. Erica got off the bus and walked home. Later, in her room, she played New Order's *Age of Consent* album over and over again on her record player. She was already infatuated with Tiala.

Their friendship blossomed very slowly. Tiala was reluctant to get involved with anyone from school—especially someone like Erica. She probably thought it would ruin her image, or maybe she didn't trust that type of girl, the type that could fit so seamlessly into a private-school hierarchy. But the friendship was inevitable if only because Erica wanted it so badly.

Finally, Tiala invited Erica to sleep over one night. It was a coup. Erica imagined them putting on makeup, trying on clothes, dancing to cool music. They didn't end up doing any of those things. It turned out Tiala had two secrets: she was a painter, and a pothead. Her room was plastered wall to wall with her own artwork—magnificent, bold paintings that made Erica's chest constrict with envy. There was an easel set up in the corner of the room, a tarp spread over the floor, and paints and brushes stacked in every corner of the room. "Wow . . ." Erica breathed. The paintings were all of women's faces, every one of them floating against a backdrop of vibrant colors; the faces were abstract and distorted, yet still defined, like reflections in a pond. But it was the way Tiala had captured their expressions that most impressed Erica—

ethereal, sad, and definitely wise beyond Tiala's age. Right away Erica felt worthless and inferior for having nothing of the sort to offer; she had no special skill or talent to bring to the friendship. Tiala was gifted. She was authentic. Her indifference in school made sense now. She was a true artist.

Tiala opened the drawer of her bedside table and pulled out a joint. "Helps me to paint," she said. "It gets my creative juices flowing."

Erica had never tried dope before. She thought maybe it could get *her* creative juices flowing too. They passed the joint between them; then Tiala started to paint, while Erica lay comatose on the tarp. She lay there for hours. In the end, pot did not get her creative juices going; it froze them like ice cubes.

As time went on, Tiala needed more and more dope to paint. And when pot was no longer enough, she moved on to new drugs. Acid *really* got her juices flowing. And coke gave her enough energy to paint into the next morning. The least Erica could do was keep her friend company. She did all the drugs Tiala did, only she never painted afterward. She just lay on her back, stoned, hallucinating, watching Tiala hard at work, painting her haunted women's faces.

And she slid. Slid down, down.

One by one Erica's former friends—the squealing ambitious clones, as she now thought of them—fell away. Erica took on Tiala's perfected indifference, the suggestion in her face that she had a far more interesting life elsewhere. Her grades slipped; her attendance dropped; she abandoned all extracurricular activities. In some ways, it was a relief. She'd lowered the bar so much, she actually felt free. There was nothing left to lose. Her parents stopped nagging about yearbook and volleyball, and at some point were just thrilled if she attended school at all.

She started shoplifting and hanging around bars on Queen Street. By this time Tiala had stopped painting. Partying was the priority now. There was one bar in particular, an old tavern. It was in the basement and smelled of stale draft beer and overflowing toilet bowls. It had once been a gay bar, but now it was always full of alternative, wayward teenagers—guys in bands who never bathed, university dropouts, drug dealers, and the like. Erica had a fake ID that said she was nineteen. As long as she was with Tiala, who really looked nineteen, she never had a problem getting in. There were always guys around them—men in their twenties mostly, misfits and rebels. Both Erica and Tiala had a natural, privileged-looking sort of beauty—rosy cheeks and wisps of clean blond hair curling around their faces, as though they'd just come in from riding horses. The Queen Street crowd was impressed with them. They were princesses and they knew it.

The turning point came early on in her last year of high school. Her grandmother called her into the bathroom one night for one of her rare but meaningful lectures. (It's always been one of Gramma Dorothy's rituals: she sets her bottom teeth on the edge of the sink, gets into a hot bath, lights a cigarette, and calls in a family member to give them a serious talking-to.) That night, Erica was sitting on the closed toilet seat while her grandmother puffed away on a Matinée. Finally, through a cloud of smoke, she said, "You know what worries me most about you, Erica?"

Erica didn't respond. She was being sullen.

"It's that you have no backbone. That you're a follower." She paused for a moment, and then leaned over and poked Erica in the chest. "Is there *any*thing genuine in there, darling?" she asked.

Erica ran out of the bathroom, devastated. She could bear her mother's disappointment; that hardly bothered her. But her grandmother's opinion mattered. That Gramma Dorothy thought she had no backbone was more than a little disturbing. It troubled her to the core; it festered.

Not long after that, she began to grow bored with anarchy. Thankfully, very few things could sustain her interest for too long, and even her idol, Tiala, was beginning to lose some of her sheen. Erica was different from Tiala in one fundamental way: Erica had values that had been ingrained in her—values she could not entirely shake, no matter how low she sank— and as a result, she understood consequences. She just wasn't the hard-core lost soul that Tiala was. When it came down to it, she couldn't hurl herself over the edge with as much abandon. There were lines she would not cross; her family, with all their shortcomings, kept her somewhat tethered to reality.

So she made a commitment to her education and decided to curb the partying. She also made an effort to get into U of T, which meant pulling away from Tiala as much as possible. By Erica's last year of high school they had drifted apart, except for the occasional weekend of debauchery.

"I haven't seen you much the past few weeks," Tiala said to her at the end of one of these weekends. The sun was already coming up. It was the middle of December and they were lying side by side in a Christmas tree lot near St. Lawrence Market. They were tucked under this big Scottish pine, the branches a shield from the rest of the world. They were coming down off acid; neither could remember how they'd wound up at the market.

"I had finals," Erica said.

"Oh."

The air smelled like pine. It was soothing.

"Do you ever wish you celebrated Christmas?" Tiala asked. She pulled some pine needles off the tree and held them under her nose like a mustache.

"I never think about it."

"I wish I did. But it's too hard on my mother, with the drinking."

Erica felt sorry for her; she was always feeling sorry for Tiala lately. *When a friendship deteriorates to pity, it's time to walk away.* That's what she was thinking. She could finally see now that Tiala's craving was for numbness. And ever since Tiala had abandoned her art, she had lost her value as a friend. Erica just wanted to be rid of her.

"Do you think Jesus ever got high?" she asked Erica.

"I've heard that he did."

"I miss you," Tiala said.

"Me too." Erica was lying. She wanted to get away. It was like breaking up with a boyfriend.

"I've got more."

"What?"

"Acid. Here—" Tiala pulled out two more tabs.

Erica felt weary. She knew this was all over for her; there was something purposeful stirring inside her. A longing for meaning. She knew, at last, that she was beyond this. "I can't. I have to go home. You should go home too."

"Home?" Tiala had moved into her own apartment, a wretched little bachelor at Jane and Finch. She shared it with two guys—a drummer and a bassist from a band called Furry Gonads.

"Let's share one more hit," Tiala said.

She was so eager, it made Erica feel guilty for having grown up. It also made her sad. What had happened to that

self-confident, passionate painter? She'd had such potential! Nearly four years had passed, but Tiala was a different
sort of girl now; the kind whose future was written on the
wall. Her cool indifference was no longer to be worshipped;
it was embarrassing. There was no one left for her to be
indifferent to.

Erica stood up. "I'm going, Tee."

"Whatever." Tiala put the tab of acid on her tongue and
swallowed it. She leaped to her feet and started walking off,
out of the Christmas tree lot. She had her invincible face on.

"You should start painting again!" Erica called after her.

Tiala never answered. She just kept walking.

Erica still thinks about her, though, the way you think
about people who you suspect have come to a bad end. She's
heard things over the years from mutual acquaintances—that
Tiala moved to Australia, that she got married, that she went
to Africa with the Peace Corps, that she died. It's all possible,
but she doesn't know if any of it is true. Mostly she wonders
if Tiala still paints. To this day, what troubles Erica most is
the injustice of someone like Tiala being bestowed with such
a magnificent talent, such a rare and true gift, and then
pissing it away.

As for Erica, she went to U of T for two years of an
aimless arts program dabbling in poetry, pottery, drama—
none of which took. Then she transferred to Ryerson, where
she studied journalism. That didn't pan out, so she traveled
through Europe for a while, then settled in London for a year.
She worked at Tower Records, the Rock Garden Café, the
Crabtree & Evelyn in Covent Garden. When she came back
to Toronto, she bought herself a used camera and threw
herself into photography. For her twenty-fifth birthday, her
father paid for her certificate program at the International

Center of Photography in New York, thinking that she would come home afterward and get a photojournalist job at a local newspaper.

Can she blame them for their lack of faith in her? She's the little girl who cried wolf. Every new interest she latches onto is supposed to be the One, the way people convince themselves that every passing fling is a soul mate. And each time, she convinces herself and everyone in her family that *this is it*.

But it never is.

It took thirty years to blow her credibility with her family. If her credibility with Paul is already shot, what hope is there of keeping him? And if she can't get her act together, where is there to go from here but down?

Jessie

"No. No way," she tells her assistant, Auben. "I don't want to do a bar." She leans back in her swivel chair, shaking her head.

She's looking at the picture of Allan on her desk. He's wearing his suede jacket, the one from the eighties. She's always hated it on him. It has big shoulder pads and too many zippered pockets. It's a bad picture. His hair needs cutting. It's thinning near the temples and then puffing out like dark horns on top of his head. And his glasses are too large for his face. Again, a holdover from the eighties. He's like that, though. When he buys something he likes, he keeps it for decades. It's not cheapness so much as a fundamental loathing of change. He gave her the picture, framed, when she moved her business into the loft. It was a gesture. She appreciates that.

It's almost three and she's got to pick Ilana up from day care and then Levi up from kindergarten, which he now attends all day to accommodate her work schedule. (Guilt, guilt, guilt.) Secretly, she always dreads the end of the workday. Not that she doesn't miss her babies, but she prefers being at the office to being at home. Home, in the end, is the place that contains her marriage. Here at the office, she is busy and preoccupied, surrounded by women she can relate to. Here, her fears are quiet, her thoughts are focused and neutral. Even the guilt recedes (though never vanishes). She loves this place, the business *she* created—the one and only thing in her life she is sure she does well. She loves the shelves above her desk, lined with her favorite books: *50 Tips for Managing Paper Chaos; Taming the Paper Tiger Software; Home Management Made Easy; Clutter No More!*

She netted nearly fifty thousand dollars last year and the company is still growing. She started out by herself, organizing kitchens and closets for her friends. She's got a gift for it, which Allan teases is the one positive by-product of her having obsessive-compulsive disorder. Hence the company's name, OCD. It's supposed to stand for Organizing Consultant & Designer, but those in the know get the inside joke. Demand for Jessie's service grew through word of mouth. Within months, she was booked to organize the biggest houses in Rosedale, Forest Hill, and the Bridal Path. She was doing their closets, their kitchen pantries, their children's playrooms, their medicine cabinets; she was designing special storage and shelving units for houses that were being built. Soon she was organizing the offices of major corporations and hiring employees to help her with the work she could no longer manage by herself. Now OCD is housed in a nine-hundred-square-foot loft at Yonge and Eglinton where Jessie oversees a staff of four women. And she still manages to get home by four every afternoon to greet her kids.

"It's good money," Auben says. "Really good money."

"To do what, though? How do we organize a bar?"

"We won't be organizing the bar, Jessie. We'll be doing their office."

"Do you know it?"

"What?"

"This bar? You're that age."

"What age?"

"The clubbing age."

"So are you. We're the same age, remember?"

"Not really," Jessie says, sighing. "I'm middle-aged." Auben, on the other hand, is single and hip and still likes to go out. "Out" being to bars, as opposed to the occasional Saturday night movie when her parents will watch the kids, or else a family dinner at Grazie. Auben is what a twenty-nine-year-old *should* be: eager, optimistic, willing.

"I'll call them and set up an appointment," Auben says. "You can check it out and then decide."

"What's it called again?"

"Ooze."

"Is that a dumb name or am I really out of the loop?"

"Both. This is a good opportunity, Jess. This guy owns about half a dozen bars and restaurants in Toronto. If he likes you, who knows what it could lead to."

Auben goes back to her desk and makes the call. She is actually an old friend who also happens to be anal, meticulous, and über-organized. She was the only person in university whose notes Jessie could borrow. When the business started taking off, Jessie called Auben and offered her a job. Auben was giving riding lessons out in Pickering at the time, but had been thinking about moving back to the city. That was two years ago, when neither of them could have predicted just how successful OCD would become. Apparently, it fills a need. It turns out most people are secret slobs who can't be bothered to try, or are simply incapable of, managing their personal clutter. What a relief to have an attractive Jewish woman show up and do it all for you.

"Tomorrow at two," Auben tells her as she hangs up the phone.

Jessie pulls out her Day-Timer. "Where is this place?"

"Richmond and John. The guy's name is Skieth."

"Keith?"

"*Skieth*. Like 'he skieth down the slope.'"

She writes it down in her Day-Timer. *Skieth. Ooze. 2 pm.* It makes her feel ancient.

She isn't sure if her middle-age syndrome is the result of motherhood or marriage. She knows other married women who don't feel that their youth is over. But these other women are not married to Allan. He makes her feel unbeautiful, unremarkable. He is so blasé about her that she has become blasé about herself. He likes to have sex regularly, but that has nothing to do with *her*. It's more a necessary function, something he is required to do as a man but could probably do with *any*one. And frankly, she can't even remember a time when he *was* excited about her, or even especially turned on by her. Not even when they were engaged. He's just not that sort of man. He isn't romantic or flirtatious. His views on women are about as primitive as it gets: they are child bearers, housekeepers, companions. They have a purpose. She knows this because he doesn't ogle other women. He doesn't make crude remarks about them or get excited by large breasts or swaying asses. Nothing. Estelle says it's because he's a doctor. She thinks he's become immune to their bodies and their manipulations. Like calloused hands. He doesn't *feel* things for women, doesn't have longings. What he's got are urges. She's learned over the years that there's a difference between the two.

She often goes back in her mind and reviews the circumstances that led up to her accepting his proposal. She was only twenty-one. A marriage proposal from an older man—a *doctor*—was simply something she couldn't pass up at the time. She was attracted to his self-assurance, his competence.

She knew he could take care of her. Besides, what if an opportunity like that never presented itself again? And she knew how her parents would react. It was a feat, really. Everyone said so. Catching a thirty-year-old doctor while she was still in university. Wow. People were impressed, envious. It filled her up with something—the thing she had always striven for: approval. And with that came acceptance. She felt proud of herself, superior. She was guilty of gloating, flashing the ring around to her U of T friends, who still thought getting to cut the line at a bar was an achievement. She felt sorry for them; their futures were so uncertain. What if they never got proposed to? What if they wound up spinsters? It was something she'd never have to be concerned about. It was all mapped out for her and, in that way, it was such a relief. One less thing to worry about. It was resolved.

She finished her last year of university while Lilly planned the wedding. The reception was held at the Four Seasons. That whole time transpired in a haze. Even now, looking back on it, it's a blur. *She* was a blur. She remembers studying a lot and getting fitted for her dress and choosing plates, but there was a hazy, dreamlike quality to it all. Where was Allan during that time? She must have seen him, spent time with him; they must have had some kind of relationship. She thinks they went out for dinner a lot. She remembers a variety of expensive restaurants. He was always trying to impress her, and that pleased her. He was generous, too. He didn't haggle over the bill at the end of the meal or skimp on tips the way some of his friends did. All these things stacked up well for him, for their future.

In retrospect, there was nothing sentimental or spontaneous about their courtship; Allan turned thirty, probably decided he needed a wife, went looking, and selected her. It was more of a strategy than a romance. Jessie happened to fulfill his criteria. She was pretty, educated, Jewish, and young enough to be molded. His parents liked her, his colleagues respected her, and she wasn't overly ambitious. Above all, she knew what he wanted was a mother for his children. He was ready to start producing and made no secret of it.

There again, she performed extremely well. She got pregnant on their honeymoon, which was the worst thing that could have happened to her. She'd wanted to wait a few years to get used to Allan, to grow up, to convince herself that motherhood was something she was capable of. She was nowhere near ready at twenty-three. (She wasn't even ready at twenty-five, when she had Ilana.) But with Levi, she was really petrified, not even certain she wanted children at all. Of course she'd always said she did— otherwise Allan wouldn't have married her. What normal woman *doesn't* want kids?

Whenever she tried to share her doubts with Allan, he would just brush them aside. "Oh, Jessie," he'd say, laughing. "Stop thinking about it."

Oh, Jessie. Come on, Jessie. For crying out loud, Jessie. That's all she heard for nine months.

But what if she miscarried? What if she died during childbirth? And if she did survive, and the baby was healthy, *then what?* What if the child died of SIDS, got hit by a car crossing the street, got molested by a teacher, fell off the monkey bars in the playground, got leukemia? What if her kid drove drunk? Or had unprotected sex? Or overdosed on drugs?

She made herself so crazy she actually contemplated leaving the baby with Allan and fleeing the country. But she had an obligation, she had a role. Her whole life had been about living up to—or surpassing—expectations. It was what she did best. She never disappointed, she accommodated. *Appearances. Appearances.* Lilly's voice in her head, reminding her. It was always for the *yentas* in the Hadassah. For Milton, it was the fans. There was always someone to impress, and somehow, it was more Jessie's burden than either of her sisters'. She took it upon herself; she wanted the praise all for herself.

People know she's neurotic—there's only so much she can hide—but what they don't know about is the monster inside her. It breathes fear in her skull, spreads worry through her body like chemical warfare, whispers at her in the dark. It tortures her every moment of her life. But on the outside she is perfectly groomed and wears designer outfits and balances work with child care impressively and is married to a doctor and lives in a detached house in a nice Jewish section of North Toronto.

She is someone who is always admired by other women. Which, of course, has always been her intention.

Estelle

*S*he staggers into her apartment sometime after ten. Astrid kept her late again, going over the goddamn *Taxi to Tijuana* trailer until she could recite the lines by heart. If it weren't for Russell Hirsch, her current job would be cause for crisis. But Hirsch has got her demo reel and he is considering her for an editing job on his new movie and she is feeling utterly impervious to Astrid.

She grabs a Coke and the container of Breyers from her freezer, and goes up to Peri's. He answers the door, wearing a tie-dyed shirt, jeans, and Birkenstocks. His toenails need clipping. "Ever hear of nail clippers?" she remarks, sounding more like Lilly than she wants to. It must course through their blood, the instinct for disapproval.

"Have you heard anything?" she asks him. "From Russell?"

"Yeah. About that. You don't exactly have a lot of experience."

"Is that what he said? So you spoke to him?" She can feel the thinly constructed walls of her self-confidence beginning to collapse.

"I ran into him yesterday."

"And you didn't tell me?"

"He's planning to call you himself. Look, this is for a legit studio. He wanted you to have at least one feature under your belt. The studio would never have gone for it otherwise."

"How am I supposed to get a feature without already having a feature?"

"Luck."

*L*ater, after a long bout of self-indulgent weeping, she fires up her computer. Probably not the best time to check her J-Date status, but the vindictive, self-destructive part of her is hoping to add insult to injury; to compound her misery and *really* have a good wallow. Wallowing in self-pity, especially in one's bed with a large Domino's pizza, is surprisingly comforting. (More comforting than being hurled out into the real world anyway.) Now she'll have twice the ammunition. Not only is her career going nowhere, but of course no one from J-Date has responded to her—

Surprisingly, there's a new e-mail. This time from J-Date access code 54987. Screen name: the Wandering Jew. She reads the e-mail and then immediately calls up his picture on the J-Date Web site. But instead of a picture, there's just a black box. He's chosen to remain anonymous. In other words, he's either obese or has to spray-paint hair on his head.

Spirits dampened, she reads his profile:

My Screen Name is the WANDERING JEW *and I am a* 37-YEAR-OLD MALE FROM TORONTO, ONTARIO, CANADA.

My hair is BROWN *and my eyes are* BROWN *and I am* 5'11" *tall. My body style is* FIRM & TONED.

I am SINGLE *and have* NO CHILDREN.

I am REFORM *and* GO TO SYNAGOGUE ON HIGH HOLI-DAYS *and* I DON'T KEEP KOSHER.

My astrological sign is SCORPIO.

My personality traits are EARTHY, ECCENTRIC, FLEXI-
BLE, SENSITIVE, ROMANTIC, SPONTANEOUS.

The activities I enjoy are COOKING, SCRABBLE,
CAMPING, JOURNALING.

I like these kinds of music: FOLK, CLASSIC ROCK.

My favorite cuisine is TUNISIAN, LITHUANIAN.

I usually read FICTION, NONFICTION, NEWSPAPERS.

I like the following pets: LOVER OF ALL ANIMALS.

My pet peeves are: PEOPLE WHO REFER TO GOD AS
"THE GOOD LORD."

More about me: I LIKE THE NEW THICK KIT KAT BAR. I
HATE TELEVISION, CHEWED GUM IN ASHTRAYS, AND
SMOKERS. I LIKE TO BE OUTDOORS. I AM AN AMATEUR
SOMMELIER.

More about my perfect date: SHE'LL BE FUNNY AND
CREATIVE AND INTELLIGENT AND NEVER ASK ME IF SHE
LOOKS FAT.

Our first date should be as follows: AN IMMEDIATE
INTELLECTUAL CONNECTION. HOURS OF CONVERSATION AT
A FABULOUS RESTAURANT. A LOT OF LAUGHTER. A THICK KIT
KAT BAR FOR DESSERT. A PASSIONATE KISS GOOD NIGHT AT
HER FRONT DOOR.

Estelle closes the J-Date file on the Wandering Jew and
returns to his e-mail. She rereads it with mounting curiosity.

*Estelle. I can't believe you're still single. I've always
had a crush on you and thought for sure someone
would have snapped you up by now. Check out my
J-Date stats and e-mail me if you're interested in
getting together. I'll come to you. WJ.*

He *knows* her. She starts racking her brain. Someone from Toronto? She can't remember anyone from high school who might have had a crush on her, certainly no one from Ryerson. Maybe Jessie or Erica will remember someone from Russell Hill—a fat little misfit who had a crush on her? Imagine.

Still, she is buoyed. He knows her and likes her. *It's in the bag*. So they're a bit different. Big deal. She can quit smoking, quit TV, stop asking people if she looks fat, and look up the word *sommelier* in the dictionary.

Dear Wandering Jew. I'm intrigued. WHO ARE YOU??

Erica

A young Japanese woman approaches the newsstand and rises up on her tiptoes to get a better view of the cigarettes lining the wall.

"Can I help you?" Erica asks her.

"Which ones are the fashion designers smoking?" she asks. "Which are the trendy cigarettes?"

Erica grits her teeth. "How about Marlboro?"

"We can get Marlboro in Japan."

Erica sighs. Her head hurts from too much squinting. Welcome to the lobby of the Paramount Hotel, where art deco literally translates to "no lighting." The entire lobby is dark, and because everyone—guests and staff alike—wears black, you can hardly make out anyone or anything without squinting. All she can see are shadowy blurs in motion.

"How about Merit Light?" the Japanese tourist asks.

"Very trendy," Erica responds, and she hands over a pack.

Having returned to her old job last week, she now wonders which is the lesser of two evils: being a kept woman, or selling trendy cigarettes to tourists at a trendy hotel in the dark. The truth is, her guilt and low self-esteem about her writing necessitated coming back to work. If Paul keeps insinuating that her writing is just a hobby, she'd better have some source of income to contribute to her own upkeep.

Just as she's about to resume reading *Death Comes for the Archbishop* (she's at the Willa Cather section of Paul's reading list, which is sandwiched between Wharton and Faulkner, in no discernible order) she spots that actor who plays twins on *All My Children*. He's wearing a black leather jacket, black leather pants, a black turtleneck, and a black scarf. If it weren't for his white hair, he would be invisible. She squints again, trying to make sure it's him.

"It's him."

Erica turns her attention to the customer standing in front of her—a young guy wearing a cream-colored cable-knit sweater with jeans. She loves men in cable-knit. It's so autumnal. He looks like he belongs on some New England Ivy League campus, or else on a yacht, like he should smell of ocean or something.

"Trust me, it's him," he says again.

"Who?"

"The guy from *All My Children*," he says.

Erica laughs. "You recognize him?"

"He plays the twins," he says, plunking a pack of Extra on the counter.

"Just the gum?" she asks him.

He nods. "You don't remember me," he says, handing her a five-dollar bill.

"It's so dark in here . . ." she says apologetically.

"It's Mitchell."

Still nothing.

"Mitchell Dorfman? From the Upright Citizens Brigade?"

"Oh! You were in my improv class—"

"Right."

"I'm sorry. I just . . ."

"It's pretty dark in here." He pops a piece of gum in his mouth and makes no move to leave. "How have you been? It's Erica, right?"

"Right. I'm great. . . ." All of a sudden she becomes extremely self-conscious about her surroundings—specifically that she is standing behind the cash register at a newsstand, selling gum and cigarettes—and she is mortified. He's sort of cute too (though rather young), which intensifies her shame. He's got straight, black hair that reminds her of the hair-cuts the boys had in Estelle's elementary class pictures—sort of longish and unstyled and shapeless, like Scott Baio's. He's got long dark lashes and girlish cheekbones, giving him a kind of prettiness that suits his short, slim frame. He looks about eighteen. She notices a tattoo on the inside of his wrist—a letter or a symbol. She has no explanation for why she finds this sexy, but she does.

"I'm just working here part-time while I get my portfolio together," she tells him, with no provocation.

"Photography, right?"

"No. Writing. I'm applying to the MFA at Columbia."

"I thought you were a photographer," he says, confused. "Hadn't you just finished a photojournalism program?"

Why does he know so much about her? She couldn't have picked him out of a lineup two minutes ago and yet he's fully up-to-date on her academic career.

"I didn't quite finish it," she admits, "but yeah, I was at ICP right before I joined UCB." (She is acutely aware of the fact that her résumé is becoming increasingly humiliating, indefensible, and schizophrenic.) "But, um, writing has really always been my 'thing.'"

"So you didn't go on to level two," he remarks.

"Level two?"

"With the improv classes."

"I wasn't very good," she says. "Besides, I need to be concentrating on my writing."

He nods, probably placating her. She feels herself flush.

"Well," he says, mercifully wrapping up their awkward banter. "I'm meeting someone in the bar. . . ."

"You sure you're old enough?" she says, half teasing but also fishing for his age.

He looks slightly bruised. "I'm twenty-seven."

"Oh," she fumbles. "I didn't . . ."

"I know. I look young. It's . . . Don't feel bad."

But she does. She feels bad because she works at a newsstand, because she is a sham, and because she likes his cool seventies haircut and that odd symbol on his wrist.

"Anyway," he says. "See you later."

She manages a smile.

*L*ater, on her break, she goes into the bar to see if he's still there. She spots him in the back corner, sitting with a woman in a black catsuit. (Are catsuits in? she wonders.) She watches him for a moment, then leaves.

She barely remembers him from the improv class, which is a good thing. It means he didn't stand out for being embarrassingly bad—as many were. It also means she was still in the blind, compulsive, all-encompassing, madly-in-love stage of her relationship with Paul—the stage where no other man on the planet existed.

That she has *now* noticed Mitchell Dorfman does not bode well for the current stage of her relationship with Paul.

Jessie

"*M*mm. That was nice, eh?"

She nods mutely, blinking back tears. Allan rolls over and puts his pillow between his legs, a habit she used to find sweet.

"Night," he murmurs, already drifting into sleep.

How easy for him. She lies there for a while, listening to the even ticking of the grandfather clock on the landing. Sometimes it lulls her to sleep, other times—like now—it torturously measures each and every minute of the long night. She knows when she won't sleep; knows when her mind won't turn off, when her fears will thump and rattle inside her skull, hour after hour until the sun comes up.

Was there ever a time when she enjoyed making love to Allan? She can't remember. She isn't a sexual person, that's always been her excuse. She doesn't blame Allan, doesn't think it's because he's especially selfish or simply not good in bed. How would she know anyway? It's true he doesn't go out of his way to find out what turns her on, but if it were ever put to her, she wouldn't know how to respond. She doesn't know her own body; it's as strange to her as if it were not attached to her head. Perhaps it *isn't*. Certainly, there's a disconnection. She knows that much. Her body is something to work at and control, to keep slim and toned, to keep clean. The way you upkeep your home. It would be a risk to let go, to relinquish herself to its needs and desires—if in fact there are any locked away inside. She thinks of her body as something that has to be reined in. Besides, Allan has never asked for more than she's given; he makes no demands on her body. Just lie there, endure the epic thrusting, feign pleasure, and then go to sleep.

She occasionally wonders if she's missing out on something, something wild and exquisite. But you can't miss what you've never had. (Then why the urge to cry afterward? Why does she find herself holding back tears when he's finished? What untapped part of her *knows* there's more to it?)

Once in a while she wonders how Allan can assume she's always satisfied. Is it denial? Arrogance? Ignorance? Or a combination of all three? She marvels at his ability to accept her performance at face value. She *knows* she's a disappointment in bed. But then, he's always been a loyal enthusiast of the status quo.

After an hour of listening to Allan snore, she slips out of bed and goes downstairs. She boils water for chamomile tea and sits down at the breakfast counter. It's almost one. Only ten o'clock in L.A. She reaches for the portable phone and calls Estelle.

"Hey, Bean," she says wearily.

"Isn't it past your bedtime?" Estelle says.

"Insomnia."

"Ah. Are you ever able to shut that brain of yours off?"

"Rarely."

"So what's up?" Estelle says. They both know Jessie never calls without a reason.

"Nothing really."

"You okay?"

Jessie sighs. How do you broach the topic of sex with your sister, when *you* are the one who's been married for years? When you've already got two kids and the world assumes you must know what you're doing?

"Any bites on J-Date?" she asks, procrastinating.

"A couple."

"Any potential?"

"I had a great date with a screenwriter," Estelle says. "We really hit it off."

"What's his name?"

"Ronnie Weinrock."

"Aren't you afraid some serial killer will answer your ad? I mean, you don't know who these lose—" She bites her tongue.

"Losers are?"

"I don't mean it like that. . . ."

"Right."

"Well. So this J-Date thing might be your salvation, eh?"

"I'm looking for a man, not salvation."

"Is there a difference?"

"Hopefully."

"Have you slept with any of them?" Jessie asks, maneuvering for a smooth segue.

"Of course not."

"Oh."

"Is something bothering you, Jess?"

"Have you ever, um . . ."

"What?"

"Nothing. Look, I'm tired. I should try to get some sleep."

"Are you okay?"

"I don't know. I'm always tired. It makes me irrational."

"Take a sleeping pill."

"Are you nuts? I don't take pills."

"They're harmless."

"I don't think I'm a good wife," Jessie blurts.

"That's ridiculous. You're the perfect wife."

Jessie lets out an ironic laugh. "I'm not a good mother, either," she confesses.

"But you take such good care of your kids."

"Isn't there supposed to be more to it than that? I don't think I've bonded with them." She's talking about all of them now, her entire family.

"Now you *are* being irrational. Where's this coming from?"

"I don't know. I worry that I'm . . . I don't know. Empty inside. Like I have no real love to give."

"Don't say that."

"It's true, Bean." She is back to thinking of her sexuality, about how it's so forced and hollow. There's nothing *beneath* it. No emotion or passion. Sometimes her whole life feels that way. Like she's following a script and uttering all the lines but the performance isn't heartfelt or genuine. "I have to go," she says, feeling suddenly embarrassed. She hates that she just laid herself out like this, made herself vulnerable. Now Estelle has a leg up on her. Now Estelle knows there's a crack in the sheen.

"Jess, this isn't like you."

"I'm just sleepy. I was up at five this morning. I get crazy this late—"

"You don't sound like yourself," Estelle says.

What does she usually sound like? What do they expect from her? "I don't feel like myself either," she says. "Look, I'll call you next week."

"Jess—"

"I'm just tired, Bean. Really."

She hangs up and stares at the phone for a while. She said too much. She shouldn't have made that phone call; she shouldn't do *anything* this late at night. She goes over to the kettle and fills her mug with boiling water. She adds milk and a teaspoon of sugar and then has a sip. She forgot the damn tea bag. She dumps the hot sugary water down the sink and goes back upstairs to check on the kids. She sits down on the edge of Levi's bed and strokes his head. His ratty old stuffed mouse, Topo Gigio—a hand-me-down from his father—is next to him on the pillow. His breathing is light and even, his narrow chest rising and falling peacefully. So precious when he's asleep, his mouth open slightly and his little arms flung out at his sides. She rubs her nose against his soft skin. Baby smell. Is this *love,* or just a relentless urge to protect him from the world? How would she even know the difference?

She arrives the next day at Ooze, which is a big black cave that reeks of beer and cigarettes. She worries vaguely about what the secondhand smoke will do to her lungs if she takes the job. Her boot heels stick to the floor as she makes her way over to the bar, where a short, stocky bartender is hoisting bottles onto the counter.

"I'm looking for Skieth," she says.

"Jessie Jaffe?"

"That's right."

"I'm Skieth Ellis."

"You're Skieth?"

"I am."

"Oh. I thought . . . I just assumed—" She hadn't been expecting someone so young, let alone someone so unpolished.

"I'd be . . . ?"

"Out of college," she jokes.

Skieth laughs. "I got my MBA from U of T in ninety-five, if you want credentials."

"You're the owner?"

The guy owns half a dozen bars and restaurants all over the city, yet he looks like he belongs inside a boxing ring. He's got a square, smashed face with a crooked nose, deep-set blue eyes, and a thick neck. Certainly not her idea of a venture capitalist.

"Let me show you the office," he says.

She follows him across the dance floor to the back of the bar. She can't stop staring at him, can't stop trying to put him into context. He doesn't fit. He's rough, a bit scary. His back is as wide as a fridge. She has to keep reminding herself that he's a client. A potentially *great* client. And yet here he is wearing a pair of shredded Levi's and scuffed Doc Martens boots with a tight black "Ooze" T-shirt stretched thin across his muscles. His blond hair is shaggy and bleached at the tips; there are tattoos on his massive forearms. She doesn't know how to act. He's someone she would be intimidated by on the street; someone she would label and dismiss.

"I love this idea," he tells her. "I love it."

"What?"

"This thing you do. Organizing people. It's a great idea."

"I'm not the first one to do it."

"No? I've never heard of it before."

"Did someone recommend me?"

"You did my sister's best friend's house. Lara Goodman?" (He knows a Jewish person! She feels calmed by that. Reassured.) "She said you were fantastic."

"She did? That's nice to hear."

"Anyway. It's a great idea. There's a lot of potential."

"For what?"

"For expansion. Like you could be the Martha Stewart of organizing or something."

She laughs off the idea.

"I'm serious. There's a lot of room for growth here. Like training a team of people to do what you do and going national. Have you thought about any of that?"

Jessie shakes her head. "I just do this to keep busy. I've got two kids."

He looks at her thoughtfully. "We can talk about it later," he says. "First things first."

He shows her into the office, which is a small maelstrom of chaos. "My manager is a total slob when it comes to paperwork," he explains. "I mean, look at this."

Skieth holds up an overstuffed file folder, fat as a phone book. "Do you know what this file is?"

She shakes her head.

"It's his 'To File' file. It's where he puts every piece of paper that comes into this office. Bills included."

Her inclination is to suggest firing the guy, but she holds back. "No problem," she says. She opens and closes a few filing cabinets. "Do you know that eighty percent of filed papers are never referenced again?"

"Here it's more like ninety-nine percent."

"The average workplace spends about a hundred and fifty dollars in labor just looking for documents."

"So what can you do for me?" he asks her.

"My goal is to design a tailor-made system for your manager that will help him *stay* organized. Something he can live with and maintain. Obviously I'd restructure all his systems, but I'd also give him at least a couple of seminars on office management."

"If you can do *that*," he tells her, "I'd like you to do the office at my bistro too."

"Where is it?"

"On College, west of Bathurst. It was my first restaurant. My baby."

She smiles, feeling buoyed by the prospect. She isn't sure if it's the money she's excited about, or *him*. Someone who's actually interested in what she does.

"I'm sure we will," he says.

"What?"

"Work well together."

He levels his dark blue eyes at her. She's rattled by his directness. She's used to being flirted with by the middle-aged husbands of some of her clients; she can expertly shrug off their lusty gazes and offhand remarks and go about being her usual efficient self. She *knows* that kind of man—hell, she lives with one of them. But with Skieth, she finds herself tongue-tied and clumsy. He's a different kind of specimen altogether—younger, unconventional, uncharted.

Estelle

"*The Key Party* is going to Sundance in January."

"What's Sundance, Bean?"

Estelle sighs. Her good fortune is always lost on her parents. "It's a film festival, Dad."

"Good for you," he says lethargically.

He's still depressed. Gladys's health is deteriorating. Despite the chemo, her prognosis is not good. Lilly says he doesn't leave the hospital, that he's like a zombie.

"So I'll be going to Park City, Utah, in January," she says.

"Why?"

"For Sundance!"

"Do you get money for that?"

"No."

"Oh."

"Robert Redford founded it," she explains. "It's his festival."

"Robert Redford, eh? Hmm."

Impressed, finally.

"But," he adds, "shouldn't he pay you?"

Estelle closes her eyes. "It's not about the money," she says. She may as well be speaking Mandarin. He won't get it. Her father only speaks the language of *shekels*.

"Oh," he says.

"It's just the prestige," she goes on. "It's good for my . . . Never mind."

"Of course it is, Bean. I'm proud of you."

Hollow praise. He doesn't understand art. He understands entertainment and fame, but not art.

"We're worried about you," he tells her. "Your mother says the terror alert level is at orange."

"I don't even know what that means."

"I think it means extra-elevated. Jessie told me to tell you not to fly or cross any bridges and also to stay out of big crowds."

All of a sudden, Astrid Blansky shoves her face into the editing suite. "Is that a personal call?"

Estelle nods. *Family crisis,* she mouths.

"I've got the VOs for the *Mob Wars* trailer," she says impatiently.

"Give me a second—"

"We talked about your personal calls," she says with a sigh.

"Listen, I've got to go, Dad," Estelle mutters, and hangs up.

Astrid is standing there with her hands on her bony hips. She pushes her glasses up on her nose. "You're a good editor," she says. "But you can't just, you know, do whatever the hell you please around here. You're not indispensable."

"My father's not well."

"Well. Can you finish the *Mob Wars* trailer by tomorrow? The producer's breathing down my neck."

"I'll probably have to be here all night."

"Whatever it takes," Astrid chirps, handing her the voice-overs.

She'd like to hurl those VOs at Astrid's scrawny back. If it weren't for Sundance keeping her spirits alive, Estelle would probably quit Just-A-Trim, get on a plane back to Toronto, and take a job in Canadian TV.

She orders Szechuan into the editing suite for supper. While she's shoveling greasy egg rolls and fiery balls of General Tso's chicken into her mouth, an e-mail comes up on her screen. It's a cryptic message from her J-Date, the Wandering Jew:

Family Emergency back home. Can't make our date.
I'll be in touch.

Obviously he's had second thoughts and his family emergency is just an excuse to get out of their date. She isn't surprised. In fact, deep down, she almost hopes so. She doesn't want to be disappointed again. She isn't a good dater. She's too insecure, too desperate. It's never been easy, not even when she was younger.

Her first boyfriend didn't come along until her second year at Ryerson. His name was Eli Guberman. They dated on and off for nearly two years. She lost her virginity to him but for some reason their relationship never congealed into anything substantial. Finally he broke it off to go out with an Italian girl. He always had a thing for Latinas.

Estelle's path to the altar has not been as swift or seamless as Jessie's was. Yet it has occurred to her since the late-night phone call that the grass in Jessie's yard may not be as green as it once seemed; maybe the life Estelle has coveted since the moment Jessie announced her engagement is really no better than her own. And although Estelle is worried about her sister—not excessively worried, but somewhat concerned— she's secretly relieved to know that the perfect veneer of Jessie's life has a crack, and that Jessie is a lot more vulnerable than she's ever let on.

After she polishes off her Chinese takeout, Estelle skulks

down the hall to invite Sally for a cigarette. They ride the elevator downstairs. Outside, the sun is beaming down on them. It's warm for November, with barely any wind. Ah, California. Never mind her stalled career in L.A.; she wouldn't go back to slushy gray Toronto for anything.

"Astrid is so vindictive," Estelle whines. "She's probably going to sabotage my career. She's one of those petty, easily threatened women."

"Don't worry so much about Astrid."

"But she's like a bouncer," Estelle rants. "Power-hungry and self-important."

"You'd do well to stay on her good side," Sally warns, lighting up a Marlboro. "She's connected to a lot of producers. Besides, this is just the beginning, you know."

"Of what?"

"Your career. Focus on Sundance. Soon you won't even remember Astrid's name."

"I hope so. I don't know how much longer I can do movie trailers. It's creatively stunting."

"Don't be high and mighty. We all have to pay our dues."

Estelle has noticed that people over the age of fifty are always spouting that worn-out cliché. *What* dues? Why can't an artist simply dive headfirst into creative glory without first having to toil in the soul-destroying muck of dues paying?

"Any word from your secret admirer?" Sally asks, changing the subject.

"We were supposed to have a date this week," she says. "But he canceled. He's got some family emergency in Toronto."

"And he still hasn't told you who he is?"

Estelle shakes her head. "Nope. I guess I'll find out when and if we meet."

"And when will that be?"

"His e-mail was pretty vague. He'll be in Toronto indefinitely. He didn't say why."

"I'd be bursting at the seams. You have no idea who it could be?"

"None whatsoever."

Erica

"*I abhor* happy endings!" Paul exclaims. "I mean, why pander to the lowest common denominator of your readership?"

Everyone in the class shrinks back as his tone gets louder and more aggressive with each rhetorical question.

"Life isn't happy!" Paul states emphatically. "Loose ends are never tied up, are they? We get enough happy endings in movies. Can literature not remain sacred? The short story should be thought-provoking, complex. It should end in such a way as to make you *think*. Remember thinking, ladies and gentlemen?"

Erica's face is red-hot. All she can think is, *He will pay.* This rant he's on is at *her* expense, and, oh, how she will make him pay for it later on.

"Now, Erica," he says, turning his attention back to her story. "Why did you settle for a happy ending in this piece?"

Is it just her, or did he spit out the word "piece" the way one spits toothpaste into the sink? "It felt right," she mumbles.

"A more provocative ending is the difference between a pleasant enough, inoffensive, amateur short story"—he holds up her story and waves it in the air—"and a publishable work of some literary merit."

"I just thought they should stay together," Erica says meekly.

"Norma and Walter would *never* stay together! He's a picaro, a wanderer. But that's beside the point. Why do we have to know either way? The outcome should be left to our imagination. I'd cut this entire paragraph and end right here—"

He bends over his desk and starts making slashes all over the page. "A short story should be opaque—"

"Says who?" Erica challenges.

Paul stops what he's doing and looks up.

"I actually think there's a good balance between Norma and Walter," someone suggests. "I like that they stay together. They're like ying and yang."

"Yin," Paul corrects grumpily.

"I agree," another student chimes in, coming to Erica's defense. "Their relationship is, like, the one stable thing throughout all the chaoticness."

Paul winces. "You mean *chaos,*" he mutters limply. And although Erica would love nothing more than to have his approval, she can't help feeling slightly vindicated by the support of her classmates.

"*L*ook," he says. "Don't get me wrong. This is your best work yet. *By far.*"

"It is?" They're heading home along Broadway. It's one of those blustery November days and the damp cold has penetrated right through the cloth of her trench coat. The wind whipping in off the Hudson River doesn't help either, and despite her anger, she is huddled against Paul for warmth.

"Of course it is," Paul assures her. "Norma and Walter are very well drawn. I mean, they're believable. I buy them as a couple. That's quite an achievement."

"You didn't give the impression that you liked it in class."

"Aha!" he cries, stopping abruptly in the middle of the street. "You took my critique personally! You reacted to your boyfriend in there and not to your professor!"

"You *are* my boyfriend," she points out. "We live together. It's kind of hard to separate the two."

"Well, you'd better learn how," he says. "I wasn't any harder on you than I am on my other students. It doesn't do you any good for me to stroke your ego and spare your feelings. I want to mold you into a real writer, Erica. In that classroom, I'm your *teacher*. Our personal relationship is of no consequence in there. And the truth is, your ending sucks. The bones are there, but you have to change the ending."

"Some people liked it."

"Oh yes," he mocks. "It balanced out the 'chaoticness.'"

Erica can't help giggling.

"Listen," he says, putting his arm around her. "Let's order in some Chinese food and curl up in the den and figure out how to improve that ending."

"I'm working at eight."

Paul looks at his watch. "We've still got a few hours to squeeze in some takeout and some editing."

"Will that be as my boyfriend or as my teacher?" she teases.

"The snuggling and eating Chinese takeout will be as your boyfriend," he says. "The editing part will be as your teacher."

"And afterward?"

"In bed, you mean? Naturally I'll be the teacher."

She punches his chest playfully.

"I forgot to put Alice Munro on your reading list," he says parenthetically. "That'll be your homework assignment for this week—to read a collection of her short stories."

She looks up at him and opens her mouth to say something. She is about to point out that she doesn't want homework assignments from him when they're outside the classroom, in the same way he doesn't want his girlfriend *inside* the classroom. Sometimes they both lose track of where the relationship begins and the mentoring ends; they're both guilty of changing their minds about it on a daily basis. But in the end, all she says is "I'm more in the mood for Vietnamese *pho*."

*L*ater, at the Paramount newsstand, Erica rebels and eschews Willa Cather in favor of *In Style* magazine. It goes without saying that she wouldn't dare bring home an entertainment magazine—*People, Us, Entertainment Weekly,* et cetera, all of which are verboten—lest she should give Paul fodder for one of his vainglorious rants. (Of course all those magazines pander to the lowest common denominator of American consumers. . . .) So she reads them at work instead.

It's a quiet November night. The New York Marathon was last weekend and the hotel has been relatively empty ever since. Besides, it's cold out. Every time someone comes through the front entrance, a brutal gust of wind blows in. Erica would have given anything to stay home tonight, cuddled on the gigantic shabby-chic couch in the den, being spoon-fed beef *pho*.

Earlier they worked on her short story for a while, and then they started to fool around. Paul managed to get her shirt off, but they never finished. She had to get to work. She almost called in sick, but having just gotten her job back, she felt it was too soon to start playing hooky. And so she left

Paul lying half-naked on the couch, surrounded by loose sheets of paper and cartons of Vietnamese food, with Paula Cole's sultry voice crackling over the speakers.

"I love our life," she told him, right before she left.

He pulled her down on top of him and begged her to stay.

"I can't," she whispered. "Believe me, I'd love to."

"I'll get this ready to send out," he said, pointing to her newly revised short story with its unhappy, opaque ending. "I just want to make a few more small changes," he added.

She kissed him, feeling grateful for his help; grateful that he deems her writing worthy of his efforts. Maybe she *has* finally found her calling.

"Grab a twenty from my wallet," he said. "I don't want you taking the subway home alone."

She got up off of him and left, feeling happy and full.

"I love our life too!" he called after her.

And now there's an hour left of her shift. The lobby is virtually deserted, even for a Tuesday night. She finishes the *In Style* magazine and reaches for an *O*. (Another secret she keeps from Paul: she adores Oprah. Sadly, even Oprah fans are lumped into that vast category of intellectually bankrupt morons who offend him on every level.)

"Hi, Erica."

She looks up and there's Mitchell Dorfman, with his sexy seventies hair and a rosy complexion from the cold.

He cups his hands together and blows on his chapped red knuckles. "Shit, it's cold out there."

She assumes he's got another date with Catsuit. This must be "their place." He probably wants a pack of gum too. He'll probably start coming here all the time to buy gum before he goes off to meet Catsuit in the bar, and Erica will have to make small talk with him and swallow her humiliation over her degrading job. God must be punishing her for some past transgression.

"I, uh, I was just passing by . . ." he says.

"You were?"

"I work near here."

She waits a beat for him to choose something—some gum, a chocolate bar, a newspaper. But he doesn't ask for anything. He just stands there.

"When do you get off?" he finally asks her.

"In an hour."

"I could wait."

"For what?"

"For you to get off. We could grab a drink and catch up."

"Catch up on what?"

He laughs easily, which makes her laugh.

"We could just grab a drink, then," he says.

Her first thought is of Paul, at home laboring over *her* short story, probably waiting for her to come home so he can run her a bath and get in the tub with her. Her second thought is that a drink with Mitchell Dorfman is alarmingly enticing. He's watching her expectantly.

"You probably want to get home . . ." he says, almost retracting the invitation.

"I can't stay out too late," she tells him.

He looks not entirely sure if she's accepted his offer or not; she isn't sure if she has either.

"I'll wait for you in the bar?" he says.

"Sure." *Sure?* What demon is controlling her voice? As he walks off, she grabs her cell phone from her purse and calls Paul.

"Hi, baby."

"Hi, love." His voice sounds groggy. "Are you almost done?"

"Almost, but I'm going to grab a drink with an old friend after work. I won't be too late."

"Who?"

"Mitchell. From the Upright Citizens Brigade."

"The improv thing?"

"Mmm."

"Okay, love."

"I won't be late."

"I'll be asleep."

"I won't wake you."

"Your story is ready to go. I prepared the envelopes. I chose six literary reviews that I think are suitable—"

"Go back to sleep," she says softly.

She can hear him purring. He hangs up.

She closes up the newsstand at midnight, and then goes into the lobby bathroom to put on some lipstick and comb her hair. Her breath smells like Vietnamese *pho;* she gropes around in her purse for a lemon SMINT. She stares at herself in the mirror and wonders what the hell she's doing. And then she goes out to meet Mitchell Dorfman in the bar.

"What are you having?" he asks her. She can barely see him in the dark. (The bar is actually darker than the lobby.) The tiny candles flickering in frosted glasses do little to illuminate the room.

"I'll have a glass of red wine," she says.

He flags down the waitress and orders a carafe of merlot. "Is that okay?" he says. "The carafe?"

"Sure." *Sure. Sure. Sure.*

The wine arrives and he pours some for her and then some for himself, and then they clink glasses.

"So where do you work?" she asks him.

"My office is at Sixth and Forty-fourth."

"What do you do?"

"I invent games. Don't you remember? We all had to introduce ourselves in that first class."

She shakes her head. "I probably wasn't paying attention," she admits. "What kind of games? Like Monopoly and Trivial Pursuit?"

"Sort of. My father and I have a company. Have you ever heard of Quote Unquote?"

"No. But I'm not really a game person." Lilly and Milton are "game people." They've probably heard of Quote Unquote. Probably play it every Sunday with the ladies from the Hadassah and their husbands.

"If you stay up late enough on a Sunday night," he tells her, "you'll see the commercial for it on channel seven. 'Quote Unquote, a game of who-said-what.' That's the slogan."

She smiles, finding the whole thing kind of charming and wacky.

"We're working on a new one for the toy fair in February," he says. "It's called Red-Handed. It's a game of celebrity scandals. I spend all my time these days immersed in the lives of Lana Turner, Roman Polanski, and Bob Crane."

"Who?"

"From *Hogan's Heroes*?"

He has nice lips. She's watching them move as he talks; the words are coming out of them and floating off somewhere and she can barely hang onto them: *Buffy from* Family Affair, *Fatty Arbuckle, blah blah blah* . . . He could be an Abercrombie &

Fitch model. It occurs to her, and not for the first time either, that beauty has a terrible, lulling power over her.

"So are your real career aspirations to be a stand-up comedian or to be on *Saturday Night Live*?" she asks him.

"Naw. Improv is something I do for fun. It's a good release."

"I think I'm too self-conscious," she tells him. "I mean, I like watching improv, but not participating in it. I was always kind of mortified in class."

"That's probably because you've got the shame gene. But if you like watching it, we could check out Asssscat 3000 together. It's that long-form improv show at the UCB Theater. It's got performers from *Saturday Night Live* and *Second City*. It's hilarious."

"What is this?" she interrupts, pointing to the tattoo on his wrist. It's been distracting her.

"My tattoo? I've come to think of it as the symbol of my teenage idiocy."

"Why?"

"It's embarrassingly pretentious."

"Just tell me what it is."

"It's an ancient rune," he admits. "This particular one is Algiz. It symbolizes protection. Like a shield, you know? Warding off evil." He laughs sheepishly. "I thought it was very cool when I was seventeen."

"I like it," she says.

He notices her wineglass is empty and refills it. "I'm glad we hooked up," he tells her. "I figured my chances were pretty slim."

"Your chances?"

"My flirting in class didn't really seem to get anywhere with you."

"What flirting?"

"Exactly," he says.

She feels herself blush and wants to come back with some clever quip, but draws a total blank. He tucks a long strand of black hair behind his ear and has a sip of wine. She's got that reeling feeling, like she's about to tumble headfirst into something dangerous and irrevocable.

I live with someone, she tells him.

But she only says it in her head.

Lilly

*S*he's sitting in the den by herself, sulking. Milton calls the room the Padded Cell, because it's all done in pale neutrals—bone-white walls, cream-colored carpeting, matching white-slipcovered couches, and antiqued-white furniture. Lilly finds it serene, but in order to keep it serene, everyone else is forbidden to set foot in here unless they've showered and are wearing the little Chinese slippers she keeps just outside the door.

As she gazes at the Inuit sculpture on her coffee table, she grows more enraged by the minute. Five little children carved out of what? Soapstone? Limestone? Sandstone? She can't remember. Their little something-stone arms are reaching out and they're holding a piece of cloth with a baby in the center. Gladys gave it to them for their twenty-fifth wedding anniversary. It came with a piece of paper, a photocopy of a letter written by the queen of England or one of her minions. Apparently the queen owns one of these sculptures too. So big deal. *October 15, 1977. Her Majesty is delighted to accept this carving at the start of her Silver Jubilee visit to Ottawa and thought the scene of the Eskimos at play was charming. . . .*

What bullshit. Everyone at their anniversary party had gone berserk over it. As usual, Gladys had outdone herself. The whole night became about *her.* "Do you know how much these things are worth?" Milton kept asking Lilly. Even after everyone had gone home, he kept staring at it, running his

stubby fingers over the smooth stone. "Isn't it so thoughtful?" he kept murmuring.

Lilly just nodded and smiled, but she'd wanted to heave it
across the room.

She squints at the clock on the VCR but can't make out
the time from where she's sitting on the couch. She gets up
and inches closer to it, until the numbers begin to take shape:
1:17 A.M. and still no Milton. He's been at the Princess
Margaret Hospital for days, sitting by Gladys's bedside with
her frail hand clasped in his.

She pads quietly down the hall to her room. She removes
the bedspread, folding it neatly and placing it on the suede
settee by the window. One by one she removes all the throw
pillows and decorative shams and stacks them neatly on the
dresser. Then she closes the raw silk drapes, which are
puddled on the floor as per her decorator's suggestion—
"Puddling is the rage."

Alone in bed, she sobs into her pillow to muffle the noise.
God forgive her, she can't wait for Gladys to die. Once upon
a time, Milton had been crazy about Lilly. Always singing to
her, buying her little stuffed animals from his friend Larry
Pinsky, the toy salesman. Whenever she got into his car, there
was a little plush bear or rabbit hidden in the glove compart-
ment. He used to take her to the Stork Club, to hear his
friends sing. At some point in the night he'd jump on the
stage and start crooning to her. "Zing Went the Strings of My
Heart" or that famous Judy Garland song—she can't remember it now. God, she loved it. It was always her favorite. What
was it?

He only had eyes for her then. He was infatuated. Even
persuaded her to give up her virginity in the backseat of his
Packard! They'd been on the show together about a year by

then and she was wildly in love with him. His voice, his sense of humor. She'd never met anyone like him before. When she was growing up, her house had never been filled with laughter; her father had been a stern, serious man. So when Milton came along, she was totally susceptible to his rambunctious charm, his pranks and pratfalls, his carefree spirit. He made her laugh. God, he was funny! Outrageous, shameless. What he lacked in manners and class, he made up for with his boundless energy.

Right after she got pregnant during the second season of their TV show, they enjoyed about three months of marital bliss. She was still working and hadn't told the CBC brass that she was expecting, so she had Milty and her singing career and a baby in her belly, and her life was marvelous. But the day came when they had to divulge their secret. The CBC leaped into action to find a replacement for her. Dozens of girls auditioned with Milton but not one of them had the kind of chemistry they were looking for.

Until Gladys.

Milt was instantly taken with Gladys. She had something about her. He was always taking her out dancing after the show while Lilly was home with her nose in Estelle's shitty diapers. There were no more "frolicking Wednesdays," as Milton used to refer to their designated lovemaking night. No more visits to the Stork Club, no more plush toys.

He swore up and down that it was innocent with Gladys, that they were just good friends. And Lilly is the kind of person who makes a choice to believe what people want her to believe. She hates confrontation. She's still avoiding it with him.

She hears her bedroom door open and she sits up. "Milt?"

"It's me," Dorothy says. "I heard you through the walls."

Lilly sniffles. "I'm fine."

Dorothy comes into the room and sits down on the uphol-stered bench at the foot of the bed. "You'll have him back soon," she says.

She's taken out her false teeth for the night, the ones on the bottom row. Lilly hates seeing her mother without those teeth. It makes her look damaged, decrepit. There's some-thing vulgar about it.

"I never told you this before," Dorothy goes on, "but your father had someone."

Lilly looks up, surprised. "Really? And you knew about it?"

"He didn't try very hard to keep it a secret. In those days, there wasn't a question of divorce. Where would I have gone?"

"Did you say anything?"

"One day I threatened to tell *you* about his affair. You were about twelve at the time."

"What happened?"

"As far as I know, he ended it. I don't think he ever saw her again."

"Why?"

"He cared what you thought of him," Dorothy says. "He didn't want to lose your respect."

Lilly crawls across the bed and lays her head in her mother's lap, something she hasn't done since she was a child.

"It was his family that mattered most to him," Dorothy says. "When he absolutely had to, he was able to give up the woman like that—" She snaps her fingers.

Lilly closes her eyes. "I'm afraid with Milton it would be the other way around."

Erica

The phone rings and Erica reaches over and smacks the alarm clock, inadvertently turning on the radio. Much to her confusion, Billy Joel starts singing "Piano Man." The phone keeps ringing.

"What's happening?" Paul moans. "Stop all the noise—"

Disoriented, Erica opens her eyes. She clumsily reaches for the receiver, trying not to disturb Paul, whose head is on her breastbone. "Hullo?"

"Darling?"

It's her mother.

"Muh, it's not even six," she complains.

"Did I wake you?"

Erica fights back the rage. "Of course you woke me. What's wrong?"

"They've captured Saddam," she says.

"What?"

"The Americans. They captured Saddam Hussein. Turn on CNN."

"Turn on CNN," Erica tells Paul.

He reaches for the remote and turns on the TV. Sure enough, there's Saddam Hussein, looking like a homeless man, having his tonsils examined by a doctor.

"Is everything okay at home?" Erica asks her mother.

"We're all fine." Lilly's voice is stoic.

"How's Gladys?"

"She's hanging on, but they don't think she'll live through the holidays."

Erica sighs. "Poor Daddy," she mutters, stroking Paul's hair.

"You'll come in for the funeral?" Lilly asks.

"Of course."

"I hope it's safe to fly. The terrorists might try to retaliate now. Make sure you book Air Canada."

"How's Gramma?"

"Oh, her bursitis is flaring up. You know her shoulder. It's been very damp here."

Paul is bored with CNN now and starts kissing her belly button.

"I wish this was over," Lilly confesses. "I miss your father. He hasn't been home in so long. . . ."

"It will be soon," Erica consoles distractedly. "Listen, I should go now."

"Do you have school?"

"Work."

"The newsstand?" Lilly asks, trying to keep her tone light. "You're back to that?"

"Yes, Muh."

"Have you heard from Columbia yet? Did you get accepted to the master's program?"

"I'll know in the spring."

"And what about the professor?"

"You mean Paul? What about him?"

"Will it be official soon?"

"I don't know. Let me ask him." Erica holds the receiver to her chest and says, loud enough for her mother to hear, "Paul, will we be official soon?"

"Define 'official,'" Paul mumbles.

Into the mouthpiece, she says to her mother, "Define 'official.'"

"You know exactly what I mean," Lilly says bleakly.

"Just keep me posted about Gladys, all right?"

After she hangs up, she curls into Paul's arms.

He zaps off the TV. "Open the rubber drawer," he says.

"By 'rubber drawer' do you mean the drawer of this bedside table?"

"Whatever. It's the rubber drawer. Come on, pass me one."

"What for?" she asks, nuzzling his chest. He rolls on top of her and they kiss. She likes the smell of his breath in the morning, as long as he hasn't eaten anything garlicky the night before. Paul is a man with virtually no bad odors—not his breath, his armpits, or even his feet.

"Gladys is dying," she informs him between kisses.

"You knew that," he pants.

"I know. But it's going to happen *soon*. My father's keeping a vigil. . . ."

Paul's mouth is on her breast now. He doesn't seem very interested in Gladys.

"Are you going to come to the funeral with me?" she asks him.

He stops what he's doing and meets her eyes. "That depends."

"On what?"

"On when it is."

"Well, when would it be most convenient for you? Maybe Gladys can arrange to die around your schedule."

"Hey, hey. Calm down."

"I want you there with me, Paul. I want you to meet my family."

"At a funeral?"

"Yes. This is nonnegotiable."

"I beg your pardon?" he says indignantly. "Nonnegotiable? I've got deadlines, Erica. I'm not saying *no,* I'm just saying I need some notice."

"Notice?" she cries. "Are you saying Gladys's death might conflict with your oh-so-sacred writing schedule?"

"Don't sound so resentful. I don't like what you're insinuating."

"What am I insinuating?"

"That my writing takes precedence over you."

"Doesn't it?"

"Of course not. But it's not like she's a family member, Erica. She's a friend of your father's. I hardly think my presence is required at her funeral, let alone appropriate."

"I *want* you there," she sulks. "That's why it's appropriate."

Paul rolls off her. "Let's just see, all right? I've got that Barry Diller feature to finish for *The New Yorker,* and my review of the new Jimmy Carter novel. It's just hard for me to—"

But she is already out of the bed, throwing his waffle robe on and slamming out of the room. She goes into the den and sits down on the couch. The coffee table is littered with his books—*Prize Stories 2003: The O. Henry Awards; Four Films of Woody Allen; Writers on Writing: Essays from The New York Times.* The amazing thing is, he's reading all of them at the same time, not as an assignment, but for pleasure. No matter how pissed off she is, Paul's mind—and his intellectual appetite—never ceases to impress her.

The short story she's been working on is lying on the table too. Gazing down at it, she isn't sure anymore if Paul's red scribbles in the margins are derisive and mocking or thoughtful and encouraging. She rereads some of them, and this time they have the effect of irritating her. *What does Norma see in Walter?* Paul has written. *He has no redeeming qualities! Too much internal dlg. SCHMALTZ!! Is this necessary? Self-indulgent! Tighten. Expand. Show, don't tell. Norma too one-dimensional? Convoluted. Pedantic. Irritating. WHY?*

It's that last one—the *WHY?* in bold, block letters—that finally pushes her over the edge and causes her to rip the story into shreds.

She picks up her journal and starts writing.

> *Paul is a selfish prick. I am living with a self-important self-centered ass who thinks a book review is more imp than a death in my family. Why do I keep picking men whose "art" comes before ME? With Ryan it was the same bullshit. His photographer's block was always the central priority of our relationship. My very existence was an imposition on his depression. He was totally unavailable, just like Paul is unavailable because of his Writing (with a capital W)—*

Erica puts down her pen. She considers leaving the journal open on the table, alongside the torn bits of her story, hoping Paul will find it and be brazen enough to read it. She changes her mind and leaves the room. She leaves the apartment. But no matter how far away she tries to get from him, *WHY?* still throbs in her head.

Jessie

*O*ut of the blackness, the phone rings. Jessie sits bolt upright in bed and fumbles around on the bedside table to answer it. Her heart is pounding. The alarm clock says five A.M. *Only catastrophes happen this early,* she thinks. At least the kids are safe. Her thoughts immediately go to her parents and then, agonizingly, to her sisters. Silent prayers. *Please God please God.*

Allan is moaning now. "Who . . . ?"

She knocks a half-filled glass of water onto the carpet before finally grabbing hold of the phone. "Hullo?" Breathless, nauseated.

"Jessica?" It's Lilly, sounding tearful. *Dear God, not Daddy.*

"What, Muh? What is it?" Panic is rising up in her. Her heart is racing furiously.

"It's Gladys. She passed away."

And then the relief washes over her. Her breathing slows down and she flops back against her mattress.

What is it? Allan is mouthing.

"Gladys died," she tells him. "When, Muh?"

"A half hour ago maybe? I'm not sure. Your father's at the hospital. I'm worried about him, Jess." She starts to cry then—hard, anguished sobs that don't fit with someone like Lilly. "I'm scared," she whimpers.

"What's to be scared of?" Jessie asks. "He knew it was coming. We all did."

"It's like . . . it's like *he* wants to die too. He's given up."

"He's just grieving, Muh. I think you should go get him. Bring him home."

"He won't let me," she says. "I said to him, 'Milton, I'm coming to pick you up,' and he said, 'I don't want to come home.' He thinks he can bring Gladys back to life or something."

Jessie sighs. Allan has already rolled over and gone back to sleep. Sensitive guy.

"Go get him," Jessie says firmly.

"Should I throw him over my shoulder and carry him out?"

"I'll go," Jessie relents. "I'll bring him home."

"A part of him died with her," Lilly laments. "You haven't lived with him all these months. You don't know."

"Muh, calm down."

"Why didn't he ever just leave me?" Her voice is childlike, uncomprehending. "Why, Jessie? We both could have been happy at least."

"He loves you, Muh. Don't talk like this."

After a while, Jessie finally manages to get her mother off the phone. She climbs out of bed and locks herself in the bathroom. She showers, puts her robe on, brushes her teeth, combs her hair into a ponytail. Then she leans against the sink and waits to cry. She feels it there, ready to come up, a good bout of sobbing. Not because she loved Gladys, not because she grew up with her and will miss her, but because she knows her mother is right.

But she doesn't cry. She stands there like that, perched over the sink, staring down at the green toothpaste stains, and the tears simply do not come. Instead, it's the usual emptiness. It's as though she is only capable of terror or utter indifference. Nothing in between.

She saw them together once, her father and Gladys. It's an image in her mind that won't budge; won't fade or recede or become even remotely less painful than it was the day she spied on them. Maybe her silence has kept it alive, preserved its vividness after all these years. Maybe she should have told someone, one of her sisters or her grandmother. Perhaps that might have alleviated her burden. But as a child she thought that if she kept it a secret, it wouldn't *be*. She was trained by Lilly, after all. If she was the only one who knew about it, then it really didn't happen, did it? Then the family was okay. All that was required of her to maintain normalcy was that she keep her mouth shut.

It was the least she could do for the rest of them, especially for her mother. Protecting them came naturally for her. It was part of the persona she'd forged for herself: part of being blindly obedient, never stumbling and always striving for perfection, which was something that she always believed to be totally attainable. She had to make her mark somehow. (Classic middle-child syndrome, probably.) Erica was the spoiled baby, and Estelle was so outgoing, so boisterous and demanding. Estelle always had to be heard and seen and she accomplished those things with wit and *chutzpah;* she fearlessly strode down one unconventional path after another, and while perhaps she didn't always get the attention she wanted, she got it nevertheless. Used it up, is more like it.

In hindsight, maybe she handled the situation with Gladys and her father all wrong. After listening to Lilly tonight, it occurred to her she probably should have spoken up a long time ago, back when there was still a chance for Lilly to get out. Lilly probably deserved more.

The worst part of it is, it happened in their own home.

With Lilly upstairs, entertaining *his* friends. Jessie remembers her mother milling about the living room, circling the clusters of guests, smiling a tangerine-lipped smile, doling out hors d'oeuvres from a silver tray. And Milton was nowhere to be found.

"Where's Daddy?" Jessie asked her sisters. She was eight at the time. The three of them were sitting at the top of the staircase, peering down at the party through the banister. It was New Year's Eve. Her parents were ringing in the New Year with a big bash, full of CBC people and other singers and musicians like her father. It was past midnight and Jessie and her sisters had been sent to bed. They'd been allowed to stay up until midnight, but now they were supposed to be sleeping. Instead they were huddled upstairs, spying. Jessie remembers there was disco blaring from the stereo—ABBA and Chaka Khan and Donna Summer. People were doing the bump over in the corner where Lilly and Milton had cleared away two love seats to make room for a dance floor. Lilly had even laid down a plank of wood, which she'd bought at Pascal's. She didn't want the new rust-colored broadloom carpet getting stomped on.

"Look at them!" Estelle giggled, pointing to the dance floor where two middle-aged women were bumping their fat bums against each other. "They're trapped in the seventies."

"Mummy looks like the maid," Erica remarked.

Jessie was preoccupied looking for her father. She hadn't seen him since he sent them to bed almost an hour ago. "Off you go, you three *yentas!*" he'd said. "Up to bed. It's time for the grown-ups now." He'd tucked them in and kissed them good night, his breath smelling like turpentine.

He had disappeared by the time they snuck out to the banister.

Jessie stood up and crept down the stairs. "Where you going?" Estelle whispered after her. "You can't go down there! We'll all get in trouble!"

Jessie ignored her and kept going. She slipped through the living room unnoticed and went down the stairs into the basement. Why? What was she expecting to find? She had a foredoomed feeling—maybe she *always* had that feeling, even if it was uncalled for; maybe she was born with it—that felt like a tightness in her solar plexus. She was worried. She had radar for catastrophe and had always had misgivings about Gladys Gold. It had occurred to her, sitting up there by the banister, that Gladys was also missing. So she snuck down into the basement, which was a rec room for the kids—it had beanbag chairs, an old couch from the sixties, a TV set, a pinball machine, stacks of board games, and Barbies lying naked in a pile—and she stood there in the dark listening for something. She was barefoot and shivering, it was so cold. There were two rooms off the rec room; one was the laundry room and the other was a storage room, full of memorabilia and old junk Lilly couldn't part with. Both of those doors were closed now. (Lilly wouldn't have wanted anyone at the party to see inside either room, certainly not her dirty laundry or her dusty old *tchotchkes*.) Jessie went over and stood just outside the laundry room. She couldn't hear anything from inside, so she went over to the storage room. She put her ear to the door and waited. No one was talking but she could hear something. Movement. Shuffling. Hard breathing. She was sure of it. Then a *thud* from behind the door, like a box falling over. And then muffled laughter.

Startled, Jessie went over and crouched behind a beanbag chair. She was just little enough not to be seen. And it was dark, no one would see her anyway. She stayed there motionless for what felt like hours. In retrospect, it may have been only minutes. She was frozen, scared.

Eventually they came out.

Her eyes had adjusted to the dark by then and she could see their shadowy figures, her father behind Gladys. He zipped up the back of her skirt and then kissed her neck from behind. She lowered her head and let out a soft moan as he nuzzled her hair.

"You go up first," he whispered in her ear.

"How long have we been down here?"

"Everyone's drunk. No one will have noticed."

"Lilly's not drunk."

"Just go up and blend in."

She turned and kissed him on the mouth before scurrying up the steps. Alone in the dark, Milton sighed. Not a happy sigh, not a sigh of contentment or pleasure. Jessie's impression was that he was sad. Unbearably sad. He rubbed his forehead and then, as an afterthought, closed the storage room door. Finally he went upstairs.

Jessie waited behind the beanbag chair. She was still, so still. When she finally got upstairs, Lilly nabbed her by the kitchen as she was trying to sneak back up to bed.

"What are you doing up?" Lilly asked sternly.

Jessie blinked but couldn't find her voice. She was angry with her mother, but she didn't know why. Perhaps for being so clueless? For not *knowing?* For leaving it to Jessie to find out?

"Get upstairs this minute," Lilly said. She wasn't in a particularly good mood, not for someone throwing a party on New Year's Eve. She wasn't lenient with Jessie, that's for sure. "This *minute* or no gymnastics next week."

As if Jessie cared about gymnastics anymore. Nevertheless, she went straight to bed. She marched past both her sisters and said, "Mom's coming up and she's mad."

Estelle and Erica scampered off to their rooms in a hurry. Jessie got into her bed and lay there all night, wide awake, worried, confused. All she could think was that if it came to choosing between living with her mother or living with Milton and Gladys, she would run away or maybe kill herself. But she vowed she would never tell anyone; she didn't need to spoil everything for the rest of them. Besides, maybe them knowing would make it more real.

This way, she thought, it might just go away.

Now she splashes water on her face and goes downstairs. She gets in her car and heads downtown to retrieve her father from the Princess Margaret Hospital. He probably won't want to go back to the condo—Lilly would be too much for him now, with the guilt and the resentment—so she'll have to bring him back to her place. Allan won't mind. No one ever minds having Milton around.

"You wouldn't have recognized her at the end," he says.

Jessie is looking out the window. Her street is slushy and wet, the sky a dull gray. Dirty snowbanks line the road. The view out there is damp and bleak, virtually barren of beauty. Same as inside. She hates seeing her father in pain, hates hearing about Gladys's cancer—the images of which will keep Jessie up at night. She'll worry about dying a similar death or, worse, that one of her kids—*Stop*. Doesn't her father realize she is *not* the person to be unloading this on?

"I'll get you another Ativan," she tells him.

"I don't want . . ." But his voice trails off as she leaves the room.

She's got to get him back to sleep; it's the only peace she gets. He's been at her house for two days, immobile in Levi's twin bed, and she's been too afraid to leave him alone. She imagines coming home and finding him hanging in her bathroom. Her thoughts are so morbid, but she is powerless against them. So she hasn't been to work since Monday and Auben is manning the office and her appointment with Skieth Ellis has already been bumped twice now. Lilly is frantic. "Why won't he come home to me?" she keeps asking. As though Jessie has the answer.

In the bathroom, she dumps an Ativan into the palm of her hand and fills a plastic cup with tap water. How lucky for Estelle and Erica that they don't live in Toronto, that they are free of all the family crises. It always falls to Jessie to handle the problems, to keep the ever-unfolding dramas to herself. They're both flying in today for the funeral, but they'll never know what they missed these past few days. They won't have to live with that image of Milton's face the night she brought him home from the hospital.

She brings him the Ativan and sits down on Levi's bed. "Here, Daddy. Take this."

"Another one?"

"It's been six hours."

He obediently swallows the pill. "I'm going to miss her," he whispers.

"I know."

"We had a good friendship. . . ."

"You've still got Mummy, and us. Your grandchildren. It'll get easier."

She wants to ask him, *Did it last this entire time?* Some part of her has always wanted to believe that when she caught them that New Year's Eve in 1986, it was a one-shot deal. Drunk at a party, they'd gotten carried away. Or, at the very least, that the affair had eventually tapered off into a deep but platonic friendship. Maybe it did. But seeing him like this, she wonders. Could it be they were lovers for thirty years? And if so, why the hell didn't he just leave Lilly? But she can't ask him now. Or maybe ever. He is her father, her daddy. There is a danger in knowing too much about your parents, about their personal—*sexual*—lives. And how would she ever face Lilly if she knew?

Gladys is gone. It could be a fresh start, if only he'd *allow* it.

His eyes are fluttering shut. She leans over and kisses his cheek, which is rough with silvery stubble. His hair smells dirty and his breath as he snores is sour. She feels sorry for him, lying there so forlorn and hopeless. Her pity is not so much over the fact that he's lost Gladys, but that he never truly *had* her.

Milton

*H*e opens his eyes and the first thing he sees is a photograph of his grandson, about age two. In it, Levi is lying in a pile of autumn leaves, grinning a giant smile up at the camera. It was Milty who took the picture. He remembers it vividly, a beautiful September afternoon, one of the rare days when Jessie had let him and Lilly babysit. They'd brought Levi to Sunnybrook Park, fed him McDonald's (which of course they never told Jessie), and then bought him a pile of toys at Top Banana.

God, Milty treasures that child, maybe even more than he does Ilana. Because Levi is the first grandchild, because he's a boy. Milton's eyes well up now, looking at the picture of his beautiful Levi. What more reason could he need to pull himself out of this bed and get dressed and go back to his life?

His mind is still groggy from the Ativan and all the sleep, but for the first time since Jessie drove him home from the Princess Margaret, he feels strong enough to face the day. Maybe even to face Lilly. He knows it's not fair, what he's doing to her. Poor woman, waiting in that condo day after day for some sign that he loves her, even just a bit.

And he *does*. She's his companion, his wife, the mother of his children. But not the great love of his life, never that. Still, they've managed. They've stuck it out and they'll hang in there till the end. Now he needs to let her know that, he needs to reassure her. Besides, he's got no one else. Lilly is it; she's the one that's left for him.

He checks his watch. Five in the morning. The house is quiet, still. He pulls on his clothes from Monday night— the night Gladys passed away. Jessie washed and pressed them, then draped them neatly over the back of a chair. He'll shower at home in his own bathroom. Lilly will pick out a suit for him to wear to the funeral tomorrow; she'll toast a couple of bagels for him with Cheez Whiz and raspberry jam. Suddenly he's ravenous.

Downstairs, he scribbles a note for Jessie. *Feeling better. Gone home to be with Mother. See you at the funeral. I love you.*

He calls a cab and waits outside on the front step. It's still dark, but the cold fresh air is heavenly. A gust of wind swirls around him and he zips his jacket right up to his chin. He's crying again; he can feel the hot tears dribbling down his face. How will he get through her funeral? And the *shivah*? And the next however many days without the sound of her voice in his life . . . ?

The cab pulls up in front of the house and he takes a deep breath, goes down the stairs. One foot in front of the other. One minute at a time. His heart is broken and there's an emptiness now, a deep, deep void inside him, as though there's nothing left to look forward to. It was like that when he lost his parents.

But he healed then and he will heal again. It will take time, but he's got his family to help him. Three beautiful daughters, two grandchildren, and a wife who loves him.

Lilly

*W*hen she hears the door open at five-thirty in the morning, she rushes out of the kitchen into the foyer. Her heart is pounding. "Milt?"

He comes through the door looking disheveled and sheepish. She has an urge to throw her arms around him but she holds back, not sure it's what he wants. Besides, she's angry with him. Three days since he's been at Jessie's and not even a phone call.

"Oy, you smell. Haven't you bathed?"

He hangs up his coat in the closet and says, "I'm hungry."

A good sign. "What do you want? I can make scrambled eggs. I've got bagels in the freezer."

"Sure."

"With Cheez Whiz and jam?"

He nods.

"Orange juice? Coffee? I can make you Ovaltine."

"Coffee."

"All right. Get in a shower and I'll make breakfast. And don't sit on the bedspread in those clothes."

He heads off down the hall toward their bedroom. Lilly goes back into the kitchen, feeling purposeful and relieved. She pulls a bag of St. Urbain bagels out of the freezer and slices two of them down the middle. She pops them into the toaster, humming.

It's going to be okay, she thinks. She's got him. He's

eating, he's showering, he's home. She looks at herself in the stainless steel fridge and fluffs up her hair. Her roots are coming in; she's let herself go a bit. She's still in pajamas and slippers (why didn't she put on her pretty pink robe?), but at least her hair is combed and her teeth are brushed.

When he comes into the kitchen, freshly shaved and scrubbed clean, she lays his plate down in front of him and fills up his mug with coffee. His eyes are red and puffy and there are splotches on his cheeks, but at least he's *here*. Let him mourn, as long as it's under her roof where she can keep an eye on him.

"I thought I'd bake a poppy loaf for the *shivah*," she tells him.

No response.

"To help out."

"She wasn't even Gladys at the end," he tells her.

Does he think she wants to hear this?

She pulls up a chair and sits down beside him. She touches his hand. He flinches.

"She was just a skeleton," he continues. "Her eyes were vacant. She wasn't there."

Lilly purses her lips. "The girls are flying home today," she reminds him.

He looks up. "They are?"

"Of course they are. They want to be here with you."

"But Estelle has that thing, that Flashdance festival."

"She'll be here. Allan is picking her up at the airport. Erica's taking a train, so she'll walk over from Union Station."

After taking a few sporadic bites of his bagel, Milton pushes his plate away. Not so hungry after all. His head flops down and he starts to sob. "I was going to try to be better today," he mumbles. "For you. I got up and I got dressed and I . . ."

"Why don't we go to the market and buy some food for supper?" Lilly suggests. "We have to feed our girls. We can—"

She stops midsentence. Milton is looking at her, baffled.

"Or I can go by myself." She gets up and stands over him for a moment. "Are you finished with this?"

When he doesn't answer, she snatches his plate away and drops it into the sink. "You wish it were me, don't you?" she asks him, hurt. She can't help it, can't restrain herself.

He shakes his head. "I wish it was neither of you, Lilly."

"I'm not so sure." She sniffs.

"Please, Lilly."

She runs the tap over his plate and puts it in the dishwasher. "Do you feel like roast beef tonight?" she says. "I'll pick some up at the market. Or I can do fish."

"Whatever you want," he murmurs. He drags himself out of the kitchen, down the hall.

She hears the bedroom door close as she's wiping the counter with Fantastik.

Estelle

*E*stelle's head feels hot and floaty, as though it's come unhinged from her neck, but she prefers that drugged feeling to the abject fear inspired by the orange terror alert level and five hours of relentless turbulence. So, two Gravol pills and half a dozen glasses of airplane wine after taking off from LAX, she arrives at Pearson Airport feeling zombielike and disoriented. And there, waiting for her, to her horror, is brother-in-law Allan, with his glib overtanned face and showoffy suit.

"Where's Jessie?" she asks him, planting a flat peck on his cheek.

"She took Ilana to the doctor."

"Again?"

"It's a preventive measure against this new influenza outbreak. Hey, have you lost weight?" he asks her.

"No," she says woozily, handing him her carry-on bag. "I gained ten pounds over the holidays. You must just be remembering me fatter." She's never flattered by the "you've lost weight" comment. The literal translation is "You're not quite as obese as I remember you." Especially coming from him.

"Do you have any luggage to pick up?" he asks her.

"No, I thought I'd wear *this* every day for the next two weeks."

He looks irritated. "You can take those wheely suitcases

on board, you know. It saves a hell of a lot of time. You don't have to wait around for your bags."

"I don't have a wheely suitcase," she informs him. His face is so brown from their trip to Barbados, it looks like a football. "I'm surprised Jessie lets you lie out in the sun like that," she says. "What with the UV rays and all. I'd have thought she'd make you wear SPF one thousand or something."

"She saves that for the kids," he says. "She wouldn't waste it on me."

After she collects her suitcase, Estelle follows Allan out to where he's double-parked at the taxi stand. The air is freezing; it gives her a jolt. "January in Canada," she mutters. "I'd forgotten how miserable. It was sixty-eight in L.A. when I left."

"I'm taking the 427," he informs her. "It's the fastest route."

She looks at him strangely. As if she cares how they get there. Does he want her approval?

They drive in silence for a while. They've got almost no common ground between them, so conversation is a challenge.

Finally Allan says grimly, "Your father's not doing too well."

"He and Gladys were very close."

"Jessie's not going to the funeral, you know."

"What?" She turns to face him. "You mean I flew three thousand miles and Jessie's not even *going?*"

"You're surprised?"

"She should be going for Daddy. He needs us right now. Besides, Gladys was practically part of our family."

"That's part of the problem, isn't it?"

*   *   *

*S*he finds her mother in the kitchen, elbow deep in cake batter. Lilly's wearing an oversize pink sweatshirt belted at the waist with black leggings and Chinese slippers, circa 1984.

"You're here already?" Lilly says. "That was fast."

"Allan speeds."

"I'm baking a poppy seed cake for the *shivah,*" Lilly explains.

"*You're* baking a cake for Gladys's *shivah?*"

"What's wrong with that?"

"Isn't that hypocritical?"

"Why? She was your father's business partner. What would it look like if I didn't help?"

"Right. What would it look like."

"You'd rather I do a jig on her grave?"

Estelle sighs. What she wouldn't give to be at Sundance right now. "Where's Daddy?"

"In bed," she says, dumping the batter into a loaf pan. "Inconsolable."

She slams the cake into the oven and leans up against the counter. Her shoulders slump forward. She turns to face Estelle, looking weary and defeated. Even her smooth lasered eyes look old again. Estelle has a momentary pang of pity for her.

Then Lilly says, "Should I make my asparagus roll-ups?" (Another Kraft concoction. Asparagus roll-ups: asparagus tips rolled up in white bread with Cheez Whiz, then baked.)

"I think the poppy seed cake is plenty."

"Are you keeping that hoop in your eyebrow for the funeral?"

"Jessie's not going, you know. To the funeral."

Lilly shrugs, looking quite smug. "That's her prerogative."

"I'm missing a great career opportunity to be here with Daddy," Estelle complains. "And Jessie's just going to abandon him now?"

"Stop feeling so sorry for yourself," she says, and rushes out of the room, leaving Estelle alone to lick the bowl and the wooden spoon, which she was never allowed to do as a kid.

"She's just upset about your father."

Estelle turns to face her grandmother, who is wearing her uniform floral housedress from the sixties and a pair of brown hand-knit slippers.

"Is he as bad as she says?"

"He doesn't come out of the bedroom," Dorothy explains. "He sleeps all day and he won't eat. He's taking it hard, your father."

"It's understandable. They've been friends forever."

"Lilly takes it personal. She thinks his grief means he doesn't love *her*."

"Jessie's not going, you know," Estelle says spitefully. Like a tattletale.

"Jessie's doing what she has to do," Dorothy says. "And you're doing what *you* have to do. Why should it bother you what your sister does?"

"Because I'm missing Sundance. . . ."

"So what? This is family."

*P*ity the person who had to cover the mirrors in Gladys's apartment for her *shivah*. The whole place is mirrors—mirrored ceilings, closets, walls; two entirely mirrored bathrooms, a mirrored coffee table in the living room, mirrored corridors, and mirrored sliding doors in the foyer.

"What did she die of?" someone mutters. "Vanity?"

Estelle, Erica, and their grandmother squeeze into the vestibule and remove their coats. They took a cab from the funeral because Milton didn't want to bring his car. He and Lilly went in the limo with the immediate family. Now Estelle hangs her coat up and goes off in search of her parents. She finds Milton propped up on a sofa in the den, puffy-eyed and despondent. He's lost weight; his face looks gaunt and pale. A few feet over, on straight-back chairs lined up against the wall, are Gladys's son, Joshua, and her two sisters, Dorothy and Frieda. Estelle goes over to pay her respects.

"Thanks for coming," Joshua says. "I know it's a long way from L.A."

She kisses him on both cheeks. She hasn't seen him in years, maybe seven or eight. She thinks the last time was at one of Gladys's Rosh Hashanah parties, right before he left for South America. He's a year older than she is and when they were kids they were always dumped in the playpen together. As they got older, they were constantly being "set up" and encouraged to "hang out." Milton probably hoped they'd wind up together one day, but beyond early adolescence, he never pushed it. Maybe he figured Joshua could do better.

Joshua's been traveling since he graduated from university. If she remembers right, his degree is in English Lit. Not much to do with that, other than travel. He was always kind of nomadic, a bit of a loner. He was sensitive, hippieish, environmentally conscious. Probably vegetarian. He's not bad to look at; his dark wavy hair and Malcolm X glasses compensate for a fairly big nose, and he has a smile that seems impossibly wide for such a narrow face. But she prefers a man with a life plan. A little ambition never hurts a man's attractiveness quotient.

"I'm sorry about your mom," she tells him, welling up. She liked Gladys more than her sisters did. Gladys was always kind to her. Gladys was a woman who could appreciate charisma and personality. Estelle never felt inferior or overlooked by Gladys.

"I'm a little worried about your father," Josh says.

They both look over at Milton, who is staring vacantly at a framed eight-by-ten black-and-white photo of himself and Gladys back in their *Young Entertainers* days. Lilly bustles past him, carrying a tray of asparagus roll-ups. She throws him a sidelong glance but does not go to him. She seems nervous, agitated. Estelle thinks she's wearing too much makeup.

Estelle is jostled over to the side by more well-wishers. Joshua smiles at her and promises they'll catch up later, when there are fewer people. But sometime after the dinner buffet is laid out, Lilly insists on leaving, and so Estelle never gets a chance to talk with him.

On her way out, she tells him she'll drop by again during the *shivah*.

"He's gotten cute," Erica remarks when they're going down the elevator. "He's grown into his features, don't you think, Bean?"

Estelle shrugs noncommittally.

"What's Josh doing these days, Daddy?" Erica asks.

"He teaches English."

"Where?"

"Wherever. Japan, France, Thailand. He moves around a lot."

"He's single?"

"He was engaged to a Thai girl," Milton says. "But it didn't work out. The wedding got called off. Gladys was relieved, too. Her name was Bam."

They come off the elevator and Lilly asks the doorman to order them a cab. When it arrives, they all pile in, the five of them in their heavy coats and winter paraphernalia.

Dorothy takes up half the backseat and Erica has to squish onto Estelle's lap. They pull onto St. Clair, and Milton slumps down in the front seat and starts to cry again. Estelle looks over at her mother. As they leave Gladys behind, Lilly looks almost serene.

Erica

Paul's friends are the usual mixed bag of New York literati, professors, and playwrights that always make Erica feel like a poser. They are Amory Huber, Paul's middle-aged gay editor; Janice Schatzky, the sister-in-law of Paul's London agent and a researcher for *Ripley's Believe It or Not;* Jad Mahroum, an associate professor in Middle Eastern Studies; and Jillian Clapton, the one among them who stands out for her unrivaled ability to turn Erica's self-esteem into Play-Doh. Aside from being the successful author of two bestselling nonfiction books—*Puke: The Mystique of Bulimia* and *Oprah Is My God: Icons as Spiritual Leaders*—and one of the few noteworthy feminists of her generation—X; she was born in 1970—Jillian also happens to be gorgeous and clever and frighteningly aware of her power.

In one of their earlier encounters, they were discussing literature (what else?) and Jillian asked Erica the name of her favorite book. Thinking fast, Erica tried to come up with something that would sound neither too pretentious (Proulx, Homer) nor too broad (*Tuesdays with Morrie,* or anything else ever featured on Oprah's Book Club). She ended up saying *The Shabat Goy of René-Charles.*

Naturally, Jillian had never heard of it.

"My grandmother wrote it," Erica explained boastfully.

"And that's your favorite book *of all time?*" Jillian pressed, in an "is that your final answer" tone.

"I don't know about *of all time,*" Erica recanted. "But it's special to me."

Jillian didn't seem all that impressed. Neither did she divulge *her* favorite book of all time.

This afternoon, Jillian sits across from Erica wearing low-rise jeans, a crisp white shirt, and a shiny silver dog tag around her neck with the engraving *Please return to Tiffany & Co New York.* Her blond hair is tied in a long, thick braid that rests on her left shoulder like a pet snake. "I've got an idea for my next book," she announces.

They're all crowded into one of the booths at the Abbey, a neighborhood pub popular among students in SoCo—the area south of Columbia University—looking for cheap draft beer and erudite banter. Amidst the stained glass windows, woodblock prints, and dark wooden booths carved to look like church pews, locals who predate the pub's fifty-year lifespan mingle with Ivy League preppies reading their Lit textbooks at the bar. It's also a favorite hangout of Paul and his friends, who, in Erica's opinion, seem to want to recapture some element of their own college days.

"Winter in Tolmezzo," Jillian divulges. "That's my working title."

"A travel book?" Jad says, and it comes out sounding like a condemnation.

"Why not?"

"Harriet won't go for it," Paul says disparagingly. Harriet Stange is their literary agent and the one who introduced Paul and Jillian. She was trying to set them up romantically, but it never took. Erica thinks they might have slept together, although Paul continues to deny it. (Knowing Paul, there's no way he could be platonic with a woman like Jillian unless he'd already had her.)

"Listen, it's perfect," Jillian is explaining. "I've always wanted to spend a year in Italy. Have you *seen* the Carnic Alps? I'll be able to ski and write, and I'll use a grant to pay for it."

The rest of them are looking indignant because they know that getting a government grant is as simple (and guaranteed) for Jillian as withdrawing money with her ATM card.

Just then, a pair of college students—two girls of about nineteen—sidle over to Jillian and thrust a copy of her book, *Puke,* on the table in front of her. "Can you sign this for me?" one of them asks. "I'm in the middle of reading it and I had it in my knapsack and, like, here you are! I mean, how weird is that? Would you mind?"

"Have you got a pen?" Jillian asks. The girl rummages through her knapsack and pulls out a pen. Jillian signs the front page of the book and hands it back to her groupie.

"Thank you *sooo* much!"

Jillian smiles benevolently; the two girls drift off, examining Jillian's coveted autograph.

"I have an idea for your next book," Janice says, her tone right on the edge of sardonic. (Janice, a dabbler in theater, aspires to write the next *Vagina Monologues,* so her job at *Ripley's* is a demeaning and stifling drudgery that precludes her from celebrating or encouraging the success of anyone else—especially the likes of Jillian.)

She reaches across the table and tugs on Jillian's Tiffany's necklace. "How about *The Gentrification of SoCo*?" she says.

"Morningside Heights has always been this way," Jillian defends.

"How would you know? You're *part* of its gentrification."

"Are you calling me a yuppie?"

"Face it, we're all Upper West Side yuppies," Amory

acknowledges. He lifts the pitcher of beer and dumps more of it into his glass.

"I'm not the one going off to spend a year in the Alps," Janice mutters.

"If she can swing it," Jad says, "why shouldn't she?"

"Talking about gentrification," Amory continues cheerily, "I paid ninety bucks for the Blissage Seventy-five yesterday."

"The what?"

"Seventy-five minutes of shiatsu and Swedish massage at Bliss. And I ran into Diane von Furstenberg while I was there. She was getting a deep-sea detox."

"Name-dropper," Janice chides.

"Did you ask her about Barry?" Paul asks. "I'm writing that article—"

"Barry who?" Jillian asks.

"Of course I didn't ask her about Barry. I just *ogled*. I was starstruck. Even with clay on her face, she's a goddess. She must be in her sixties. What a life she's led . . . you have to give her credit. She was a has-been for two decades and look at her now. I love a comeback story—"

"Barry who?"

"Diller. Her husband."

"She's the new Tina Turner," Amory gushes. "I've wanted to meet her since seventy-six. . . ."

"Let's all say who we'd most like to meet!" Jillian pipes up excitedly. (She loves these kinds of parlor games. Last week she made them play the Mixed Metaphor Game; they had to go around the table besting each other *ad nauseam*.)

"Let's go around the table!" Jillian chirps.

Erica's instinct is to flee. Paul says Nabokov. Amory says Oscar Wilde (postprison). They continue around the table. Frida Kahlo. Audrey Hepburn. George Orwell. Akira

Kurosawa. It comes to Erica and she decides to tell the truth. She says, "Sarah Jessica Parker."

They all look at her. The only one who won't look at her is Paul. He's too embarrassed, or else too angry. She was supposed to say someone important, someone historically noteworthy and artistically influential, but she doesn't care. Fuck them.

"My name is Erica and I love *Sex and the City*," she jokes. They're still watching her. (Most of them don't own TVs.)

"I have to go," she says, standing up. "I'm meeting someone. . . ."

"Who?" This from Paul, who is suddenly interested in her.

"I told you. I'm going to see that improv show at the Upright Citizens Brigade." She bends down and pecks him on the forehead. "I won't be late."

And as she leaves them all sitting in their booth at the Abbey, discussing Orwell (did he predict or influence the future?), Erica suddenly can't wait to get to Chelsea.

She makes her way to Midtown and wanders along the Avenue of the Americas, checking addresses against the business card in her hand. The plan is to meet Mitchell at his office, and then they will head over to the theater together.

She stops when she comes to a high-rise on the corner of 44th. Inside the building, she checks the directory on the wall for M&M Games, and then rides the elevator to the nineteenth floor. She's surprised to discover that Mitchell's office is bustling with activity—employees on the phone, computers on every desk, games stacked from floor to ceiling. It's all very businesslike and efficient. She was half expecting to find a workshop full of elves.

She finds Mitchell hurling darts at a dartboard. The TV is tuned to an update of the Martha Stewart trial on CNN. It's all he could talk about the last time they spoke—the number of currently unfolding celebrity scandals. "Can you believe it?" he had gushed in reference to Michael Jackson's troubles. He couldn't have been more excited. "It's like God's telling us we're on the right track with our new game. Michael Jackson, Robert Blake, Kobe Bryant, Martha Stewart . . . The timing couldn't be better for us to be launching Red-Handed at the toy fair!"

She stands in the doorway now, watching him hurl a few darts, and then teases, "Is this a busy time?"

"The pros of self-employment," he says, turning toward her. "Hey, check this out." He hands her a pile of metal rings and wooden blocks. "It's the prototype for Chi Yi. A game of meditation."

"You came up with this?"

"We're putting together ten prototypes for the fair."

A man who looks to be in his late forties comes up behind Mitchell and thrusts out his hand. "Larry Dorfman," he says. "Mitchy's father."

"Dad, we talked about you calling me Mitchy in front of my friends."

"Right."

Erica laughs. The first thing she notices is that Mitchell is a clone of his father—both slim and dark and more pretty than handsome. They look like brothers.

"You're the writer?" Mitchell's father asks her.

"Aspiring."

"We're all aspiring to something," he says.

They take her on a tour of the office, introducing her to their coworkers—most of whom are friends and family—and stockpiling her with games. *Take this one, take that one, you'll love this. . . .*

"How did you guys get into this, anyway?" she asks them, playing absently with the Chi Yi rings.

"When I was about twenty," Mitchell explains, "I started collecting quotes. It was just a hobby of mine. I literally had hundreds of them. Then about five years ago, my father and I came up with this idea to incorporate all my quotes into a game. Once we had the strategy down, we decided to get a prototype made. Next thing we know, we're taking orders from Wal-Mart and Toys 'R' Us. My dad quit his advertising job and here we are."

"It's not every day you get an opportunity to go into business with your son," Larry boasts.

Mitchell looks at his watch. "We'd better get going," he says. "The show starts in half an hour."

"Don't forget this—" Larry tells Erica, and he hands her the shopping bag full of games.

She imagines herself arriving home with them all and showing them to Paul. He loathes board games! She feels bad accepting them, knowing that they'll wind up in the incinerator, but she doesn't want to come off as ungrateful.

"It was nice to meet you," Larry says.

Just as she turns to leave, she catches him winking conspiratorially at Mitchell, which unnerves her. It means she's conveyed to one or both of them that there is some level of interest on her part; it means that Mitchell has probably expressed *his* interest in her to his father. It means that despite her best intentions to have a completely innocent friendship with Mitchell Dorfman, she is inadvertently setting herself up for what could be an awkward and unpleasant situation down the road. Why then, despite the unsettled feeling in her gut, does that wink between father and son leave her feeling so giddy and victorious?

"*H*ow do you feel about a kosher restaurant?" he asks her. They've just come out of the improv show, and although she's starving, the thought of a kosher meal doesn't exactly inspire her.

"You keep kosher?"

"I try to."

"Sure, then," she says, somewhat shocked. "That's fine. Wherever."

He looks relieved. They take a cab to West 72nd, a shabby, bustling Jewish haven where she's always felt surprisingly comfortable. He leads her inside a kosher Italian restaurant called Provi Provi. Having never been to a kosher restaurant before, Erica can't help staring at all the Orthodox and Hasidic Jewish men who are rocking back and forth with eyes closed in intense prayer, while their wives watch patiently across the tables, waiting to eat.

"How did you like the show?" Mitchell asks her after they're seated in one of the booths.

"I think I've realized that I don't actually like improv," she says. "I mean, the whole thing sort of . . . it stresses me. Just watching it makes me uncomfortable, you know? Because I feel embarrassed for the performers."

"Really?"

"I was tense through the whole show tonight, especially when that really unfunny woman was on."

"The redhead?"

"It's like watching gymnasts perform on the balance beam. I can't look. I guess that's why I left the Upright Citizens Brigade."

"You're not the only one who's dropped out," he says. "Remember Carlene?"

Erica hates that she's a "dropout." Even being an improv dropout implies that she's some kind of quitter.

"The one with the big hair and the nails," he reminds her. "You must remember Carlene."

"Long Island Carlene?"

"Right. Well, she's in beauty school now. Barry Berger's School of Glamour and Beauty."

She knows she's meant to find this amusing, but she wonders, is beauty school really that much "funnier" than selling gum and smokes at a newsstand? Is Carlene's dream of becoming a makeup artist any more ridiculous or far-fetched than Erica's dream of becoming a writer? (In point of fact, it's probably a lot more attainable.) And suddenly, Erica sees herself as she imagines Mitchell must see her—the way he views Carlene, as a laughingstock.

"So is it hard?" she asks him, changing the subject.

"Is what hard?"

"Keeping kosher."

"This is going to sound corny, but it's actually one of the very few spiritual things I do in my life," he says. "I can never be careless about what I put in my mouth, you know? I always have to be very conscious of not mixing dairy and meat, so every time I have to check a label or prepare my food, I'm reminded of *why* I do this. So, no. In that sense, it's not hard at all."

"Why do you do it?"

"I guess I started doing it out of respect for my sister," he says. "Miriam's a rabbi. And then, along the way, it started to have real meaning for me. Now it's a ritual that connects me to God. It reminds me three times a day who I am and where I come from."

"Is your family Orthodox?"

"Conservative. Orthodoxy doesn't recognize women rabbis."

"I didn't even realize there *were* women rabbis," Erica admits.

"It's relatively new. Amy Eilberg was the first woman to be ordained. That was in eighty-five."

The waitress brings them their food—two platters of ravioli—and refills their wineglasses.

"Is your family religious?" Mitchell asks her.

Erica bursts out laughing. "Uh, no," she responds. "Religion has never been . . . it's never been anything."

"That's too bad."

"Why? We have different values, that's all. Music, literature, success . . . that's what we worship in my family."

"In mine too," he says. "We just make a point of acknowledging God's hand in all those things."

Flustered, Erica stabs one of the raviolis on her plate. She can't think of anything to say.

"Why don't you come over for Shabbat dinner on Friday?" he asks her.

"I can't."

"Why not?"

She racks her brain. "Because I live with someone," she finally blurts.

"I'm just inviting you to Shabbat dinner with my family. You don't have to sleep with me afterward."

"I know that . . . I just . . . I wasn't sure if I've been clear."

"I'd like you to experience Shabbat with me."

"Are you trying to convert me?"

"Into what? You're already Jewish."

"But I've never . . . we've never lit the candles or anything. We don't do that in my family. We're liberal. We work on Saturdays. . . . I don't even know what it's all about anyway."

"I can only explain it the way Miriam once explained it to me. Shabbat is like stepping out of time," he says. "It's a reprieve from your crazy schedule, from work stress, from thinking about the future. . . . The more you celebrate it, the more precious it becomes. The beauty of it is, you're not just *allowed* to escape from the real world for a day. It's a requirement."

In the end she accepts his invitation, not because she finds him attractive or charismatic or full of surprising twists, but because she is genuinely enticed by the prospect of celebrating Shabbat. The way he describes it makes it sound like something quiet and simple, sacred—the opposite of her family's loud, misguided version of a Jewish holiday (which is all food, no spirituality). Something about Mitchell's Sabbath piques her interest.

And it doesn't hurt that she does find him attractive, charismatic, and full of surprising twists. The guy is kosher, spiritual, tattooed, and hot—a combination she never would have imagined possible.

Estelle

*P*eri stubs out the joint and flops back against the sofa. "Do you want to have sex?"

Estelle mulls it over. They've had sex before. Not great sex, but "friend" sex. Comfortable, funny, pressure-free sex. What it lacks in passion it makes up for in convenience.

"Will you try to get me an editing job on a feature? At least make it worth my while. I've got decent credentials. I'm an Avid expert. My work has been shown at Sundance. I'm even willing to sleep my way to the top."

"I'm hardly the top, baby. Sleeping with me is like sleeping your way to the lower middle, at best."

"You want to order in?" she asks him.

If her scale is to be believed, she's packed on ten pounds since Gladys's funeral. (An above-average weight gain, even in the aftermath of a visit home.) She's one glazed doughnut away from a size fourteen. But who cares? All J-Date responses have dried up. Even Internet dweebs aren't interested. And Wandering Jew has, apparently, wandered off the planet.

The phone rings just as she's about to pick it up to order food. It's Astrid Blansky.

"Are you busy?" she asks Estelle.

"I've got a guest over." Calling Peri a "guest" is a bit of a stretch, but she doesn't want to have to drag her ass into work on a Sunday, which is exactly what Astrid is going to ask her to do. She's made Estelle go in the past two Sundays in a row, just because she can.

"I'd like us to get together," Astrid says. "If you've got time later."

"Get together?"

"I need to talk to you."

"It can't wait till tomorrow?"

"It can," she says mildly. "But I think you'll probably want to do it today." Her tone is so cool, so indifferent. Estelle makes a face for Peri's benefit, but he's not paying attention.

They agree to meet at the Coffee Bean & Tea Leaf in Santa Monica. Estelle hangs up and turns to Peri. "That's it," she says. "She's firing me."

"How do you know?"

"I just know," Estelle says. "She wants to tell me today, so I don't have to slither out of work in front of my coworkers tomorrow. She'll act all gracious about it, like she's doing me a great kindness. It's so Astrid."

"So don't go."

"I have to go because she wields all the power. She *knows* people. I can't burn my bridges and she fucking knows it."

It was a hard enough leap from the psychic hotline to Just-A-Trim, but she was finally in the door. She was editing! And now she's back to square zero, thanks to that bitch. "I got cocky," she mutters. "I shouldn't have been so cocky. Astrid probably smelled it."

*A*strid is waiting for her inside the coffee shop. There's the usual endless lineup at the counter, which Estelle bypasses. She sits down with Astrid.

"You're not getting anything?" Astrid says.

"I don't like the coffee here."

"You don't like the Ultimate?"

"Not really, no."

Astrid looks dismayed. She's wearing a backward baseball cap with two long braids hanging down to her shoulders. She's eating some sugary cake with two inches of icing. She's one of those people who are constantly plying themselves with sugar and never putting on an ounce. She's tall and gangly—all the more reason for Estelle to loathe her.

She says, "I saw that documentary you edited."

"What did you think?"

"Honestly? It was a bit amateurish. Interesting idea, though. And I thought your editing was excellent."

"You did?" High praise from the likes of Astrid Blansky.

Astrid nods. "I thought the editing made it as good as it was."

Estelle doesn't know what to say. It's certainly an odd segue into being canned.

"I've told you before," Astrid says. "You're a fucking good editor."

"Thanks."

"I know a producer," she says languidly. She takes a bite of her cake, savoring it. "I was at a premiere last night and he came up to me afterward. He's looking for an editor for an upcoming movie. He asked me if I could recommend someone."

Estelle's pulse starts racing.

"I told him about you," she says. "He wants you to send him your demo reel right away. He's pretty keen."

"Oh my God. Who is he? Would I know him?"

"We've edited a couple of his trailers. Remember *Army Brats*?"

How could she forget? It was one of those low-budget teen gross-out comedies. A night in the lives of six horny army brats. *Porky's* meets *An Officer and a Gentleman*.

"He's the king of the tasteless teen flick," Astrid says. "But his movies make money."

"Whatever. It's a feature—that's all I care about. I really appreciate this, Astrid."

"Look, I'm a postproduction supervisor," she explains. "When producers ask me for recommendations, my reputation is on the line. I'm going to recommend someone who I think is the best person for the job."

Estelle nods gratefully. Her joy is somewhat tempered by shame. She had Astrid all wrong.

"Having said all that," Astrid concludes, "you're fired."

Jessie

*S*kieth hands her a check. She tries not to look at it before folding it and tucking it into her purse, but she is dying to have a peek. They had settled on a fee for the work she completed at Ooze and for the seminars, but he also promised to tack on a deposit for the work she is going to do at Skieth's. No specific amount was discussed, but he assured her it would be generous. Skieth's is a bar, restaurant, and cigar lounge on three floors. Triple the clutter, triple the paperwork. Triple the money.

"When do we start?" he asks. He's standing behind the bar at Ooze; she's sitting facing him on one of the stools.

She opens her agenda book and starts flipping pages. "I've got two commitments over the next two weeks—two homes that I absolutely have to do myself," she tells him. "So if you want to start right away, I can send Auben on Tuesday, or—"

"I'd rather wait for you," he says.

Not an unusual request. It doesn't *mean* anything. Most of her bigger clients prefer to have Jessie on the premises. It makes them feel important, like they're getting the best, the CEO herself.

"So, then, how about the third week of February?"

"I'll be here," he says, smiling.

"I was thinking of something that might be of help to you," she says. "I was planning to schedule a second seminar with Steve sometime next month and I thought it might be more cost-efficient for you if I did it with *all* your managers. I mean, I know most of them are not as disorganized as Ooze was. . . ."

"No, it's a great idea. Let's set it up."

She scribbles something down in her Day-Timer and looks up at him. "I'll let you know a little closer to March."

"I love your card," he says.

"My card?"

"Your business card. 'Organizing Consultant and Designer.' Very clever."

"Most people don't notice."

"Do you have it?"

"What?"

"OCD."

"Probably. Well, yeah. Obviously."

They laugh together and then linger awkwardly over the bar. He turns around and starts pouring two drinks, vodka-and-tonics.

"What are you doing?" she asks nervously.

"Making you a drink."

"I have to go pick up my kids."

"In two hours!"

"Still."

"One drink."

"I don't drink."

"Come on. Let me make you a drink."

She slides off the stool. "I can't."

"Do you ever let loose?" he teases.

"No."

He pushes the drink across the bar at her. "One toast, to a successful business relationship."

"I'm leaving now, Skieth."

"You'd really walk out and not have a drink with your number one client?" He smiles expectantly at her.

She likes his smile. It's the only time he's ever handsome.

"I'll call you about the seminar," she says, turning to leave.

"My staff will be so excited," he quips. "Hey, Jess?"

"Hmm?"

"Thanks. You did a super job. Really."

She can tell he doesn't want her to go. In a way, she doesn't want to go either. Go to *what?* Day care, kindergarten, supper on the table, small talk with Allan, screaming at the kids to behave, bathing them (did you brush your teeth?), begging them to just go to sleep, *West Wing* in bed with Allan, lying awake all night thinking about Skieth, about the slope of his thick neck when he bends down, his broad shoulders under his tight T-shirts, even the tattoos on his arms. There's something seedy and yet sexual about him.

"All right," she concedes. "Just the one drink." She takes a sip of it and grimaces.

"Too strong?" he asks.

"I shouldn't be doing this. I have to drive."

She wonders fleetingly what it would be like to live one minute of her life without worrying about consequences. Without always thinking, *I shouldn't, I shouldn't, I shouldn't.*

"What are you thinking about?" he asks her.

"Nothing."

He looks unconvinced. "I know this wasn't on your schedule for today, wasn't in your plan—"

"I guess you think you know me," she says. "Look, I have to be somewhere. An appointment in Leaside—"

"Right. Just finish your drink at least—"

"We'll talk soon," she says, sliding off the bar stool.

When she gets halfway across the bar, she turns back. To say something? To have another look? But he's already gone back into his office.

Outside, she leans up against her car and takes a breath. She tries to clear her head; to clear *him* from her head. That image of him sitting there at the bar, pleading with her to finish her drink, keeps gnawing at her. He looked so wounded, so rejected. She wanted to stay, and that scares her more than anything.

Erica

*T*he Dorfmans live in a brownstone on the Upper East Side, a tall, narrow building with enough of a front yard (by New York standards) for a small garden in the summer. Mitchell's mother, who is a pediatrician, runs her practice out of the basement, and the family lives on the top two floors. There are two entrances, one at the basement with a gold plaque on the door—SARAH CHANA DORFMAN, MD—and one at the top of a short flight of concrete steps.

Erica knows all this because Mitchell is explaining it to her as they approach the brownstone. "It's like on *The Cosby Show*," he says. "Remember how Dr. Huxtable had his practice in the basement of their house? My mom has the same setup."

"So you're like the Jewish Cosbys."

"Except my father isn't a lawyer."

Before Mitchell even grabs hold of the knocker, the door is flung open by a diminutive woman with jet-black hair and reddish-brown eyes the color of goulash.

"I could see you guys coming up the walk," she says, drawing Mitchell into her arms. She plants a kiss on his cheek and another on his forehead, and then examines his face. She smiles at him tenderly. "I was watching for you from the kitchen."

"She used to do that when I was little," he says affectionately. "Every day after school, I'd look up and see my mother's anxious face in the kitchen window."

Mrs. Dorfman turns to Erica. "I'm Sarah. Mitchell's mother. Come in." She pulls them both into the foyer.

"I smell brisket."

"I've also got roast chicken and kasha warming on the stove, for after synagogue. You're wearing a suit, Mitch. I'm impressed."

"It's easier than dealing with Miriam," he says.

"You look adorable," she says, leading them into the kitchen.

And Erica has to agree; Mitchell *is* adorable in his navy blue suit, with the yarmulke pinned to the back of his head. He looks like he's about to be bar mitzvahed—looks barely a day over thirteen.

The hallway walls are covered with family pictures—formal portraits, school and graduation portraits, bat and bar mitzvah pictures, wedding photos. Erica pauses to study them. Lilly never did care to expose their family to guests by hanging pictures on the wall; she always thought it was one of those déclassé Jewish customs. Besides, it clutters up the decor and leaves holes in the walls. That's what albums are for.

Miriam is waiting for them in the kitchen. She jumps up to greet them as they walk in. Erica is startled by her appearance. She's wearing a long khaki skirt with a gray turtleneck and high-heeled boots, and her long dark hair is pulled back in a ponytail. She's pretty and young and normal-looking, meaning you'd never know by looking at her that she was a rabbi.

"I've heard so much about you," Miriam says, shaking Erica's hand.

"Oh?"

"Mitchell's been talking about you."

"Miriam—" Mitchell looks embarrassed.

"Mitch, you wore a suit!" she exclaims.

Mitchell pulls Erica off to the side and shows her the

table, which is already set with fancy china and candles and two loaves of challah bread covered in white linen napkins. "These are the two Sabbath candlesticks," he explains softly. "And this is the kiddush cup."

"Do you follow all the Shabbat rules?" she asks him.

"Not like Miriam," he admits. "She won't watch TV or turn on the lights or ride the bus. I'm not that strict."

"You didn't tell me we were going to synagogue," Erica says.

"I didn't?"

"I haven't been to synagogue since my cousin Amy Rosenberg's bat mitzvah in eighty-one. I was six."

"What about the Jewish holidays?"

Erica shakes her head. "We used to just stay home from school and watch soaps."

Mitchell gets a strange look on his face—a blend of incredulity and something like pity. "That's too bad," he says. "Maybe tonight will spark something."

She laughs at his earnestness. He doesn't know her at all.

*J*ust before synagogue, they all go into the kitchen to say a prayer, which Erica hopes won't take too long because she's starving and wants to get the whole religious part of Shabbat out of the way.

Miriam pulls two white candles out of the drawer.

"Do I just stand here?" Erica whispers in Mitchell's ear.

He nods, watching his sister prepare the candles.

"We're starting right now?"

"It's almost sundown," he says.

Miriam hands Larry a pack of matches. He strikes the match. "This first candle represents one part of the fourth commandment," he explains to Erica. "*Zachor,* meaning 'remember' the Sabbath day to keep it holy. And the other is *Shamor,* meaning 'observe' the Sabbath to keep it holy."

He lights both candles and everyone closes their eyes. Then Larry says, *"Baruch ata adonai elohainu melech ha'olum asher kidshanu b'mitzvotav vetzivanu l'hadlik ner shel Shabbat koddesh."*

All of a sudden, Mitchell reaches for her hand. She lets him. As Mitchell's father continues to recite the Shabbat prayers, the outside world slowly begins to ebb away. A peaceful, joyous feeling begins to wash over her, and she is momentarily uplifted.

"Shabbat Shalom," he murmurs. One by one, they all repeat it. *Shabbat Shalom.* When it comes to Erica, she says it, as naturally as if she'd been saying it her whole life. "Shabbat Shalom."

After a feast of brisket, chicken, kasha, gefilte fish, and *kreplach* soup, the Dorfmans linger around the table, mostly divulging their family secrets to Erica. (Among other things, she learns that they call themselves the Dwarfmans because they're all so short; that as a kid, Mitchell actually had shots to make him grow; that Robbie, the eldest brother, married a Maronite Christian from Beirut who refused to give their newborn son a bris and who has, to their great shame, saddled them with a grandson who has a foreskin.) All this over coffee and cheesecake.

Finally, Mr. Dorfman excuses himself to go have a nap, and Miriam and Mrs. Dorfman start clearing the table. They refuse to let Erica touch a plate. "Go be with Mitchell," they say.

Outside, side by side on the front steps, Erica says, "That was nice. I thought it would be weird, but it was very comfortable."

"Good. Maybe you'll be inspired to keep celebrating Shabbat on your own."

She looks at him for a moment, certain he must be joking, and then realizes by the look in his eyes that he is entirely serious. "I'm not really into all this," she says apologetically. "I don't even know if I believe in God."

"I didn't always."

"What happened?"

"I went to visit Miriam in Israel. Rabbinical students spend their third year studying in Jerusalem, so she invited me to spend my spring break with her. One morning we went to the Western Wall. I'd written this question for God on a scrap of paper—sort of as a joke, you know? I'd written, 'Are you for real?'"

He laughs at the memory.

"I should mention," he says, "at the time I was a complete fuckup."

"In what way?" she asks him, intrigued.

"You know, the usual. Bad crowd, bad attitude. Drugs."

"Really?" She thinks of her own past; it's something they have in common.

"So anyway," he continues, "I was at the Western Wall and I wrote, 'Are you for real?' on this piece of paper. Then I folded up the paper till it was the size of my thumbnail and I shoved it into the crevice between two stones, among all the other thousands of notes in there. I couldn't see Miriam because she was over with the women, but she'd told me to pray after I gave away my question. So I stood back and the guy beside me opened his Torah. I was kind of peering over his shoulder. I remember the sun burning a hole in my back. It was scorching. My T-shirt was stuck to my back as though it had been hosed wet. My eyes were closed.

Frankly I thought I was going to pass out. I certainly wasn't expecting an immediate answer to my question—"

"Don't tell me you got one."

"I was standing there beside this stranger. He was deep in prayer. I was feeling pretty humbled and reverential—I mean, it *was* the Western Wall, and even for a nonreligious Jew with an attitude problem, it was quite an experience. And then all of a sudden there was this vibration under my feet. The ground heaved and rumbled, and we all stumbled forward. Me and this guy, we looked at each other, and then we both looked up at the sky. I remember reaching out my hand and pressing the stones. And then I heard this commotion from over where the women were. When Miriam and I found one another later, she told me the commotion was over *her*. She had fallen, passed out or something, and people had rushed over to fan her and splatter her with bottled water."

"What happened?"

"It was sunstroke, or that's what they said. People were running all over the place looking for a hat she could put on. But Miriam didn't think it was sunstroke. All the way back to her room she kept saying, 'The earth moved! He answered me! God answered me.'

"I asked her what she'd asked Him," Mitchell says. "She said she'd asked Him if she was on the right path. I think at that point she was having doubts about becoming a rabbi. Needless to say, her commitment to the rabbinate has never wavered since that day."

"And you?"

"How can I doubt His presence? I mean, the earth *did* move, Erica. Right there in front of the Western Wall of the Temple Mount—the most sacred spot in the world for Jews."

"Come on!" Erica cries. "That was just a coincidence."

"We found out later on that there'd been an earthquake in Egypt. We'd felt the vibration of it in Jerusalem."

"Exactly."

"But what caused the earthquake?" he asks her.

"Probably a crack in the earth or some perfectly valid geological explanation—"

"Or God."

"Oh, please."

"Why not?"

She shrugs. She doesn't have an answer.

"Really," he presses, "*why not?* That earthquake convinced Miriam to become a rabbi and it gave me my faith. You can choose to believe it was geology, if that's all you can handle, but Miriam and I choose to believe it was God."

She considers his words for a moment. Something about his vehemence coaxes her into almost believing him, at least into opening up her mind to the slight possibility.

*L*ater, in the cab home, she can't stop thinking about the way he'd held her hand during the reciting of the prayers. What strikes her most about Mitchell is that beneath his offbeat, improv-loving, game-inventing exterior, there is real depth. He is spiritual and soulful and completely without pretense—he likes Harrison Ford movies, he reads Stephen King, and he believes unapologetically in God.

Paul is the exact opposite; to engage in a conversation with Paul is to be lulled and swayed by his impressive, boastful intellect. He's got words upon words to fill a thousand pages, and yet beneath his surface, Erica worries there is nothing meaningful.

Estelle

*E*stelle imports a Flash animation of a pair of dancing jeans and inserts it into the spinning logo. She hates spinning logos, but Dress For Less is signing her check. She's been freelancing to pay the bills while she waits for her first feature to be shot. Through Peri's connections, she lined up a few commercials, which pay upward of six hundred bucks for a day's work. In hindsight, she never had to panic about losing her job at Just-A-Trim.

That day at the Coffee Bean & Tea Leaf, Astrid bluntly told Estelle that her attitude sucked. "You're a great editor," she said. "But your constant sulking and complaining at work is demoralizing to everyone around you."

Estelle just sat there, stunned.

"You need to do something that challenges you," Astrid went on. "You've obviously outgrown Just-A-Trim, and frankly, we've outgrown your attitude."

So there it was. She was jobless, but not without prospects. She quickly sent off her demo reel to Armando, and he called her within two weeks. She met with the director and was hired for what will amount to about six weeks of work. Armando calls the movie *Game Set Snatch,* although he knows it will be renamed when it's released. It's about four horny young guys on a professional tennis tour.

Armando knows everyone in the industry and is made of money. He's a good person to know, and as bosses go, she likes working for him a lot more than she did Astrid. She can at least *read* him; she knows where he's coming from. He's got a very simple bottom line: *money*.

In their first meeting, he told her he was Jewish, possibly as a warning. "Don't be fooled by my name," he said.

It turns out his father opened a *schmata* business in a neighborhood of New York that was richly populated with Italians. His real name was Benny Abromowitz, but he started calling himself Benito Abruzzi as a way to bolster his credibility in the neighborhood and improve his business, which ultimately led to his learning to speak fluent Italian. Years into his scam, Benny Abromowitz *became* Benito Abruzzi. He even concocted a colorful tale about his parents coming to America from Bari. In reality, his father, a rabbi, had come from Lodz, in Poland.

Armando Abruzzi is really Arty Abromowitz. His father rechristened him Armando when he was in grade school, and it stuck. After his mother passed away, there was no one left to uphold his birth name or his Jewish faith. Nevertheless, blood is blood. Make no mistake about it, Armando Abruzzi is as Jewish as they come.

Estelle rewatches the commercial. She decides at the last minute to put a one-frame strobe on the image, to make it look less like video and more like film. She backs up her project on a zip disk in case the hard drive melts—something that actually happened at Just-A-Trim and which still haunts her to this day—and closes down for the day.

At home, she changes into a velour leisure suit she bought at Value Village in Toronto, and makes herself a mug of hot chocolate. She pops *Sense and Sensibility* into the VCR—

she's seen it seven times already and could see it another dozen times (she worships Ang Lee)—and then goes over to her computer to check her e-mails. Having long since closed her J-Date file, she no longer gets that doomed, agitated feeling whenever she checks her mail. These days, the most she can expect are succinct updates from her sisters and the occasional graphic message from Peri. So she's surprised when she clicks on the mail icon and a message from the elusive Wandering Jew pops up.

> *Sorry for the disappearing act, but I'm finally in L.A. I'd love to hook up. E-mail me ASAP if you're interested.*

She e-mails him right away. He e-mails back sometime during *Sense and Sensibility*. They arrange to meet tomorrow afternoon at the Rose Café.

She's heavier than she usually is; there's no point being in denial about it. She has no idea how WJ knows her, so she has no idea how she looked when he last saw her. She couldn't have been any bigger, that's for sure. So it's all about camouflage now. She spends the better part of six hours trying on different outfits, tossing them disgustedly on the floor and then putting them back on out of desperation. She settles on a pair of black leather straight-leg pants with a charcoal turtleneck sweater and her favorite black boots with the three-inch heels. A little extra height goes a long way. She decides to wear her hair up—Lilly always says it makes her face look slimmer—and take her eyebrow hoop out. No point scaring him away.

She calls a cab to take her to the Rose. When she gets there, she scans the place for a guy sitting by himself. There are, of course, several: one extremely good looking, probably an actor. She rules him out. Another busily typing on a laptop. He looks up at her, then goes right back to typing. She rules him out. Off in the corner, there's a leather-clad black guy who looks like he's waiting for someone. Does she know any black men? She is ashamed to admit that no, she does not, nor did she ever. Ruled out. There's an older guy, about the same age as her father, sipping an espresso. Dear God, no, she pleads. Not an old friend of her father's! But then the old guy glances past her blankly, and she breathes a sigh of relief.

So he's not here yet. She was careful to arrive about eight minutes late. Eight minutes is a good amount of time; it's more than five (which is desperate) and less than ten (which is infuriating). She orders a latte and sits down at one of the high, cafeteria-style tables. Her feet dangle from the stool.

She makes a point to stare intently down into her cup of coffee, and to look natural and un-stood-up.

"Estelle?"

She looks up. "Josh?" she cries. "What the hell are you doing here?" For a moment she doesn't put two and two together, merely thinks it's a colossal coincidence that her old friend has shown up in the very same place where she's got a blind date.

"Oh my God," she breathes. "*You're* the Wandering Jew?"

He smiles and sits down opposite her. "Surprise."

"Why didn't you say anything when I saw you?"

"At my mother's *shivah?*"

"I don't know. I just . . . I can't . . . I'm totally stunned."

"Are you disappointed?"

"No," she says, looking at him in an entirely new light. And she's not. He's as attractive as she could have hoped for.

"Good," he says. "Let me get something to drink."

He returns to the table moments later with a chai tea. "I was so frustrated that we didn't get a chance to really talk in Toronto," he says, settling back onto his stool.

"I wanted to go back to the *shivah,* but I—"

"I know. Your mother."

"She was having a hard time dealing with my father's grief."

"I understand."

"How are *you* doing?" she asks him.

"I'm better," he says. "Much better. I went underground for a few weeks. Basically stayed at Mom's and went through her things, you know. I tried to get used to the idea of not having her around anymore."

Estelle touches his hand sympathetically.

"How's your dad doing?" he asks her.

"Coping, I guess. Lilly says he's still depressed."

"Goddamn cancer," he says. "It's going to get us all eventually. What do you expect, though? Look at the environment we live in."

He pauses, and then perks up. "So where do we start?"

"Would you have told me?" she asks him.

"Told you what?"

"That you were the Wandering Jew. I mean, if we'd had the chance to really talk in Toronto."

"I don't know." He shrugs. "I knew you'd be at the funeral and I wasn't sure what I'd do." He mulls it over and then adds, "I was happy to see you again, that's for sure. But I don't think it was the right time or place." .

"Why didn't you just *call* me and ask me out?"

"Come on. When your father told me you'd joined J-Date I had to build the suspense a little."

"Is that why you didn't put up a picture?"

"Of course. I only joined to hook up with you. I didn't want to ruin the surprise."

"I can't believe my father told you about J-Date."

"Forget about it. What have you been up to for the past ten years?" he asks. "I know you're editing. Your father told me a movie you worked on was at Sundance."

She's surprised by that. "He did?"

"Sure. He's proud of you."

"That's news."

"Are you working now?" he asks.

At last, the question she's been waiting for. "As a matter of fact . . ."

She tells him all about *Game Set Snatch,* although she is very careful to leave out the title. She mentions Armando's name. "Remember *Army Brats*?" she asks him.

"I was probably out of the country."

"Oh."

"I'm not a big moviegoer."

"Right. You're more into poetry."

After a few more lattes and chai teas, they decide to go back to her place and order some food. (Big bonus points to Josh for suggesting wings and not Tunisian takeout. And yay, he's not a vegetarian!) By the time they get back to her place, she's soaring. She's attracted to him *and* totally comfortable hanging out with him.

The one thing she keeps drilling him about is his career, or the lack thereof. He uses expressions like "hiatus" and "spiritual journey" and "finding himself" to qualify his current unemployed status. She feels like Lilly, with her relentless probing.

"There must be something you see yourself doing for the rest of your life."

"Traveling."

"What's your ultimate ambition?"

"To publish a book of poetry."

"What about getting a PhD and becoming a professor?"

"I'm not an 'academic.' A bachelor's was enough for me."

So it goes, back and forth all night. He'll be describing some beautiful coastal village in Portugal and she'll say—thinking about that book about Tuscany that was on the best-seller list for ages—"Why don't you write a travel book?"

"I don't like nonfiction," he responds.

"But to earn a living . . ."

"I make money teaching English as a second language."

"It's just so nomadic."

"Exactly."

She suspects that his yearnings to drift aimlessly around the world—what he calls his "wandering soul"—are sympto-matic of a paralyzing fear of commitment. Commitment to one single career, a home, a stable relationship. And yet he was willing to marry someone, the Thai girl who called off their wedding at the last minute.

"You were going to live happily ever after in Thailand, though, weren't you?" she asks him.

He dunks a clump of soggy fries into the container of hot sauce. "Bam was like me," he explains. "Very restless. We talked about seeing the world together. Maybe on bicycles."

Estelle groans inwardly. On bicycles? Ugh. "What happened?" she asks.

"We had planned to get married on Railei Beach. Just the two of us in a Buddhist ceremony. She never showed up."

"Oh no—"

"I sat on the beach for eight hours, till the sun went down. No Bam."

"How awful."

"There was always the possibility of it," he says. "She was like that. I told you. She was restless. A free spirit."

"Have you spoken to her since?"

"I never saw her again. I left Phuket the next morning."

"Maybe that's why you chose her, Josh. Maybe *you* didn't want to settle down, so you picked someone you couldn't count on."

"Probably. At least I can say I tried."

Estelle goes quiet. What's left to say? Here she is on a date with someone she likes very much, the first man she's connected with in ages, and he's basically warning her that he is incapable of commitment, let alone of staying in the same country for longer than a few months. It's a dead end.

"What's wrong?" he asks her.

He's so gentle and laid back, qualities she finds soothing. She wishes he would scoop her into his arms and whisper a string of promises in her ear.

"I guess I'm . . . I don't know. Sort of disappointed," she tells him. "I'm having a great time tonight, but I feel like the sand is going to run out on the hourglass."

"What do you mean?"

"I don't want to go on a few dates and start to really connect and then have you announce that you're heading off to Papua New Guinea."

"I've been there already."

"You know what I mean."

"You think if we had something special I could just pack up and leave?"

"I don't know," she says sulkily.

"I just haven't met the person who could make me settle down yet," he says. "It obviously wasn't Bam."

He moves in close to her then and kisses her lips. It's a soft kiss, unhurried and a bit tentative. They grew up together, after all. It's hard to extract Milton and Gladys, let alone the past, from the equation. His mouth is hot. Her lips are burning. She isn't sure if it's passion, or suicide sauce.

Jessie

Skieth lives in one of those minimalist lofts in the Merchandise Building, the kind with barn doors dividing the rooms, impossibly high ceilings, and the authentic concrete floors you'd find in a warehouse. The front of the loft is all windows, overlooking downtown Toronto, and the rest of the walls are exposed brick.

When she gets there, he's got a fire going and a few candles lit. Music playing on some high-tech stereo, but she has no idea *what* kind of music. Techno, maybe. Something young, new. His art collection, which is impressive, is not hung but sitting on the floor, leaned up against the walls. Magnificent paintings, black-and-white photographs, sculptures.

"Wow," she says, handing him her camel-colored wool coat.

"Take a look around," he says.

There's an open-concept kitchen with a modern teak breakfast counter and stools that are not so much stools but works of art. "Philippe Starck," he says, noticing her admiring them. The appliances are (predictably) stainless steel, like her mother's. Like those of everyone else in Toronto who has a decorator. The barn doors that separate the bedroom are open, exposing a platform bed covered in a simple white linen duvet cover. There's a white metal-and-glass night-table next to the bed, and on it, a sleek, curvy chrome lamp, also Philippe Starck.

As always with Skieth, his home is nothing like what she had expected. She imagined him living in squalor. Not caring at all about art and decor and fancy stools. She thought he'd have a snake for a pet.

"I can't believe this loft needs organizing," she comments. "There's not a *thread* out of place, Skieth."

"My fridge is sort of a mess."

She looks at him dubiously.

"Would you be offended if it was a tactic?"

"If what was a tactic?"

He smiles at her with that charming "I'm infallible and I know it" smile. "To get you to come over."

She feels her face get hot. She's not even angry, though she *wants* to be. Her thoughts are conflicted, racing. She's flattered and embarrassed and has no idea how to respond. She should leave. She should snatch her coat and storm out, thoroughly insulted. (But is this not playing out exactly as in one of her many Skieth fantasies?) She feels herself slipping, but into what? Lust?

"You're kidding," she says.

He shrugs sheepishly. He's wearing baggy army pants and a ratty sweater; hasn't shaved in what looks like days. He doesn't belong in this loft, in this clean, pristine setting. It's too formal, too put-together. And yet she knows it's all part of his strategy.

"So the whole thing about having to meet here in the evening because of work . . . ?"

"I did have appointments all day," he admits.

"Right."

"I can't believe this is the first time one of your clients has fallen for you," he remarks.

Fallen for her? "My clients are all women," she says. "I'm married, Skieth."

"I know that."

"So, then . . ."

"I just thought maybe . . ."

"What?"

He shrugs.

"This isn't very . . . professional," she says. But she makes no move to leave, just stands there facing him. She's stepped into his trap and now her foot is caught.

"I'm sorry," he says, but he obviously doesn't mean it. He's smiling at her knowingly, awaiting forgiveness.

"This is awkward," she tells him. "Our working relationship is—"

"Our working relationship will be fine. Don't worry about that."

"I'd better go."

"Jessie, let me make you a cup of coffee at least."

It's after eight. The kids are probably sleeping; Allan must already be camped out in front of *Larry King,* waiting for the latest on Scott Peterson. What was she thinking, coming here so late? Blow-drying her hair for him and putting on jeans (which she knows makes her ass look great) and spritzing herself with perfume? She's not *that* naive. But she thought they'd play the game first; thought they'd flirt and tiptoe around this budding attraction, sneak meaningful glances at each other. Under the guise of working, it would have been *safe*. She wasn't expecting such forthrightness, hadn't wanted him to be so damn brazen and honest right out of the gate. Now she's at a disadvantage. If she stays, she's got no excuse other than the truth: she's staying because she *wants* to be with him, not because she's being paid to organize his closets. She'll be exposed.

She gives in. "All right, I'll have a coffee." (So unlike her; she knows she's on dangerous ground now.)

He goes into the kitchen and pulls a tin of Illy coffee out of his pantry. "Espresso? Cappuccino?"

She laughs.

"What?"

"I just . . . I never would have pictured you making cappuccinos. I never imagined you living like this."

"Have you been imagining me?" he asks her.

Always a clever comeback with him. He always keeps the edge.

"I'm fairly civilized," he says. "Once you get to know me."

"A cappuccino would be nice."

She sits down on one of the incredibly uncomfortable, impractical stools at his breakfast counter.

"They're not very comfortable," he cautions. "Why don't you have a seat on the couch."

She goes over to the white leather couch and sinks into it. He starts steaming milk and she's thankful for the noise, so that for the moment they don't have to strain for conversation. All she can think is, *What am I doing? What the hell am I doing?*

"Cinnamon?"

"Sure."

She watches him sprinkle the cinnamon onto the frothy foam and she gets this wild surge in her chest; a surge of desire that momentarily makes her want to leap over the breakfast counter and tear his clothes off. She tries to calm herself down. It hits her then—with a certain measure of amazement and alarm—that she has managed to get to twenty-nine years old without ever having experienced this. "This" being the feeling of having utterly no control, no *will*. For once, her body is ruling her head and she is indifferent to consequence. What freedom! She's never felt more powerless or aroused. And even though she's scared shitless, it's a thrill. A rush.

It's just a cup of coffee, she reminds herself.

He hands her the mug and sits down beside her. "I added a bit of Bailey's," he tells her. "For flavor."

"What's this we're listening to?" she asks him.

"It's the soundtrack to *Run Lola Run*."

"Oh," she says, vaguely remembering hearing about that movie. (Estelle would have seen it. Estelle, who is hip and knows what's going on in the world; who is *of* her generation . . . unlike Jessie.)

"You like it?" he asks.

"It's a bit thumpy."

"Thumpy?"

She laughs at herself, feeling stupid. She's such a mother, a clueless old dork. "I don't listen to music much," she says apologetically.

"You must like something."

(So they're going to discuss music. She is totally out of her element. She should be home with Allan, picking his underwear up off the floor, nagging him, *safe* where she belongs.)

"I like . . ." (*Who*? Who *does* she like to listen to? She has no idea. Which raises the question, *Who is Jessie?* She only knows Allan's music. She doesn't mind some of his CDs—the Carpenters, Fleetwood Mac. . . . But are they too outdated?) Out loud she says, "Carole King?" Phrasing it as a question, rather than a statement.

"Ah, a classic," he says. He gets up and goes over to his newfangled CD player, searches through an impressive collection of discs, slides one in. *Tapestry.*

Something inside her swells.

"Better?"

She nods, wondering what it is about her that he likes. She's so uptight, so . . . unfun.

"When did you get married?" he asks.

"When I was twenty-two. Seven and a half years ago."

He's shaking his head. "So young. Don't you worry you missed out?"

"On what?"

"Experience."

"What do I need experience for?"

"So you can be sure."

"Sure of *what?*"

"That you're with the right person."

"I don't think anyone is ever sure," she says. "You make a choice and you stand by it. No one's perfect. There's no one perfect person."

"I disagree."

"Well, you're still young and optimistic."

"I'm your age."

"After you've been married seven years and have two kids, then we'll be the same age."

"That's pretty presumptuous."

"You'll see. Being a parent changes your perspective."

"You think I'm still immature?"

"Sort of."

"So having kids ensures maturity? *All* parents are mature?"

"That's not what I'm saying," she fumbles.

"I've done a lot of things in my life."

"But *I* can't just go clubbing every night and stay out till four in the morning when I feel like it."

"That's your definition of immaturity?"

"Maybe *immaturity* isn't the right word," she says. "I'm just telling you, I guess I feel older because I have more responsibilities."

"*Different* responsibilities."

"Whatever."

"Your problem is you've put yourself in a box, you've labeled the box, and you never let yourself step *out* of that box."

"And what box would that be?"

"Mother, wife, organizer. Always in control, always doing the right thing."

"What's wrong with that?"

"Nothing. But you're more than that," he tells her. "You're *allowed* to be more than that. You're allowed to be other things too, you know."

"Like what?"

"You tell me."

"I'm everything I want to be."

"Are you?"

What else *could* she be? Certainly not something sexual. Not a *woman*. Not those things *and* have her family. "Being a mother is everything," she says. "It's all there is, really. And that's how I like it."

"Even though you always say you feel old and boring?"

"Motherhood precludes everything else in my life. Everything else that I *am*."

"But do you enjoy it?"

The question is a knife in her abdomen. She wants to flee. How dare he? He with his nightclubs and his freedom and his selfishness. Only a single man could ever ask such a thing, could be so flat-out ignorant.

"Are you asking me if I love my kids?"

"I know you love your kids," he says, sounding exasperated. "I'm asking you if you ever want to step outside your life for a moment, just to try something else."

"Some*thing* else, or some*one* else?" she counters. She notices that his thigh is touching hers, just lightly. The flesh under her jeans heats up but she doesn't shift her leg away from him.

"Either one."

"Who doesn't?" she answers. "It doesn't mean I have to act on it."

"I'm not talking about anything drastic," he says. "Just a minor change of attitude."

She's never thought about her "attitude" before, didn't even realize she brought any particular attitude to her life. She never consciously *decided* to feel old and asexual; never chose to think of herself as unattractive and dull and prudish, or virtually out of the running as a woman. Those feelings were just there, from the beginning. Maybe as far back as her teens, long before she even bore her first child. And she's accepted them, the way Allan accepts them in her.

"Let's go out," he says brightly.

"I can't go out."

"'I can't, I can't, I can't.' It's always the first thing out of your mouth. Why can't you?"

"Just because."

"Eventually you will. I don't take no for an answer," he warns. "You'll see."

"I see already."

* * *

*O*n her way home from Skieth's place, her mind goes back again and again to the same question. A question for which she has no satisfactory answer.

Does she enjoy motherhood?

Erica

She presses her face up against the window and watches the train pull out of Buffalo. She looks at her watch. Four hours left to Toronto. Paul is snoring beside her; he has that gift of being able to sleep anywhere, even upright in a chair while the two kids behind them are on their second hour of playing Yahtzee. Every time the dice smash against that little plastic table, Erica gets a stabbing pain in her frontal lobe.

The trip to Toronto was Paul's idea. Saturday morning, the day after her Shabbat dinner with Mitchell's family, Paul brought her a cup of coffee in bed and said, "Let's go to Toronto next weekend. It's time I meet your parents."

Just like that. It seems all she ever had to do was pay less attention to him and spend more time with another man. Presto, instant cooperation.

The dice come crashing down on the table again. "Yahtzee!"

Erica pulls her ski jacket over her head. She shoves her fingers in her ears. She curses herself for not remembering to bring spare batteries for her Walkman. She curses Paul for being in a coma and also for not shelling out the money for plane tickets. And in the midst of all her rage, she thinks of Mitchell, and she remembers the way they sat outside on the front stoop of his parents' brownstone talking until one o'clock in the morning—about their families, about reli-

gion—and her rage subsides a little. She smiles, remembering his story about the earth moving in Israel.

*W*hen they arrive at Union Station, Paul mutters something
about it lacking character. "Nothing like Penn Station, is it?"
he says, and for some reason she takes it personally and gets
annoyed.

She leads the way, heading east along Front Street, past
the Flatiron Building, which she points out to him. "It looks
like New York a bit," she says. "Don't you think?"

Paul raises an eyebrow, obviously not seeing any similar-
ities. He's not the least bit impressed.

When they come to her parents' condo on the corner of
Church Street, she notices with some embarrassment the new
Pizza Pizza restaurant, with its gaudy orange-and-white-
striped awning, and wonders how long before the entire city
consists of nothing but condo buildings and Pizza Pizzas and
Starbucks, and how long before Paul goes on one of his fran-
chise rants.

They're ceremoniously buzzed into the building and up
they go to the sixth floor. Lilly accosts them in the hallway,
before they even reach the front door.

"Have you eaten? I made Porcupines." (Porcupines: balls
of ground beef and rice baked in V8 juice.) Erica glances
over at Paul and winces. No doubt he will have much to say
about Lilly's Porcupines, later on in bed.

"Muh, this is Paul. Paul, Lilly."

One thing about Lilly, no matter what she thinks about
Paul—that he's too old for Erica, that he's a pervert for sleeping with one of his students, that he's not Jewish, et cetera—
she would never be anything less than warm and cordial to

him. She will always opt for making an impression in lieu of showing her true feelings. Today she is in fine form—her hair freshly colored, her lips gleaming with coral lipstick, a trendy silk scarf around her neck. If anything is bothering her, it doesn't interfere with her performance. She embraces Paul as though he's her long-lost son and fusses over him in vintage Jewish-mother style.

"Can I get you some wine, Paul? A beer? A Porcupine? Make yourself at home here. Have a seat. Milton will take your bags into Erica's room. How was the train, Paul? Was there a hassle at the border? Did you sleep?"

"Someone was playing Yahtzee behind us the entire trip," Erica complains.

"I'll make coffee, then," Lilly says. "That'll perk you up."

Paul seems pleased with the idea, until Lilly says, "Hopefully Milton bought the Sanka." At that point Paul shoots Erica a desperate, beseeching look. (He hates instant coffee. He grinds his own beans and uses one of those old manual espresso makers.)

Erica finds Milton in his den, watching a Montreal Canadiens hockey game on one of the French channels. He always prefers to watch hockey in French; says it reminds him of his childhood in Montreal. He looks up when he hears her and a smile breaks out across his face. Erica rushes over to him and jumps on his lap. She hasn't seen him since the funeral. He still has a sadness about him—a slowness to his movements, a flatness in his eyes. His spark is gone, replaced with a heavy resignation that hangs in the air around him. They go out into the living room together.

"Milt, did you buy the Sanka?" Lilly asks.

"It's in the freezer," Milton says.

Erica glances nervously at Paul. He looks horrified. Sanka

from the freezer! "We don't drink instant coffee," Erica says apologetically, not meaning to sound like a snob but wanting to spare Lilly the trouble of preparing it and Paul the trouble of forcing himself to drink it.

"Since when don't you drink instant coffee?" Milton asks.

"I don't know. We just prefer real brewed coffee. It's not a big deal."

Milton shrugs. Paul looks uncomfortable.

"We could go downstairs to Starbucks, then," Lilly suggests. "It's right across the street. I'm sure they serve brewed coffee."

"Why should we pay eight bucks for a cup of coffee?" Milton says indignantly. "I refuse to break a ten-dollar bill for a cup of coffee that tastes like caramel and hazelnuts."

"Milton—"

"I agree with Milton," Paul says. "Starbucks isn't real coffee. It's just another example of our Gap-ified American culture. Frankly, you don't see coffee franchises all over Europe, do you? But here, you package poor-quality coffee in a recycled cup with a familiar logo, add some chocolate syrup and shredded coconut, and *boom*—everyone's got to have it. I'll take an old-fashioned cup of Joe from a dingy Greek café over the iconic sewage that Starbucks serves any day."

Erica can feel her neck itching already, an affliction that flares up whenever she's stressed. Paul has rendered Milton and Lilly silent—no small feat on his part—with his coffee sermon. Erica can see that Lilly has no idea what to say next, or how to proceed. She will be afraid to make a new suggestion now. If something as benign as coffee can elicit such an impassioned response, she certainly won't want to bring up the potentially explosive topic of wine.

"I'll have a glass of water," Erica says, and she prays her mother doesn't bring out the Brita, which Paul thinks is a conspiracy intended to fool ignorant consumers into believing that all that stands between them and the E. coli bacteria is a five-dollar plastic filter.

*T*here are two types of Chinese restaurants in Toronto: the ones in Chinatown, and the ones Jewish people go to. Naturally, Erica's parents drive all the way to North York for safe, Jewish-friendly Chinese, even though they live a few blocks away from Chinatown. This astounds Paul, who loves authentic dim sum and can't understand why anyone would drive half an hour *away* from Chinatown for Chinese food. Erica's neck is painfully itchy; red welts have sprung up from all the scratching. And it's only their first night in town.

"I tried to read your book," Milton is saying to Paul, between bites of his egg roll. "But all that legal stuff confused the hell out of me."

"Dad—"

"No, it's fine," Paul says graciously. "It's a valid criticism."

"Do you have some background in law?" Lilly asks him.

"No. I did all my research on the Internet."

"I thought it was very good," Gramma Dorothy says. "Very well written."

"Do you have a new book coming out soon?" Lilly asks. "Are you working on something?"

"I've got some ideas. I may do a collection of themed short stories, much to my agent's dismay."

"Why don't you write a mystery?" Milton asks him. "Those mystery books are a gold mine."

Paul smiles politely. "Mysteries aren't my bag," he says. "Mystery writers are slaves to their plots. As a writer, I find that confining."

"You find plots confining?" Milton says.

"Rigid plots, yes. The construction of a mystery has to be meticulously laid out and I just don't write that way."

"But *could* you?" Milton presses. "I mean, if you had to?"

"If I had to? Well, I suppose I could, but . . ."

"So if you *could,* why wouldn't you?"

"To what end?"

Milton looks perplexed. "Money!" he roars. "And fame. I'm not saying you don't earn a nice living, but if you could earn from one book what Stephen King earns—"

"But that's not why I write," Paul says. "That's never been my motivation."

Milton shrugs. "I'll never understand why someone who *can* do it, doesn't just write a good commercial mystery. It doesn't mean you can't also write your kind of book—"

"My kind of book?"

"Arty. Highbrow. Not that there's anything wrong with that, but what's so bad about writing for the masses once in a while?"

Erica notices the vein in Paul's temple begin to pulsate. The word *masses* usually has the Pavlovian effect of setting him off.

"I've had this argument with my mother-in-law a million times," Milton continues. "Did you know Dorothy was a poet?"

"*Is* a poet," Lilly corrects. "You don't just stop being a poet."

"She stopped getting published is what I mean."

"Milton, not all of us care about the things you care about," Dorothy says. "I never wrote for recognition or money. That may be why you sang and made records, but that's not how it is for—"

"For who? *Real* artists?" Milton finishes.

"I never claimed to be a real artist," Dorothy says. "Poems come out of me. That's all."

"Beautiful poems," Lilly adds.

"Do you still write?" Paul asks her.

"When I feel like it," she says noncommittally.

Then Lilly says, "How's *your* writing coming along, Erica?"

"Erica is going to be a real talent," Paul answers, beating Erica to the punch. "Her diamond needs some polishing and she could use a little more discipline, but I have faith in her."

"Do you think she'll get accepted to the writing program at Columbia?" Milton asks him.

"Dad, Paul has no idea if I'll be accepted," Erica says irritably. "He's not the one who decides."

"But he must have some pull."

"Why do you assume I need Paul's 'pull' to get in? Maybe I'm good enough on my own." She pouts. Much to her embarrassment she can feel herself rapidly regressing.

"Connections never hurt," Milton defends. "It's got nothing to do with your talent."

"We've sent some of her stories out," Paul tells them.

His choice of the word *we* makes Erica even more miserable. She can see how it must look to her parents; like she is the marionette and Paul is behind her pulling the strings, making her dance and perform and, more literally, write.

*L*ater, when Erica and Paul are getting ready for bed, Gramma Dorothy knocks on her door. "Put him to bed and come in the bathroom with me," she says conspiratorially.

Erica nods, heavyhearted. You don't say no to one of Gramma Dorothy's bathtub sermons, but nothing uplifting has ever come of them. Erica kisses Paul's forehead and promises to join him in a bit. Then she morosely goes to the bathroom, where she can already hear the tub being filled.

"Close the door," Dorothy says, as Erica walks in.

She does as she's told and then plunks down on the closed toilet seat lid. Dorothy thrusts her hand under the tap to test the temperature. When it's sufficiently scalding, she dumps a capful of bubble bath into the water. Then she removes her clothes, and finally her bottom teeth. Looking at her naked, Erica shudders, the way she always did as a child. She used to wonder, *Will that happen to* my *body?* And she still wonders the same thing. No matter how much she loves her grandmother, old age—exposed in all its nakedness, under the harsh, fluorescent bathroom lighting—is unforgiving.

Dorothy slips underwater and leans her head back against an inflatable white pillow. She lets out a small sigh. "Pass me a cigarette."

Erica hands her grandmother a Matinée. Dorothy lights up and the smoke rises and mingles with the steam in the air. The humidity and smoke and the smell of lily-of-the-valley bubble bath all lull Erica back to a time when these rendezvous were a regular part of her life.

"He won't marry you," Dorothy says, her voice coming suddenly out of the steam.

"How do you know?"

"I just know."

"Maybe I don't want to get married."

"What *do* you want, Erica? Do you know? Are you even close?"

"I want to write," Erica answers, her voice quavering.

"Since when?"

Erica looks away. Before she can stop herself, tears are rolling down her cheeks. "Not everyone is born knowing what they want to do, or even what they're good at," she says. "I've had to figure it out."

"You've been figuring it out for a long time."

"It's not my fault. Everyone else in this family has a gift for something. Lilly and Milton are singers. You're a writer. Estelle is a whiz at editing. Even Jessie has a talent that she's turned into something successful. What have I ever been good at?"

"I don't think it's a question of being born to do just one thing," Dorothy counters. "I think it's also a question of commitment. We've all had to commit to something. *You* have to commit to something, but I don't think you've ever been willing to do that."

"I'm committed to writing now."

Dorothy is silent.

"You don't know what it's like," Erica whimpers. "Being the only one in the family who's not good at anything. How am I supposed to express myself when there's absolutely nothing to express?"

"Everyone has something to express. You just haven't found the right outlet."

"I have! I've chosen writing."

"Paul chose writing for you."

"You're telling me to commit myself to something, but then you're telling me it shouldn't be writing. I don't understand."

"I think it should be something that is meaningful to *you,*" she says, exhaling a couple of smoke rings. "Not to your boyfriend."

"What, then?" Erica cries. "What other artistic outlet is there that I haven't already tried?"

"Maybe that's what you're afraid of," Dorothy says, sitting up in the tub. "Uncovering that maybe you're not an artist."

"What does that leave?"

"You have to answer that for yourself. Jessie found her answer. So did Estelle."

"Paul has faith in my writing," Erica mutters. "He thinks I could be good at it."

"He also thinks you're young and attractive and he's smitten with you right now. And maybe you are good at it. But do you even like writing? Do you enjoy it? Erica, have you ever considered that maybe you can't commit to anything because you're looking in the wrong place?"

"This family makes it so hard. . . ."

"Makes what hard?"

"All that matters to you is talent and achievement. I'm sorry I can't create anything. I wish I could. I *want* to! I feel like there's something inside me that wants to come out . . . I just don't know what or how. I wish there was a way for me to get things out the way you can just write a poem, or the way Daddy can sit down at the piano and sing. . . . What's a person like me supposed to do?"

"No one in this family ever imposed anything on you. No one said you had to be something you're not."

"Didn't they? Didn't *all* of you?"

"How?"

"By being who you are. You just don't understand. How could you?" She stands up and turns to leave. "You have a passion for something," she tells her grandmother. "You'll never understand what it's like *not* to have a passion."

Estelle

"*M*aybe we should tell them in person," Josh says.

They're lying in bed under a tent of newspapers. Josh is scribbling in his journal.

"You mean go to Toronto?" Estelle cries. "No way."

"Whatever you want."

"My family's bad for me," she says. "Like eating fried foods. I'd rather just call them."

"It's your decision," he says. "I'm going to have a shower." He kisses her forehead and slides out of bed.

She watches him go into the bathroom, admiring his naked body. He's a little thin and lanky, but he's rock hard and in good shape. Long-limbed and sinewy.

Picking up the phone she dials her parents. She's got that excited, jittery feeling in her chest because she knows her father is going to be thrilled. Finally, *she* will be the daughter to bring home the biggest prize: Gladys's son! She isn't sure how Lilly will take the news, whether Estelle's getting a man at long last will supersede the fact that he's got Gladys Gold's blood coursing through his veins.

She's disappointed when Lilly answers. She wanted to get to Milton first.

"Hi, Muh."

"Estelle? How's your movie?"

This is something she can get excited about: a real

Hollywood picture. She hasn't stopped talking about it since Estelle told her the news. Not that Estelle's complaining. Her status within the family has skyrocketed.

"I haven't started yet," she says. "Next week, Muh."

"It's so exciting. We rented that Armand Assante movie, the one you told us about. *Army Brats*?"

"Armando *Abruzzi*," Estelle corrects irritably.

"It wasn't very good. But he didn't have *you* directing."

"Editing."

"It takes *chutzpah* to do what you're doing," Lilly says. "Eh, Milt?"

Estelle can hear her father mutter something in the background.

"So," Estelle says. "Anything you want to ask me?"

"Did you go to Jenny Craig like I suggested?"

"Not that."

"What, then?"

"For the past ten years, every time I speak to you, you ask me if I'm seeing anyone. . . ."

"You met someone?" Lilly exclaims.

"I've been seeing someone for about a month." What she doesn't mention is that Josh has actually been living with her the whole time, with no plans to find a place of his own. She's just happy he's staying in one place. He's even hinted at looking for a job.

"What does he do?" Lilly asks.

Why is that always the first question? "He's an English professor."

"Is he tenured?"

"Actually, he's not a professor exactly. He's a teacher."

"A high school teacher?" Less impressed now.

"No. Well, no. He teaches English as a second language."

"To immigrants?"

"I guess."

"You mean like Josh Gold?"

"That's the funny part. See . . ." She takes a breath. "It *is* Josh. He got in touch with me through J-Date—"

Silence.

"Muh?"

"Not you, too."

"What?"

"Infatuated with them."

"Them who?"

"The Golds! That's who."

"I thought you'd be happy. He's a nice Jewish boy, he—"

"He's a bum, Estelle! He's a drifter."

"He is not a bum. He's a very spiritual—"

"Spiritual doesn't buy you a house or a car."

"I can buy my own—"

"What are you going to do? Follow him around the globe?"

"He's not going anywhere."

"What could you possibly have in common with him? You're so driven and hardworking."

"We have a lot of the same interests," she says defensively, and it's not so much a fib as an exaggeration. They aren't exactly two peas in a pod. For instance, she loves movies and TV, and dislikes any kind of outdoor activity, i.e., inline skating, cycling, beach volleyball, walks, jogging, and swimming in the ocean. Josh can't stand TV and refuses to indulge in even the odd episode of a quality show like *Will & Grace* or *Law & Order*. He was mortified when he caught her watching *Maury Povich* one afternoon. (She didn't tell him that not only is she a huge Maury fan, but also she and Peri have, on numerous occasions, been part of the studio audience.) He's also fanatical about inline skating, cycling, playing volleyball, going for long walks, jogging, and swimming in the ocean. But they manage to find their common ground; they make concessions.

"Is it serious?" Lilly asks.

"It's moving fast," Estelle admits. "But that's because we've known each other our whole lives. We have a comfort level that usually takes a long time to develop, you know?"

More silence.

"Let me talk to Daddy."

Lilly sighs and then Milton comes on the phone. "What is it, Bean?"

"I'm seeing Josh."

"Seeing him?"

"He's living with me."

"Like a roommate?"

"No. Like a boyfriend."

"Gladys's Josh?" he cries. "You and Joshy? I always thought he liked Erica."

Estelle winces; her father's words pummel her chest. "Go figure," she retorts, her voice full of bravado. "Muh doesn't seem very happy about it."

"Josh is a little lazy. She's right about that. But you can work on that."

"He's not lazy," she says. "He just likes to travel."

"Gladys supported him, you know. She spoiled him. He has to go out and get a *real* job, Bean."

"He will."

"But he's a nice boy. He's someone who can probably make you happy."

*   *   *

*J*osh comes out of the shower and puts on a pair of shiny cycling shorts. "How about a bike ride?" he says.

She forces a smile. "But it's Sunday," she reminds him.

"And?"

"It's our day to rent movies and order in."

"It's gorgeous outside. We can't shut ourselves in and hibernate!"

She looks longingly over at her TV set. She gives in. "Okay. But do you have to wear those shorts?"

"They're racing shorts," he tells her. "They've got the padded rear."

She gets out of bed and starts rifling through her dresser for some piece of clothing that won't get caught in the spokes. She settles on a pair of cutoff army pants.

"We have to get you some new gear," Josh says.

"Gear?"

"And I was thinking," he goes on, "that we could learn how to surf."

Jessie

She smears some pink lip gloss on her lips and then wipes it off with the back of her hand. She decides to go with something more dramatic, that deep brown Mac lipstick she bought but never wore. Allan hates when she wears makeup, so there's some satisfaction in applying it now for someone who will appreciate it.

She still doesn't know how Skieth managed to convince her to go out. *Out!* To a club, like a teenager! Something Estelle would do. But he asked her and, to her own astonishment, she agreed. Maybe he put something in her orange juice on Wednesday afternoon. Or maybe it was the things he said to her—not his usual boasting or smooth maneuvering. She was labeling files for him at Skieth's when he came into the office and sat down. He seemed distant, distracted. For once he wasn't quizzing her about her life or firing off his usual disconcerting questions. He was depressed and off his guard.

She asked him what was wrong, thinking she'd get some trite response—a problem with his staff, the bad weather, a hangover.

Instead, he said, "My father came to see me at Ooze last night."

"Did you have a fight?"

"Not the way you're thinking. He came to drink, not to see me."

"Oh."

"He's an alcoholic. He shows up at my bars, thinking he can drink all night, on me of course. It always ends badly. Usually my bouncers have to throw him out kicking and screaming. It's pathetic."

Jessie looked up from the files.

"He left my mother when I was about twelve," Skieth went on. "He'd go months without getting in touch with me. After a while, he disappeared altogether. For four years, all through university, I never heard from him. Then he shows up one night after I'd opened this place. Suddenly, I was his free booze ticket. At first I let him drink all he wanted. I was so happy just to have him back, you know?"

She nodded, trying to understand.

"I'd pretend like we were great pals. Me and my dad, having a few drinks at my bar. I was kind of proud. But then it started getting ugly. Every night he'd harass my staff, or cause fights, and he'd end up passed out at the bar. I'd have to put him in a cab. It was embarrassing."

"What made you decide to own *bars*?" she asked him. "I mean, with him being . . ."

"I don't know. Probably to prove to myself I'm not like him, that I'm stronger."

She thought of all the mornings he'd shown up at work hungover, and wondered if he was as strong and unlike his father as he thought he was.

"Or maybe for revenge," he muttered. "Who the hell knows?"

"What happened last night?"

"The usual. He showed up early at Ooze, before the bouncers were even at the door, and he went up to the bar. My bartender refused to serve him, so he started ranting and raving, calling me a fucking asshole. I had to get Darius to throw him out the back door."

Skieth looked so forlorn while he was talking, Jessie wanted to cradle his head in her arms. She was melting. . . .

"They all know he's my father," he said. "It's fucking humiliating."

"It's nothing for *you* to be ashamed of."

"You've never seen my father drunk. When I was little, I used to have to sleep in the bathtub. I'd bring my blanket and pillow into the bathroom and lock the door. It was the only place I was safe from him."

Jessie looked down, not knowing what to say.

"Seeing him now just brings everything back up," Skieth continued. "It's like I can't move on with him showing up every night, you know? Just by being around, he won't let me forget."

"Do you have a close relationship with your mother?"

"She remarried another alcoholic. I don't speak to her."

Jessie wanted to offer up a tragic story of her own, to show him solidarity, but there was nothing she could say. Lilly and Milton were pretty harmless by comparison. She's never known true suffering, other than what she puts herself through.

"You should feel pretty good about what you've accomplished," she told him, in a pat, reassuring tone that she knew smacked of Lilly. "In spite of everything."

He looked at her strangely. "Let's do something," he said. "Let's just go somewhere right now."

"I can't."

"Of course not."

"No, really," she said. "I have to be at a seminar at four."

"How about Friday night, then?"

She thought about Allan, about having to take Levi to karate on Saturday morning. "All right," she said. "Friday."

"What's with all the war paint?" Allan remarks, coming into the bedroom.

She ignores him. He's been grouchy lately, ever since his book fell out of the top ten on the national bestseller list. That and the critical beating he took in the *National Post* last Saturday, in a feature that slammed his diet, among many others, including *SugarBusters, The Zone,* and *The Carbohydrate Addict's Diet.* But none of them was more ridiculed than Allan's green tea diet.

"So where're you going?"

"I don't know. Auben chose the place."

"Since when do you go out for drinks, anyway?"

She doesn't respond.

"You're wearing those?"

She looks down at her black Dolce & Gabbana pants. "What's wrong with them?"

"Aren't they a bit snug in the rear?" he asks, examining her from behind.

"They're supposed to be."

"You should do a week of green tea," he suggests. "As a cleansing, to take off that excess . . . bloat."

She closes her eyes. "Allan, please."

"Sorry, sorry. I know you're sensitive."

She opens her eyes. He kisses her head and stands behind her, so that they're both looking into the mirror.

"Don't stay out too late," he says. "Remember Levi has karate tomorrow morning."

"Why can't you take him?"

"I've got that doubles match at Mayfair."

What would happen if she simply failed to show up by tomorrow morning? Allan would probably leave the kids alone and go play tennis anyway.

"Have fun," he says, on his way out of the room, now that he's already sabotaged any potential for that. She can hear him galloping down the stairs, the TV going on in the den. Her muscles start to relax.

"Mom?"

She turns around. "What are you doing up, Peanut?"

Levi steps tentatively into her bedroom. "I can't sleep," he says. She notices that his pajama top is on backward—the tag is sticking out from under his chin.

"Lift up," she says, pulling the top over his head and then putting it back on the right way. "Why can't you sleep?"

He shrugs.

"Go back to bed and try again."

"Do I have to go to karate tomorrow?"

"You like karate. Why wouldn't you want to go?"

Another shrug.

"What is it, Levi? Now or never." She looks at the clock guiltily. She's meeting Skieth in half an hour.

"Sensei yelled at me in front of the class last time," he tells her.

She crouches down in front of him. "Why?"

"Because I can't remember the *kata*."

"Why can't you remember it?"

"Because it's hard."

"I hear what you're saying," she tells him, remembering one of those books on parenting she just read. *Be sympathetic. Let the child know you understand him.* "I understand it's hard, but that's not a reason to give up."

"And then he said my patch was sewn on the wrong side of my *gi* and if it isn't fixed by tomorrow I'll have to do fifty burpies."

"And you're only telling me *now?*" she cries.

"I don't want to go anymore."

"We paid six hundred dollars for those lessons."

"But I'm afraid of the sensei!"

Looking closely at him now—maybe for the first time all week—she can see there are dark purplish circles under his eyes. She pulls his limp body closer to her. "Have you been worrying about this since last Saturday?" she asks him, her heart breaking. She imagines him lying in his little bed every night, unable to sleep; lying there awake in the dark, dreading his Saturday karate lesson, agonizing over that troublesome *kata*. He nods miserably.

I've created a monster, she thinks.

"Get me your *gi*," she says. "I'll move the patch."

He looks up at her, blinking tiredly. "What about Sensei Fortunato?"

"I'll talk to him tomorrow when I drop you off."

He acquiesces reluctantly and pads down the hall to retrieve his *gi*. While she's waiting, she calls Skieth's cell phone to tell him she'll be late. Family emergency.

She gets to the Courthouse at around ten. It's an old courthouse that's recently been converted to a bar—a much classier one than Ooze. She finds Skieth downstairs in a loungey area, sitting in an upholstered armchair by the fireplace. He's dressed up in a collared shirt and black pants. It becomes him, makes him look like the success he is. His face brightens as she approaches.

"I thought you weren't going to show," he tells her. "I was sure you'd back out."

"Here I am."

"Everything okay at home?" he asks, concerned.

She never did explain what *sort* of family emergency was holding her up. "Oh yeah. I just had to do some last-minute sewing."

"That constitutes an emergency?"

"In my house it does."

He looks at her thoughtfully and then says, "Let's go upstairs."

On the third floor, there's a bar and a spacious dance floor, surrounded by couches and coffee tables. Another fire blazes in an imposing stone fireplace. Skieth has ordered them drinks—for him a vodka-and-tonic, for her an amaretto sour. Whenever she's at a party, usually for one of Allan's book launches, she'll indulge in one or two amaretto sours, which to her taste like lemon meringue pie.

"So in Niagara Falls," he's saying, "there's this strip club where you get up onstage and lie down on your back with a penny in your mouth, right? Then these strippers try to take the penny out of your mouth . . . with their *breasts*."

Just hearing him say the word "breasts" makes her heat up. "And that turns you on?" she asks, incredulous.

"Sure. Do you know how much skill that requires? Using their tits like that?"

She gets a flash of herself kneeling over Skieth, trying to lift a penny out of his mouth with her breasts, and it makes her flush. She flags down the waiter and orders another lemon meringue drink.

"Do you go alone?" she asks him. "To the strip clubs?"

"Sometimes. When I'm lonely," he says, snuggling in a

bit closer to her on the couch. He smells so good. Nothing identifiable, just "man" smell—a commingling of hair product and skin, maybe a trace of cologne, but nothing over-whelming.

"You okay?" he asks her.

"I'm fine," she says. "Why?"

"Well, I know you're out of your safety zone."

He touches her hand and she shivers.

"Will you dance with me?" he asks. "And don't say you can't."

She follows him onto the dance floor and he puts his arms around her, bringing her right up against his pelvis. It's a fast song, but they dance slow. Her face is on his massive shoul-der and he tickles the back of her neck as they sway back and forth. She closes her eyes; she can feel his hard-on against her lower abdomen. Now she's the one who pulls him closer. That feeling of pending danger that always infuses her time with Skieth has disappeared, leaving only a kind of surreal numbness. Because this is not reality. Reality is so far away, so blurry and indistinguishable.

She has finally managed to escape her life, her *self,* for the first time ever. Her head is so quiet, peaceful. Maybe it's all the alcohol; or maybe it's Skieth's reassuring presence, his strong arms around her, his broad chest, the smell of him which is so different from Allan's smell.

"I want you to come back to my place," he says.

She's shocked to discover that she's wet between her legs. "I don't know," she breathes.

"It's getting a little late to turn back, don't you think?"

"I guess so," she murmurs. And all of a sudden, reality starts encroaching on her fantasy and she's embarrassed to be one of those women, those bad-marriage women who have affairs. She is *Jessie Jaffe!* She is not weak, not a failure, not a slut! And yet, here she is.

He pulls back from her then, forcing her to look him in the eyes—those bottomless, melancholic blue eyes that render her inept. Before she can even get her wits about her, before she can *get back control,* his lips are pressing down on hers, his tongue flicking around inside her mouth; he's got one hand rubbing her hair, the other on her behind, caressing it. And then that thread of reality is gone again and there's no one in the world other than her and Skieth.

She realizes then that she is a person without loyalty. She has succumbed to a stranger. Not even a beautiful stranger either, not a gallant prince worthy of her fantasies. But a man with muscles and tattoos and a square face and big rough hands that could crush her.

There's a feeling like a balloon floating up from her belly into her throat. The music, the people dancing in her periphery, Allan and the kids—these all fall away in an instant. She is weightless, levitating; her fingertips tingling. *But I'm Jessie Jaffe* is just a distant echo in her skull.

She never really knew who Jessie Jaffe was in the first place; no point in clinging to her now. The booze, Skieth's mouth, her own unfamiliar desire—this is all she's got now. The old Jessie is irretrievable.

Erica

"*I* owe you," he says. "I owe you big-time."

"But I'm not wearing the costume."

"No, you have to. It's part of it. It'll be fine."

"I can't. It just . . . it goes against everything . . . I don't do costumes."

Mitchell takes her hand. "You have to," he says. "That's the whole point."

She looks down at her hand clasped in his, but she doesn't pull it away.

"Sorry," he says. And he lets go.

There's a moment of confusion, awkwardness. She has no idea what she's doing. A favor for a friend? That's the premise, of course. That's the "understanding" they've reached. Mitchell needs a date for his cousin's bar mitzvah and she's going to help him out of a bind. Nothing sinister about that. Paul hardly seemed to care when she asked his permission. And the fact that the post–bar mitzvah party is taking place at Medieval Times in Lyndhurst, New Jersey, had Paul in stitches. As she was leaving, he called out, "Have fun, my wench!"

So much for jealousy. Which raises the question, If Paul is okay with her posing as Mitchell's date for one afternoon, why is *she* so uneasy about it?

"Maybe it'll actually be fun," Mitchell says. They're in a rented car, on their way to the East 23rd Street Synagogue of

Flatbush, where his sister Miriam is the second rabbi. He pulls the Medieval Times pamphlet out of his suit-jacket pocket and hands it to her.

" 'Guests feast on a four-course medieval banquet,' " she reads, " 'while watching brave knights compete in games of skill, dangerous swordplay, and an authentic jousting tournament.' "

"See," he says. "How great does that sound?"

"Remind me why I'm doing this again?" she asks as they enter the Brooklyn Battery Tunnel.

"So that I don't have to be subjected to the Dorfmans' litany of questions about why I'm still single. Do you know what it's like to attend a Jewish celebration without a date?"

"I have an idea," she says.

"On the self-punishing meter, the dateless bar mitzvah is second only to the dateless wedding. At least with you here, I won't have to get high beforehand."

"I thought you reformed when you found God," she teases.

"Since when are spiritual faith and smoking the occasional joint mutually exclusive?"

*M*itchell and Erica are seated in the red section of the twelve-thousand-seat arena. They are in full medieval regalia—or at least what passes for it on the cheap: red polyester capes and red paper crowns on their heads. Serving wenches in bonnets and elaborate medieval dresses are handing out plates of food. Below in the stadium, the knights are stampeding past on their horses, waving their swords in midair. The red side is winning, and even Erica has succumbed to the whole thing. She finds herself repeatedly leaping to her feet along with the rest of the crowd every time a red knight wins a jousting match.

There's even been a moment or two when she's caught herself laughing unself-consciously; but then Paul's disparaging voice pops into her head and jolts her back to reality, and she'll think cynically, *I'm making an ass out of myself.*

Mitchell, on the other hand, has been the one consistently cheering the loudest. Not so long ago, Erica would have judged him harshly for his unrestrained enthusiasm, his absence of ego, and his complete *willingness* to make an ass of himself; she would have assessed those traits as shortcomings and been embarrassed by him. But now she finds herself somewhat awed by his lack of cynicism. And she almost— *almost*—doesn't want the day to end.

A fter the bar mitzvah, they drive back into the city without saying much. He pulls up in front of her building and turns off the ignition. "So, thanks," he says, turning to face her. "I couldn't have done it without you."

"Don't repeat this to anyone, but I had fun."

"You did?"

"In an 'I'll never do that again' sort of way."

"On the bright side, I'm sure it gave you great material for a story."

"A literary masterpiece about a bar mitzvah at Medieval Times?"

"Do you only write literary masterpieces?"

"I don't write much of anything," she confesses. She leans her head against the window and gazes up at her apartment. "I'm not so sure that it's the great passion of my life."

"Does it have to be?"

"It should be. It is for Paul. He eats, drinks, sleeps, and breathes writing."

"So I suppose only 'great artists' have passion."

"I think people should be passionate about what they do, yes."

"I wouldn't say I'm passionate about making games, but I earn a nice living from it. I *am* passionate about the Mets, and about smoked meat from the Second Avenue Deli. That doesn't mean I'm about to make a career out of either of them."

"I guess I've always just wanted to fall in love with something, you know? To absolutely love what I do, be great at it, and earn a living from it."

"I'd be happy just to fall in love with *someone,*" Mitchell says, looking away from her.

"That's never been my problem," she admits. "Speaking of which, I'd better get home to Paul."

Mitchell starts the car. "My aunt Mona thinks you're adorable, by the way."

"Which one is she?"

"Big bouffant hair and Botoxed face?"

"Which one?"

Mitchell laughs. "I wish that what they thought about us was actually true," he mutters.

"What do they think?"

"That we're a couple."

"Mitchell—"

"I know. I don't want to pressure you. It's just that . . . it's like . . . imagine you finally found something you love to do, and it's exactly what you've been looking for, that great elusive passion. But for whatever reason, you couldn't have it. It was off limits. How would you feel?"

"Frustrated, I suppose."

"I guarantee it would be worse than never finding it at all," he says. "I can tell you, it *is* worse."

When she gets up to the apartment, she finds Paul pacing the hallway. "I thought something happened to you!" he says, as she comes through the front door.

"Are you pacing?"

"I was worried."

"You never pace."

"It was supposed to be an afternoon bar mitzvah. It's almost eight o'clock, love. Usually you call."

"It was too loud in there."

He pulls her close and embraces her. "I missed you. I was lonely all day. Let's have a bath," he says, leading her by the hand into the bathroom.

He kneels and turns the brass taps. "How was it? Was it ghastly?"

"You would have thought so."

"What did *you* think?" he asks her, turning around. And crouched there on his knees, staring up at her expectantly, he looks impossibly vulnerable.

She rushes over to him and cradles his head. "It was awful," she assures him. "I couldn't wait to get home."

"What took you so long, then?"

"I was stranded in Jersey. I had to wait till it was over."

Paul wraps his arms around her waist and holds her there, like a boy clutching his mother. He unfastens her skirt and then undresses himself. They get into the tub, she between his legs. He splashes hot water down her back and massages her neck.

"You're spending a lot of time with him," he says.

"I was just doing him a favor. It didn't seem to bother you when I left this morning."

"I guess I've had all day to think about it."

"Think about what?"

"Where is it going exactly?"

"We're just friends."

"So you keep telling me."

"It's true."

"He must be in love with you."

"He's not."

"Of course he is. There's nothing not to love."

"I love *you*," she murmurs.

The bath fills up and she turns off the tap. Paul lights a candle. Then she leans her head back against his chest.

"Erica?"

"Hmm?"

"I'm jealous of him. Do you think you could stop spending time with him, please?"

She wants to answer yes; wants to promise him. The last thing she wants is to hurt Paul. But the mere contemplation of not seeing Mitchell anymore causes something inside her to plummet. The truth is, she wants to keep them both; they each have something special and amazing to offer her.

"I don't like how long it's taking you to respond," Paul says dejectedly.

And because he's the man she lives with and the one who takes care of her—and especially because he's the man whom she worshipped until not so long ago—she says, "Of course I'll stop hanging out with Mitchell. If that's what you want. It's no big deal at all."

He exhales loudly, but she isn't sure if it's a sigh of relief or of resignation.

Estelle

*B*arese Films is on La Brea, just south of Santa Monica Boulevard. It's still in West Hollywood, not too far from where she lives. It's also one block over from Tim Burton Productions, which is on Formosa. Who knows? Maybe one day Estelle will bump into Tim going for a coffee at the Formosa Café!

"Who's Tim Burton?" Josh asked her, when she told him.

"Edward Scissorhands?" she said, deflated.

"I must have been—"

"I know. Out of the country."

At Barese Films she has her own editing suite, which she's already put her touches on. Pictures of her and Josh taped to the walls, her Hello Kitty mouse pad, scribbled Post-its full of her ideas stuck to the desk, the twenty-inch monitors, and the vector scope. She realizes now, more than she ever did at Just-A-Trim or even doing freelance commercials at Splice, that she is truly in her element in the editing suite; she is at her creative best when choosing between a circle-wipe transition or an edge-wipe transition, when she's removing an irritating breath that precedes a clip of dialogue, and even when she's adjusting her white levels to balance the color. She even loves the soothing hum from behind her in the tower, the room where the computers are, and she actually leaves the sliding glass doors open so she can hear all the noise from the Beta machines, the hard drive, and the sound panels.

It's still early, but so far she hasn't seen much of Armando, which is fine by her. That's how it is with producers; they're like ghosts. At most, the director—a nervous wisp of a guy—comes and sits with her every once in a while, but mostly he defers to her creative judgment. She's got some cool ideas and he knows it. He also knows Estelle was handpicked by Armando, so there's no point trying to wield any illusory power. All in all, it's an ideal situation for her feature debut. Too bad the movie is such a stinker. But, she keeps telling herself, it's one step up on the rung. If she does a good job, who knows where it could lead? Armando might recommend her to *any*one. Opportunities abound in L.A. when you know a big-shot producer. Now she's just got to wow him with her editing.

"Knock, knock."

She looks up from her computer. "Hey!" She leaps up and into Josh's arms. "How was the flight?"

"Fine. I missed you." They embrace. He smothers her face with kisses. "Have you been smoking?" he asks her.

"Oh, I had a drag off someone's. . . ." (She hopes he can't see her pack of Marlboros sticking out of her bag. It was just a treat while he was away.)

"Let's go for a walk," he says. "It's a beautiful day."

"Sure. Hang on." She saves her sequence onto a zip disk and turns off the screen.

Outside, the sun is blazing. Spring in L.A. is paradise, like summer back home but without the cramping humidity. She thinks the palm trees perfume the air, but Josh insists palm trees have no smell. They walk up La Brea to Santa Monica Boulevard.

"You hungry?" he asks her.

"I could eat."

They go into Best Price Chinese Fast Food, a restaurant she frequents far too much. She consumes so much peanut oil that her bowel movements smell like Skippy.

"Good news," he says. They're eating Kung Pao chicken out of the container as they walk. (Josh hates sitting for too long.) "I got a job."

She looks up at him, startled. "Doing what? You mean back home?"

He only went back to clear up some legal business relating to his mother's estate. He's been left a substantial chunk of money, which he's been living off for the past few months. Estelle had no idea he was also going to look for a job.

"It fell into my lap," he says. "A friend of mine just launched a literary magazine and he needs a coeditor."

"Doesn't that pay, like, ten cents a week?"

"Look, it's not about the money. My mother left me plenty to live off for a long time."

"But don't you want to earn your own living?"

"I want to follow my heart's desire."

She groans. He looks wounded by her reaction.

"It's a dream come true for me, Estelle. It's the only thing I can imagine doing for an indefinite period of time. Hell," he says, "I may even get to publish some of my own poetry!"

Hoorah! she thinks. He's leaving her to get a goddamn poem printed in one of those pretentious magazines that no one on earth will ever read. *The Annieopsquotch Quarterly* or *The Ploughman's Ass*.

"I thought you'd be happy. . . ."

She tosses her Chinese food into a garbage can and quickens her pace. "Happy? You're fucking leaving me!" she cries.

"No," he says. "I want you to come with me. I want you to marry me and move back to Toronto with me."

She stops cold and stares at him. "What?"

"You heard me. You're it for me. You're the one. I want to marry you."

"So soon? It's only been a few months—"

"We've known each other forever," he reminds her. "I'm thirty-seven years old. Trust me, I *know*."

Her film career flashes before her eyes. The Golden Globe, the Oscar, schmoozing with Julia Roberts outside the Mann Theater . . .

"Is moving back to TO negotiable?" she asks him.

"Estelle, you're one of those people who can do anything you put your mind to. You win people over. You could have a successful career *any*where—"

"Not a film career."

"Do you know how many movies are being shot in Toronto these days? It's Hollywood North!"

"Josh—"

"It's so much harder for me. I just can't. . . . I don't have your . . . I'm shy and I'm not a go-getter."

"There must be a literary magazine in L.A."

"L.A. literary magazine. That's an oxymoron."

"Seriously."

"This is a great opportunity for me," he says. "Michael Shulman is an old friend. He really needs a coeditor. It's right up my alley. Besides, after *Game Set Snatch*, you'll essentially be out of work again."

"But Armando's already got another movie on the back burner. Do you know what kind of money I could be making soon?"

"Oh. I didn't realize your soul was for sale."

"Good God, Josh. Don't be so sanctimonious. This is L.A., for Chrissake. They take our souls at the airport."

"So what are you going to do?" he fires back. "Make teen gross-out flicks for the rest of your career?"

"Maybe."

"How noble."

"I'm not trying to be noble!" she cries. "And speaking of noble, how noble is living off your dead mother's money?"

She watches in horror as his expression goes slack and his face turns sheet white. She wants to snatch back the words and stuff them back inside her big ugly mouth. "I'm sorry," she pleads. "I'm so sorry. I'm sorry, sorry, sorry. . . ."

He turns away from her and starts heading toward home.

"Josh!" she calls after him. "Josh, wait!" She catches up to him. He won't look at her, won't speak to her. They've never fought before. She's never seen him angry (wasn't sure he was even capable of rage).

"Josh, please. I'm so sorry. I didn't mean it. I . . ."

He keeps walking. She's terrified. Scared he'll go home, pack his things, and she'll never see him again. Next thing you know, she'll get a postcard from Sri Lanka. There's always the possibility of it with a guy like Josh. He's her Bam. Every day with him is a gamble.

She follows him as far as she can, but knows she has to get back to work. Armando is paying her four hundred bucks a day and she can't just take off to resolve a personal crisis.

"I didn't mean it," she sobs. She wipes under her nose. "I love you and I'm proud of you for following your heart." She gags a bit on that one, but she's at the groveling point of no return. "Maybe I'm jealous!" she cries after him.

This gets his attention. He stops and turns to listen.

"You know, jealous of your integrity," she says. "I admire

that you're willing to do something you love, regardless of the size of the paycheck."

"That's not what you just said."

"I know. Maybe I wish *I* had the courage to pursue my heart's desire. . . ." (She's pretty sure she heard that on *Oprah* once. It appears to appease him.) "Rather than keep on editing these trashy movies." (She dares not admit to him that for the first time in her life, she finally feels like she *is* following her heart.)

"You don't respect me," he whines. "You think I'm just screwing around, living off my inheritance."

"No, I don't. I know that you're trying to figure things out."

"I *did* figure things out! I found a job and I found *you*. I've got things figured out, finally. The two biggest commitments I've ever made in my life. You know how scared I was to ask you? To accept that job?"

"I'm not the first person you've proposed to."

"No," he says. "Just the first one I *meant* it with."

She drops her head guiltily. "I'm sorry," she mutters.

They part ways and he heads off toward Larabee.

She takes a deep breath. "Josh?" she calls out.

He turns around again. "What?"

"Yes."

"Yes what?"

"Yes, I'll marry you. I'll marry you and move back to Toronto."

Jessie

*S*he bangs down the phone without leaving a message.

"Jessie? Is something wrong?"

Jessie looks up. She didn't realize her assistant Auben was standing there, watching her.

"Sorry, I just . . ."

"Who've you been trying to reach? You've picked up that phone a hundred times this morning."

"Have I?" Jessie says, distracted. "I'm, uh, trying to reach Allan. He's supposed to pick up the kids. . . ." Her voice trails off. It feels like only lies come out of her mouth these days. Lies to Allan, the kids, her parents, Auben . . . *I am Jessie Jaffe! I don't lie!*

The truth is, she's trying to reach Skieth. Skieth, who slept with her and hasn't called her since. Skieth, who gave her her first orgasm and then disappeared. Skieth, who pursued her until she relented and then dumped her after he got her.

She's left dozens of messages—most of them under the pretext of some work-related matter. Still nothing. The bastard's got call-display and is obviously call-fucking her off. Not only has she lost him as a lover, but she's lost one of her most lucrative clients—and she was only halfway through his extensive collection of restaurants and night-clubs!

Of course, this is God punishing her. Self-pity is wasted. She deserves what she's getting.

She dials Skieth's number again, this time aware of Auben lurking only a few feet away. She leaves an overly casual message. "Hi, Skieth. Jessie Jaffe. I've been trying to reach you for a few weeks now in regards to that second seminar we had discussed for your office managers. Give me a call. My schedule's pretty tight so I'm waiting for your confirmation so that I can—"

The machine cuts her off midmessage. She wants to scream.

"Still no luck with that?" Auben says.

Jessie glares at her.

"Maybe he's away?"

"Why don't *you* try calling him?" Jessie says, brightening. Yes, yes. Auben will call, so he knows it's really about work. She can at least salvage his business.

"But you just left a message," Auben reminds her.

"I know, but . . ." How can she explain? "I just can't be chasing him down now. I don't have time. I've got too much on my plate. I'm passing it on to you, the whole project. So you keep trying him if we don't hear back from him by tomorrow. Call him from your cell—"

"Does he owe us money?"

"No. He paid me for the work at Skieth's, but he mentioned he wanted me to do one of his other restaurants— on Front Street, I think. So we should stay on it."

"We don't want to harass him," Auben reasons. "Maybe he's run out of money."

"We shouldn't give up so easily."

"Did he leave a deposit for the next job?" Auben presses.

"No, but . . ." Jessie sighs, exasperated. She wants to

shove Auben up against the wall and tell her to mind her own goddamn business. "Just call him tomorrow from your cell, okay? No, on second thought, never mind. I can't just pass him on to you," she says. "He'll be offended. He's too important. I'll go find him myself."

"But you just said you had too much on your plate—"

Jessie slams her Busy Woman's Daily Planner on her desk and stands up. "We can't *lose* him," she seethes.

"Are we in financial trouble?" Auben asks, looking worried.

"No, why?"

"You're just so . . . desperate. I mean, if the company's in trouble, if we need his business this badly . . ."

The room starts swirling around her. Auben's voice turns into one long, high-pitched whine. Her mouth is moving but Jessie can't hear the words. It sounds like that noise the TV makes when the channels go off the air.

"The company's fine," Jessie manages to say. "I have to go out. Print up the spreadsheet for the Rubenstein house, okay?"

Auben nods solemnly.

*O*utside, it's pouring rain. She doesn't have an umbrella so her hair goes flat and droopy in the time it takes her to get from the office to her car on Dunfield. So much for looking radiant when and if she ever finds Skieth.

She decides to try Ooze first, then work her way north, stopping at all his clubs and restaurants if necessary. She's waited patiently—voice-mail messages aside—for three weeks. Three weeks she's been walking around like a zombie, not eating, unable to focus on work, unable to pay proper attention to her own children. She can't get Skieth out of her head. She relives their night together over and over again, replaying every word he said to her, every look, every touch; the way they made love in the foyer of his loft because they were too horny to make it to the bedroom. The front door was barely closed and he was pulling her Dolce & Gabbana pants down around her knees. She surprised herself by attacking back with equal ferocity, hoisting his shirt over his head, rubbing her hands all over his bare chest, pressing herself into him until they practically fell backward.

The first time they did it, on the floor by the front door, it was rough and hard and fast. They were hungry, rushing. Her own voice kept coming out of her in wild shrieks; it was like she was out of her body. Some previously dormant, uninhibited version of herself took over. When it was finished, she lay there in a heap, in shock. Looking down at their entwined bodies, the crumpled condom and their clothes strewn around them like in a movie, she didn't recognize herself.

Then they went into the bedroom and he peeled off the linen duvet and pulled her down on top of him. They did it again, this time slowly. It took her a while to figure it out, to know exactly how to move for *her* utmost pleasure. He helped her, he was patient. "Suck on my nipples," she told him, shyly at first and then more authoritatively. Then she was screaming, "Don't stop! Don't stop!" so afraid he would quit and push her off just as she was building toward her first orgasm. And then she came, in a frenzy of panic and tears and near hysteria. She started laughing, brushing tears off her face. He kissed her lovingly and caressed her tangled hair, as though he was proud of her. Or maybe he was proud of himself. She collapsed on top of him and for a moment she thought she would never go back home to Allan. How could she?

"I didn't know it could be like that," she said into his shoulder blade. He was rubbing her back. He didn't make an issue of it, didn't embarrass her.

They did it a third time, a little while later. Finally, at about twelve thirty in the morning, she told him she had to go.

"Okay," he said.

In retrospect, that might have been the first red flag. He didn't persuade her to stay; didn't beg or plead for her to cuddle with him, or wait till morning. Just "Okay."

He made her a cup of coffee for the road—no offer of a cappuccino, no Bailey's for flavor—just a straight cup of instant coffee. (Another red flag?) Then he walked her to the door—he was wearing pajama bottoms and no top and it was all she could do to keep her hands off his chest—and he kissed her good-bye on the mouth. Nothing too passionate, but it was soft, tender.

"I want to do this again," she told him bluntly. (Was that her first big gaffe?)

He smiled. "Anytime," he said.

"When?"

"I'll call you tomorrow."

"Promise?"

He nodded, kissed her again. She was soaring, giddy. She floated out of his building and into her car. It crossed her mind again that maybe, if Skieth insisted, she would leave Allan.

Allan was snoring away in bed when she got home. She had a long bath, giggling to herself and reminiscing, and then fell asleep dreaming of Skieth.

And then nothing. No call the next day, or the next. She waited four days before calling him, and then left a terse message about business. He never responded. Instead, the manager from Skieth's on College called to arrange an appointment. It took her a full week to organize that office and never once did she cross paths with Skieth. In the end, it was the manager who handed her a check for the balance. Signed by Skieth, but not personally delivered.

So she left more messages, some more straightforward than others, depending on her frame of mind.

"Maybe you're away so call me when you get back. . . ."

"Just thinking about you. . . ."

"I'd love to see you again. . . ."

"I need to schedule that seminar with Steve. . . ."

Nothing.

She has rationalized his snub a thousand different ways. Perhaps he was so overwhelmed by his feelings for her that he had to back off because he knew ultimately she'd never leave Allan; or maybe she's the first woman he's ever truly been in love with and he's scared shitless; or he was so racked with guilt over wrecking her marriage that he fled; or he was stabbed at Ooze and left in a Dumpster (she's always hearing about nightclub stabbings on Citytv); or maybe his father killed him in a drunken rage. . . .

She parks in a lot on John Street and rushes through the rain to Ooze. It occurs to her now that she may be about to humiliate herself, but for the first time in her life, she doesn't care. Somewhere along the way (probably during that first orgasm) her pride evaporated. All that matters is that she *sees* him. And hopefully once he sees her, he'll remember how attracted he was to her.

"Skieth?"

He looks up from his bottles. Something passes over his eyes. Panic? Dread?

"Hey, Jessie."

"So you're here," she says accusingly.

"I'm always here."

"I've left messages," she says, unable to keep the venom from her tone.

"Oh?"

"Listen," she says, deciding to play it cool, to keep the focus on business. "I don't know what's going on with us, but at this point, I want to know if you're going forward on a professional—"

"I don't think we should," he cuts in.

"But you said . . . you said . . ."

"What?"

"That we . . . that 'it' wouldn't affect our business relationship."

"That was before we slept together."

"If you're uncomfortable," she says, "I'll send Auben to finish the other places."

"Do you really think that's a good idea?" he says in a patronizing tone.

"I value you as a client," she says, moronically. She is trying to appear professional but knows she sounds like a jilted lover. Which is what she is. She is groveling.

"I appreciate that, but it would still be awkward."

"So what you're saying is, you don't ever want to see me again?"

"Jessie, you're married."

"That didn't bother you *before!*" she cries.

"In good conscience—"

"Oh, please!"

"Seriously, we had a great night together, but where did you expect it to go? Do you want to have an ongoing affair or something?"

Yes! That is exactly what she wants! But she doesn't say anything.

"Because I'm not into getting involved with a married woman," he says.

"Then why did you pursue me?" She can feel tears bunching up in the corners of her eyes.

"I'm sorry if you misread me."

"Misread you?"

"The timing's off," he tells her. "I just can't do this right now."

"Do what?"

"I told you. The extramarital thing. It's too . . . complicated."

"I'm just asking you to keep doing business with us," she snivels. But they both know she's lying.

"It's not a good idea." He bends down to pull a few more bottles out of a box, his way of dismissing her. All she can think is that she wants to go backward and retrace her steps, do them over. She wants to rewind back to that day when he was confiding in her about his father, to the way he used to look at her, ask her about her business. Back to when *she* was holding all the cards.

How did they go from *that* to this?

"I thought we were so great together," she says, throwing her last shreds of humility at him.

"We were," he agrees. "We totally were. But—"

She stands there, waiting. *But . . .*

"Now it's over."

Erica

She ceremoniously places the two white candles in her new candelabra and then stands back to admire her table. She bought the candelabra for herself this afternoon, with the intention of using it only on Shabbat. It wasn't exactly a decision she made, to continue celebrating Shabbat by herself; it was more like an evolution. It just felt like the next right step in her life: to create a special routine for herself—something spiritual that she can continue to grow into and perhaps even pass on one day.

She hasn't got the blessing memorized yet—she still has to read it off a scrap of paper—but something about the simple ritual makes her feel indescribably calm inside. Ever since Shabbat dinner at Mitchell's, she's wanted to recapture that feeling of being connected to something. She may not know what it is, or how to describe it, but she knows it's there when she closes her eyes and those two candles are burning on the table in front of her. So for the past couple of Fridays, while Paul's been out drinking at the Abbey, she's lit the candles quietly and alone.

She's not about to give up TV and driving and electricity for Shabbat, nor is she anywhere near dragging herself to synagogue, but for now, lighting the candles seems to provide her with some comfort. If nothing else, it connects her to Mitchell, whom she misses more than she would have thought possible.

She holds up the piece of paper on which she's copied out the Shabbat blessing, and just as she's about to read it out loud, she hears the front door open. There's some noise from the hallway—laughing and banging—and she recognizes a woman's voice over all the rest. *Jillian.*

"Erica?" Paul's voice. "You home, love?"

She can tell right away he's drunk. Instinctively she blows out the candles, just as he bursts into the kitchen.

"What're you doing, lover?" he asks.

"It's Shabbat."

"Beg your pardon?" His face is flushed.

"I was just . . . lighting the candles for Shabbat."

"Since when?" he asks. "Did I miss something?"

"It's not a big deal."

"All of a sudden you're religious and it's not a big deal?"

"I'm not religious."

He looks confused, but not unhappy about the discovery. "I think it's adorable," he says. "But how come you didn't invite me?"

"I don't know."

"Is it because I'm not Jewish? I can convert," he teases.

"Who's here?" she asks him.

"The gang. You don't mind, do you?"

She shrugs, looking down at her ruined Shabbat dinner.

"We came here to smoke some pot," he announces. "Apparently Jillian's new boyfriend gets the most amazing pot. She's got a giant bag full of it."

Erica starts clearing off the table. Paul puts his arm around her.

"I'm sorry, love. I had no idea about this. Otherwise I wouldn't have invited them."

"I know."

"Will you join us?" he asks her.

"Just let me wrap up the chicken," she says, relenting. In the absence of God, a giant bag of amazing pot will do quite nicely.

"*A*tom Egoyan."

"Interesting choice."

"He's Canadian, isn't he?"

They all look at Erica, as though she's to be given a certain measure of credit for sharing the same nationality as their favorite director.

"I'm not saying he's the best director of our generation," Jad goes on. "But his films are very hypnotic. Cinematic poems, if you will."

"He certainly has his own unique voice—"

Good God, Erica thinks miserably, now they're going to spend an hour lauding Atom "plots are for morons" Egoyan and kill her buzz.

"*Exotica* was a masterpiece," Jillian purrs. "Cerebral, yet totally visceral."

"Put some music on," Amory tells Paul.

"Oh, let me," Jillian says, jumping to her feet. "How about some jazz?"

Another buzz-kill.

"Jillian, this *is* good pot," Paul remarks.

"I told you. Kai gets the best stuff."

"Jillian's dating a character from the *Real World,*" Janice mutters.

"He's a Rhodes scholar," Jillian says defensively, as she scans Paul's CD collection. She finally settles on Mickey Tucker's *Blues in 5 Dimensions*. A real stoner classic.

"I'm thinking of renting a cottage on the North Fork this summer," Amory announces. "Anyone interested in doing a time-share?"

"Count me out," Jillian says. "Kai and I are going to India."

"What's happening with your travel book?" Erica asks her. "The one about the Carnic Alps?"

"My grant application was turned down," she says matter-of-factly. "Which is actually a total blessing, since I've met Kai."

Bullshit, Erica thinks. Phony bravado. God, she hates Jillian. She hates Jad and Janice and jazz for that matter, and she realizes (in a moment of pot-induced clarity) that all things evil begin with the letter *J*. What she'd love right now is to get out of here, lock herself in a dark room, and blast Pink Floyd into a pair of headphones.

"Would you excuse me?" she says.

No one even notices her leave the room. The last round of toking has suddenly knocked them all into a silent stupor.

She grabs a couple of her old CDs and disappears into Paul's office. Alone in the dark, having escaped from all the Evil Js, she instantly feels better. She turns on a lamp and starts shuffling around Paul's desk in search of the headphones. Not sure where he keeps them, she pulls open the top drawer and notices a letter addressed to her from Columbia. The envelope has already been opened.

She sits down in Paul's swivel chair and reads the letter. The fact that Paul read it first is humiliating enough, but not quite as unforgivable as the fact that he's kept it from her for—she checks the date, does the math—five days!

Being stoned upon discovering a rejection letter from the program of one's dreams might a) defuse the blow and stave

off all feelings of failure until one's head is clear, or b) inten-
sify all feelings of failure and worthlessness, and precipitate
what's commonly known as a Bad Trip. Naturally, Erica, who
at the best of times is never very far from feelings of worthlessness and failure, descends into the darkest, most morbid
place a stoned person can go: her head.

It's bad enough Paul's known about her rejection from
Columbia for five days and apparently feels so sorry for her
that he still hasn't figured out how to tell her—but what gives
him the right to open her goddamn mail?

If all the Evil Js weren't sitting in her living room, she'd
go out there and give him shit. But she can't face them right
now. What if Paul's already told them she wasn't accepted to
Columbia? What if they've known all along?

What if they knew before *she* did?

Jessie

*T*he room is dark. She starts gasping for breath. "Allan? Al?" She can't breathe. She's hyperventilating.

Allan flicks on his bedside lamp and sits up. "What?" he asks, squinting at her. "What's wrong?"

"I—can't—breathe."

She's clutching her throat and crying. Her chest is heaving.

"Hang on."

Allan leaps out of bed and tugs open the window, letting in a gust of damp April wind. He goes into the en suite bathroom and comes back out with a glass of water. "Here. Have a sip."

She tries to drink but ends up choking. She starts convulsing. "I can't breathe!"

"You're having another panic attack," he tells her. "It's not physical. Calm down."

He pulls her against his chest and smoothes her damp hair. "Deep breaths. Breathe in deeply, Jess. That'a girl. Calm down. It's happened before. We know what to do."

She tries to inhale as deeply as she can, but her breaths are still quick and shallow. Her heart is palpitating. "I'm having a heart attack!" she wails. "Allan! I'm scared! Call 911!"

"Jessie, you're not having a heart attack. It's an anxiety attack. Just like the others."

"No!"

"I want you to take one of the Ativan that Dr. Belzberg prescribed."

"No!" Her whole body is trembling. She's sure she's dying. "No pills!" she growls.

"All right, then, deep breaths. Jessie, listen to me. Breathe in. Right from your diaphragm, and expel. That's right."

"Mummy, what's wrong?" Levi is in the doorway, whimpering.

"Levi, go back to bed," Allan says calmly.

"Is Mummy going to die?"

Allan forces a reassuring laugh. "Of course not, Peanut. She just has a sore throat. She's having trouble swallowing."

Jessie tries to calm herself, tries for Levi's sake to get her breathing even. "I'm fine," she croaks. "I promise."

"You said you were having a heart attack," he accuses in a panic-stricken voice.

"No, Peanut," she murmurs. "You didn't hear right."

Her breathing is returning to normal. Slowing down. Her body is relaxing. "Get into bed and I'll be right there to scratch your back," she tells him.

He disappears from the doorway and she worries for the umpteenth time what she must be doing to him.

"What started it?" Allan asks.

She can't tell him. She can never tell him.

"It was *ER,* wasn't it? You know you can't watch that show," he scolds. "It was when they brought in the kid with the hanger in his throat, wasn't it?"

She nods limply.

Allan is shaking his head. "I knew it. I *told* you. No more *ER.*"

When she's as calm as she can ever hope to be, she crawls out of bed and shuffles down the hall to Levi's room.

He's waiting for her on the bed, sitting up with Topo Gigio in his arms. She sits down beside him and scoops him into her arms. He starts to cry.

"You said for Daddy to call 911!" he sobs.

"I know, baby. I just got scared for a minute because . . . my throat hurt so much. But I took some medicine and now I'm all better."

"Why are you always scared, Mummy?"

"That's just how I am."

"Do all mummies get scared like you?"

"Of course they do." (Why should he think his mother's a freak?)

She manages to get him under the covers and then scratches his back until he falls back to sleep. Watching him now, she gets a powerful surge of guilt; it comes up on her like nausea. There have been days during the past few weeks when she thought she could leave him—all of them—if Skieth had asked her to. If he had called and said, "Leave your family and come be with me," she *would* have.

Then she got to thinking about AIDS. Thinking that Skieth must sleep around a lot, and maybe he isn't always careful and that *she* might have AIDS now too. That was the realization that led to her first panic attack. She was lying in bed alone, thinking, as usual, about the night she'd slept with Skieth. She was wistfully reliving it, *again*. Every detail, in slow motion. And then something began to gnaw at her. The condom. The way it was lying there in a soggy puddle on the floor; then the other two in the bed.

It hit her then. What if one of them had *torn?* What if there had been a hole? What if he'd put it on wrong? What if his semen had dribbled out the sides and got inside her? Knowing now that he's a womanizer—she suspects he's slept with hundreds and hundreds of women, probably strippers and prostitutes and any old skank he might have picked up in a club—she's convinced there's a high probability he's got AIDS.

It would be a beautiful punishment for her—God's retribution. Isn't that how He works?

The more she thought about it, lying there in her empty bedroom, the more she had trouble breathing. She started freaking out. Hyperventilating. Her heart was banging against her chest and she thought it was a heart attack. She was by herself with no one to calm her down. Allan was with the kids, visiting his parents at their cottage in Collingwood. So she called 911. By the time the paramedics arrived, she was flailing on the bed, sobbing. But she was breathing, her heartbeat was regular again. She was okay. Still, they brought her by ambulance to the hospital, and the doctor diagnosed the anxiety attack. She took a cab home at five in the morning and huddled in a bath, crying and shivering and worrying about AIDS.

Since then, there have been two more panic attacks, including tonight's. And not a single moment when she hasn't been consumed with dread and guilt and abject terror. But here's the bigger irony: she could never, *ever* clear up the matter by going for an AIDS test. She would sooner kill herself than subject herself to waiting for those results. She visualizes that moment when the doctor would tell her, "You're HIV positive, Mrs. Jaffe," and that's when her breathing goes haywire. Where once she used to replay Skieth's flirtatious words over and over to herself, now all that echoes in her head is, *You're HIV positive, Mrs. Jaffe.*

Worse yet, she can't even unload this burden on Allan. Usually she goes to him with all her fears and worries, and he manages to reassure her and convince her she's being irrational.

The next morning, Levi comes into the kitchen, frowning. "Are you better?" he asks her.

"I told you I was better last night."

He sits down at the kitchen table.

"Where's your sister?" she asks.

"Daddy's dressing her."

Jessie turns back to the stove, where she's stirring a pan of scrambled eggs. She grabs a handful of grated cheddar and dumps it into the soupy mixture.

"I made fresh orange juice," she tells him.

"I know."

She turns around suddenly and catches him sipping orange juice from a glass that was on the table. *Her* glass. Without thinking, she lunges at him and jerks the glass out of his hands, knocking it against his teeth and spilling juice all over him. He starts wailing.

"Don't *ever* drink from my glass!" she screams. "Do you hear me?" She's shaking all over as she pulls him out of his chair and starts wiping his mouth with her hand, slapping his back to get him to spit up the juice.

"Mummy!" he cries. *"Stop!"*

She can see he's scared to death, but she's got to get the juice off his lips. *Her* contaminated juice! My God, what if she's passing AIDS on to all of them? Every time she kisses them now, or puts a Band-Aid on one of their bloody wounds, or washes their hair . . .

Is she going crazy?

"What are you doing to him, Jessie?"

Allan pulls her off Levi and pushes her up against the wall. Ilana is bawling in the background. In the confusion, the orange-juice glass shatters on the kitchen floor. A piece of it cuts Jessie's finger and droplets of blood spurt onto her shirt. She looks down at her own blood and writhes, as though it were acid burning her flesh.

Estelle

*I*t wasn't enough for Milton to fly the whole family to New York for Jessie's thirtieth birthday; he also had to put them up at the Hilton and make dinner reservations at Tavern on the Green. Nothing less than a spectacular table in the Terrace Room for his precious Jessie! (Estelle is bitterly mulling this over as she is led to the stunning oasis on the terrace, which is all Waterford crystal chandeliers, hand-carved ceilings, and bright bouquets of fresh flowers on every table.) There's a view onto Central Park that's the next best thing to actually eating *in* the park and the Terrace Room's even got its own private garden off the terrace.

"How's this?" Milton asks, knowing full well he's outdone himself.

Jessie smiles appreciatively, and yet something about her graciousness seems forced. She appears to be in one of her moods—tense, distracted, irritable. She's probably worrying about her kids, or her business, or terrorism. The more random or abstract the threat, the more Jessie likes to worry. She looks as though she's lost about twenty pounds since the last time they saw each other (putting her at a size minus-two). Estelle gasped when they were reunited at the hotel yesterday.

"Are you sick?" Estelle asked her.

Jessie flinched and looked up at Allan. "I'm fine," she said. "I'm just tired from the drive. . . ."

Even Erica didn't look convinced. She shot Estelle a concerned, "to be discussed later" look.

"I'm not sure we should say anything about our engagement tonight," Josh whispers in her ear as they enter the Terrace Room. "It's Jessie's night—"

Estelle rolls her eyes. "What better time to tell them than when we're all here together? It's not like this happens very often."

Besides, she's been holding on to her news for seven weeks. It was no small feat either, but she wanted to be sure of Josh's commitment. She was afraid of announcing her engagement and then having him flee on her. (That would have sealed her reputation as the family's relationship loser.) So far, he's passed the test. In the last two months, he has become her best friend, her partner, all those amazing things a future husband is supposed to be. And he loves her. God, he loves her so much! The way he looks at her, laughs at her jokes, admires her success; the way he bolsters her when she's in her dark tunnel of self-loathing. She doesn't want to live without those things, not ever again.

She finished her work on *Game Set Snatch* (no word yet on a release date or a new title) and felt bittersweet about wrapping up her first feature. Armando was pleased with her work, but in the end, she had to adhere to *his* ideas about which scenes stayed in the final version and which were cut. Creatively, she was extremely limited. Josh said that's how it would always be in Hollywood. So they're going to stay in L.A. until her lease runs out at the end of August, and then move back to Toronto. In the meantime, she'll try to make as much money as possible freelancing, and Josh will coedit his magazine from California.

The first thing Milton does once they're seated is order a bottle of Dom Perignon 1983—which, at over four hundred dollars a bottle, reconfirms his unabashed favoritism toward Jessie—and another bottle of white zinfandel.

Now that Estelle has decided to hijack the party with her little announcement, she's delighted with Milton's choice of champagne. She glances over at Josh and winks.

"Hey," she says, spotting a famous-looking person in the corner. "Isn't that Charlize Theron?"

Everyone turns to look and unanimously decides that it's not Charlize, but just another stunning blond New Yorker in a spectacular Chanel suit.

"They sure don't look like that in Toronto," Allan remarks, to which Jessie sulkily mutters, "Thanks."

Estelle orders the beluga caviar for an appetizer. "When in Rome . . ." she says merrily.

Lilly says, "It comes with blini, crème fraîche, and melted *butter,* Estelle." Her facial expression is dangerously close to panic.

"I can read, Muh."

"But that's so *heavy,*" she warns. "You won't be hungry for your second course."

"Don't worry about my appetite," Estelle snaps. She orders the roast prime rib of beef as her main course, which comes with caraway spaetzle and green olive tapenade. Wow.

"I'd like to make a toast to Jessie," Dorothy says, holding up her flute of champagne. *"Mazel tov!"*

"Happy birthday!" Milton echoes.

"One more year and all our babies will be out of their twenties," Lilly laments.

"Thank God," Milton says.

They all clink champagne flutes, and Estelle is suddenly

moved by the moment to blurt her news. "Josh and I have an announcement," she says quickly, not wanting to lose the momentum of the toast.

Everyone turns to look at them. Lilly's eyes are as wide and shiny as loonies.

"We're getting married."

Lilly lets out a scream that sounds a bit like "yeehaw!" Milton leaps up from the table and rushes over to Josh, shaking his hand and tousling his hair, gushing, "Welcome to the family, son!"

More *mazel tov*s from Gramma Dorothy.

"Congratulations," Paul says, and pats Josh on the back.

"Let's see the ring," Jessie says. It's all she can do to muster up a sputter of enthusiasm.

Estelle pulls the ring out of her pocket—she hadn't wanted to show it prematurely—and slides it onto her finger. It's a one-carat diamond on a platinum band, very understated and elegant. It belonged to Gladys, but she doesn't tell them that. Doesn't want to upset Lilly and set Milton off crying, just as he's beginning to move on. She asked Josh if he'd given it to Bam when he'd proposed to her and he said no. Adamantly *no*. He never would have given his mother's ring to Bam. Estelle felt that boded extremely well for his sincerity in wanting to marry *her*.

Jessie and Erica lean over the table to see the ring. "Hmm," Jessie says. "It's very clean." ("Clean" meaning small. Jessie's ring is two carats, but never mind.)

"What a wonderful day this is," Gramma says.

"It's really Jessie's day," Josh mutters apologetically. But no one is listening to him.

"Estelle is getting married!" Lilly trills. "Have you set the date?"

"We're thinking December."

"That gives you plenty of time," Lilly says. "You can definitely lose that little bit of tummy by then." ("Little bit of tummy" meaning forty pounds.)

"She can try my diet," Allan pipes in.

"Does Vera Wang make a size-fourteen dress?"

"We need another bottle of champagne!" Milton declares. He hasn't been this jovial and spirited since Gladys was diagnosed.

"We're also moving back to Toronto," Estelle tells them, still building on the frenzy of good news. "Josh got a job editing a magazine."

"A magazine!" Lilly exclaims. "A real magazine?"

"A literary magazine," Josh says modestly.

"An editor!" Milton roars. It may as well be *Time* or *Maclean's*. "Now that's a step up from teaching English to immigrants."

"Maybe you can publish some of Erica's stories!" Lilly says.

Erica's smile freezes on her face. She looks uncomfortable. And although Estelle feels a stab of sympathy for her little sister, she is determined not to let anything derail her perfect night. It doesn't matter what she had to do to get it, or how long it's going to hold out; all that matters right now is she's got her parents' approval and it's delicious.

"Our Bean is coming home," Lilly says to Milton. She squeezes his hand, the first sign of affection between them in months.

Estelle catches Jessie's gaze. Is there something there in her eyes? A hesitation? A flutter of resentment for horning in on her day? A warning? Estelle can't be sure. She will not let that bother her either. This is her moment of triumph.

Erica

"You haven't told them yet?"

Erica is slumped in the backseat of the cab, her head leaning on Paul's shoulder. She doesn't answer him. She's not in the mood to talk. She's had enough conversation for one night. Jessie's birthday and Estelle's engagement have sapped her, and she just wants to feel sorry for herself in peace.

"Erica?"

She ignores him.

"Erica."

"No, Paul. I haven't told them."

"They'll understand, love. It's a tough program to get into. It's extremely competitive and you haven't been writing all that long. I can talk to them if you like, explain—"

"I'm surprised you didn't forward them a copy of my rejection letter before I found it."

"That's not fair."

"It's not? I'm confused about what's fair and what's not. Is it fair for you to read my personal mail and hide it in a drawer?"

"I thought we were done with this."

"Maybe *you're* done with it."

The night she found the rejection letter, she waited in Paul's office until his friends had left. By the time he came looking for her, the pot had worn off and she was ready for a confrontation.

"What're you doing in here?" he asked her.

She was sitting in the dark. She had the letter in her hand.

"Reading," she said.

"In the dark?"

She stood up and crumpled the letter into a ball. She threw it at him. He knew what it was right away, without even having to uncrumple it.

"Love—"

"What gives you the right to open my mail?"

"I've never opened your mail before."

"Why'd you open *this?*"

"I thought it was an acceptance letter. I wanted to be the one to give it to you. I was going to hang it on the wall and surprise you—"

"Bullshit."

"I thought it would be more special if I gave it to you," he said, groveling. "I honestly thought it was going to be an acceptance."

"Even if it had been, you still had no right!"

"I guess I was so excited, I didn't think it through. I just sort of tore it open—"

"Do *they* know?"

"Who?"

"Your stupid friends. Did you tell them?"

He looked at her as though she'd gone mad. "Of course not. Why the hell would I tell them?"

"Why wouldn't you? Were you too embarrassed?"

He looked trapped. "It's none of their business."

"Apparently it was none of *my* business either."

"I'm sorry," he said, coming toward her. "I didn't realize you'd be this upset."

"You kept it from me for almost a week!" she ranted.

"And you didn't think I'd be upset? When the hell were you going to tell me?"

"I was waiting for the best time."

"*You* shouldn't get to decide that. It makes me feel like a child!"

He seemed about to say something, but he let it drop.

"And it's illegal, you know! Stealing mail."

"Oh, for God's sake, Erica. Now you're being irrational."

She sat back down at his desk and started to cry. "I hate your friends," she sobbed. (Maybe she was still a bit stoned.)

"What do they have to do with this?"

"They're part of it."

"Part of what?"

"This!" she cried, throwing her arms up in the air. "This life! This world I don't belong in!"

"Of course you belong here—"

"No, I don't! And there's the proof!" She pointed to the crumpled rejection letter on the floor. "There's the proof that I don't belong, Paul."

"Big fucking deal about that. So you didn't get in. Lots of great writers don't get accepted into writing programs. If you're going to throw in the towel after every rejection, you may as well give up now."

"Spare me the whole 'Ernest Hemingway was rejected seventy-four times before he got his first story published' sermon. Please."

Paul sighed and she could tell she was reaching her limit with him. He was exasperated with her. Not just with her reaction to the rejection letter, but with everything. He was at the same point her parents and her grandmother had reached ages ago. She could see it in his face: he was on the brink of losing faith in her, of giving up on her entirely. In that instant, the tables turned. Suddenly, she was afraid; afraid of losing the last person in her life who had hope for her future.

"What should I do now?" she asked.

"Try again," he said. "That's what writers do."

He came over to her, and this time she let him put his arms around her. She buried her face in his sweater.

"I'm sorry I opened it," he whispered. "I really thought it would be an acceptance."

"I know," she said. And whether she believed him or not no longer mattered. It was beside the point. The important thing was to keep fooling him into thinking that she could still become something.

Now she lifts her head off his shoulder and slides to the other side of the cab.

"You're just upset because the spotlight wasn't on you tonight," he says.

"I'm upset because no one in my family thinks I'm capable of getting a story published without nepotism . . . and they're *right*. I'm upset because no one thought I'd get into the fucking writing program at Columbia in the first place and *they were right*!"

Paul looks nervously at the cabdriver. "We'll finish this at home," he mumbles.

"Why?"

"I'm too tired for another one of your pity parties," he says. "If you're so upset about the rejection, why don't you stop whining about it and start writing, for Chrissake? Getting you to write the few stories you did submit was like pulling teeth. And I'm the one who wrote the proposal *and* the synopsis. You want to be a writer so badly? Then *write*."

"You didn't think I'd get in, did you," she accuses.

He looks away.

"Did you?"

"No, I didn't!" he flares. "And not because you don't have the talent, but because you don't have the heart."

*W*hen they get up to the apartment, Paul goes directly into the bedroom and closes the door. Left alone in the hallway, Erica stands there fuming. She has a sensation of being paralyzed. She can hear him brushing his teeth, opening drawers, climbing into bed. She makes no move to either join him or find something else to do. She doesn't know what to do with her anger. She wants him to be punished; he should have to pay for trying to control her, for forcing his life down her throat, for bullying her into writing, and for being disappointed in her. But mostly he should pay for not having succeeded in turning her into an artist. She trustingly put herself in his hands and yet even he, with all his clout and his credentials and his *Who's Who* of New York connections, could not manage to pull her into his circle. But how can she retaliate?

She opens the door and finds him lying in bed, reading. He doesn't look up from his book. His indifference makes her feel powerless. She goes over to the bed and stands beside him, watching him read. He makes a point of ignoring her. She wants to rip the book out of his hands and hurl it across the room. She notices a pile of his notes on the bedside table. Notes for a new book. Lately, he's been waking up in the middle of the night to jot down ideas. They'll both be sleeping and then all of a sudden he'll flick on the light and start scribbling away, writing out whole chapters and character sketches as if they'd come to him in his dreams. She is torn between loving him for it and resenting him.

Without uttering a word, she slips under the covers and crawls between his legs. She pulls his pajama bottoms down and kisses his inner thighs. He doesn't let on that he wants her to continue, not at first, but when she looks up she can see he's stopped reading and the book is flat on his chest. She knocks it onto the floor and he groans.

She pulls off her shirt and smothers her breasts against his groin. He pushes her head down and she teases him by flicking her tongue all over his abdomen, his hips, his thighs. He raises his hips off the bed, again and again, pleading with her. And when she finally takes his penis in her mouth, he lets out a loud yelp of pleasure and defeat.

Early the next morning, she leaves Paul splayed across the bed and creeps down the hall to the den. She retrieves her address book from the top drawer of Paul's antique secretary and flips through it, looking for a phone number. She feels awkward about making the phone call, but desperate enough to talk to someone.

She has a whole speech planned out in her head, but the moment it comes time for her to actually say it, she freezes up. "Um, uh, hi," she fumbles. "This is, uh, Erica. Erica Zarr?"

Silence on the other end.

"Mitchell's friend Erica?"

"Oh! Erica! I haven't seen you since the bar mitzvah."

"I know. I haven't been . . . I haven't seen Mitchell much lately."

"How are you?"

Erica takes a breath. "I'm okay. But I was wondering . . . this might sound weird, but do you think I could come to see you sometime?"

"I'd love that. Is there something in particular you want to talk about?"

"Um, just about everything. I'm sort of lost right now and I just thought—"

"Sure. Absolutely."

"Do, um, do people do this?" Erica asks nervously.

Miriam laughs. "You mean do people talk to rabbis about their problems?"

"Yeah."

"Well, Jewish people do."

"I'm feeling pretty overwhelmed lately," Erica confesses. "I feel like something is missing, or I'm missing something, and I just don't know where to look anymore. Does that make sense?"

"Of course it does."

"I didn't think it would be this way."

"What?"

"My life."

Miriam is quiet for a moment. "Can you come to my synagogue?" she says. "Why don't we start there?"

Jessie

*S*he catches her reflection in the kitchen window and shudders. Her chin is jutting out like an icicle and her face is drawn; even her collarbone is protruding through her sweater. The pimples up and down the side of her face don't help, nor do the gray circles under her eyes or the pale splotchy skin on her cheeks. She's barely thirty and she doesn't look a day under forty-five.

The chronic worrying is wreaking havoc, more now than ever before. Before the incident with Skieth, there were always so many things to obsess over—such a vast pool to choose from—that she was at least able to stay afloat, flitting from one passing fear to another. Jack of all fears, master of none. Now there is just the one; looming, feeding off itself and growing, like the disease inside her body.

New York was a nightmare. She drifted through her birthday weekend in a trance, unable to pull off her usual phony upbeat demeanor. She was worried about the kids too, having entrusted them for three days to her in-laws. What were Allan's parents feeding them? Did they strap them safely into their car seats? Did they childproof their house like she had asked? Still, she was barely able to manage them herself, not in Toronto, and certainly not in New York. In some small way it was a relief to be free of them for the first time in six years. Alone, she was able to suffer in peace, without having to tend to them, appease them, keep them entertained.

There was just her family, cloying as always. *What's wrong, Jess? Are you sick? Is the business okay? Are you and Allan okay? You don't seem yourself. . . .*

Work stress, she kept saying. It was her mantra all weekend. She wouldn't go shopping with them, wouldn't go to Bloomingdale's, ABC Carpets, or Barneys. Didn't even offer up much of an excuse, either. In the hotel room, alone with Allan, she would lie inert on the bed, staring vacantly up at the ceiling. She kept drifting farther and farther away, turning inward. Allan was in a panic. "What's happening?" he kept asking. He was pleading with her. "What's going on? The panic attacks, this depression, *what is it?*"

She couldn't answer him.

"Is it a nervous breakdown?" he asked. The TV was on in the background, *Judge Judy*.

"I don't know."

"It's finally happening," he said. "Your neuroses are finally catching up to you. You're doing too much." He was being authoritative, doctorly. "You're a person who needs as little stress as possible. It's too much for you, the business and the kids. Something's got to give. You obviously can't cope with this much going on in your life."

She nodded limply.

"You've got to cut back," he informed her. He was pacing back and forth in the narrow space between the bed and the TV set.

"Cut back on what?" she said. "The kids?"

"Of course not. On work. It's time to let go."

"Why should I have to give that up?"

"You obviously can't manage both. And the kids aren't going anywhere."

"I'm not good for them."

"That's true," he conceded. "But maybe if you were home full time, you'd recoup some of your precarious sanity."

She was too exhausted to argue. Allan was entirely on the wrong track, but how the hell could she tell him she thought she might have AIDS?

"Everything will be okay," he promised her.

And his self-assurance, his certainty in the matter, almost soothed her.

Since getting back from New York, she has struggled to keep busy. She decided on the drive back to Toronto—she wouldn't fly—that if she didn't have a single free moment to *think,* she might survive. So she booked a dozen new clients and threw herself into the preliminary shopping for Estelle's wedding dress. At night she works till after midnight, sitting by herself in the kitchen, just her and her laptop. Then she takes an Ativan—much easier than she had thought it would be, popping strange pills—and falls gratefully into a deep, manufactured sleep. She's fuzzy and disoriented the next day, but even that's better than the alternative.

But despite all her efforts to have no thoughts, to not indulge in worry, it still niggles at the back of her mind, waiting to prey: not just the possibility that she's got AIDS, but that she will transmit it to someone in her family.

"You coming to bed?" Allan calls out.

She turns off the light in the kitchen and goes upstairs to the bedroom. Allan's waiting for her under the covers. He looks eager, horny. He thinks she's better lately because she hasn't had a panic attack since before New York and because she is at least functioning again.

She gets into bed and rolls over on her side, offering up her back to him. He rolls her back around and starts kissing her neck. His lips travel up to her mouth and she pushes him away violently. "Don't," she says. His touches, his breath, they make her feel sick.

"Come on," he pushes.

She slaps his hand away. "I said get off."

"What's the matter with you?" he fires at her. "It's been three months."

"Leave me alone, Allan. Please."

"Is that *it?* We're never going to have sex again?"

"Maybe."

He sighs, giving up. "Are we finished?" he asks her. "Is that what this has all been about? The panic attacks, your moods? Is it *me?* Do you want out?"

"Of course not."

He gets out of bed, grabs his pillow and the wool blanket from the foot of the bed, and stomps out of the room.

*I*n the morning, Ilana crawls into bed beside her. "I'na snuggle," she says, curling up against Jessie's body. She pops her thumb in her mouth and closes her eyes. Jessie strokes Ilana's long yellow ringlets. She hasn't cut her hair in over a year, can't bring herself to chop off those curls.

Ilana looks up at her and says, "Don't be sad today, okay, Mama?"

Which makes Jessie cry. Ilana reaches up to touch her mother's wet cheek but Jessie nudges her hand away.

"Don't touch me," she says. What if the disease is in her tears? What if there's a cut on one of Ilana's little fingers?

Ilana's lip starts to tremble.

"What's the matter with you?" Allan accuses.

Who knows how long he's been standing in the doorway, watching? He strides over to the bed and lifts Ilana's resistant body out of Jessie's arms. He smothers her tiny face with kisses and carries her away.

When he comes back minutes later, he closes the door behind him. "What are you doing to them?" he asks.

"What do you mean?"

"You've barely touched them in months. You don't show them any affection anymore. You've become . . . a monster. What kind of a mother are you?"

"It's because I don't want to . . ." She's on the verge of confessing. How else to restore herself in his eyes? It's not that she doesn't love them; it's *because* she loves them. She has to protect them, keep them safe from *her*.

"Don't want to what?" he prods.

"I don't know."

He is shaking his head gravely. The look on his face scares her. "I don't like what's going on in this house," he says. "I can handle what you're doing to me—pushing me away, ignoring me. But not what you're doing to *them*. I can't let you destroy them."

"I'm not—"

"You're sick, Jessie, and it's affecting Levi and Ilana. They're always upset. They feel abandoned by you; they worry about you. It's not normal. They're four and six, for God's sake! I can't let you take this family down with you."

She puts her hands over her ears and lowers her face.

"Will you get help?" he asks her.

"It won't do any good," she whimpers. "No one can help me."

"You have to do something or else—"

"What?"

"Or else I'm leaving," he says. "And I'm taking the kids with me."

She looks up at him blandly, unmoved. She knows he's all talk. All bravado. He would never take the kids. They're too much for him. He's too selfish. He's just hurling threats to shake her up, and she knows it. He *knows* she knows it. And it isn't working.

She doesn't care anymore.

Maybe he thought she would panic or plead, fight for them. But the truth is, if he ever did it, if he ever followed through on his threats, she'd probably be relieved.

Estelle

"*W*e should have eloped."

"I told you so."

She's snuggled up to Josh on the Hide-A-Bed in the guest room. They've been in Toronto for a week. They flew here directly from New York so that Estelle could begin the first leg of her job hunting. Since they've been back, Lilly and Jessie have monopolized her time, dragging her to just about every bridal shop in the greater Toronto area.

"She'll be able to take this in, right?" Lilly keeps asking the ladies in the dress shops. "She's going to lose weight by the wedding."

No problem, no problem, they all assure Lilly. Brides always lose weight before their weddings. That's why the final fitting is done one week before the ceremony.

"What if I *gain* weight?" Estelle asked one of the dress-makers.

The woman looked baffled. Lilly was horrified. "Don't even joke about that," she hissed.

So far, she hasn't found anything she feels good in. She tried on a couple of dresses that made her feel like a giant, fluffy meringue. Every time she puts something on, Lilly's face registers disappointment. "Once that little bit of tummy is gone . . ." she'll say. But it's no use.

She should have listened to Josh. He wanted to get married on a cliff somewhere, maybe Ireland or some other exotic place with cliffs. Just the two of them. "That's too much like you and Bam," Estelle had said, ruling it out. "We should have a traditional wedding in a synagogue."

In retrospect, the big Jewish wedding is what she thought her mother would want. It was just another way to win Lilly's approval, to top Jessie's gargantuan wedding at the Four Seasons. Her way of saying, *See, I can have that too!*

And now she is paying in spades for her cowardly, sniveling neediness. Lilly's already bought half a dozen Martha Stewart wedding books and is making lists ad nauseam of videographers, violinists, and caterers. Yesterday, she took Estelle to Ashley's to register for china.

"What do I need china for?" Estelle whined. "I only eat takeout and things I can nuke."

"That explains *this*—" Lilly snipped, and then grabbed a fold of skin under Estelle's chin. "Now just pick something so you don't wind up with a closet full of useless gifts."

"Why can't people just buy me what they *want* to buy me?"

"You remember that hideous painting of fruit I had in our old kitchen on Russell Hill?"

"Yeah."

"*That's* why you register. That was a wedding gift from your father's cousin, Florence. Now pick a china pattern."

Estelle eventually settled on a Moroccan-inspired set in red and gold, but Lilly vetoed it. "It's too gaudy. In two years you won't be able to look at it."

Lilly ended up choosing something more contemporary— white with a platinum rim. The salesgirl kept pulling out different pieces—gravy boats and teapots and serving platters in all shapes and sizes.

"Who's going to spend four hundred dollars on a teapot?" Estelle said. "I don't even like tea."

"You have to have all the components or else it's not a set."

The salesgirl nodded emphatically. They were at Ashley's for over three hours, mulling over cutlery and salad tongs and useless knickknacks Estelle couldn't give a shit about. And when it was all over, and Estelle was on the brink of smashing a plate or two over Lilly's skull, Lilly said, "Now we have to register you for the linen shower!" And off they went to Lilly's store on Mount Pleasant to choose sheets.

"It's months away," Estelle muttered in the car. "Why are we doing this now?"

"Because you're here now," Lilly said. "Besides, it's just enough time. You'll see. We'll still be running around in a panic the day of your wedding. And don't forget about the bridal show in September. You'll be back by then?"

Estelle looked out the window. She wanted to escape. Not just from the car, but from the whole predicament. From her own wedding. It was beginning to feel like a sentence.

"*I* want to go back to L.A.," Estelle complains.

Josh kisses her forehead. "Just one more week," he reminds her.

"But Jessie and Lilly want to take me dress shopping *again* today. And then Lilly wants you to go 'approve' the sheets and the china she chose for us. As though your opinion matters."

"It makes her happy."

"What about me?" Estelle sulked. "What the hell am I going to do with platinum china? Or three-hundred-thread-count sheets that I have to hang to dry?"

"Just look at it as your gift to your mother. Let her do her thing. If she wants to have input on your dress, is it such a big deal?"

"But I can find one myself," she says. "I can't stand the way she and Jessie look me up and down whenever I try something on."

"They just want to be included."

"Jessie just wants to gloat. *She* looked like Princess Grace on her wedding day. Her dress was a size four."

"Who cares what her dress size was?"

"What else matters more than how you look when you're walking down the aisle?" Estelle shoots back.

"How about who you're marrying?" he reasons.

She snorts indignantly.

"You suffer from bondage of the self, Beany."

"Please don't start with the twelve steps."

Josh used to go to Al-Anon. He had an ex-girlfriend who was an alcoholic. Once when Estelle was complaining about the lineup at Starbucks, he said to her, "Let go and let God."

He still likes to use the jargon, which drives her ballistic.

The phone rings somewhere in the house. Moments later, Lilly is jamming the portable in her ear. "It's your sister."

"Bean?" Jessie says.

"Hey, Jess. I'm still in bed."

"What time are we meeting?"

"Um, I don't know," Estelle says evasively. Lilly is standing over her, waiting. "I sort of have to start looking for a job."

"Bean, trust me. It's better to start dress shopping early. Especially because you're not a standard size."

"I'd rather get it in L.A.—"

"You need our help," Lilly cuts in. "You can't just buy it on your own."

"I've been choosing my own clothes for some time now."

"Exactly!" Lilly thunders.

"I can go with her," Josh says.

"You're the groom!" Lilly cries. "You can't see the dress."

"Listen," Jessie says. "I'll get some work done if we're not meeting up. Just let me know."

Estelle is caught between wanting to please them and wanting a day off from their joint scrutiny. She's had all the public humiliation she can take. "I have an appointment at Citytv," she lies.

Lilly leaves the room, shaking her head. Estelle hangs up.

"I didn't know you had an interview with City," Josh says.

He can be so dense. He has no concept of the deceptive inner workings of the female mind.

"I don't," she snips. "But I *will*. I'm going to go down there and try to set something up. I've edited Bubble Video in the States. Citytv owns the rights in Canada. I figure with my Avid experience, it's a good in."

"That would be great, eh? Working at MuchMusic or something?"

Estelle shrugs. "It's TV, though," she says. "It's not film."

Erica

Paul has "fixed her up" on a date with Jillian. They're going to an empowerment training session in TriBeCa. It's supposed to be a spiritual retreat, meditation instruction, and self-esteem-building workshop all rolled into one that was founded by some quasi-famous West Coast motivational speaker named Josette Fonseca. Paul seems to think it will help Erica; he offered to pay for it and he asked Jillian to invite her personally—which caught Erica off guard, and before she knew it, she'd accepted.

The decision to go was partly the result of having been cornered, but also partly out of curiosity. Her rejection from Columbia was a setback—it certainly precipitated an all-time low—but the fact is, she's always been in search of some unknown X-factor that would presumably transform her life or her character, or possibly both. Whether or not that X-factor will be meditation, improved self-esteem, and/or "spirituality" (whatever that means these days), she is at least willing to start exploring.

Mitchell is the one who first inspired her to be more open about this sort of thing. Ever since their conversation at his parents' place, she's been more and more mindful of his life philosophy: we simply don't know who or what will lead us down the path to some kind of fulfillment. And when she spoke to Miriam at the synagogue that afternoon, it was more of the same thing. Miriam encouraged her to pray and meditate, to get quiet enough so she can access that unfulfilled part of herself and actually *listen* to what it's telling her. Miriam kept asking her, "Who are you, Erica?" And she couldn't come up with an answer. She's a year shy of thirty and has no idea where she belongs, what she should be doing, or what she even *wants* out of her life.

For Mitch and Miriam, it was an earthquake in Egypt that provided their answers. Who knows what it will be for Erica? And if Jillian Clapton happens to be *her* conduit, so be it. She's desperate enough to find out.

They meet at the Canal and Franklin subway station and greet each other with strained, phony pleasure. They don't like each other, so formalities are tough. Jillian is wearing leather pants and a cashmere cowl-neck sweater, which pisses Erica off. How the hell is she supposed to meditate in leather? Erica is wearing a tracksuit, which she figured would be conducive to sitting in the lotus position all day.

"Are you going to be comfortable in that?" she asks Jillian.

"Probably not, but I'm meeting Kai afterward. You'll get to meet him."

They walk for about fifteen minutes until they come to a historic cast-iron industrial warehouse on Duane Street. "Wait till you meet Josette," Jillian says. "She's fabulous."

"Does she live here?"

"She lives in Vancouver. She's renting this space for a month while she's on tour in New York. It's a share."

"On tour?" Jillian makes it sound like this Josette woman is a rock star.

The old warehouse has been totally renovated and converted into artists' lofts. The lobby is filled with paintings and sculptures and art-deco furniture that remind Erica of the

Paramount Hotel lobby, only brighter. They ride the freight elevator up to the loft, and although she wouldn't trade Paul's Upper West Side luxury apartment for this, she has to admit the whole scene is pretty cool, if you're into upscale, artsy bohemia. Erica can appreciate its trendy, downtown appeal, but she still prefers park views and luxury apartments with doormen.

The inside of the loft is breathtaking, with fifteen-foot ceilings, skylights, tall windows, and a spiral staircase that leads up to a rooftop garden. There are two bedrooms off an absolutely massive living space. The sun is flooding in, illuminating the honey-colored wood floors and all the artwork on the walls.

"The woman who owns this loft is a painter," Jillian tells her. "She's really quite good, if you like urban contemporary."

Erica is instantly drawn to one of the paintings—a moody image entitled *The Artist's Space*. Upon closer scrutiny, the abstract strokes of rich color reveal themselves to be a corner of an artist's studio, with soft pink light coming through a loft window. It evokes a feeling of comfort and familiarity, of reverence for the space in which the artist creates. Just looking at it, Erica has a real sense of the painter's connection to her surroundings. The painting itself stirs in her that same blend of awe and envy that Paul's writing does; it makes her feel both touched and excluded.

Erica follows Jillian up the staircase to the terrace. Outside, a motley group of women are mingling and hugging in the garden. Erica hopes they're hugging because they know each other, not because it's one of those strange customs among the spiritually inclined. A fortyish woman who looks like an older Alanis Morissette is handing out bottles of Evian water and yoga mats. She's got long, dark hippie hair parted down the middle and she's wearing black leggings with an oversize sweater. She looks like the type who probably spells women with a *y*. She recognizes Jillian and they hug, which startles Erica. She never pegged Jillian as the hugging type.

"Josette, this is my friend Erica. Erica, this is Josette Fonseca."

Please don't hug me, Erica is thinking, just as Josette pulls her into her arms.

"I guess we can start," Josette announces to the women. "I think everyone's here now."

All of a sudden, the women gather into a circle and hold hands. Everyone seems to know what to do except Erica. Jillian grabs hold of her hand. Their eyes are all closed, so Erica closes her eyes.

"Let's just take a moment to acknowledge the Great Spirit," Josette says. "Great Spirit, we humbly call upon you for guidance today, to shower us with your light and your love. We surrender ourselves to you this morning to do with us whatever you will."

Erica opens one eye and looks around. No one is laughing. She can't believe it.

"Let's start by getting to know each other," Josette continues.

They all sit down cross-legged on their yoga mats. Erica takes great pleasure in watching Jillian struggle to cross her leather-encased legs.

"Let's go around the circle and introduce ourselves by saying our names and one thing we really, *really* like about ourselves. I'll start. I'm Josette and I'm compassionate."

"I'm Miranda and I'm a good mother."

"I'm Leah and I make a great bulgur casserole."

All the women laugh. Erica is panicking. This is more shame-inducing than improv. She can't decide what to say about herself.

"I'm Carol and I'm a good listener."

More laughter.

"I'm Jillian and I'm a good writer."

"I'm Erica and . . . I . . . I . . ." It's not that she can't think of anything; it's that she's too embarrassed to utter anything out loud. "I have pretty good skin. I mean, people have told me I do—"

"Don't justify," Josette admonishes gently.

Jillian looks at her.

"I'm Freddie and I'm an optimist."

"I'm Petra and I'm a survivor."

Some of the women clap. They finish going around the circle and no one else gets in trouble for justifying.

"Before we start working with the tools, I'd like to know what you hope to get from this workshop. So let's go around the circle again and share what brought you here."

Miranda again. "The other day I was watching MTV with my son," she begins, "and a Madonna video came on. My son made this remark about how Madonna is a cougar. Apparently a cougar is an older woman who's trying to act young. I don't know why, but it made me feel demoralized. I mean, I think Madonna's unbelievable. She's an icon. And still gorgeous for her age. But my son thinks she's just this old lady. That's the world we live in. I mean, obviously that's how the world perceives me too. I'm a cougar, I guess."

"Did you hear what you said there?" Josette asks her. "You said 'gorgeous for her age.' You're programmed, too! Just like your son."

"You're right!" Miranda gushes. "That's why I'm here. I don't want to perpetuate my self-loathing by buying into this patriarchal bullshit. I don't want to think of myself as a cougar! I want to reappropriate that word. . . ."

Erica is gazing at the view of New York. How hard would she fall from this height? she wonders. Would it kill her if she jumped? Could it be worse than this?

"Menopause is what brings me here," Leah confesses.

She might break both her legs, but she could make a full recovery. . . .

By the time it's Erica's turn to share, she surprises herself with her frankness. She tells them she got rejected from the writing program at Columbia and that she feels like a loser and doesn't know what to do with her life, and they all seem to like this a lot and they smile at her encouragingly and Josette thanks her for being so honest. Being downtrodden seems to be the way to earn respect.

Josette moves on to teaching them about their "tools." According to the *Fonseca Empowerment Training Handbook,* the two most vital tools for survival are the Invisible Protective Shield and the Emotions Screen. "The Protective Shield is a sort of safety bubble made of shimmering light," Josette explains. "In a difficult situation—a confrontation, for instance—you'll want to get into the habit of erecting your shield before you react, which will deflect all negative energy back to the offender. Erect before react. *Erect before react.* That's the key. Similarly, in a crisis of any kind, you should go inside—meaning retreat into a meditative state—and turn on your Emotions Screen, on which will unfold, in movielike fashion, the range of all the negative emotions you're experiencing in that moment. The idea being that when you can witness your emotions objectively, you can observe them and then let them pass, rather than be overcome by them."

Sounds simple, Erica thinks.

"Now, that's the theoretical overview," Josette continues. "Let's actually go in there and use these tools that will be with you for life. This is what's called an *active* meditation, which you can do anywhere, anytime."

While everyone is presumably deep in meditation, Erica sneaks off to go to the bathroom. She doesn't really have to go, but her attention span is too short for her to stay focused on the white light that is supposedly flowing up through her kundalini. Plus her ass is killing her.

When she gets downstairs, there's a woman making coffee in the kitchen.

"Oh, hi. Don't mind me," the woman says. "I live here." She looks up and smiles.

Erica does a double take. "Tiala?" she cries.

"Erica? Oh my God!"

They practically run to each other, arms flung out. "You're in New York?" Erica says, hugging her.

"This is my place. What are you doing here?"

"I live on the Upper West Side. God. I can't believe it. . . . We haven't seen each other since . . ."

"Grade twelve?"

They both laugh. Erica remembers that last night they were together—Tiala strutting off, high on acid. Off to God knows where or what kind of life. To *this* life, in fact, which is a damn lot better than Erica would have predicted.

They pull apart and look each other over. Tiala looks exactly the same. Still beautiful in that ethereal way that always made Erica's breath catch.

"This is your place?" Erica asks, incredulous. "You're the artist?"

Tiala nods modestly. "It's my studio, but I exhibit other artists here too."

"I'm so glad. I mean, I'm so glad you kept painting. I wasn't sure . . ."

"No. When we left off, I wasn't exactly . . . it took me a while to find my way. But what about you? What are you doing? Do you want coffee? Or, shit, you're in the middle of Josette's workshop. You probably have to go back up there. We could meet afterward?"

"I can't go back up there," Erica says. "I'm just going to have to live the rest of my life without a Protective Shield."

Tiala lets out a robust laugh, the same one that once made Erica worship her. Tiala pours them each a cup of coffee and they go into her bedroom and close the door. The bedroom is also Tiala's studio. There's a ladder that leads up to a second-story loft, a cozy space where Tiala spends her days painting. There are canvases and easels and empty cans full of brushes on the floor, a paint-spattered stereo on a long pine table littered with drawings.

"What's it like?" Erica asks her as they're climbing down from the loft.

"What's what like?"

"This life."

"I don't know. I like it. I'm happy. I get to paint and show my work. I earn a living."

"I'll say."

"What about you? When did you move to New York?" Tiala asks. "I've thought about you so often. Wondered what you wound up doing."

"You say 'wound up' like I should know by now."

"Don't you?"

Something about Tiala makes it easy for Erica to come clean right away, to just be herself. It was always like that with them. No pretense, no bullshit. No need to impress Tiala the way she had to try to impress other girls. Tiala never had those expectations. She never cared about the things other people cared about; she never gave a shit about status.

"I moved here to go to the photography institute," Erica says.

"You're a photographer! Fantastic!"

"No. I didn't stick with it. I met someone in the meantime and now we're living together, so I stayed in New York. I'm sort of trying to figure out what to do with my life now. I took a writing workshop at Columbia. Paul's a writer . . ."

"You're not working?"

"I'm working at the Paramount Hotel. Part time."

Rather than responding with the usual "poor you, you're going nowhere" look that Erica generally notices on people—i.e., her family, Paul's friends, et cetera—Tiala's expression seems to be one of curiosity. "I have an idea, if you're interested," she says.

"What?"

"I need someone to manage my studio," she says excitedly. "You know, to coordinate the exhibits, handle the money, keep the space organized. That sort of thing. At the moment, it's just me and some artist friends. We're sort of like an ad hoc committee, but it's taking up way too much of my time."

"But I'm not qualified."

"Of course you are. I need a smart, capable person who has some level of interest in the art world. Besides, you can try it out, see if you like it. It's a great environment. It's chaotic, creative, challenging. It's never boring, I promise."

"Can I think about it?"

"Of course. I mean, if it's money—"

"No—"

"Because I can afford to give you a competitive salary."

"Tiala, I sell gum and cigarettes part time. Believe me, I'm not doing *that* for the money."

Tiala smiles. "I'm so glad we ran into each other," she says. "Even if you don't take the job, we have to stay in touch."

On her walk back to the subway, Erica mulls over the possibility of managing Tiala's studio. The idea appeals to her for a lot of reasons. For starters, she would have a certain measure of responsibility and a variety of tasks to keep her stimulated; she'd be connected, even peripherally, to the art world; and she would certainly feel good about telling people what she does for a living. If she's truly open to finding a career she loves—which is what she *claims* to want—then she has to accept that it might not be a creative one. That's what her grandmother tried to tell her that night in Toronto.

And yet she's still ambivalent. She can't help feeling slightly disappointed with her options, as though taking a job managing an artist is tantamount to settling, or somehow conceding. It would mean, once and for all, relinquishing the dream of actually becoming an artist. And what would happen to all those artistic aspirations, the ones she's been clinging to forever?

If they could just fall away and be easily forgotten, who would she be?

Jessie

*T*his time when she finds him standing behind the bar at Ooze (as she knew she eventually would), she is void of emotion. She's here to take care of business; to face the demons.

"I need to talk to you," she tells him.

He looks about to say something, or perhaps to roll his eyes, but something in her tone stops him cold.

"What about?"

"I think we might be HIV positive," she blurts.

His face goes a sickly white. He swallows nervously. "You're HIV positive?" he says in a thin voice.

"Only if *you* are!"

"What?"

"I was thinking about it, about the condoms we used. How do we know they were sturdy?"

He looks confused. "What are you . . . Did you have a test?"

"No."

"So, what's the problem?"

"I don't even want to think about how many women you've slept with, Skieth. And if the condom broke or something—"

He lets out a long sigh and runs a hand through his spiky blond hair. "Holy—" he breathes. "You scared the shit out of me."

"How do you think I feel? *You're* the one who's so goddamn promiscuous!"

"I don't have AIDS, Jessie."

"How do you *know?*" she cries. "You go to strip clubs and sleep around—"

"I get tested. Fuck. What are you doing here? What's this about? Are you trying to get back at me?"

"When did you get tested?"

"I get tested every year."

"When?"

"In January. Christ. What's the matter with you?"

"How many women did you sleep with between your last test and me?"

"None. I got tested in January, for Christ's sake. You and I slept together in February. There was no one in between."

"Bullshit."

"Jessie, I don't know what the hell you think of me, but I don't have sex three hundred sixty-five days a year. I was seeing someone last fall and we split up right after Christmas. She was the last person I slept with before you. I got tested in January and then I was with you, like, barely three weeks later. If you want, I can fax you the results."

"Do you swear?" She's crying now, relieved and embarrassed and suddenly aware of how irrational and unbalanced she is.

"Of course I swear. Shit. I'm always careful."

"Because I have a family, and what I did . . . I mean, I can't even sleep with my husband anymore, Skieth. And I'm destroying their lives over this . . . so worried I'm going to give them . . ."

He comes out from behind the bar and pats her back while she cries. "I'm sorry," he says. "But I promise. I'm super-careful. You don't have to worry."

"Are you sure?"

"Why don't you just get a test and see, if you don't believe me."

"I can't. I'm too scared."

He's looking at her now, not with longing as in the old days, but with pity.

"Have you slept with anyone *since* me?" she asks him.

"Jessie—"

"Well, if you're sleeping around *now,* how can I believe you didn't sleep around right before me?"

"I've slept with someone—I mean, I'm sleeping with someone—but I'm dating her. I care about her. I've been with her for over two months."

"You're dating someone?"

"She's a teacher. A kindergarten teacher. She lives in my building."

"You're dating a kindergarten teacher?"

He nods.

"Oh."

"Jessie—"

"I'm sorry I scared you," she says. "I was so sure. . . ."

"Mira wanted proof too," he confesses.

"Mira?"

"My girlfriend. She wanted to be sure, you know? I can understand that, with my lifestyle. She wanted to see the results."

"Did you tell her about me?"

"Of course. I told her I'd been with one married house-wife since my last AIDS test and that was it. She was pretty relieved."

One married housewife?

"Feel a bit better now?" he asks.

She nods mutely. Naturally, she's overwhelmed with relief. But she also feels rejected and depressed. "Thanks."

"No problem," he says, returning to his bottles of liquor. "Take care, eh?"

Take care, eh. Was there ever a more impersonal dismissal?

When she gets home, the house is empty. Ilana's at day care and Levi's in school. Allan agreed to pick them up; he's been a lot more accommodating since what they now politely refer to as her "meltdown." Which has been one of the only positive side effects of the past few months.

She runs a bath and fills it with seaweed bubble bath. She feels oddly calm as she sinks down into the tub and lets the hot water envelop her. No, not calm. Ambivalent. The AIDS panic has been alleviated, there's that. But what else has changed? She is still a *married housewife,* a bad mother, a neurotic wreck trapped in a cage. And there's still Allan. The hysteria of the past few weeks was a distraction. She randomly plucked something to obsess over and now, in its aftermath, her life is exactly what it was before—barely manageable. And she's probably done irreparable damage to her babies, not just these past few terrible months, but since the day she brought them into this world.

She has failed them. Jessie Jaffe, the perfectionist extraordinaire, has damaged her children. It's harder to say whether or not she's ruined her marriage, too. What was there to ruin? Her little affair with Skieth made one thing abundantly clear: she was—and still *is*—deeply unhappy. Maybe she failed *herself* by picking Allan, or by letting him pick her. Skieth was probably right. With no prior experience, how could she have known there wasn't a better man out there for her?

So far, Allan hasn't acted on last week's threat to leave her. Part of her wishes he would, and that he'd take the kids with him too. As it is, she's just biding her time until the next calamity crops up. And with children, there is always a calamity in store, down the road. She just can't physically stomach it anymore. They're better off without her.

Would it be so terrible if she walked away from them? She would miss them. Of course, she would miss them. But there would be relief; she'd be free of that crazed need to protect them. If she was gone, maybe they'd at least have a chance at some semblance of a normal life. Playing in the grass, touching pennies, eating McDonald's, sleeping over at friends'. What will she do to them if she *stays?* Levi is already a walking time bomb, a six-year-old defeatist, a cynic. And Ilana is moody and temperamental, overly sensitive.

Is she capable of just packing a suitcase and walking out the door? She's heard stories before about mothers who have done that. They just disappear. Auben's cousin's wife did it; she told her son she didn't want to be his mother anymore and she *left*.

Could she do it? Could Jessie Jaffe—not even so much a name anymore, but a *title*—walk away?

Estelle

"*I* brought home supper!" he says, coming into the apartment with two tantalizing, grease-stained paper bags. "Smoked meat and fries."

Her heart soars. He lays the paper bags down on the coffee table and kisses her on the mouth. She's surging—with love and hunger. Occasionally a little voice screams in her head that a love of food is their only shared passion, the singular common interest that sustains their entire relationship. Even Tunisian food will do in a pinch. Occasionally, she racks her brain to list all the things they both like to do. Snuggling, spooning . . . and eating. Somehow, it always comes back to food.

But they *are* compatible. They must be! For one thing, they rarely fight. (He's a pacifist; he is only ever wounded by her, never the one who wounds.) Besides, she doesn't want a partner who is just a replica of herself. She doesn't need a man to encourage her to laze around in front of the TV all night watching *Survivor* or *Who Wants to Be a Millionaire?*, or to waste money on a *Saturday Night Fever/Staying Alive* double feature (Josh has never seen either). Nor would she want a man whose ambitions clashed with hers, who was competitive and petty and threatened by her success. She tells herself she's much better off with someone at the other end of the spectrum, someone who complements her, who forces her to go for a walk on the pier or go antiquing on Montana.

Her horizons could certainly use broadening. So what if she hates to travel? She'll learn to like it or else Josh can go off by himself when he gets an urge. Short separations are good for a marriage. And she doesn't need someone who is her match in irony and sarcasm, someone who is sharp-tongued and cynical. His easygoing optimism is an inspiration. Besides, her Scrabble game, and vocabulary, have vastly improved.

Here's what matters: he adores her. His love is the only unconditional love she has ever known. When it isn't irritating, it's absolutely cleansing. Opposites attract, damn it. And so they have. He is her simple, sweet-tempered, nature-loving pet. He is not a man of gravity or biting wit, but he compensates with his sensitivity and capacity for devotion. He brings home supper in greasy paper bags and feeds her french fries with his fingers. She has dreamed her whole life of finding a man as tender and compassionate as Josh. (Hasn't she?)

"How was your day, Beany-Baby?"

(This is a new thing, the nickname. He's put his own stamp on Bean and by God she hates it.)

She tears open one of the paper bags and gets her hand on some of the hot, soggy fries. "I got a call from a producer at Citytv," she tells him.

"That's fabulous news!" he cries. "Finally!"

"His name is François Montpetit," she says. "He's originally from MusiquePlus in Montreal."

"Great, great."

"He wants to meet me as soon as possible," she says, pulling out her smoked-meat sandwich. She's weak-kneed from the smell of mustard and caraway. "He's producing a new show for the fall called *D-TV*."

"D-TV?"

"D for 'Design,'" she explains. "It's a weekly exposé on the fashion industry. They're looking for innovative editors. He was pretty excited about my résumé."

"That would be super!" Josh enthuses. "A new show!"

She smiles halfheartedly, feeling a bit resentful over his superkeen reaction. It bugs her the way he so desperately wants her to find a job she likes in Toronto. It's his own guilt. He knows she really wants to stay in L.A., so his boundless enthusiasm for Citytv is beginning to grate.

Meanwhile, his job at the literary magazine is off to a rocky start. He's already locked horns with Michael Shulman over just about everything: how much to charge, which direction to take it in, what to call it. Josh wants it to have a travel slant. Michael thinks that will be limiting. Thus far, they've agreed on a name for it: *The Foulwind Review,* after Cape Foulwind, a spectacular, rugged coastline on New Zealand's South Island (Josh's description). She has noticed that in his own slippery and persuasive manner, Josh somehow always manages to get his way.

So far, *The Foulwind Review* is still scrounging submissions from friends—amateur poems and short stories brimming with Can Lit pretension. But Josh is happy and money for him is a nonissue, thanks to Gladys's substantial wealth. When Estelle feels a little critical of him in that regard, she has to remind herself that Milton still pretty much pays her rent.

"So, are you going to Toronto?" he asks her.

"I guess. I told François I'd call him as soon as I book my flight."

"Fantastic. Coke or 7UP?" he asks her, opening the fridge.

"Coke. What'd you do today?"

"I ordered my tux," he says, sitting down beside her. "I did it over the Internet!"

Sometimes it's as though he wants her to pat his head and say, "Good for you!" when he accomplishes even the most banal task.

"Don't you have to try it on?" she points out.

He frowns. "I provided all my measurements."

"And that's it now?"

"I'll have a fitting in Toronto a few days before the wedding," he says. "Do you think that'll be okay?"

"I guess so." She leans over and wipes a glob of mustard off his chin. She still hasn't found a dress yet and the wedding's in three months. Lilly is having panic attacks over Estelle's inability to find a dress and her lack of weight loss. She's threatening to fly to Los Angeles and physically drag Estelle to a gym and a bridal shop, in that order.

"Would you come with me?" she asks him, out of the blue.

"Where to?"

"To buy my dress."

"But your mother said—"

"Never mind what Lilly says," she snaps. "It's our wedding. I want *you* to like my dress. That's all that matters to me. I don't care if you see it."

"Really?"

"I've been looking at this dress on Melrose," she says. "It's not really a wedding dress, but it's beautiful. It's ivory with a beaded bodice and chiffon skirt, and it's got an Empire waist, which would be really flattering on me."

"What's an Empire waist?"

"It's old-fashioned, like the dresses from *Sense and Sensibility.*"

"The novel?"

"The movie!"

"It was a novel *first*," he says smugly. "You have read it, right?"

"No. Have you seen the movie?"

"No, but I've read—"

"You never saw *Sense and Sensibility*?" she cries.

"I just told you, I read the book. I don't like movies made out of classic—"

"But it's not the same! Oh, never mind," she says, disappointed. "Will you come with me?"

"Of course," he says, laughing at her. "I'd love to come with you, Beany-Baby."

Lilly

"*M*ilt?" she calls out, letting herself into the condo. She hangs her keys on the peg in the foyer. Work at the linen store was a mob scene today and she's got a terrible headache. Can't even remember when it started. She's not in the mood for more of Milton's grumpiness and self-pity. "You home, Milt?"

She finds him in bed, watching an old videocassette of *The Young Entertainers Showcase*. The first thing she does is rip the big pillow out from behind his back. "I told you never to use these for watching TV!" she rants. "They're six-hundred-thread-count shams! They're for decoration."

"It's a pillow, for Chrissake. What's the point of it if you can't lie on it?"

She goes over to the TV and turns it off.

"Hey!" he protests, sitting up.

"I thought we were finished with this," she huffs.

"Too bad."

"Too bad for you."

"Leave me alone."

"You want I should leave you alone?" she threatens. "Fine. How about I just leave, period."

"Don't start."

"I deserve better than this. I've put up with a lot, Milton. Don't you think I've been more than fair? Letting you wallow around the apartment all these months, pining?"

"I'm not pining. I'm reminiscing."

"Either you pull yourself together," Lilly threatens, "or you can pack your bags."

He sighs, flopping back against the pillows.

"She's gone, Milt. I'm the one that's left. You'd better deal with it."

"I am dealing with it."

"You call this dealing?" she accuses, yanking the video-cassette out of the VCR and hurling it onto the bed. "How many times have you watched these?"

"You don't understand."

"It's not normal behavior." She sits down on the edge of the bed. Her head is throbbing. The Motrin she took are having no effect. "Milton," she says, in a far-off voice. "Why didn't you just leave me? Why?"

He doesn't answer.

"I'm asking you," she pushes. "I know Gladys is the one you wanted. Everyone always says, 'But he stayed with you, didn't he?' I want to know why."

"Let it go, Lilly."

"You're all talk! I want to know why you never left me."

"Because she wouldn't have me!" Milton blurts. And in the stunned silence that follows, she knows there's no going back. The game, the pretending they do, it's over now. The charade is irretrievable. "If you want the truth," he goes on recklessly, "I begged her to marry me! For years I begged her and she wouldn't hear of it. I told her I'd leave you and she refused. She liked it the way it was."

"How was it?" Lilly asks him, her voice trembling.

"Having me around," he confesses, "but keeping her independence."

"Having you around?" Lilly whimpers, her body sagging.

It's like the wind's been punched out of her.

Milton nods.

"All the time we were married . . . ?" she manages to say.

"Lilly, you knew. Don't act like you didn't know. Besides, the question isn't why did I stay. It's why did you?"

Lilly closes her eyes. Why? Denial, fear, responsibility. All those things. She is a master pretender. She pretended it away. Of course she knew. But some part of her clung to the fact that he'd never attempted to divorce her. *He must love me. He must.*

"I stayed for the children!" she tells him.

"Bullshit. You stayed out of selfishness."

"I stayed out of *selfishness?*" she cries, leaping to her feet.

"Who else did I have?" he says violently. "Not you, Lilly! Your world has only ever been big enough for your mother and your daughters."

"That's not fair."

"They come first with you, Lilly. They're who you put all of yourself into. Me, I get the dribbles left over. And I never complain. I give you your space. I understand about your mother, how you need to have her around. But maybe I had to look elsewhere to feel a bit important."

Lilly is shaking her head. "Don't you put this on me. Don't swing the blame to justify your disloyalty to this family!" She runs from the room then, not knowing where to go. Her mother is upstairs at the pool doing her laps; she'll be home any minute.

She goes into the den and looks around. She grabs the Inuit sculpture and, without thinking, smashes it onto the parquet floor. A couple of stone heads roll under the couch.

"Lilly?" Milton cries out. He comes running into the room, barefoot in his underwear, looking frightened. "What happened?" He immediately crouches to pick up the pieces of the shattered sculpture. "Are you out of your mind?" he cries. "Look at the floor!"

It's scratched and dented where the carving landed. He just paid to have it all rebuffed last year.

"Oh God," he moans, staring desperately at the mess. "Do you know how much this carving was worth?"

"Oh, yes!" Lilly answers. "I know how much it was worth!"

"Maybe I can glue it back together," he says, still crouching. "Help me clean this up."

She watches him trying to collect all the tiny stone limbs and it makes her feel weary. "Let go," she whispers. "Just let go already."

Erica

She spreads the contact sheets out on the pine table and hunches down over the magnifying loupe. They're in Tiala's bedroom, up in the loft where she does all her painting. "This one's not bad," Erica says, moving aside to let Tiala have a look.

"This one's good too." Tiala points to another of the images and hands back the loupe. "They're amazing. You did a great job."

"My parents will be pleased that all those photography lessons they paid for weren't a complete waste."

That she is using her state-of-the-art Nikon camera and her modest talent in photography to design a flyer for Tiala's next art exhibit is beside the point. What matters is that her new job allows her to incorporate just about every hobby she's ever dabbled in, and at last, all her scattered creative interests are finally serving a purpose. Even writing. Last week, she photographed Tiala's paintings. Today she's designing a flyer. Next month, she'll be curating the show. It certainly hasn't been dull.

They've turned the second bedroom into an office with just the bare necessities—a desk, a computer, and a telephone—and they're planning to buy a backdrop and a flash system so that Erica can eventually do all the photography "in-house." The next crucial step is for Erica to meet the accountant and start learning the business of running a studio.

"I want to show you a couple of the fonts I picked out," Erica says. "If we go with this shot, I think the overall look of the flyer should be more whimsical. I was looking at the one from your last show. It was more moody and gothic—"

"I agree. Let's stay away from gothic. My new series is very soft, very fluid. I want the flyer to reflect that." She studies the fonts and says, "I like both. You choose."

The canvases for Tiala's new show are spread all over the studio. She paints almost around the clock. She is driven by something beyond ambition and rational motivation. She is obsessed with color and light, the way a fine black ox-hair brush leaves its mark on the canvas. And Erica is as smitten with her as she was more than a decade ago.

They've spent time catching up. Hours stolen here and there, over lattes and cigarettes, or else while Tiala paints. Tiala's life since high school hasn't been nearly as seedy or dramatic as Erica once imagined it would be. In her early twenties, she fell in love with an artist from New York and moved here to be with him. But his art always came first. She was an afterthought. They got married, and then divorced a few years later. By then she had rediscovered her own love of painting, and she's never stopped. She's also never fallen in love again. Too time-consuming, she says. Love—especially the kind that fails—saps her creativity. With Erica it's the opposite. Failed creative pursuits sap her ability to love.

The buzzer sounds in the studio and Erica climbs down the ladder of Tiala's loft and leaves her bedroom. "It's probably the courier," she says. She grabs a manila envelope from her office and opens the front door. The transparencies she shot have to go to the graphic artist's to be scanned by the end of the week. But when the elevator door opens, it's Mitchell Dorfman who emerges onto the landing.

"Hey," he says, as though she'd been expecting him.

The sight of him after all this time throws her off-kilter. Her heart beats faster; her face feels hot. She's nervous. "What're you doing here?" she asks him. "How did you know . . . ?"

"Miriam."

"Miriam?"

"My sister. Your rabbi."

Her cheeks flush. For some reason, she's embarrassed by her recent visits with Miriam, the way one would be embarrassed about seeing a shrink. "Isn't there some kind of rabbi–client privilege?" she says.

"What's the big deal? Lots of people talk with their rabbis."

"She's not my rabbi. I just . . . I like talking to her."

"She mentioned you've been to see her a few times," Mitchell says. "That's all. She doesn't tell me what you talk about."

"She told you where I work—"

"I guess she didn't think it was a secret."

"It's not a secret," Erica says defensively.

"So, uh, can I come in or do I have to stay out here?"

"Of course you can come in."

They go inside and Mitchell looks around, examines some of the paintings. "Nice," he says. "She's good."

"We went to high school together. Her name is Tiala."

"This is a great space."

Small talk. Her worst nightmare. Especially with Mitchell. She hates that they've become awkward with each other.

"So what do you do here exactly?" he asks.

"A bit of everything," she says. "I guess officially I'm managing the studio. But I get to do some creative stuff. . . ."

I photographed some of her paintings. I'm designing the flyer for her new exhibit. I'll be writing a blurb about her."

He smiles. He's cut his hair; it's supershort, like an army buzz cut. No more seventies hair, but it suits him. He looks older, sexier. Goddamn him for looking so good. "So maybe you've found your thing," he says.

"Maybe." She grabs two Cokes from the kitchen and hands him one. "So what's up, Mitch? I mean, did you want to talk to me about something? Do you need a date for another bar mitzvah?"

It's not that she doesn't want him here, or that she wouldn't love to spend the afternoon catching up and rekindling things; it's just that it took her a long enough time to get over their friendship. It's been like giving up cigarettes. Slowly, slowly she was just starting to forget about him, the way you can forget how good a cigarette is with a cup of coffee. Seeing him now is like taking that first sweet drag again. It somehow feels illicit. And yet she can't help feeling as though she's the one who instigated this visit; that it's what she's wanted all along: to be chased by him, and found.

"I miss talking to you," he says.

"Mitch—"

"I know you don't want to hear this, but I just had to come . . . I mean, I couldn't live with myself if I didn't at least tell you—"

Erica looks toward Tiala's bedroom. "Let's go for a walk," she says.

They ride the freight elevator downstairs and head toward Duane Park. "What does Paul think of your new job?" Mitchell asks, out of the blue.

"He's happy that I'm happy," she says. "Why?"

"Just that he was so keen on you becoming a writer."

"I can still become a writer. I could write in my free time—"

The truth is, when she mentioned the job to Paul, the first thing out of his mouth was, "What about writing?"

"I can still become a writer," she said defensively. Just like she said to Mitch and her parents and her sisters. "I'll write in my free time."

Paul didn't look at all convinced. "As long as you're not going to give up on the writing," he said, "I think working in a gallery is a fine idea."

A fine idea. He keeps calling it a "gallery" too, no matter how many times she reminds him it's a studio. And lately, when she gets home at night gushing about her day at the studio, he smiles patronizingly, as though he's just waiting patiently for her to grow disenchanted and drop it. Presumably the way she drops everything. But maybe she's just imagining that, putting her own biased slant on it. Maybe he *is* happy for her, in his self-absorbed way. It's so hard to tell with Paul what makes him happy and what disappoints him.

Erica and Mitchell sit down now, side by side on one of the park benches.

"And do you?" Mitchell asks her.

"Do I what?"

"Write in your free time?"

"I didn't get accepted into the MFA program."

"So?"

"That sort of dampened my enthusiasm for the whole writing thing, if ever there was any real enthusiasm to begin with. I don't know anymore. Maybe it was Paul's dream for me, not mine."

"Does he tell you you're amazing anyway? Whether or not you're a writer?"

"Let's not go there—"

"I just want to know. Because you are. And he should."

She's staring down at the grass, doing everything in her power not to look at him. She just can't. "You know," she says, "I've . . . I've been lighting the candles on Shabbat."

"You have?"

She shrugs. "I try. Paul's usually out on Friday night, so I do my little ritual thing. I light the candles and have my supper. It's nice."

"So it worked."

"What?"

"My brainwashing."

"I guess so."

"You're going to synagogue, celebrating Shabbat. . . . Next you'll be keeping kosher."

"Don't get excited. It's like you said. It's just a few minutes of peace in my week. That's all."

"That's plenty."

"I'm still not sure about God," she admits. "But Miriam is helping me with that."

"You know why I came to see you today, right?"

She doesn't answer.

"Are you going to look down there the whole time we talk?" he says. "Why won't you look at me?"

"I can't."

"Why?"

"I don't know." And she doesn't. Doesn't know what will happen if she looks up at him, at his face, into his eyes. Would she love him if she did?

"I know you don't want us to hang around together anymore," he says. "I respect that. Well, I've tried to. And I've been pretty good about staying away and giving you space. But I just keep thinking, if I don't just give it one last shot, you know, I won't be able to live with myself."

"Give *what* one last shot?"

"Us. I don't know. Telling you how I feel before I give up and walk away for good."

"There's nothing to walk away from," she says, lying.

"Bullshit."

"We went to an improv show. I went to a bar mitzvah with you. It wasn't anything—"

"It was," he says. "We both know it was."

"I promised Paul I wouldn't do this with you."

"You participated in this," he whispers. "You helped create it, Erica, no matter how much you pretend you didn't."

"You're saying I led you on?"

"You did more than lead me on. You made me love you. So either it was part of some perverse game, or else you have feelings for me too. Because I didn't dream this all up. I know I didn't."

"I didn't do anything on purpose," she tells him. "I like being with you. I just didn't think about the consequences . . . for any of us."

"Are you happy with Paul?" he asks her. "I mean, are you happy enough?"

"Happy enough for what?"

"I don't know." He shakes his head miserably, runs his hand across the top of his buzz cut. "I guess happy enough not to even want to know what it might be like with me."

She looks up at him then and for a split second she is tempted to blurt the truth: no, she's not happy enough with Paul; yes, she is curious about where a relationship with Mitch could lead. Not only curious, but preoccupied with the possibility. She's thought about him incessantly over the past few months, imagining them together in every conceivable way—as friends, as lovers, as a couple. Even at night, lying beside Paul, or sometimes in his arms, she's wondered. . . . What would Mitchell's arms around her feel like? His body against hers? What would they whisper to each other in bed late at night?

Maybe her expression reveals what she's thinking—more than she's willing to let on, anyway—because without any provocation, he leans over and kisses her. It's a short kiss, his lips on hers for a single moment; uncertain, hopeful. He doesn't give her time to stop him or let him go on. Instead, he pulls away quickly and lowers his head.

She can't think of anything to say, so she reaches for his hand. His fingers are cold. She holds them, not quite ready for him to leave. They're not finished yet. *She's* not finished with him. Whether it was fantasy or calculation, she has always known that she would succumb to her attraction for him—at the very least experiment with it before letting him go. That he came to her first is pure chance. The truth is, she would have sought him out if he hadn't come to her. Her friendship with Miriam was one small way for her to stay tethered to him. What else made her tell Miriam about her new job, including the name of Tiala's studio? They all know she was just leaving a trail of bread crumbs for Mitchell. And all he did was follow it.

"Now what?" he says.

"I really don't know," she answers.

"I guess you have to make a choice."

Suddenly her grandmother's words come back to her. *You have to commit to something.* Straightforward enough instructions, when they applied to her career. But this is her love life. Choosing one man means losing the other. And as always, she is utterly incapable of making that kind of choice and standing by it. She wants them both; she wants it all. She wants everything. She always has. The idea of ruling out possibilities has always terrified her.

"I can't tell you what you want to hear right now," she says. "But I . . . I guess I do have feelings for you. I just don't know what to do with them."

"If you have feelings for Paul and you also have feelings for me, maybe you need to think about what kind of life you want, and which one of us can give it to you. Maybe that will help you decide."

She leans her head on his shoulder. And she knows it *is* a question of commitment—of committing not just to the right man, but to the right package.

Estelle

"What do you think of vellum?" Lilly asks.

"I'd love one right now," Estelle mutters.

"Not Valium. *Vellum.* For the invitations."

"Whatever."

"We could have gold engraving on it. I think that would be classy. What do you think?"

She doesn't care! Doesn't give a shit. That's what she'd like to tell Lilly. Vellum, parchment, purple construction paper—she doesn't give a shit. "It's just an invitation," she says weakly. "What's the big deal?"

"The invitation makes an impression," Lilly explains. "It sets the tone of the whole wedding."

They're sitting in Lilly's kitchen, having another "wedding tête-à-tête." Lilly's got her giant overflowing binder on the table; it's neatly divided into categories. Music; Flowers; Photography; Caterers; Dresses. Then there are subcategories. Violinist; Band; DJ; Table setting; Boutonnieres; Bouquets; Hors d'oeuvres; Main course; Wedding cake. She needs the Dewey decimal system to catalogue everything.

She makes a vague pretense of having Estelle be a part of the discussion, but she's already made most of the decisions on her own. She just wants Estelle to authorize everything—which means a sporadic, indifferent nod whenever necessary.

Estelle's only reprieve from Lilly's zealous wedding planning is when she's safely back in L.A. But she had to come to Toronto again this weekend to start looking for an apartment. They're moving back at the end of the summer, and if they haven't got a place they'll have to move in with her parents.

The good news is, she's got that job editing *D-TV* at MuchMusic all lined up. She met with the producer, François Montpetit, and he offered her a nine-month contract. It appeals to her on a certain level and it won't be nearly as mind-numbing as editing movie trailers. Still, in some ways, it feels like a step down.

Josh took her out to the Border Café to celebrate the job offer. He acted like it was the greatest coup of her career. She reminded him that it was a notch or two below what she'd achieved in L.A.

"You can't really compare Canadian TV to Hollywood movies," she said. But he doesn't understand that she's achieved something monumental in L.A.; that she managed to insert herself into a world that is virtually impenetrable. He just wants to go on believing that they're moving back to Toronto as much for her as for him.

Lilly shoves a piece of paper at her and says, "Here's a mock-up of the menu."

Estelle looks it over and frowns. "It's a bit pretentious, isn't it?"

"How can food be pretentious?"

"What's spicy yellow dahl dip?"

"I don't know," Lilly says indignantly. "It's from Martha Stewart."

"And poached mozzarella in gazpacho? Will people eat that?"

"They'll admire it."

"I think the orange pistachio–black olive biscotti with chile-lime aioli is a bit much."

Lilly snatches back the menu. "Oy, I've got a headache again. I don't know why I bother showing you any of this."

"Maybe because it's *my* wedding?"

"Well, you don't seem very enthusiastic."

"It's like you're planning this for someone else, not me. None of this has anything to do with me."

"What do you want, then?"

"I want a candy table instead of desserts."

"A candy table?"

"With bowls of jelly beans and Mike and Ike and Smarties. It'll be fun."

"It's not a *birthday party,* Estelle. Who ever heard of a candy table at a wedding? That's tacky."

Estelle is on the verge of launching into a tirade when Josh and her father come into the kitchen. They're wearing jogging suits and dripping sweat onto the slate tiles.

"How was your run?" Estelle asks them. Lilly is already getting up and grabbing a bunch of paper towels.

"Painful," Milton pants. "I think I had a heart attack along the way."

Josh slaps Milton's back. "My mission when we move back is to get your father into shape," he tells Estelle.

"I'm going to check on my mother," Lilly says curtly. She thrusts the paper towels at Milton and says, "Wipe up your sweat."

Estelle doesn't press to know the particulars of what's going on between her parents. They aren't speaking much and Lilly keeps leaving the room whenever Milton shows up. Every time his name is mentioned, it seems like Lilly's mood deflates. Estelle assumes it has to do with Gladys. It always does.

"Lilly?" Josh says. "Wait a minute." He looks over at Estelle. "We wanted to ask you guys something."

Lilly reluctantly sits back down.

"Beany and I were wondering," he says, looking back and forth between Lilly and Milton. "Well, it would mean a lot to us if you two would sing a duet at our wedding."

Lilly makes a face. "I don't sing," she says. "I haven't sung in years."

"Muh, you have a great voice," Estelle says.

"How would you know?"

"I've heard you singing around the house when you thought no one was around."

Lilly waves her hand in the air dismissively. "I'm not singing in front of anyone."

"I think it's a great idea," Milton says.

"You would," Lilly sneers. "Any opportunity to show off."

"Lilly, it would really mean a lot to us," Josh says. "I mean, I always thought my mother would sing at my wedding—"

His voice breaks off and Estelle can see tears in the corners of his eyes. She gets up and puts her arms around him.

"I'll think about it," Lilly says.

"I'll forgo the candy table," Estelle promises, "if you do the duet with Daddy."

Milton

"*P*ass me the sauerkraut juice," Dorothy says.

Milton hands her the measuring cup and watches her dump the juice into the pot. The kitchen is filled with the smell of browned onions and Polish sausage.

"Now the sugar."

She's teaching him to make sauerkraut soup. He's been cooking a lot lately, partly because Lilly has stopped and partly because he finds it soothing. He's been reading cookbooks and watching Emeril Lagasse on the Food Network. He's experimented with a few dishes and his mother-in-law says he's got "a knack."

She stirs the soup and looks at him. "Now get me the eggs," she tells him. "And the milk and cream."

He goes to the fridge and starts pulling out the eggs and milk. The heavy door swings closed as he's trying to maneuver the ingredients and he drops the eggs on the floor. "Goddamn it," he mutters. He hates Lilly's appliances—the big stainless steel monsters that are supposed to be modern and trendy. What ever happened to white appliances and linoleum floors? But Lilly always has to have the newest trend. Her kitchen is gleaming and cold, with big slabs of slate on the floor. Faygie Rosenberg, the decorator, chose them. Milton never could understand why they had to pay someone to tell them how to furnish their own home.

Besides, in the end it was Lilly telling the decorator what to do. Slate floors, steel appliances, pots dangling from the ceiling that he keeps clunking his head on. He thinks it's not a kitchen meant for cooking—now that he's actually cooking—it's meant for showing off. But he's never said anything to Lilly. He just inhabits her world.

"We can still use them," Dorothy says.

He doesn't argue. There's no point. Dorothy crouches with her spatula and scoops all the broken eggs into a bowl. She dumps two of them into a separate bowl for her soup and covers the rest with Saran Wrap.

"I'll make omelettes with the rest," she tells him.

Lilly comes in as Milton is mopping the floor. She's wearing a new aqua-colored suit with a scarf tied around her neck. He wants to tell her she looks good, but they aren't speaking. She'd think it was insincere. A contrived attempt at making amends. Maybe it would be, too.

She puts her purse on the kitchen table and comes over to inspect what they're doing.

"I'm teaching your husband how to make *kapusniak*," Dorothy says.

Lilly frowns. He's used to the moods by now. She doesn't indulge him with her laughter anymore; she won't even nag him.

It's lonely without her. He misses his wife—the nagging, the gossiping, the bossing. He misses the way she used to put his vitamins on the breakfast table every morning, the way she used to lay the dental floss on the bathroom sink so he wouldn't forget to floss before bed. He misses hearing about the broads who shop at her linen store. Mostly he misses her smile with the smudge of lipstick on her front teeth.

Lilly kisses her mother's face and rubs her back. The gesture, which is so utterly natural for Lilly, suddenly fills him with guilt. He's realized recently that it's a remarkable quality in her—the *way* she loves. It's an all-encompassing love that tends to bleed into controlling, but it comes from a place of purity and good intention. He sees that now. And that's what he used against her. Instead of pleading for forgiveness, which he should have done, he took her most noble attribute—her loyalty to her mother and children, her bottomless capacity for love—and he used it as his weapon.

Dorothy beats the eggs and milk and adds them to the soup.

"I'm going to have a nap," Lilly says.

"What's wrong?" Dorothy asks. "You never nap in the middle of the afternoon."

"It's this headache."

"Still with the headaches?"

Lilly nods wearily and leaves.

"What headaches?" Milton calls after her.

Dorothy just gives him one of her looks.

*T*hat night, Milton falls asleep in the den. He's been sleeping on the couch a lot recently, with the lumpy pillow and the spare blanket that gives him a rash. It's still better than lying beside Lilly, with her stiff back in his face and her muffled crying.

He wakes up to the sound of Lilly's voice coming from the bedroom. He sits up and looks around, disoriented.

"Milton! Milton! Mother!"

He stumbles off the couch and hurries down the hall to her. His neck is stiff and his back is aching. He collides with his mother-in-law outside his bedroom.

"What time is it?" he asks.

"Two," Dorothy says, looking worried.

"Milton?" Lilly's voice is small, frightened.

They find her sitting up in bed, with her bare legs splayed out in front of her.

"What is it?" he asks.

"I'm tingling. My hand and my leg are tingling. I'm numb!"

"You're slurring," Dorothy says, alarmed.

"I can't . . . talk . . . properly," Lilly tells them. "My . . . mouth isn't . . . working right—"

"Let's go to the hospital. Can you walk?"

"I can't . . . feel . . . my leg."

"I can carry you," he says.

She clasps his hand urgently. "I'm . . . dying, Milton."

"You're not dying." But there's something in her face that makes him believe her.

"I knew . . . something was . . . wrong," she moans. "Ten days I've . . . had this migraine. Blindness in . . . one eye and then . . . the pain would come—"

"We'll go to St. Michael's," he says. "It's the closest."

Ten days his wife has had a migraine and he didn't even know. Hadn't had a clue.

*T*hey take a cab rather than an ambulance because Lilly doesn't want a scene in front of the concierge. They get dropped off on Shuter Street and then, at the hospital, have to wait four hours in the emergency room. When Lilly is finally told to go to one of the small, curtained-off rooms, she is half-asleep and has to be pushed in a wheelchair. She's left there for another hour, until a young doctor—Dr. Fung—shows up to examine her.

"She's numb," Milton explains.

"Where?"

"Her leg and her arm."

"My . . . fingers," Lilly puts in groggily.

"Right or left?"

"Right. I'm . . . tingling all down . . . my right side."

"And you can hear she's slurring her words," Dorothy says.

"She may just be tired," Dr. Fung says, scribbling notes on his clipboard. "What kind of tingling?" he asks her. He shines a light in her eyeballs and peers into them.

"I don't . . . know," she mutters. Her voice is drowsy, fading. "I can't . . . feel anything . . . in my fingertips . . . and thighs."

"Is it possible you fell asleep on them?"

"She's been up four hours now," Milton says irritably. "That's a long time for her leg to be asleep."

"Is it getting worse?" the doctor asks Lilly.

"I don't think so."

"Has it improved?"

Lilly looks confused.

"She's had a migraine for ten days," Dorothy explains.

"Have you had migraines before?"

"Never," Dorothy says. "Never before."

"I'm going to send you upstairs for a CAT scan."

"CAT scan?" Lilly cries. "You think . . . it's a . . . brain tumor?"

"Let's see what the CAT scan turns up," Dr. Fung says, disappearing behind the curtain. Leaving them without any hope or reassurance.

A few minutes later, a nurse wheels Lilly away. Milton and Dorothy are alone in the waiting room.

"I didn't know," he admits, his voice full of remorse. "I had no idea." He looks away from his mother-in-law, trying to hide the terror in his eyes. "What if I lose her, too?" he whimpers.

Dorothy purses her lips. She's white, trembling.

"We fought the other day," he confesses. "It was terrible. I said terrible things."

"Oh, Milton." Dorothy is disappointed. "Not over Gladys again."

He nods miserably.

"What are you doing to her?" Dorothy whispers.

The results of the CAT scan come in around eight in the morning. Negative. They wake Lilly up—she fell asleep on a gurney—to tell her.

"Thank God," she murmurs, but her eyes never open and when she talks, it sounds like her tongue is too big for her mouth.

"Just let her sleep," Dr. Fung says.

"What about the numbness?"

"I think she probably fell asleep in a funny position and panicked," he says. "She was already anxious about the migraines."

"So that's all that's wrong with her?" Milton's willing to buy it. She's been under stress lately, thanks to him.

"The CAT scan is negative," Dr. Fung says. "I'll give her a prescription for Zomig, for the headaches. She should be fine."

"And the slurring?" Dorothy says.

"She just needs sleep. A good long sleep."

By the time they hail a cab outside, Lilly is already in a deep sleep in her wheelchair. Milton has to carry her into the car, then into the elevator at home, and finally into bed.

Her limbs are heavy, limp. Her eyes are half open. Milton deposits her on the bed and pulls the duvet up.

"Lil? Do you still have a headache?"

No answer.

"Do you want a Zomig?"

"Let her sleep," Dorothy tells him. "Keep an eye on her."

Milton turns off the light and lies down beside Lilly. He hears his mother-in-law shuffling out of the room. "She'll be fine," he calls out to her. But his voice sounds desperate.

*I*t's noon when he wakes up. The first thing he does is lean over and check on Lilly. She's still asleep. He rolls her over to face him and her eyes flit open, but she doesn't seem to recognize him.

"Lil?"

He moves closer to her and realizes the bed is wet. He pulls down the duvet. "Dorothy!" he cries.

His mother-in-law comes running.

"She wet the bed." Panic now.

"Wake her up!" Dorothy tells him.

He tries shaking her, jostling her inert body around violently. Her head lolls from side to side but she doesn't stir. Her eyes are still open, but vacant. And then all of a sudden her body starts convulsing. White froth oozes from the corners of her mouth.

Dorothy is screaming in the background. She's on her knees, rocking back and forth. Milton lunges for the phone and dials 911. Everything happens in a blur. Some time passes—he doesn't know how much—while they wait for an ambulance. Lilly's body is still convulsing. He tries to hold her still, but it's futile. He rolls her onto her side and tries to grab hold of her tongue to keep her from choking on it, but it's like grabbing a slippery fish. That's when the two paramedics burst into the bedroom. They tell Milton and Dorothy to wait outside. They close the door. They're in there with Lilly and it feels like forever that Milton and Dorothy have to wait. Dorothy is inconsolable, frantic. Milton just feels in a daze.

If she dies, the last real conversation they had was about Gladys. The last words he uttered to his wife of almost forty years were about another woman.

"Why my Lilly?" Dorothy wails. "Why?"

"I was too wrapped up in my own . . ." His voice trails off. They aren't speaking to each other so much as just speaking out loud. Desperately hurling words out to fill the air.

Finally the paramedics come out, carrying Lilly through the apartment on a stretcher. There's an oxygen mask on her face; her body has stopped convulsing. Other than that, they know nothing.

"What happened?" Milton asks them, following behind.

"She had a seizure. We're taking her to St. Michael's. One of you can ride in the ambulance."

"You go," Milton says to Dorothy.

Alone in the house, he searches for his keys. At the last minute, he decides to bring a nightgown for Lilly, for when she wakes up. And her hairbrush and toothbrush, her makeup case. He shoves everything into a duffel bag.

Let her live, God, and I'll do better. But he isn't even sure he deserves a second chance.

Jessie

*S*he gets off the elevator in a trance and wanders around the ICU corridor looking for her family. She's vaguely aware of Allan behind her. They left the kids with the next-door neighbors. There isn't even space in her head right now to worry about them.

"Over there," Allan says, pointing to a small waiting room. "I see them."

Jessie finds them huddled together on two vinyl couches. They're all there. Milton, her grandmother, Josh, and Estelle. Erica is on a plane right now, flying in from New York.

She goes right to her father and puts her arms around him. "How is she?"

"Still in a coma."

Jessie quivers. Worrying about the worst possible things that can happen to your loved ones is nothing like actually living through those things. In a way, the imagining is worse. What surprises her now is that she is functioning. She is standing upright, speaking, walking, staying calm. She is managing.

"Do they know what happened?"

"They're not sure. It could be encephalitis, or a stroke."

"A stroke? But you said the CAT scan was negative—"

"It was. They don't know, Jess."

"There's bleeding in her brain," Estelle whimpers.

"What does that mean?"

"Brain damage."

"That's not for sure!" Gramma says.

"Could she die?" Jessie asks.

No one answers her.

"Could she die?" Jessie repeats, her voice near hysteria.

"We're waiting for the results of the MRI."

"I'm going to see her."

"I'll come with you," Estelle says.

And they walk hand in hand through the sliding glass doors of the ICU. Lilly is in the first bed on the right, attached to tubes and beeping machines. Her eyes are wide open, vacant. She doesn't see them standing over her.

Jessie turns away and starts to cry. To see Lilly lying here in a coma, hooked up to all these contraptions, makes her feel as fragile as she's ever felt in her life. If Lilly—her invincible, resilient mother—can wind up this way, then everything is precarious; no one is safe.

She turns back, half expecting Lilly to sit up, rip the tubes out of her mouth, and say, "Wait till the *yentas* in the Hadassah hear about this!"

"She doesn't see us," Jessie says.

"She goes in and out. I said something before and she smiled. But then she was gone again."

Jessie leans over her mother and touches her forehead. "Muh?"

Lilly's eyes move all over the ceiling. The giant tube in her mouth looks as though it's tearing her lips open.

"She's too young for this," Jessie laments.

"*We're* too young for this," Estelle says.

And Jessie knows exactly what she means. For the first time in their lives, they aren't under the protection of Lilly's omnipotent care.

*   *   *

*D*r. Blume shows up in the evening with the results of the MRI. "There's a clot in Lilly's sagittal vein," he says solemnly.

He's got wild white hair that reminds Jessie of the crazy scientist in *Back to the Future*. And yet she feels oddly reassured by him.

"What's the sagittal vein?" Milton asks.

"It's the central vein that runs between the parietal bones," Allan cuts in.

Jessie glares at him.

"What's happened," Dr. Blume continues, "is that she's had a very rare type of stroke. With a common stroke, the clot occurs in the artery. Lilly's clot is in the vein, which is why it didn't show up in the CAT scan."

"And the migraines?"

"Probably weren't migraines at all. The pain in her head was likely a result of the pressure from the clot. So when she was seizing yesterday, that's when the clot tore and bled."

They're all looking at each other, not understanding what any of this means.

"What's the prognosis?" Josh finally asks.

"We've put her on heparin, which is a blood thinner. Hopefully, that'll help to shrink the clot."

"Hopefully?"

"The next few days are critical. All we're hoping for at this point is that she stabilizes. We just want the bleeding to stop so that she doesn't deteriorate. That's what the heparin is for."

"So if she stays the same, that's a good sign?"

"A very good sign."

"Could she improve?" Milton pushes.

"Maybe ten percent of people with this kind of stroke actually improve right away. But it can happen."

"Will she walk again?" Jessie asks. "Or talk?"

"We'll have to wait to see the extent of the brain damage."

The words hang there heavily between them. *Brain damage*. Words that are totally incongruous with someone as capable and in control as Lilly.

*T*hey sit there in the waiting room for hours, until Milton finally sends them home sometime after midnight. He lies across one of the couches and covers himself up with his sweater and tells them to turn off the lights as they leave.

Jessie lets Allan pull her away. She can't even fathom how she's going to tend to her kids. But she needs sleep. She's like a zombie. She hates leaving her father here like this; hates the idea of Lilly in that ICU, alone.

Erica

*S*he tries uttering a prayer in her head—nothing too formal, nothing she would ever say out loud, but something sincere. *God, I'm not ready to lose Lilly. Let her live.*

She's sitting in a synagogue on Bathurst.

While Paul was showering this morning, she called Miriam in New York. She had to sneak into her father's office to do it, but she desperately needed to hear Miriam's voice. "What am I going to do?" she kept sobbing. "What am I going to do?"

"Have you tried praying?" Miriam asked her.

"No." She sniffled. "I've never really prayed before."

"Your mother's never had a stroke before either," she said. "Maybe you could go to a synagogue. That might help."

So here she is. What does one say to God anyway? *I've never called on You before, but now I'm in trouble. If You let my mother live, I promise to go to synagogue more often, to drop coins in the hands of the homeless when I pass them on the street, to never lie again. . . .*

What do you say to God when you're not even sure He exists? She is reminded of that book she read in her teens, *Are You There, God? It's Me, Margaret*. It was her favorite. She loved all those Judy Blume books. It occurs to her that she's never loved reading as much as she did back then. This is what she's thinking about, while Lilly lies in a coma at the hospital? This is her best effort at prayer?

Maybe her stumbling block is not so much a lack of faith as anger. She's angry with God. Why Lilly? Why *her?* Catastrophe is for other families. And why now, when her personal life is already more than she can handle? She hasn't told anyone about her little secret yet. She doesn't have the heart to lay her news on them right now. Doesn't have the courage either—even to tell Paul.

She closes her eyes. She remembers this one time when she was about four; there was a terrible blizzard and she was trapped inside her nursery school. All the children were sitting in the corridor, lined up against the wall, waiting for the snow to stop so they could be sent home on the bus. Most of the kids were crying; the teachers were trying to calm them down. Outside, it was a complete whiteout. Erica was terrified she'd be trapped in the school for days. She was whimpering alongside her classmates, wondering where her sisters were, if her parents were all right.

And then the front doors burst open and there was Lilly, wearing Milton's shiny silver Ski-Doo suit and covered head to foot in snow. She strode down the corridor in her giant white fur boots and took Erica in her arms. Then she bundled her up and led her away. Erica remembers looking back at all the other children and feeling sorry for them; she knew then what kind of mother she had. It made her feel elated and proud.

Lilly had brought a toboggan with her and she plopped Erica down on it and pulled her all the way home to safety. When they got inside, Lilly made her a hot chocolate with marshmallows. And then she left her with Gramma Dorothy and went back out to get Estelle and Jessie at the elementary school. That was Lilly.

Who would they all be without Lilly there to define them? How would they go on in her absence? Without her, achievement would be almost futile; the striving, the jostling for approval, even the rebellion would be pointless. Erica realizes guiltily that so much of what motivates her is this underlying mission to push Lilly's buttons, to rub her the wrong way, to goad her, and ultimately, to make her take notice. She sees now how powerful a presence Lilly still is in her life. And how integral. She is the mother in the shiny silver snowsuit dragging her babies through a blizzard to safety.

All of a sudden, Erica knows exactly what to pray for. She touches her stomach, which is still flat, and she utters one last silent prayer. *God, please let my child know her grandmother.*

Jessie

"*I*s this machine supposed to be beeping like that?" Dorothy asks, examining Lilly's IV bag of heparin.

Jessie looks up from her *People* magazine.

"It's fine," Milton says. "It's just the dosage changing."

"I'm going to get a nurse," Dorothy mumbles, and she leaves the room in search of some poor beleaguered nurse to pester.

"By the way," Milton says, "they think they know what's wrong with her blood. It's called— Hang on, I wrote it down." He pulls a Kleenex out of his pocket. The name is written in dark brown lipstick, probably from Lilly's purse. "Factor Five Leiden."

"Factor who?" Jessie says.

"She's missing a protein in her blood or something."

"That's what caused the stroke?"

"Her blood is thick and clotty. They think she's had it her whole life."

"I'd like to speak to a doctor about it," Jessie says.

"She's got about ten, so take your pick."

There's a rotating roster of doctors, each with his or her own theory about Lilly's blood. You never see the same one twice, never get two matching diagnoses or prognoses.

"You girls have to get your blood tested too," Milton says matter-of-factly. "It's hereditary."

Jessie feels the color drain from her face. "What do you mean?"

"You have to take a blood test," Milton says. "Your mother might have passed this bullshit down to you."

"What about my kids?" Jessie cries.

"Them too."

Jessie looks back and forth between her father and her mother—her mother who continues to lie there inert and comatose.

"At least you'll know," Milton rationalizes. "Isn't that something you'd want to know?"

She can't use her cell in the hospital so she rushes out of the room and heads down the corridor to a pay phone. She calls Allan at home.

"We might all have my mother's blood disease," she tells him hysterically. "Even the kids!"

"What blood disease?"

"I don't know. It's what caused my mother's clot. It's hereditary."

"So you'll get tested," he says. "Why panic before you even know?"

She wants to scream, *Don't you know me?* "But what if the kids have to go on blood thinners for the rest of their lives?"

"Jessie, get them tested first. Then we'll worry."

"You're not the one who'll have to schlep them back and forth to the hospital—"

"When are you coming home?" he interrupts.

"After supper."

"What am I supposed to make the kids?"

"Make them eggs or give them a can of soup."

This whole situation with Lilly has required a terrifying abdication of control on her part, both at work and at home;

she's had to close her eyes, take a breath, and hand over the reins to Auben and Allan. Even relinquishing control over the kids' menus has required great effort and even greater restraint.

"I'll take them to McDonald's," Allan says, sounding put out.

"Just open a goddamn can of soup," she says tightly. "They've never had McDonald's before. God knows what'll happen if they—"

"Listen, if you're not here, Jessie, you can't dictate what I feed my own children. Plenty of kids have eaten a Big Mac and survived."

"Fuck you," she snarls, and hangs up.

When she turns around, her grandmother is standing behind her, looking concerned.

"What's the matter?" Dorothy asks.

"Nothing."

"Did you fight with Allan?"

"That doesn't matter."

"It should, shouldn't it?"

"I'm worried about this thing with the blood," Jessie says. "What if I have it?"

"So you have it. Then you can prevent something bad from happening like it did to your mother."

"I know, but—"

"But nothing. Why don't you go home to your family? You've been here all day."

"I don't feel like going home."

"What kind of a thing is that to say?"

"Never mind."

"Is it because of Allan?"

"That's part of it."

"What's the other part?"

"The kids."

Her grandmother gives her a look, a blend of incomprehension and disdain. If they were at home, she knows she'd be called into the bathroom for some straightening out.

"I'm doing a bad job," Jessie tries to explain.

"A bad job?"

"Raising them. I'm not good at it. I'm . . . I don't know. Ruining them."

"Ruining them? You're their mother!"

"I'm a terrible mother."

"Stop talking like this. You're just upset about your mother. You're not rational."

"I'm never rational. I'm always worried. It's just so hard all the time—"

"Of course it's hard," Dorothy says harshly. "That's what motherhood is. You just do your best and that's all any mother can do."

"I've thought about leaving," Jessie confesses.

"Leaving Allan?"

"Leaving all of them." The words are out before she can stop herself. Right away she knows she's made a fatal error in judgment.

Dorothy scowls. Her whole body stiffens. "Don't talk like that," she hisses. "You're blessed to have those children."

"But it's the truth—"

"Don't you dare tell me you've even contemplated walking out on your own babies. Especially with your mother lying in there—" Dorothy's voice breaks and she stomps off down the corridor, toward Lilly's room.

Jessie wants to run after her grandmother and promise her that she would never actually do it; that these are just fleeting, meaningless doubts in her head. But she can't. She can't even pretend.

*O*utside, she takes a few gulps of fresh air before getting into her car. When she drives off, she has no clear idea where she's going to go. Not home, though. Not there.

Her hands are trembling on the wheel. She's still reeling. Why does she feel so embarrassed and ashamed? She hasn't done anything wrong. Not yet.

She shouldn't have said anything; it's not the sort of thing you tell people—especially not your grandmother! She would never tell anyone else, not friends or colleagues. Not Auben. People would look at her differently, treat her differently. They would think she was a monster. Her whole life she has sought respect, above everything. Why would she sabotage herself by revealing her darkest thoughts? And to her grandmother!

I'm evil. That's what she's thinking. Lilly could be paralyzed, could be a vegetable, could die . . . and here she is still thinking about herself. *Her* worries, *her* fears, *her* problems, *her* troubles.

She turns onto the DVP heading north and accelerates. And then the inevitable thought occurs to her: What if Lilly is already gone? What if she's gone *forever?*

A feeling of utter purposelessness washes over her. The quest for everything in her life has always somehow been for Lilly. It was Lilly's expectations that fueled her pursuit of good behavior, success, achievement. Again and again it had to be proven—to Lilly, to Gramma Dorothy, to the *yentas* in the Hadassah, to the entire world—that the Zarr girls were not just worthy, but impressive, enviable, remarkable. The world had to know that Lilly Cynamon had created three bright stars.

So much energy over the years, gone into impressing people. Showing off. Bragging and accumulating and gloating. Marrying a doctor, starting a business, having beautiful, healthy, well-adjusted, well-behaved children. It occurs to her now that maybe all those things were done merely to make an impression, and not because any of it was ever in her heart. It seems so ridiculous now to have constructed a life based on its admiration value. Because if anyone actually knew the truth about her—that she is a fraud—she would have the respect of precisely no one.

She reaches for her cell phone. Better at least call Allan and tell him she won't be home for a while. He should put the kids to bed. In the middle of dialing her number she stops, tosses the phone onto the other seat. What's to tell him? *Where am I going?*

She thinks about her mother lying in that hospital bed and she is suddenly overwhelmed with pity for her—not because Lilly's in a coma, but because of the life she's led right up until her coma. What must it have been like for Lilly to watch her husband fall in love with another woman—a more famous woman, a more talented woman, a *real* star—while she was home raising his children?

Jessie knows intuitively that there is still so much left for Lilly to prove—to herself, to Milton, to her daughters, to her mother. (Gramma Dorothy never could understand Lilly's pursuit of all things shallow; things like fame, recognition, money, glitz.) Lilly wasn't done yet. That kind of obsession is bottomless, Jessie knows. Jessie hasn't got there yet either. That's Lilly's legacy.

Jessie's on the 401 now, going east. Maybe she'll drive to

Montreal. Get a hotel room and stay there indefinitely. Hasn't she just been biding her time anyway, waiting for some reason to take off and abandon her family? She needs to get away and think, to be alone.

Why?

Her mother's had a stroke. Why the hell is she in her car driving away from her husband and her children? Shouldn't she be turning *to* them, for support?

Her entire life has been one long identity crisis—one which she has kept well hidden from the rest of the world. Until Skieth. Ever since the affair, she hasn't been able to keep her confusion on the inside, where it belongs. More than ever before, she began questioning everything about her life. Questioning her motives, her parenting skills, her ability to love. Her purpose. *Everything.* The possibility of losing Lilly is yet another catalyst in the ongoing dissolution of her persona.

Now she's thinking about Skieth, and now Lilly, and now her husband, and now her own children. . . . Her mind is racing. They're all there, jumbled together in her thoughts. Entwined how? What was it about Skieth that so quickly unraveled her world? Why *him?* She supposes it wasn't so much him, but her. She was ready for it to happen. Ready for anyone to come along and blow her wretched existence to bits.

And in their own way, each of them has accomplished just that. Skieth with his cock and his fleeting attention. Lilly with her stroke. There's no going back now. No going back to the old life.

But what can she take with her into the new one? Allan? The kids? OCD—the company *and* the mental illness? Or do they all need to go?

She turns off the highway. Exit 440. PORT OF NEWCASTLE. She follows the road to the water. She passes a harbor full of boats, a small beach. Who knew this was here? A little New England–style oasis off the 401. She continues along the lakeshore, hugging the water. The sun's almost down; it'll be dark any minute. But right now, the view is breathtaking. She winds around a bend in the road and the sandy beach turns into rocky cliffs that overlook Lake Ontario; it stretches out into oblivion like the ocean. The houses along the cliff are a mixture of styles—ostentatious mansions; log cabins; Tudor houses with winding driveways and fancy wrought-iron gates; farms; suburban bungalows. It doesn't know whether it's city or country. And yet it's magnificent. She parks the car and gets out in front of a darkened house—one of the bigger ones with an untended, overgrown lawn. A safe bet no one's there. She crosses the lawn, stepping through weeds and bush, till she comes to the edge of the cliff. There's a wooden rail fence, to keep people from falling one hundred feet onto the rocky beach below, and a rickety path of stairs leading down to the water. She starts going down the stairs, clutching tightly to the railing. It's almost pitch black now, except for a thin stream of light coming from the neighbor's porch.

She arrives on the beach sweaty and breathless, having fought her way down through jutting rocks and tall, prickly weeds. The lake is calm and still, rippling occasionally when there's a gust of wind. The sky is clear and she can see better now for the moonlight. She sits down on the sand to catch her breath. It occurs to her with a wild surge of fear that she is alone on a beach at night and if anyone suspicious is lurking around her, she'll have a hell of a trek back up the cliff to safety. She was fearless the whole time she was descending the staircase, her mind focused on nothing but getting down to the water. Her thoughts were free of the usual doomsday clutter and incessant warnings of danger. But now she's here and reality has set in. Still, she suppresses the urge to retreat. She stays put on the sand. She knows this is a "moment."

Jessie has not let herself have many "moments" in the past. Has never taken the time to just be. To sit quietly, alone and undisturbed, and . . . well, hokey as it seems, reflect. Meditate. Look at the water and the moon and smell the air. These are things Jessie Jaffe never does.

Her life may be in shambles, but that's up there, back up on that cliff. Back in reality. Down here, it's just blank. It's dark and scary and spectacular. A serial killer could be hiding behind one of those boulders, or the Loch Ness monster could rise up from the lake and swallow her whole, but goddamn it she's going to have this moment.

The surprising thing is, she comes to no earth-shattering conclusion about anything. No epiphany or nature-inspired revelation. She does not hear God speaking to her, offering any profound guidance. Instead she does the craziest thing.

She masturbates. Thinking of Skieth, she does it right there on the beach. And when she's finished, she feels at once elated and ashamed and relieved and still terrified to lose her mother; and of course she still has no idea what the hell to do about her life.

Estelle

*T*he phone rings first thing in the morning and she just lies there, resigned to the most catastrophic news. She had a feeling all night. She's been preparing herself for it: preparing herself for death. For Lilly's death.

"How does it feel when your mother dies?" she asked Josh in the middle of the night.

She could feel the tears sliding down his cheeks, but he didn't answer. He just held her. They held each other.

Now the phone. All her mental preparations fall away. Now that it's actually a possibility, now that it's tangible, she can't face it. *I can't do this,* she's thinking, as Josh grabs the phone. *Can't lose my mother.*

"Hi, Milt." Even Josh is prepared. There's a readiness in his voice.

Estelle closes her eyes. She feels herself floating up, away from herself. From reality. So here it is. This is what it feels like. Her first tragedy.

"She did what?" Josh says. He breaks into a smile.

Estelle sits up. "What? What is it?"

"I can't believe it." Josh is laughing now.

Estelle starts to laugh. Her bones go limp with relief. "What?" she cries.

"She kicked her leg in the air," Josh says. "Your mother moved her leg."

"She's out of the coma?"

"We'll be right there, Milt." Josh hangs up and flops down on the bed. "She's attentive, she's awake. She recognized Milton and Erica. She's responding to the doctor."

"What does Dr. Blume say?"

"He says we can be very pleased. It's more than what they were hoping for. She's improved on the heparin."

Estelle jumps out of bed. "That's my mother," she says, laughing. "Only ten percent improve later on and of course Lilly is one of them. Why wouldn't she be?"

"*L*ook," Lilly is saying, as Estelle comes into the room. She's pointing at something in the air. "Look at the fireflies."

Estelle gets choked up just hearing her mother's voice again. She rushes over to the bed, and her father and grandmother move aside. She crouches over Lilly. "Hi, Muh," she says tenderly. She kisses Lilly's face and smoothes her damp hair. She feels a great surge of relief and love and it really hits home that she might never have heard Lilly's voice again.

"Hi, Bean," Lilly croaks. The big tube is out of her mouth, but her voice is still scratchy and weak. "Can you see the fireflies?"

"You're hallucinating, Lil," Milton assures her.

"I see them," Lilly argues. "They're all over."

"How do you feel, Muh?"

"I had a caesar."

"A seizure?"

"Caesar," she repeats laboriously.

"I know. It was a stroke."

Lilly's eyes well up and she's crying. "I can't feel my arm."

"It'll come back," Dorothy tells her.

Erica and Jessie burst into the room then. They surround Lilly, smothering her with kisses, crying and laughing and stroking her.

"I've lost weight," Lilly boasts.

And for a moment there is this fleeting hope that she is exactly the same as before, her personality intact; that she is unchanged by the stroke and will be up and about, running their lives as always.

But then she starts to cry again and in a childlike voice, she whimpers, "I can't feel my arm."

And Estelle knows that this is not the same Lilly at all. For the first time ever, insomuch as Estelle can remember, Lilly is terrifyingly vulnerable.

A few days later, Lilly is transferred to the Traumatic Brain Injury Clinic at Sunnybrook. Ever since the stroke, their lives have all been put on hold. Routines have been interrupted; sleeping and eating have become vague necessities. Their world is the surreal microcosm of the hospital; their single priority is Lilly's recovery. Estelle wants, more than anything, for her mother to just get back to her old self. It somehow feels essential to their family's survival that Lilly should get back on her feet as quickly as possible and reclaim her role as the strong, meddling, critical beacon she's always been. Estelle is sure it's what they all want—Milton, Jessie, Erica— because without Lilly in that role, they are all disoriented. As a family, they've lost their bearings.

Estelle stops at the Neuro Café and buys herself a hazelnut coffee. She pays Kathleen, the cashier, and heads back to Lilly's private room, wishing that she didn't know Kathleen's name. When you know the cafeteria staff personally, you've been spending too much time in the hospital.

Selfish as it is, she wants her mother well and on track to a full recovery so she can get back to L.A. She is anxious to get away from all this—the hospital, her family, Lilly's sickness. She is just waiting for confirmation that her mother will officially be "okay," so that life can seamlessly return to its former version of normal.

The most recent MRI shows that the clot in Lilly's head has shrunk considerably. This is great news. Her legs are moving and, although she has trouble remembering a lot of words, her speech is improving daily—all of which bodes well for her recovery.

But the doctors are still concerned about her blood. They are now relatively certain that she's got a rare blood disease. The hematology team is still doing extensive testing, drawing her blood regularly in the hopes of confirming that the disease was in fact what caused her stroke. And she is still hallucinating and having miniseizures. She'll be feeling fine and then all of a sudden her leg will go numb and her tongue will feel thick and she isn't able to speak. The seizures last about half an hour before the numbness subsides and she can talk again.

The prognosis at this point is still murky. Her right arm and hand are completely paralyzed. The doctors aren't sure she will ever get the feeling back. The longer the paralysis lasts, the dimmer are her chances. She'll also have to be weaned off heparin and put onto Coumadin, another blood thinner which she will have to take for the rest of her life. (A pain in the ass, she complained.)

In light of all that, Estelle knows it is still premature to be planning her escape. She feels a bit ashamed of herself, and yet all she wants is for Lilly to be her old self. She wants everything to be as it was, and fast.

"Did you get one for me?" Josh asks her, ogling the cup of coffee in her hand.

"Oh. I forgot. Sorry."

She sits down beside him in the lounge. "You can have a sip of mine," she says, handing it to him.

"You okay?" Josh asks her tenderly.

And for no reason at all, she wants to flick him on the forehead. Just gets an urge to give him a flick right in his concerned face, the way her father used to do on her leg when she was little. He called it giving "fadoopers."

"What are you thinking about?" he asks.

Shut up, please. She would give anything for him to stop talking.

"Eh, Beany-Baby? What's up?"

His tenderness, his sympathy, it's too fucking much sometimes. She wants to be alone. She hasn't been alone in so long; hasn't been able to sort out her feelings about Lilly's stroke, about her upcoming wedding, about having to move back to Toronto. It's hard with Josh here, coddling her and caressing her and Beany-Babying her to death. He is a smotherer. A kind, loving, doting smotherer.

"I'm fine," she says.

"You sure? You seem really distant. You can talk to me, Beany. I know you've been through a lot—"

"Lilly's going to be fine," she says, not wanting to endure his relentless compassion for the rest of the day.

"But she'll never be the same," he says gravely. "I think you have to face that."

"I don't want to talk about it."

"The Lilly you knew is no longer—"

She reaches over and flicks him on the forehead.

"Ouch!" he says indignantly.

"I said I don't want to talk about it."

"So you flick me?"

"I felt like it."

"I know you're feeling a lot of stress and sadness right now, but I'm only trying to help."

"You're trying to help me the way you think I need help, not the way I want to be helped."

"I'm doing my best."

"Don't *do* anything."

The person she wishes were sitting beside her right now is Peri. Peri would say something funny. He would talk about movies. He would insult her and be obnoxious and keep her laughing. He would be working on a script and asking her for ideas. He would ask her for zingers. He's always asking her for zingers—funny one-liners at which, he says, she is a master.

He would not let her dwell or wallow or "discuss it." The problem with Josh is he takes himself too seriously. Takes everything too seriously. She is irritated that he's her fiancé right now. Just this minute, she wishes she were alone.

"I think we should think about leaving soon."

"The hospital?"

"Toronto."

"Already? Lilly's still—"

"I don't mean today. But we have a lot to do before we move back here. A ton of shit. And once I'm back, I'll have plenty of time to care for my mother."

"You don't have to justify it to me. I understand perfectly that you have to put yourself first sometimes."

"You would," she mutters.

"What's that supposed to mean?"

"That's just what you do. You always put yourself first."

"*I* do?"

"Your career. Your magazine."

"I know you're fragile right now, Beany, so I'm going to let that slide."

"Such a martyr," she says. She's out for blood. And Josh is so easy to decimate.

He pulls his book out of his knapsack—*Meditation for Dummies*—and starts pretending to read, even though Estelle can tell he's really thinking of a million angry things to hurl back at her. She puts her headphones on to tune him out.

"Besides," he says, jerking the headset off her. "We're moving back to Toronto for *your* job too! Not just for my career!"

She replaces the earphones and ignores him. He turns back to his book.

After a while, she sneaks a sidelong glance at Josh and is overwhelmed with pity. All he's done is adore her! And she is so rotten and unlovable that she doesn't trust his love. He's probably the only man on earth who would put up with her shtick and all she can do in return is resent him.

"I'm sorry," she murmurs, using her irresistible baby voice.

He puts down his book and smiles. "I know. I know." He wraps his arm around her shoulders and presses her face to his chest. She almost expects him to say, *There, there.*

"You've been through a lot," he soothes. "And I'm the closest person to you. It's par for the course that you're going to take it out on me a little. It's natural."

"You're allowed to be mad at me," she tells him.

"You're too cute to stay mad at."

She's always wanted to be cute, to have people tell her she is cute. No one ever did. But hearing Josh say it doesn't make her feel cute. It makes her feel evil and guilty. Like he dispenses these things too easily, without warrant. The thing about Josh is that he gives in on just about everything—except for the most important things. The things she wants most, like to stay in L.A.

"One day," Josh says, "when Lilly is walking again and you've made peace with each other—"

"Peace?" Obviously they're going to talk about it now or else Josh will harass her for the next five hours. "What do you mean, made peace?"

"You and Lilly have to resolve your differences. This was a wake-up call. You almost lost her."

"You're right," Estelle says. "Do you think we could get a flight out next Saturday?"

Erica

"*I*sn't it amazing," Jessie says, "how rarely we get to do this?"

The three of them are having dinner together at Grazie, their old haunt from back when they were all still living in Toronto. It used to be their Sunday night hangout; they'd gossip and drink Morettis and pig out—Erica and Estelle were usually nursing hangovers. The pasta is great and the place is always jammed. Tonight it's especially noisy and they have to practically yell across the table to be heard.

"I can't believe how long it's been," Estelle says. "I mean, just the three of us like this. No husbands, no fiancés . . ."

"No kids!" Jessie adds.

Erica is moving her food around on her plate, hoping neither of them has noticed that she hasn't touched a single agnolotti. She's been able to eat small meals throughout the day but she can't keep anything down at night.

"When do you think Mom will be able to go home?" Estelle asks them.

"I hope they don't plan on releasing her until she stops having seizures," Jessie says. "It's too much for Daddy to handle."

"I'm thinking of going back to L.A. next week," Estelle announces. "Do you think that's okay?"

Jessie and Erica are quiet. They look at each other.

"What?" Estelle says.

"Nothing."

"I'm moving back here soon," she explains. "But I have to take care of stuff in L.A."

"I'm always the one in this position," Jessie complains. "I'm always left here to deal with the family crap by myself."

"You resent us for living in different cities," Estelle accuses. "But we made lives for ourselves outside Toronto. You made your own choices."

"I'm not saying you shouldn't have moved away," Jessie says. "But you should be here *now*. Mom is still in the hospital, for Chrissake."

"Can we not argue tonight?" Erica says. "We never get to do this anymore."

"You know, Jess, Mom isn't your responsibility," Estelle continues. "Neither is Dad. You're not obligated to fix everyone's lives and take care of everyone. You just *think* you are."

Jessie shakes her head. "Is that how you feel about Mom?" she accuses. "That it's not our obligation to take care of her?"

"It's not."

"Even if it's not, don't you *want* to?" Jessie asks her. "Don't you feel it in your heart?"

"You're the one who just referred to this situation as 'family crap.'"

"It is family crap! It's fucking awful that our mother has brain damage and that she's paralyzed. But I wouldn't dream of not being here for her now, regardless of whether or not it's my obligation. It would just be a hell of a lot easier if the two of you felt the same way."

The waiter passes by and Estelle orders another Moretti. "You sure you don't want one, Erica?"

Erica shakes her head.

"I know you think I'm selfish," Estelle goes on. "But I just don't feel the way you do, Jessie. I feel like I have responsibilities back in L.A. A job to finish. Loose ends to tie up. Rent to pay. That's where my life is and I can't stay here indefinitely. I mean, if the situation were reversed—if your job and your family were in another city—what would you do?"

"I have kids. It's different."

"Oh. So if I had kids, it would be okay for me to leave?"

"Can we drop this?" Erica pleads.

"It would be understandable, at least," Jessie says. "It would be somewhat logical."

"Then maybe I just don't have the same connection with Mom that you do," Estelle says. "Maybe if she'd been as supportive and accepting of me as she's always been of you, maybe then I'd 'feel it in my heart' to stay."

"This is a really appropriate time for Mom-bashing."

"I'm not Mom-bashing," Estelle argues. "I'm stating a fact. It's how I feel."

"I'm going to the bathroom," Erica says, and gets up from her chair. Neither of them even looks at her.

She goes downstairs and locks herself in a stall. She pees for what must be the hundredth time today and then checks the toilet paper for spotting. She's been doing this ever since she read on the Internet about ectopic pregnancy.

When she's finished, she splashes cool water on her face and leans wearily against the sink. So much for a joyous reunion with her sisters. Frankly, she'd rather be having a Brazilian wax than refereeing their fight. Between the unbearably loud acoustics, the incessant bickering, and the smell of tomato sauce, it's all she can do to keep from barfing. She wonders if it will be like this for the next eight months, and, more to the point, if it will even be worth it. Motherhood is not exactly something she's ever been sure of. It wasn't on her "must do" list, that's for sure. At least, not for the immediate future. She's ashamed of her ambivalence, but she intends to make up for it by being a damn good mother. This baby will never, ever know about her problem with commitment. The way she sees it, she's on this path now and, for once in her life, she doesn't have the option to be indecisive about it, or to back out.

When she gets back upstairs, Jessie and Estelle are both eating in silence.

Erica sits down and has a sip of water. Water is good. Drinking it, splashing it on her face, bathing in it, whatever. It may be the only thing that gets her through this pregnancy.

"What do you think, Erica?" Estelle asks her.

"About what?"

"About me going back to L.A."

"I don't want to get involved," Erica says. She pushes her plate away; the tomato smell is making her queasy again.

"I just want to know what you think," Estelle presses.

"I think you both have valid points," Erica says judiciously.

Estelle rolls her eyes. "God forbid you would ever take a stance."

"That is my stance," Erica fumes. "I think you should wait till Mom's out of the hospital at least, but I understand that you have to get back. I have to get back, too. I've got a job and a boyfriend and an apartment. I can't stay indefinitely either."

"Why aren't you eating?" Jessie asks her, noticing for the first time the untouched plate of agnolotti.

"Or drinking," Estelle adds.

"Are you pregnant?" Jessie jokes.

Erica freezes. She was going to tell them anyway, but not like this. When she doesn't answer, they both drop their forks and gape at her.

"Oh my God," Jessie breathes.

"Are you fucking pregnant?" Estelle cries.

"I was going to tell you tonight. . . ."

"You're pregnant?"

"Eight weeks."

"Are you getting married?" Jessie asks.

"Probably."

"Probably?"

"I haven't told Paul yet."

"You haven't told Paul you're pregnant?" they both scream.

"It's complicated."

"*What's* complicated? You live with him, you're pregnant. I assume you were trying—"

"That's the thing," Erica says. "It was sort of an accident. We always use condoms."

"I *knew* condoms weren't safe!" Estelle cries. "I'm going back on the pill."

"Doesn't Paul want kids?" Jessie asks.

"I'm not sure."

"You've never talked about it before?"

"He might have mentioned once or twice that he's not the fatherly type."

"Oy."

Erica decides it's best not to bring the Mitchell factor into the conversation. And Mitchell *is* still a factor; being pregnant with Paul's baby hasn't changed that. It hasn't extinguished how she feels about him (which, admittedly, is somewhat problematic). She's called him just about every night since she's been in Toronto, at least as many times as she's called Paul. She doesn't know which is making her feel worse: that Paul doesn't know about the pregnancy, or that Mitchell doesn't know.

Right before she missed her period, she was as uncertain about her future with Paul as she's ever been. In fact, she was gearing herself up to move out of his apartment, not necessarily to be with Mitchell, but to take some time to think about things. She thought it would be best to be alone for a while, to see how she felt without Paul; to see what might possibly unfold with Mitchell.

The pregnancy is a real glitch in her plans. She thinks there is some moral obligation to stay with the father of her child. Leaving Paul now—no matter how confused she is about their relationship—seems utterly selfish at this point. And yet Mitchell is on her mind. She hasn't found the willingness yet to give him up. Not even for her child.

"Why isn't Paul here with you, anyway?" Jessie asks. "Shouldn't he have come with you?"

"I told you. I didn't want to have to worry about him while I was at the hospital all day."

"He's not a dog, Erica. It's not like you would have had to feed him or take him for walks."

"He doesn't get how it works with families."

"Just like Estelle," Jessie mutters.

"God, you sound more and more like Mummy every day," Estelle gibes.

"But Paul can learn to be a family person," Erica says hopefully.

"He'd better."

Erica smiles weakly.

"Are you happy?" Estelle asks her. "Is this what you want?"

"It's growing on me. Or should I say 'in me'? I mean, it was a bit of a shock, let's be honest. But there's no question that I'm keeping it."

Jessie doesn't look persuaded. Her expression is full of everything she knows about motherhood but doesn't seem to have the heart to pass on right now. But that worried look on her face is warning enough. It makes Erica feel anxious.

"I think this is perfect timing," Estelle says. "It's exactly what Mom needs to hear right now. What better motivation to get well than a new grandchild?"

"I think it's too soon," Jessie says. "It'll overwhelm her."

"I'd better tell Paul first anyway," Erica points out.

"Well," Estelle says brightly, "once this is out, no one will even notice I'm gone."

Jessie

She comes through the door feeling elated. Her doctor called the office today with the results of her blood test and she doesn't have Factor Five or Factor Three, or any blood disease, for that matter—none of them do. But right away Allan is on her, shattering her rare good mood. He's standing in the foyer, waving his arms in the air.

"Where were you today?" he wants to know. "Marsha from the day care was trying to reach you all morning. Your cell phone was off—"

"I had a seminar," she says wearily. "I told you that. What happened?"

"Ilana had an accident and I had to leave work to pick her up—"

"What do you mean, *an accident?*" The panic, the tightness in her chest.

Levi steps out of the kitchen then. "She fell off the teeter-totter," he says. "Her lip was bleeding and there's a bump on her head."

"Where is she?"

"Watching TV in our bed," Allan says angrily. "She's fine. The point is, I had to rush home in the middle of the day and . . ."

Jessie's already running up the stairs, not listening to him. She finds Ilana sprawled on her tummy, watching *Chitty*

Chitty Bang Bang. She looks so tiny in their king-size bed. Jessie goes over to her and scoops her into her arms. "Poor baby," she coos. "Show me your lip."

Ilana thrusts out her lower lip, revealing a bloody red cut inside. "Daddy gived me a Popthicle."

"Did that make it feel better?"

Ilana nods. "Marsha thays I have a egg in my head."

Jessie runs her fingers over the bump on her forehead. Nothing too alarming. It's turning a pale bluish color. "You know you're not supposed to go on the teeter-totter," she says.

"Now I weally know why."

Jessie kisses the blue lump on her head and leaves her alone with *Chitty*.

Downstairs, Levi and Allan are waiting for her. "You have to be more accessible," Allan starts. "You have to have a pager on you in case something like this happens again."

"Daddy had patients," Levi informs her. "He had to cancel all his appointments."

"Go upstairs and watch the movie with your sister," Jessie says impatiently.

"I've seen it, like, fifty times already."

"When this whole thing started with the organizing," Allan continues, "we agreed it wouldn't interfere with the time you spend with the kids. I gave in on the day care thing, but if you're not even going to be available for an emergency—"

"Some couples compromise," Jessie says. "Some husbands help."

Levi is looking worriedly back and forth between them.

"I've been helping plenty," Allan tells her. "A lot more than you lately."

"My mother had a stroke."

"That's getting thin."

She wants to smack him for doing this in front of Levi.

"It could have been serious," he says. "What if Ilana had needed to go to the hospital?"

"You would have taken her," Jessie says logically.

"I don't like being taken for granted. I have a very busy practice."

She looks down at Levi, who is watching her expectantly. "I'd better start dinner," she says stiffly.

"Daddy said we could have Kraft dinner," Levi says in a smug, Allan-like tone.

"Then Daddy can make it." She turns around and walks out of the house.

It's bad enough having Allan lecture her, but now he's got Levi on his side. God help her if Levi turns into a mini version of her husband. She used to think she was the worst thing that could happen to her kids. Now she knows better.

She sits down on her front stoop, knowing what she's got to do. That night she drove out to Newcastle, that's when she decided. Or in some strange way, a decision was unconsciously made for her. Sitting on that beach, nothing especially revelatory came to her. No decision hit her. And yet as she was driving back to Toronto, she knew. She felt inexplicably relieved. A way out was in reach, though it was still murky in her mind, undeveloped.

Since then, she's been strategizing. Plotting. Nothing monumental, just mostly preparing herself. At first she was waiting for Lilly to get out of the hospital. Then it was getting the kids started at camp. But now the time is right. She thinks tonight will be the night. She is hating Allan just the right amount. More to the point, she is hating her life just the right amount.

She isn't even afraid. For the first time in ages, she feels clearheaded and determined. Calm. What happened to Ilana today is the clincher. Their baby has a swollen lip and a bruised skull, and all Allan can think about is that his time was compromised. Ilana's accident was nothing but an inconvenience for him. He'll have to learn how to cope better with these kinds of incidents. Soon he'll have no one to turn to.

*W*hen she goes back inside, the three of them are sitting at the dining room table eating Kraft dinners out of Tupperware containers. "My God, Allan," she says. "Couldn't you have at least given them bowls?"

"They're all dirty."

"Ever hear of running the dishwasher? All you have to do is turn it on."

"I was taking care of the kids," he says. "Now you want me to clean the house too?"

"I do it every day."

"Apparently you don't."

Seething, she goes upstairs and changes into a sweat suit. She'd like to have a bath, but Allan will probably throw a fit if she's not "available" to tend to the kids after supper. Instead, she goes from room to room, collecting all the dirty clothes off the floor and tossing them into the hamper. She shoves a load of whites into the washing machine and then goes back downstairs.

The three of them are in front of the TV, watching *The Addams Family*. Their crusty orange Tupperware containers are still sitting on the table, waiting for her to clear them and wash them.

Wordlessly, she stacks them and carries them into the kitchen, then dumps them in the sink and washes them by hand. The dishwasher's too full. She runs the dishwasher, wipes the counter, sweeps. She notices a message on the blackboard above the phone. *Treasure Guerra,* it says, and below it there's a phone number in Allan's illegible doctor's handwriting.

She pokes her face out of the kitchen. "When did Treasure call?"

"This afternoon," he says. "Who is she?"

She ignores him, goes back inside the kitchen, and makes the phone call.

*W*hen the kids are finally asleep—which is close to nine by the time she's done bathing them, brushing their teeth, nagging, pulling them off each other, getting them water, chasing them up and down the stairs, reading to them, refilling their water, scratching their backs, and flicking on their night-lights—she goes into the kitchen and boils water for tea. She feels surprisingly centered.

"Can you bring me a bowl of ice cream?" Allan calls out from the den.

She dumps two scoops of Baskin-Robbins Mint Chip into one of the hot clean bowls from the dishwasher and carries it out to him. "Thanks," he says, happy now that their roles have been restored.

"I have to talk to you," she says to him over her shoulder as she returns to the kitchen for her tea.

"After *Cold Squad.*"

She checks the clock on the oven. Ten minutes to nine. She sits down at the breakfast counter with her tea and goes over what she's going to say to him. She rehearses it in her head. It will be ugly; she's sure of it. For him, it's coming out of nowhere. Totally unexpected.

"All right!" he calls out a few minutes later. "It's over."

She goes out to the den and sits down opposite him on the love seat. She sets her tea down on the coffee table.

"*West Wing*'s on in five minutes," he mentions. "What is it?"

"Well . . ." The rehearsed speech of moments ago escapes her now. Looking at him, with his slippered feet propped up on the table and the *TV Guide* in his lap, she suddenly doesn't know how to tell him. She sees him not as the husband she has fallen out of love with—if ever she was in love—but as a guy with a comfortable routine whose world is about to be upheaved. She knows how much he hates change; doesn't adapt well to disruptions or new situations. She doesn't feel sorry for him, though; that would be too generous. But there's no vindictiveness anymore. Not like this afternoon.

"I don't know how . . ." She's nervous. "I actually rehearsed what to say, but . . ."

He looks interested now. He lowers the volume on the TV.

"It's obvious we, or, well, I haven't been, um, happy for some time," she stammers. "We haven't been happy together, I suppose. . . ."

"What're you talking about?"

"Come on, Allan. We're fighting constantly over my business—"

"When we got married we had the same vision of the future," he reminds her. "We wanted the same things. That's why I married you."

"Meaning what?"

"Meaning we agreed you would be a stay-at-home mom. We were both against day care and nannies. We were on the same page."

"People change."

"I didn't."

"You weren't the one staying home every day."

"I think I've been pretty supportive," he says. "I let you start organizing your friends' homes—"

"*Let* me?"

"You know what I mean. I thought it was a good hobby for you, as long as you were home when the kids got back from school. And then with Ilana, I even gave in on day care."

"You've been making my life a living hell for five years!" She feels some of the old rage bubble up. "Making me feel guilty, never helping out, keeping score."

"But you didn't hold up your end of the bargain."

"What bargain?"

He sighs, exasperated. "That you would be home raising our children."

"I have been, Allan. I have been."

"Not today you weren't, when Ilana needed you."

"Look, let's not have this conversation again. It's got nothing to do with what I'm telling you."

"What are you telling me?"

For an instant she considers sparing him, but then she decides it's necessary—for her and for Allan—to be truthful. About everything.

"During the winter when I was doing that bar—remember it? Ooze?"

"Yeah."

"I met someone—"

"Met someone?"

"It was the owner, the venture capitalist guy."

"The one you were always talking about? That kid?"

"He's my age."

Allan takes off his glasses and rubs his eye sockets.

"Anyway," she continues, "I sort of . . ."

How to put it? *Fell in love? Fell in lust? Temporarily lost my mind?*

"Sort of what?" he presses edgily.

"Oh God," she groans. "Allan—"

"Are you saying you're in love with someone else? Are you having an affair?"

"No. Not anymore."

"Not *anymore?*" he breathes, obviously stunned.

"I slept with him once."

Allan leaps off the couch and starts pacing in circles. "You slept with someone?"

She nods.

"Did you . . . ? Christ. You *slept* with someone? Did he have a rubber on?"

"Yes."

"The panic attacks," he says, remembering. "All through the spring you were having those panic attacks. They were because of this, weren't they? You were feeling guilty!"

More nodding. She doesn't need to tell him about the AIDS scare. That would just give *him* an AIDS scare. He's prone to neuroses too.

"I can't . . . I don't know . . ." He shakes his head, runs a hand through his desperately overdue-for-a-cut hair. "This is really fucking unbelievable," he mutters.

And then the wildness in his eyes gives way to defeat; and for a moment, she sees a vulnerability he has never exposed before. It almost makes her want to take him in her arms.

"It wasn't exactly an affair," she clarifies. "It was just one time."

"Oh. Oh. Just one time. Well, okay, then. No problem. Just the once? I can live with that. Sure."

"Allan—"

"This is a deal breaker," he says angrily. "You know that, right? I want no part of this marriage anymore and I don't care how much you fucking grovel. I've put up with a lot over the years—all your goddamn anxieties and phobias and psychoses. Your job. I've been a fucking saint! I'm the only man on earth who would tolerate your bullshit. And this is how you repay me?"

"You're right, you've been patient. You've put up with a lot. But I was unhappy, Allan. *Am* unhappy."

"Hey, so you went out and screwed some asshole. Why not?" He picks up one of Ilana's Barbies and whips it across the room. It lands in a plant, with the yellow hair cascading down the terra-cotta pot. "Did you think about the consequences, Jessie? How about your kids? Remember them? But hey, thanks for telling me now, six months after the fact."

"It just happened," she says. "It was totally out of character for me, but I've got to tell you, it changed me. It woke me up."

"Woke you up from what?"

"I don't know. Numbness. Resignation."

"Don't you understand, Jessie, that you are the source of your own misery? It's not me or the kids or your family. It's you. It's what's in your head. You're sick. You always have been."

"Maybe you're right," she says. "I don't dispute that. But the way my life is now, it doesn't help. Don't you think I have a right to try to make myself happy?"

"By screwing strangers?"

"No."

"What, then? Why couldn't you make yourself happy and still be faithful to me?"

"Because you're part of the problem, Allan! And not because you don't want me to work or because you don't help out around the house, but because I don't—"

"Don't what?"

"I don't think I love you," she blurts. "I don't think I would have chosen you if I'd had a choice."

"Was there a gun to your head when I proposed?"

"I was twenty-one, for Chrissake. You were the first one to come along and make the offer. My parents were so pleased, and it was comforting to know I'd be taken care of, and you were safe and comfortable."

"Thanks . . ."

"Allan, the truth is—and I'm not proud of this! I'm ashamed of myself, believe me—the God's honest truth is that I married you for status and security. But underneath all that, and despite all the praise from my family, there was this emptiness. I was never in love with you. I thought it was just me—"

"It *is* you. Believe me, it's *all* you!"

"No," she says. "I thought it was, but it wasn't. I thought I was incapable of—I don't know—loving. Or at least of feeling anything passionately other than fear. And then with Skieth—"

"Skieth!" He spits out the name.

"I realized that I do have it in me," she says. "Longings and passion and emotions. I never gave myself a chance to become anything other than what I thought I was supposed to be. A good student, a good daughter, a good wife, a good mother . . . I never knew myself, Allan. I still don't. I have no idea."

"Did you get this from that 'Remembering Your Spirit' shit on *Oprah*?"

Ignoring his gibe, she continues. "My whole life has been about trying to feel safe," she explains. "Everything I do, it's to feel safe. And you know what? I never, ever do. No matter what, I never feel safe. So maybe I should try something different and start doing things that make me happy."

"Like screwing bartenders."

"Like being alone."

"If you tell me you need to find yourself, I'm going to puke."

"I want to know who I'd be if I hadn't married the wrong man and had kids too young. That's all. I need to know how I would have turned out if I hadn't been following so many goddamn rules."

"And what do you want to do with the kids? Send them back?"

"Don't be a smart-ass," she says. "I know I haven't always been a great mother. And if you want to know the truth, I've thought about running away from all of you. Up until recently, I thought they'd be better off without me."

"That remains to be seen," he mutters.

"But I know that if I'm not going through my life like a robot, I can be a better mother to them. If I ever felt anything close to fulfillment, I could do better. I'm not saying I won't be afraid anymore or that I won't be overprotective and—"

"Controlling."

"But I know I can enjoy them more. I just want to enjoy them, Allan. That's all I want. The way a mother should."

"And I have to be out of the picture for that?"

"I have to be happy for that. And our marriage does not make me happy."

"It's been a real barrel of laughs for me too, let me tell you."

"I know I haven't been easy to live with—"

"That's an understatement. The irony is, in return for having invested the past decade of my life with a paranoid, controlling nutcase, I'm the one being tossed out."

"You're the one who just said you wanted no part of this marriage," she reminds him. "I thought the cheating was a 'deal breaker.'"

"It is. But I expected some resistance."

She looks away from him. She may not love him, but the end of a marriage is a sad place. Especially when there are children.

"I'll go stay with Doug until I can find an apartment," he says, almost too easily.

Doug is his newly divorced friend. He's also got two kids under ten. They'll be able to commiserate at least. Maybe Allan is relieved, too. His ego is battered, but he's probably grateful to be getting out.

He leaves the room then, and she can hear him climbing the stairs. Sitting by herself, she's astounded it's over. How relatively easy it was. She's limp with relief. She knew he wouldn't hassle her over the kids, suggest fighting for custody or anything like that. He wouldn't want them full time. He hates the daily chores of parenting—the bathing and tooth-brushing and disciplining; he hates carpooling, and dragging them to karate and gymnastics and skating; he hates the birthday parties and the playdates and the homework. He likes to feed them Kraft dinner and ice cream and watch TV with them, snuggle with them before bed, take them for a drive in his car on Sundays. But he would never sign on for full custody.

Now that it's actually happening—now that he's really leaving—it occurs to her how long she has been waiting for this moment.

*L*ater that night, when Allan is gone—with two suitcases full of clothes, his tennis gear, the small TV from the bedroom, his laptop, his old ratty pillow, and his favorite jersey sheets—Jessie goes upstairs and lifts Ilana out of bed. She takes her into her own bedroom and plunks her into the king-size bed. She rubs her nose against Ilana's skin and it smells like butterscotch. Then she goes to Levi's room and lifts him up—with more difficulty—and carries him into her bed. He doesn't stir, not even when she almost drops him on the floor.

She puts on her nightgown and brushes her teeth and then snuggles into bed, right in the middle of her two babies. Ilana's little mouth is open slightly, her warm breath on the back of Jessie's neck. Levi is snoring softly, nothing disruptive, just enough to lull Jessie to sleep.

Erica

*T*hai food, a bubble bath, and a foot massage. That was the preamble to her announcement. Now they're sprawled on the bed about to watch *The Way We Were* and she's just going to squeeze in her news before he presses play on the VCR.

"Love?" she says.

"Hmm?"

"I have something to tell you."

"You don't feel like going to the Hamptons this weekend."

"Well, no. I don't. But that's not what I have to tell you."

Paul rolls over on his side and caresses her cheek. "What is it, love?"

She takes a breath. In her rehearsals, she just came right out with it. *We're having a baby! Exclamation point!* But now that she's actually doing it, she decides on a more meandering approach.

"Love, we've never really discussed children," she says.

"Yes, we have. I told you I don't want any."

Bad start.

"No, you didn't," she says, persevering. "You told me you weren't the fatherly type."

"I'm not the fatherly type because I don't *want* kids. See how that works?"

"What if *I* do?"

"Do you?"

"Yes."

"I find that surprising."

"Why?"

He shrugs. "You've never really mentioned it. You don't particularly like kids. I mean, you always complain about them when we're picnicking in the park."

"Only when their balls and kites land in our food."

"You hate when there are children beside us in the theater."

"Because they talk all through the movie. But we wouldn't bring *our* kids to the movies with us."

"You hate it when babies cry on the plane."

"Who doesn't? Anyway, all that doesn't mean I don't want my own kids. Maybe I just hate other people's kids."

Paul smiles. "We're both too selfish for children. Look at what a great life we have. Take-out dinners in the tub, weekends in the Hamptons . . . All that would be ruined if we had kids. And I'd never be able to get any writing done."

"I'm not selfish," Erica says petulantly.

"Of course you are. You're still a child yourself."

"I'm almost thirty!"

"You don't even know what you want to do with your life," Paul reminds her.

His arguments are frighteningly convincing.

"I want to be a mother," she says.

"Let's not ruin this perfect night. We'll talk about it another time. Next year maybe."

"All right. But we'll be having this conversation with our six-month-old baby."

For a split second she thinks he hasn't heard her. Rather, she thinks he hasn't understood her, because he happily flops onto his back and presses play on the VCR. But then he sits up and jerks his head around to look at her.

"What do you mean, 'with our six-month-old . . .'?" He can't even bring himself to utter the word "baby."

"I'm pregnant."

"Oh fuck."

"That's not exactly the reaction I was hoping for."

"But we use rubbers!" he wails, sounding like a two-year-old. He reaches into the bedside-table drawer and pulls out a handful of the useless condoms. "What the fuck is the point of these things?" he rants. And then he starts throwing them across the room. "I should have had that vasectomy—"

"Paul! Stop it! You're making me feel awful." She starts to cry. "This is happening. We're having a baby. So just . . . let's make the best of it, okay?"

"The best of it? What about my writing?"

"Plenty of writers have kids. Christ."

"Children are not in my plan," he whimpers. "They never were. You knew that, Erica. And I didn't think they were in yours, either."

"Maybe not for right now, but I never led you to believe I didn't want a family down the road."

"You've never known what the hell you wanted!" he accuses. "You still don't."

"I do. I want to be a mother."

"How far along are you?"

"Why?" she asks suspiciously. "You're not thinking . . ."

"Let's talk about all our options. That's all I'm asking."

She reaches for a Kleenex and daubs at her eyes. This isn't how she envisioned it. She knew it wouldn't be a fairy tale, not with Paul, but she didn't think it would be this bad.

"Are you . . . Do you want to get married?" he asks her. "Is that the next thing you're going to tell me?"

She shrugs. "I wasn't going to force you."

He reaches for her and pulls her into his arms. "I'm sorry," he says. "I'm sorry. This isn't your fault. It's . . . it's the condom company's fault."

"Paul—"

"I just need some time to process this. I love you. I don't want you to think I don't love you. But can you give me some time?"

"Time for what? To decide if you're going to leave me? Or if you want to be in our baby's life?"

He doesn't answer her. Instead, he jumps out of bed and starts putting his clothes on.

"Where are you going?" she asks him.

"I'm going to the Hamptons."

"How?"

"I don't know, Erica. How do people get to the Hamptons? I'll take the fucking jitney."

"You're just going to leave me here alone all weekend?"

"You didn't want to come anyway."

"That's not the point, is it?"

"I need to be away from here."

"You mean away from me."

"I need to think. I need to process this."

"What the fuck is there to 'process'? I'm pregnant. It's not a trigonometry problem."

"I'll be at Amory's," he says, sliding his feet into a pair of Birkenstocks. "The number's on my desk. Or in a drawer or—"

"Don't worry," she sobs. "I won't call. I wouldn't want to disrupt you while you're *processing*."

He grabs his travel bag from the closet and shoves some clothes into it. Then he comes over to her side of the bed and tries to hug her. She pushes him away.

"I love you," he says. "This isn't about me not loving you, okay?"

"I can see how much you love me."

He sighs. "I'm sorry. I'll be back Monday."

And then he leaves.

She ends up staying in bed for the entire weekend. Paul doesn't call. Not even once. She doesn't even bother to turn on the TV. Doesn't bother to shower or eat, or answer calls. Every time the phone rings, she checks the call-display hoping it will be Paul, and then she falls back into bed, devastated.

All she can think about is that she's going to be a single mother. How will she support herself, let alone a kid? She'll have to go on welfare. Or worse, she'll have to move back home and live with her parents and raise her child while nursing Lilly. . . .

Or she could show up on Mitchell's doorstep, tell him she's pregnant with Paul's baby, and see if he's still interested in her anyway. . . .

There was a moment, right when she first found out she was pregnant, where she felt this great buoying surge of hope: the hope that everyone would finally be pleased with her, or proud of her. The hope that at last she had accomplished something worthwhile. But one by one, with each person she tells, that hope disintegrates.

She had told her parents when Lilly was still in the hospital. Gramma Dorothy wanted to know if Paul was going to convert. That was her first question. Milton wanted to know when the wedding would be. He said if they did it quickly enough, maybe the baby would never know it was illegitimate. Lilly just looked confused. Then she cried like a baby. "That child will never know what I was like before the stroke! My new grandchild will never know the old Lilly!" She was inconsolable. No one seemed especially happy about Erica being pregnant. And there was definitely a collective concern over what other people would think.

In the end, the circumstances of her pregnancy—that she isn't married, that the baby's father isn't Jewish, that her mother just had a stroke—have snuffed out any possibility of pride and joy and acceptance from her family. It will not be the way it was for Jessie. When Jessie made her announcement, Milton and Lilly and Gramma Dorothy all wept with such pure and open delight. That moment resonated with Erica; secretly, she aspired to have a moment of her own like that one day. She wanted to feel the way Jessie must have felt, to feel what it must be like to make Lilly and Milton happy. There were no glitches on Jessie's path. There never are.

Erica's mistake was in thinking *this time* it would be enough to just give them a new grandchild; she should have known there would be much more involved. Scavenging for their approval is always a more complicated proposition than she ever anticipates. Why should this time be any different? A grandchild alone is *not* enough. In the end, she has still managed to mangle everything and come up short.

*O*n Sunday afternoon, in the midst of her self-pity fest, Paul comes home. He dumps his bag on the floor and crawls into bed with her. He's got a suntan, which bothers her. But she lets him hold her. She needs it.

"Have you been in here all weekend?" he asks her.

She nods, sniffling.

"I had a terrible weekend too," he tells her.

"You have a suntan and you smell like Scotch. It couldn't have been that bad."

"I didn't come to any profound decision," he says. "I thought I would come back here and be able to tell you that I just can't do it, or that I'm fully on board."

"Is that supposed to make me feel relieved?"

"I am sure about one thing," he says. "I don't want to lose you."

"But I'm an 'us' now."

"I know. I wish I could sit here and tell you I'm excited about the prospect of a baby. Hell, I wish I could *lie* to you and tell you I'm excited. But I'm not. I still don't want children. I still haven't wrapped my head around the idea. I don't want my life turned upside down and my routines disrupted. I want my friends to be able to come over and smoke pot—"

"All right already! I get it."

"I don't know how the hell I'm going to make the adjustment. Amory says maybe when I hold it for the first time—"

"Paul. Please. Just get to your point. What are you saying?"

"Fucked if I know."

Erica moves away from him.

"I missed you," he says. "I had to come back today."

"You're fucking with my head now."

"I guess I'm saying okay to this," he says, sounding thoroughly unconvinced. "If I'm not willing to lose you, then I have to . . . to just live with this whole baby thing."

Erica lies there for a moment, not sure if she's supposed to be grateful and happy with his lukewarm commitment to her and "this whole baby thing." Is this the way it happens with other couples? Or would another man—a better man—embrace the idea of starting a family?

"I'm scared," he says. And something inside her softens.

"I'm scared too," she says.

Estelle

*E*stelle spins around in front of her mirror. In the last couple of weeks, she has managed to lose about fifteen pounds, thanks mostly to Allan's green tea diet. She looks fabulous, especially in this outfit. A silk cardigan over a low-cut red camisole, Gianfranco Ferre pants—black and shiny with slightly flared legs—and red leather boots with spiked heels. Wow. She feels grown up, sophisticated. She bought all of it for the premiere tonight. It cost a fortune—Josh was mortified when she forked over her Visa card. "We could buy a Jetta with that money," he remarked. That's his new thing. He wants a car when they're back in Toronto.

Still, it was worth it. She's so used to wearing second-hand clothes, stuff with holes and patches and the patchouli smells from other people, she never realized how good it feels to dress in style. And having lost a bit of weight, she was able to squeeze into a size ten! ("Squeeze" meaning she won't be able to breathe until after the premiere.)

Josh has decided not to go with her. It's not his scene. He's proud of her, but not enough to subject himself to an L.A. movie premiere. At first Estelle was indignant. "Then don't ask me to go to any boring literary readings with you," she told him. "That's not my scene!"

But after she thought about it for a while, she realized it was a blessing. Now Peri's going instead. He'll know who all the famous people are and will be able to keep up with her running commentary.

The movie is now called *Ground Strokes,* a title that's a little more tasteful than its former incarnation. All she can think about is seeing her name up there on the screen: Editor, Estelle Zarr. But her joy is laced with something bitter too, because it may be the *last* time she sees her name up on the big screen.

Peri was appalled to learn that she's moving back to Toronto right at the moment when her career is taking off. When she told him, he slapped her cheek—not hard, more like an Alexis Carrington slap. All drama.

"Are you nuts?" he bellowed. She was up in his apartment, sneaking a cigarette and an episode of *Road Rules*. Josh was at the pier, doing whatever it is he does down there. Cycling or inline skating—one of his tight, shiny shorts activities. It was hot and sunny, a perfect day for hibernating inside with the TV. "You can't leave," Peri told her. "Not now!"

"I have to." She was already feeling miserable about it and didn't need Peri reinforcing her doubts.

"You have to? Excuse me?"

"Josh has a great opportunity there."

"How great?"

"He's going to coedit a literary magazine—"

Peri's mouth agape. "And what's the great opportunity?"

"Peri, please. Josh loves that sort of thing. It's perfect for him."

"Let me just make sure I've got the facts straight, okay? You moved out here to edit feature films. You toiled around doing trailers and commercials while waiting for a break, and then you finally landed a gig on a mainstream Armando Abruzzi movie, and instead of using that opportunity to launch your career, you're moving back to the Great White North so your boyfriend can coedit a fucking literary rag?"

"My fiancé."

"Is this the nineteenth century, Estelle? Can he not coedit his little magazine via computer?"

"He hates L.A."

"I thought he loved it. You said he loved it here. Hell, isn't he out enjoying the boardwalk as we speak?"

"He likes that part, but everything else he hates. He hates my world. You know, the gross-out movies and how money is always the bottom line—"

"Oh, please."

"—and how everywhere you go everyone is an actor or an actress. He says it's not reality."

"So what?" Peri argued. "What's so good about reality anyway? Estelle, you love it here. You love that everyone is an actor. This is where you belong."

"I belong with Josh."

"Estelle, come on. Be rational for a second. Take off the love blinders. Do you know how hard it is to get as far as you've gotten in this town? I could understand it if— No, there's no way I could ever understand this. He's making you leave L.A. so he can edit a fucking literary magazine that probably earns about four bucks a year."

"It's not about the money."

"How subversive."

"Anyway, I got a great job in Toronto, Peri. A great job."

"Oh yeah? Doing what? Editing *The Beachcombers 2005*?" (She was the one who told him about *The Beachcombers,* one time when she was ridiculing the Canadian entertainment industry. Who knew he'd use it against her one day?)

"Editing my own show for MuchMusic," she informed him smugly. *"D-TV."*

"Congratulations," he said, "on your giant step backward."

"When and if you ever fall in love," she countered, "you'll understand why I'm doing this. Besides, I'll be close to my mother."

"The same mother who's inspired countless nervous breakdowns and fits of self-hatred?"

"She's got brain damage now. She's easier to be around. Besides," she tried to explain, "I'm making a concession for the man I love." Gag. Even as the words were coming out, she wanted to puke.

"A concession is switching your brand of toothpaste," he said. "Not abandoning a potentially amazing career."

"Look, Per, he proposed. That doesn't happen to me every day, okay?"

She takes a step closer to the mirror and adjusts her boobs in their new underwire bra—a minimizer—and then steps back again, admiring herself.

"Wow," Josh says, coming up behind her. "You look sensational."

He kisses her on the neck, then cups one of her minimized breasts in his hand. "I don't know if I want you schmoozing with all those smarmy actors."

"Then you should come," she says, secretly hoping he won't change his mind and take her up on it.

"You know I'm proud of you," he tells her. "I just can't stomach that environment. I don't fit in."

"I don't fit in either."

"Yes, you do. You fit in everywhere. You just don't realize it."

A sweet thing to say. Maybe he's right. She turns around and kisses him on the mouth. In her spiked heels, she's almost as tall as he is.

"I love you," he says.

"Me too."

When he's holding her like this, looking at her so adoringly—like she's the best thing on earth—she knows she's making the right decision. Marrying him is a far smarter choice than staying in the plastic factory. Acceptance in L.A. would always be shifty and precarious, dangerous. But Josh's acceptance is a given. It's unconditional.

*W*hen the credits roll at the end of the movie, Peri whips out his JoyCam and takes a picture of Estelle's name on the screen. Who cares if the movie was a disaster? And that everyone laughed in the wrong places and then applauded because it was over. So what? That's her name up there on the screen and that's all that matters.

"Do you think this may have ruined my career?" she asks Peri.

"It was bad," he admits. "But the editing was great."

"Really?"

"Absolutely."

She knew during the fine-cutting that *Ground Strokes* was pure garbage—though it will probably appeal to its target audience of toilet-humor junkies—but she still feels a tinge of humiliation at having helped create something so awful. "Should I be ashamed?" she asks Peri.

He snaps her picture and says, "Most definitely."

They bump into Armando in the lobby. He's beaming proudly, as though he's just unveiled a masterpiece. "Good job," he tells her. "You're coming to the party, right?"

And then before she can answer, he disappears into a cluster of important-looking people wearing sunglasses and baseball caps with the *Ground Strokes* logo.

"He seems happy," Peri says, shouting above the symphony of ringing cell phones. "Did he just see the same movie we did?"

"What does he care? He knows he's going to make a shitload of money."

They take a cab to Armando's fortress in Bel Air. It's tucked away in one of those gated communities, which they have to get to via endless winding roads, traveling deeper and deeper up into the hills. "Where do you buy groceries around here?" Estelle mutters.

The house is on a cul-de-sac, shrouded by palm trees. It's a Spanish Colonial with white stucco exterior and a mottled, orange-tiled roof. At the door, she's greeted by a bouncer wearing tennis whites and a *Ground Strokes* baseball cap.

"I'm the editor," she announces proudly.

"Invitation, please."

She searches through her purse for the invitation—a tennis ball with writing on it—and hands it over, feeling extremely important.

Inside, everything is white stucco walls and dark wood floors, arched windows with plantation shutters, impossibly high ceilings, and fans twirling overhead. In the middle of the foyer, there's a curving double-sided staircase in dark wood. They have to cross the kitchen—which is painted tomato red with white wood moldings—to get to the river-rock patio, where people are milling around by the pool. The caterers are circulating with trays of sushi and skewered shrimp and champagne. Estelle grabs one of everything.

"Look," Peri says, pointing to a brightly lit tennis court where people are playing.

"This is so Hollywood."

"It is Hollywood. Oh my God," Peri whispers, nudging her. "Isn't that the guy who played Matt on *Beverly Hills 90210*?"

"I think you're right."

"I heard he's going to be in Armando's next movie."

"Poor him."

They down their champagne and grab two more glasses as the waiter sails past. "Shit, where's the shrimp lady?"

"Over there, by the hot tub."

"Is that the guy who plays twins on *All My Children*?" Estelle says, pointing.

"I think so. Should I take a Polaroid?"

"No, you idiot. I'm the editor. Don't embarrass me."

"All right. I'm going to schmooze," Peri says. "It's my one chance to find a backer."

"Estelle!" It's Armando, coming toward her with a young, slick guy in tow. "Estelle, this is Russell. Russell, Estelle."

The guy is attractive in an arrogant, self-important sort of way. All confidence and attitude, with a cell phone and a pager dangling from his holster and mirrored Armani shades perched on his head.

"She's my editor," Armando explains, and then he's yanked away by someone else—Don Johnson? Is it possible?—and she's left alone with Mr. Suave.

"Congratulations," he says.

"Oh, thanks."

"I can't say I liked the movie—in fact, Armando produces some of the worst shit in Hollywood—but your editing stood out. I loved that pixelation sequence where the girl was trying on all those different outfits. Did you choose the music?"

"Yeah, for that particular sequence I did."

"Super. It was just super. And that freeze-frame of the guy with the tennis ball in his mouth? That was good stuff."

"Really? You think so?"

"Listen, I'm working on something right now—not quite on the scale of an Armando movie, just your average low-budget indie, but I'm looking for an editor—"

"Russell!"

They both turn around and Peri is there, holding out his hand.

"Peri. How are you, man?"

"Estelle," Peri says, excited. "This is Russell Hirsch."

"Armando already introduced us," Russell tells him.

Russell Hirsch! She wants to touch him! Just press her fingers to his face and make sure she isn't dreaming. Russell Hirsch, standing here on this river-rock patio telling her he loved her pixelation sequence.

"Actually, you have my demo reel," she tells him.

"I do?"

"I gave it to you last fall," Peri explains, cutting in. "When you were shooting *Dazed in Atlanta*?"

"Perfect," Russell says. "I'll take a look at it this week, Estelle, and get in touch with you."

"Actually, I'm . . ." She is about to tell him she's moving back to Toronto, but she decides not to. She decides to just see what will happen. Maybe MuchMusic would let her take off for a few weeks. She could stay with Peri while she's editing Russell's movie. Why close doors?

"I was just talking to the girl from *Felicity*," Peri gushes.

"Keri Russell?" she cries. "Keri Russell's here?"

"No, the other one. The one who sings. I can't remember her name."

"Estelle—"

She feels a tug on the sleeve of her cardigan and turns around to find Astrid Blansky standing behind her.

"Astrid, hi."

"How are you?"

"Pretty damn good right now. I guess I owe this all to you."

"Probably," Astrid says. "Although the movie really sucked. Obviously."

Same old Astrid.

"But I liked that part with the Bran Van 3000 song," she says. "When they're in the disco. You have great instincts for the music."

Estelle can see Russell and Peri drifting off toward the hot tub. She wants to go with them but she owes Astrid a bit more small talk. She can at least tell a few lies to make it look like she's got something fantabulous on the horizon; like she's booked solid with creative, industry-related "projects."

"So what's next?" Astrid asks her.

"Um, well. I'm going to be doing some TV. And I've got this idea for a screenplay—"

"Sally tells me you're engaged," she remarks. There's no mistaking the disapproval in her voice.

"Yup. I'm getting married."

"So you're leaving L.A.?"

"At the end of the summer."

"Strange timing, isn't it?" Astrid goes on. "I mean, with your career just getting going."

"I can come back, though. There's always freelance. It's 2004. . . ."

Astrid smiles patronizingly. "It's not the same as being here," she says. "You know that. You could direct one day, you know. I think you're making a mistake."

Estelle almost says, *So do I,* but she stops herself. She won't give Astrid Blansky the satisfaction. And yet, not voicing the thought doesn't make it any less true. Maybe she's known it all along.

She looks around and the whole scene feels like a dream—the clinking glasses, the laughter, the melodic hum of schmoozing. It's glossy; it's a thrill. And she's part of the dream, not outside of it, the way she usually is. She feels totally in her element; there's a sense that she is absolutely in the right place and doesn't have to claw her way in or grovel for acceptance. Sure, she's a bit starstruck and she'd love to get an autograph or two, but she belongs here as much as any of these people. She's the editor. And the truth is, she is more attached to *this* than to a lifetime back home with Josh. She loves Josh, but not enough. Not quite enough.

Maybe it's not so noble, this Hollywood microcosm. Maybe it's all a sexy, dangerous illusion. But right now, she fucking loves it. Loves everything about it. And there's this voice in her head that keeps telling her anything is possible.

Erica

She lingers awhile on Buckingham Road, admiring the Victorian mansions with their grand porches, their turrets and bay windows, their immaculately groomed lawns. The South Historic District near Prospect Park is one of her favorite neighborhoods in New York. She'd love to raise her family in Brooklyn, but Paul would never leave the Upper West Side. "Soul-murdering" was the last thing he had to say about it.

She turns off Church Avenue, feeling hungry. Maybe she'll grab a kosher falafel on her way back. Most of the day, she fluctuates between nausea and hunger; when one subsides, the other kicks in. Other women keep assuring her it will pass after the third month, but she doesn't think she'll ever feel herself again.

Miriam is waiting for her outside on the lawn. She's sitting under the sign—EAST 23RD STREET SYNAGOGUE OF FLATBUSH—eating an apple. Erica sits down beside her on the grass.

"So what's this big news?" Miriam asks her. "Can I take a guess?"

"Go ahead."

"You've decided to become a rabbi."

Erica laughs. And then it occurs to her that Miriam might not be joking. "No. That's not it," she says. "Not yet, anyway."

"What, then?"

"I'm pregnant."

Miriam looks genuinely surprised. It's obviously not what she was expecting. "It's Paul's?" she asks.

"Of course it's Paul's."

"Oh."

"You look disappointed."

Miriam sighs. "Does Mitchell know?"

"No."

"I mean, I'm happy for you," Miriam says quickly. "It's just that Mitchell will be crushed. He thinks . . ."

"What?"

"He thinks you guys are meant for each other."

Erica looks away.

"You were so uncertain about Paul," Miriam says. "Did you plan this together?"

Erica shakes her head, somewhat embarrassed.

"Do you think Paul will convert?"

Erica laughs again. "I doubt it. I mean, he joked about it once, when I was lighting the Shabbat candles. But I don't think he was serious."

"What about the baby?"

"I guess the baby will be Jewish, since I'm Jewish."

Miriam is quiet for a moment. Finally she says, "A Jewish marriage requires two Jews. Halacha doesn't recognize intermarriage, you know."

"What's halacha?"

"Jewish law."

"But Reform Jews have a much more liberal attitude," Erica says.

"Our generation has to keep Judaism alive, Erica. We're already an endangered species. Do you know that more than sixty percent of Jews in America have married non-Jews? Thirty years ago, it was only six percent. All these interfaith marriages are diluting the Jewish faith."

"I don't think that way," Erica says. "I understand what you're saying, but I've never been religious."

"I don't mean to sound judgmental or harsh," Miriam says, her voice softening. "It's just that I see your faith blossoming, Erica. I see a spark there. You may not have been raised with a strong faith, but you've sought it out. Why do you think you come here to talk with me so often? Why do you think you keep lighting the candles on Shabbat? It's growing inside you. You're connecting to something meaningful. That's why it's so important that you keep honoring your roots."

"I will. I'll never give up Shabbat. And I want my child to learn Hebrew and celebrate the Jewish holidays—"

"But Paul isn't Jewish. This is what you want for your child?" Miriam challenges. "A Jewish mother and a Christian father? What does your family think?"

"They're so preoccupied with my mother's recovery right now, I think my baby's religion is the last thing on their minds. Maybe before the stroke they would have made a fuss about Paul not converting—"

"So it's definite that he's not converting?"

"I haven't brought it up. I'm not even sure we're going to get married yet."

"Why not?"

"Paul's having a hard enough time dealing with my pregnancy. He never wanted kids, so . . . this is a lot for him right now. I'm not going to start pressuring him about marriage."

Miriam reaches for Erica's hand. "Are you sure about Paul?" she asks urgently. "Are you sure he's the man you want to spend the rest of your life with?"

"I sort of don't feel like I have a choice anymore."

"You always have a choice. You have a choice to marry a Jew. You have a choice to raise a Jewish child. You have a choice to spend your life with the right man. Maybe my brother is that man."

"But don't you think God's made the choice for me?" Erica says. "All these months I've been torn between Mitchell and Paul. And then, just when I decided to leave Paul, I got pregnant with his baby. Maybe that's God's way of telling me I belong with Paul."

"Or maybe God is testing you. Maybe He's put an obstacle in your path so that you have to be really committed to your choice. Isn't it possible that you're supposed to take a real stance here?"

"I'm confused."

"You're confused a lot of the time, Erica. And I don't say that to put you down. It's just that maybe you don't listen for the answers that are inside you. Some decisions can't be made intellectually. You can't pick a husband with your head. What is your heart telling you? Who do you *love,* Erica? Which one of them do you love?"

"Is this your Torah?" Erica asks her, pointing to a battered blue book on the grass.

"You're changing the subject," Miriam says. "But, no. It's my Tanakh. It's got the five books of the Torah inside, as well as the Nevi'im and the Ketuvim."

"I envy you," Erica says. "I sometimes wish I'd had a path to follow, you know? A simple path that I never doubted."

"You think I never doubted my path?" she cries. "I had doubts every step of the way. I remember right before I gave my very first sermon, I was positive I'd made a colossal mistake about the rabbinate. I didn't think I'd be able to live up to what's required of a spiritual leader. I felt like I had nothing of value to share, and that no one in my congregation would be interested in what I had to say. Then my mentor said to me, 'They don't have to applaud you, Miriam. They only have to learn from you.' And he was right. A path or a calling isn't decided by the approval you're going to get from it. It's just what comes naturally to you. It's whatever piques your interest."

"I need to tell Mitchell about this baby," Erica says. "Don't I?"

"He wouldn't care that it wasn't his. I mean, if you should decide . . ."

"You just want me in your family so you can recruit me into the rabbinate."

Miriam smiles. "I'll keep trying anyway."

*I*t is only after she leaves Miriam, after she buys herself a falafel and while walking aimlessly up and down Church Street, that she suddenly has a revelation. The revelation is this: her life could be simple if she'd let it be simple. She overcomplicates everything. She looks for nuances and glitches and loopholes in every situation; she needs a hundred people to validate every decision she makes; she searches for complexities where there are none. She is so busy searching for some kind of path—which she imagines will be all lit up with flares—that she has never paid attention to the most basic truths about who and what she is. And yet this is what she knows about herself right now: she needs some kind of creative outlet, she needs a strong spiritual connection, and she's going to be a mother. Those are three tangible things that she has already committed to and about which she has never wavered. The outcome of each one—whether she is a writer or an art curator or a photographer; whether she lights candles on the Sabbath or becomes a practicing Orthodox; whether she winds up with this man or that man—those will all fall into place as long as she's got her bearings. Spirituality, creativity, motherhood; those are her bearings. That is the infamous, elusive path she has been seeking. The rest is none of her business.

At the end of all this philosophizing, she finds herself in a cab, pulling up in front of Mitchell's office. He greets her coldly; yet she knows him. He's protecting himself. She glances at his tattoo, his symbolic shield. Who would have thought he'd need it to defend himself against *her?*

They go out onto 53rd Street. "How's your mother?" he asks her.

"She's out of the hospital. They kept her a bit longer because she had a bad cough, but she's home now. She has an eye infection. They think it's a reaction to all the blood thinners. She goes to rehab every day, so hopefully she'll be able to move her right arm soon. She's depressed, too, which is, I guess, normal—"

Erica can hear herself rambling but she can't seem to make herself stop. Talking about Lilly is a way to fill the air without saying what she is supposed to be saying.

"And how are *you?*" Mitchell asks her.

"I'm good. What about you?"

"Listen, this is awkward. Can you . . . Why are you here? I mean, have you come to any decisions since the last time we spoke?"

When she doesn't answer, he nods. "I get it."

"Mitch—"

"You're staying with Paul—"

"Mitch, I'm pregnant."

Mitchell stops cold. He looks like he just got a football in the gut. "You're pregnant?"

"It's like I was saying to Miriam, it's as though God is telling me to stay—"

"You told Miriam before you told me?"

"I guess she's like . . . my rabbi. I tell her everything these days."

"This is quite a turn of events," he mutters.

"Mitch, don't you think this is God's way of telling me to stay with Paul? Because if I was supposed to be with you—"

"Don't use God as a fucking excuse," he says icily. "Don't do that. It's a cop-out."

"I'm not using God. It's what I think. I was planning to move out of Paul's place—"

"And so now you're going to stay because you're pregnant? That's a terrible reason to stay with someone you don't want to be with."

"I never said I didn't want to be with him."

"How does Paul feel about having a baby?"

Erica ignores the question.

"That good, huh?"

"Mitch, I don't need you to be angry with me right now. . . ."

"Fuck you," he says. "You were going to leave Paul and now you're not? That's what you came here to tell me? *That* pisses me off, Erica."

"It's true I was leaving Paul," she says. "But I never said I was leaving him for you."

"That would have happened eventually," he says.

"That's pretty smug."

"No, it's not. It's just something I knew. I was so sure about us. Shit," he says, flinging up his arms. "You know why I'm angry with you? I'm angry that it took so damn little to make you chicken out of leaving what's safe and easy."

"So little?" she cries. "I'm pregnant with his child! You think that's some small, petty little reason for me to want to stay and make it work with him?"

"I think it's a disaster waiting to happen. You think a baby is going to make your relationship with him work all of a sudden? You think this baby is going to make you love him more? Make him less selfish? Less of a prick—"

"He's not a prick."

"Do you really think raising a child with a man you were on the verge of leaving is the best choice here?"

"What are my choices, then?"

"I'm your best choice."

"I can't just . . ." She doesn't bother finishing. She was going to say that she can't just let another man raise Paul's child, but in her heart of hearts, she knows Paul would be relieved. He'd probably pack her bags and send her off and count himself lucky to have sidestepped fatherhood. He'd miss her; there's no doubt in her mind about that. He'd probably cry on the couch for a few weeks with a bottle of Scotch between his legs. But when that subsided he'd find himself another student to shack up with and be damn grateful his selfish existence could go on as before.

And that's when she suddenly realizes something else about herself: she wants more for herself than a man who is just barely, grudgingly willing to be in her baby's life. She wants enthusiasm, excitement; she wants commitment.

"You're right," she says, stunned at how long it's taken her to get to this.

"I am?"

"This baby won't make it better between me and Paul," she realizes out loud. "It'll just get worse. Paul doesn't want to be a father. He was practically sick when I told him. He fled. He went to the Hamptons and drank himself into a stupor. And then he came back and told me he'd thought about it all weekend and he *still* didn't want a baby! But then he said he would just deal with it and . . . and that was enough for me! Can you believe that? I almost let that be enough!"

"You wanted it to be enough."

"The way he reacted when I told him . . ." she vents. "I was shattered. I felt like such a piece of shit. As though I'd done it on purpose to trap him or something! And I actually felt bad."

"Not to bring this moment back to me, but—"

"I need time, Mitch. I'm not leaving Paul so I can just bounce over to someone else. This isn't about choosing you over him. I'm going to move into Tiala's loft. She made the offer before my mother's stroke. . . ."

"I'm not in a rush."

"But there may be an opening down the road," she concedes.

"I'm not going to wait forever," he warns. "A few years, tops. Maybe a decade, if you're lucky."

She laughs. "I have to go home and pack now," she says. "Before I change my mind."

But even as she hails the cab, she knows there's no going back on this decision. She turns around and leans out the window. Mitchell is standing on the curb, watching her. She smiles at him, not quite sure when she'll see him again. He doesn't smile back.

Milton

*H*e finds Lilly in the den, with her wedding binder spread open in front of her. Her bifocals are perched on the tip of her nose. "What are you doing?" he asks apprehensively, not sure how she'll respond to him. Never knowing these days.

"I can't do it anymore," she murmurs.

"What?"

"The planning."

"That's okay. Estelle understands."

Lilly closes the binder. "I'm letting her down," she says. "Letting everyone down."

There's still a childlike quality to her voice—not just the slowness of her speech or the groping for words, but even the tone. It's gentler, more quizzical and uncertain. Her whole personality is like that. As though the damaged part of her brain contained everything that was abrasive, hard. There's no edge to her now. The girls keep saying she's "cute." And it's true. This frightened, helpless, disoriented woman who is so far away from the old Lilly is somehow endearing. Her neediness makes him feel important.

"Where's your mother?" he asks her.

"Swimming."

He lingers there for a moment, not sure if he should press his luck. This is the most by way of conversation he's managed to elicit in a long time. She's so depressed these days, he doesn't know how to act around her.

The therapist warned him there would be a depression. The loss of her independence, the sense of her own mortality, all that. He thought he was up to the challenge, but he never imagined it would be so difficult. That she'd be so utterly despondent. And aside from the stroke, there's everything else. The unresolved stuff about Gladys, Jessie and Allan separating, Erica getting pregnant with the German professor's baby. It's been one blow after another. In light of all of it, he thought maybe she would let him comfort her.

But she hasn't. She's withdrawn completely. He's tried everything—clowning, bumping into doors, telling jokes. But he can't penetrate her self-defeat. She hates going to rehab and having to squeeze balls all day and ride the stationary bike; hates having to do math homework and keep a journal of what she does each day. *Today Milton made me soop with crackers. It was good but he put too much salt. Jessie my dauter came over and we played Scrabble. Milton won. We went for a walk and I tripped on the sidewalk.*

What saddens him most is her listlessness. It scares him, too, watching his Lilly give up. He just wants her to smile. Aches for it.

"Where's your sling?" he asks her. "You're supposed to wear it around the house."

"In our room."

He goes into the bedroom and retrieves her sling. When he comes back, he goes over to her and puts it around her shoulder, gently easing her paralyzed arm inside it.

"I thought maybe we could choose a song," he says.

"For what?"

"For our duet. You know, for the kids' wedding."

"I can't sing," she says angrily.

"There's nothing wrong with your voice."

"Don't be a schmuck."

"You can do it."

She shakes her head, petulant. "I can't even talk properly," she says. And then she starts to cry.

"Don't cry, Lil," he says. "It's nothing to cry over." He hesitates to hold her; she'd probably push him away.

"I could have been as good as Gladys," she says. "And as successful. I just needed more time. I was still young. And now it's too late for everything. . . ."

"You were meant to be a mother, Lilly. It's what you were meant for."

He didn't used to believe in that stuff, in things that were meant to be. Destiny and God's plans and all that. Sure, he always curses God when he finds a parking ticket on his windshield or when the Canadiens lose in the play-offs. But lately he's started to believe that something is at work in their lives, something beyond his grasp and comprehension.

"You know, I did have one song in mind," he says.

"What?" she asks, wiping under her nose.

He clears his throat and starts singing to her, a song he used to sing back in the days when he was courting her. It was always her favorite, an old Judy Garland tune, "You Made Me Love You."

She looks up at him. Her face is suddenly full of recognition. Possibly nostalgia. He continues singing, his voice getting louder and more confident as he dances his way over to her. He holds out his hand, which she takes, and lets him pull her up from the couch. He pulls her close to him and they start dancing around the den, the old-fashioned way. He sweeps her across the floor. *"You made me love you!"* he croons.

He looks into her face and she's grinning. A real smile.

It occurs to him then, with a stab of guilt. Is this all he ever had to do? Could it always have been this easy?

He twirls her around under his arm, still holding on to her hand. Still singing to her. *"You made me love you. . . ."*

Lilly laughs out loud. She is a different woman today. Even if it couldn't have been this easy with her in the past, perhaps it can be now. Perhaps this is enough for both of them.

Jessie

"Don't touch the flowers, Levi. They have bugs."

She hands him one of the white folding chairs. "This goes near the *huppa*. Ask Zadie where he wants it."

It's eleven thirty. She figures people will start arriving by four. Rabbi Frieder and the violinists are supposed to be here at three thirty. She peeks into the living room, where Milton is setting up the chairs for the ceremony. The caterer and her helpers are already in the basement, preparing the appetizers. All Jessie has left to do is set up the floral arrangements around the house.

Her house is nothing fancy, just a big, cozy log cabin for the weekends. But she put the down payment on it by herself—paid for with her share of what they got for their house in the city. Allan used his half of the money to buy one of those arty lofts in the Merchandise Building—of all places. She almost passed out when he told her.

But Allan's happy. He's got a new girlfriend and a new car. She's grateful that he didn't hold a grudge for too long. They're on fairly amicable terms, except when it comes to setting rules for the children. Every second Friday when he comes to get them, she hands him a list of what meals they should eat, what TV shows they can watch, what time they need to go to bed, and which activities she's scheduled for them—but it's no use. One time she saw him crumple up her list as soon as he got to the elevator—she was spying on them as they went down the hall—and they were all laughing as he chucked it into the ashtray. She was furious. He lets them run wild. They eat all kinds of shit and stay up late watching God knows what on TV, so that by the time he delivers them to her on Sunday night, they're whiny and obnoxious and have stomachaches.

But that's part and parcel of being divorced, which Allan keeps reminding her. She can handle them spending time with Heather, the girlfriend, but what's tougher is having them out of her grasp, beyond her reach. And yet being out of the marriage is the best thing that's ever happened to her. She rents a three-bedroom apartment in Leaside with a concierge guarding the front door so she never has to worry about break-ins. And she has this house in Newcastle to escape to when the urge moves her. She loves it here. The view is phenomenal. It's right on the cliff, with two acres of land and the beach down below.

"Mrs. Jaffe?"

Jessie turns around. Treasure is standing in the kitchen, holding Ilana's hand.

"How was your nap?" Jessie asks her daughter.

"When do I walk down the aisle?" Ilana thinks today is all about her, that *she's* the star.

"After your bath," Jessie promises. "Treasure's going to take you right now."

Treasure nods and takes Ilana upstairs. At first, Jessie was terrified of entrusting the kids to a nanny, but she knew if she left Allan, a nanny would be nonnegotiable. So far, Treasure's been a savior.

Jessie goes back to her floral arrangements. She's keeping it simple. Roses and baby's breath and Queen Anne's lace in

Spode milk pitchers. When she offered to hold the wedding at her house, everyone was thrilled. Her only mandate was to keep it simple—casual dress, a couple of violinists, a fire in the fireplace, and a *huppa* in the living room, which overlooks the cliff and Lake Ontario. No more than fifty people. Lilly was relieved to relinquish all the planning. She just wasn't up to it; couldn't muster her old energy.

"One of the chairs is busted," Milton says, coming into the kitchen. "I need a screwdriver."

"Allan's old toolbox is in the basement," she says.

"What time are the girls supposed to be back?"

"They had their appointments at nine, so I figure two hours at the salon and then an hour to get up here."

"What about *your* hair?" Milton asks her, coming up to her and kissing her face. "Don't you want one of those fancy pompadours like the other girls?"

"I've got a wedding to organize," she says. "Who else is going to tell the caterers what to do?"

Milton smiles. "You're just like your mother," he says fondly. "You know that, right?"

"It's what everyone keeps telling me."

And although she's not quite thrilled with the comparison, she's somewhat resigned to it.

When she's finished the last arrangement, she does a quick tour of the house to make sure everything's neat and in place. Naturally, it has to be perfect. She's got candles burning in all the rooms and brand-new linens on the beds. She did everything in whites and pastels, with soft flowers and ruffles and sheers in the windows to expose the view from every possible angle. There are French soaps in all the bathrooms and, as far as she can tell, nothing has been overlooked. Hopefully it will snow later, which would create the perfect mood.

Jessie Jaffe is thirty years old. She is a CEO, a mother of two, divorced. She owns a log house in the country. She hasn't been with a man since she left Allan. She doesn't date. (She's too afraid of AIDS.) She had her infamous "meltdown" last spring, but she's climbing back slowly. She has a therapist who is trying to cure her fears and phobias with a new miracle treatment out of California called Thought-Field Therapy. It isn't working.

But she's still hopeful.

Estelle

*E*stelle steps into the motel room and dumps her purse on the floral bedspread. She looks at herself in the mirror and is mortified. Her hair seems to have expanded since she left the salon. She looks like Wilma Flintstone.

She turns on the TV, lights a smoke, and flops down on the bed. Peace, at last. Spending the entire morning at the hairdresser with her mother, grandmother, and sister was a sufficient dose of bonding to last her another year. All she could think about was escaping to her room at the HoJo's for a precious hour of alone-time before the wedding.

These days she's more at peace with the fact that she can love her family from a distance. It's just easier to be herself far away, rather than be who they want her to be up close. They want too much from her; they always did. They want her to look a certain way, want her to fit, want her to find someone. More than anything, they want her to be married, settled. Her singleness is like an unfinished chapter in a book they want to put away on a shelf. They don't care how it ends; they just want to be able to say they've read it.

It's not like Estelle doesn't want to oblige, but she's not willing to grasp at some random, suitable man just to appease them. She almost made that mistake with Josh and it ended in disaster. He didn't take the breakup well, especially because it was his second time getting dumped by someone he intended to marry. "Not again," he muttered, when she started to tell him. He seemed more indignant about his poor record than upset about losing her.

It was the night of the *Ground Strokes* premiere. She stumbled in at four in the morning, plastered. She wanted to tell him right then and there, before she lost her nerve. So she woke him up.

"How was it, Beany?" he asked sleepily.

"We have to talk."

He rolled over and sighed. He knew it was coming.

"I can't move back to Toronto," she told him.

"But what about your job at MuchMusic?"

"It's not the job I want. It's the job you want me to have."

"Let's talk in the morning. We'll work it out."

"No."

He turned on the light then. His hair was sticking out on top and his breath had sleep smell. Hers wasn't much better. Booze and cigarettes.

"You're just caught up in tonight," he said. "The premiere and the party. I thought this would happen."

"I can't leave all this. I had the greatest time tonight. . . ."

"It'll turn sour. I guarantee it. It always does in this place."

"I don't think you can talk me out of it, Josh."

"All right. We'll compromise, then. A few months here, a few months in Toronto. We can spend winters in L.A. I suppose I could live with that."

"No."

"No?"

"I left Toronto for a reason. For a lot of reasons. It's not where I want to be. I belong here."

"What about your mother?"

"Don't use Lilly. I can't make this decision based on her."

"Then what about *me?*" he whines.

She didn't know what to say. She hadn't thought about what she'd do if he agreed to stay in L.A. with her.

"Hello?" he said. "Remember me?"

"You should have been there with me tonight."

"You know I hate that scene."

"I know. Exactly. I'm not saying you should have been there out of obligation, but I kept wishing it was something we shared."

"Lots of couples have different interests."

"You've never seen *Sense and Sensibility.*"

"And you haven't *read* it!"

"Exactly!" she cries triumphantly.

"I'll rent the movie, for fuck's sake."

"We're just not . . . I'm not . . ."

That's when he said it. "Not again."

"We're in different worlds," she went on. "And that can be okay. Two people can bring something different to a relationship and it can still work. I know that. But . . ."

"But?"

She lowered her eyes. How could she tell him she wasn't passionate about him or about his interests and aspirations? Or that she thought his ambitions were too small? Or that he never made her laugh out loud? "Our worlds are just too far apart," she murmured.

"You're just realizing this now?" he lashed out. "Why did you let it get this far if you've been having doubts?"

"You've been so good for me—"

"Good for you? I'm not a vitamin!"

"You've loved me like no one else ever has. And my family was so proud of me."

"For Chrissake, Estelle. Are you that needy?"

She nodded miserably. She just wanted to lie down and go to sleep. Alone. "I'd been on this mission to find a husband for so long," she confessed. "When you proposed, it was just like, 'Here's your one shot, Estelle. Better grab it 'cause it may never happen again.' That's what it felt like."

"So you used me."

"I wanted it to work so badly. I wanted your love to be enough, believe me. I've been trying to convince myself for so long. . . ."

"Thanks," he sneered.

"I do love you," she offered as consolation. But she loved him the way you love a cousin. Or the son of your father's best friend. Wasn't she entitled to more?

He got out of bed then and went into the living room. She left him alone. She ended up passing out, and when she woke up in the morning, he was gone. A few days later, she found out from Michael Shulman that he was in Bali. She hasn't heard from him since.

She still misses him sometimes. She misses the humble comforts of a relationship—snuggling, ordering in, enjoying built-in companionship. But she knows she was marrying him to satisfy her parents, to impress her sisters, to show the world she could get a damn husband if she wanted one. She's wise enough to know now that being alone and independent ranks higher on the happiness scale than settling. If nothing else, she learned that from Jessie. Josh came along when she was feeling low and worthless and he picked her up, nursed her ego, and restored some damaged part of her. She will always be grateful to him for that. But she couldn't face a lifetime of trying to mold him, or of being molded.

Estelle called Lilly and told her the news over the phone. She was too chickenshit to do it in person. "Sit down and take a deep breath," she said.

"What've you done?" Lilly asked wearily.

"It's about the wedding."

"Oh, Estelle. You didn't! Did you and Josh elope?"

"Josh is gone."

"Gone? He left you? I warned you, he's a drifter."

"I'm the one who ended it."

Silence.

"Muh?"

"*You* ended it?"

"I'm sorry."

"But why, Estelle? Why?"

"He wasn't the one."

Lilly was quiet for a long time. Finally, she said, "We've left deposits, you know. For the hotel and the caterer and the photographer. And the rabbi's been booked for months."

"I'll pay you back."

"That's not what I mean," Lilly said, retracting. "It's just that it went so far. You let it go so far."

"I didn't want to cause a scandal or break your heart. . . ."

"It's his heart you should be worried about, Estelle. I only want you to be happy."

"I am happy. I can be happy without . . ."

She didn't bother finishing. She knew she wouldn't convince Lilly, not then. Lilly will always believe a woman needs a man for stability, for status.

"If it's what you want," Lilly said, relinquishing.

Her voice was full of bravado. Or maybe she really didn't mind. She had other priorities. Her fingers were still paralyzed; her blood was too thin. She just wasn't the same person who once would have thrown a tantrum over this kind of bombshell. She no longer had it in her to lay a heavy guilt trip.

"I'm sorry, Muh."

"Stop apologizing to me," Lilly said. "I'm fine. I'm just grateful I'm alive to be having this conversation."

Estelle was quiet. She felt terrible. And she knew there would be future conversations about it with her father and Gramma Dorothy and Jessie. Back in Toronto, there would be plenty of hell to pay. But right then, she had no regrets. She was comfortable on the less conventional road. It's where she's always been most herself.

Erica

*T*hey're all looking at her with dewy eyes and frozen, wistful smiles. Lilly, Jessie, Estelle, her grandmother. So this is what it feels like, she thinks. And she isn't sure if what feels so good right now is having their validation, or knowing for the first time in her life that she's made the right choice. Lilly blows her nose. They're up in Jessie's room, just about ready to start now. All the guests are here, milling around downstairs. The caterers are ready with the champagne and hors d'oeuvres. The violinists are warming up. They're going to play "La Vie en Rose" for the procession, and then "Here Comes the Bride" for Erica's entrance.

"My baby . . ." Lilly sobs. "So beautiful . . . Look at all my beautiful girls. . . ."

Jessie and Estelle are wearing pale pink slip dresses with spaghetti straps. Erica let them choose. It was more like she let them battle it out. Estelle was hoping for red or black; Jessie was adamant about everything being pastels. Estelle finally agreed when they found the slip dresses in Soho, on a weekend when they were out visiting Erica. Lilly is also in pink—a pink silk camisole and short blazer with a long black skirt slit up the leg. She looks perfect. No one would ever know she'd had the stroke—no one except the people who remember the old Lilly.

Erica blinks back tears. The fact that Lilly is here at all

to witness this wedding, and that her own baby is swoosh-
ing around in her belly—these wonders are almost too
much to bear. She knows when she sees Mitchell standing
under the *huppa,* she will not be able to keep her emotions
in check.

She still thinks about Paul once in a while. The way they
ended was more of a severing than a gentle, mutual parting.
There was no comforting feeling that the relationship had
run its natural course. And yet technically it wasn't Erica
who instigated the breakup. It was him. She got back to his
apartment that day, fully ready to tell him she was moving
out, and found him sobbing on the couch. Immediately she
went to him. She was having second thoughts. Depending
on what he might have said, she could have been persuaded
to stay.

"What is it?" she asked him. "What's the matter?" She
was stroking his hair. He was practically wailing.

"I can't do it!" he cried. "I just can't do it!"

"What?"

He was shaking his head despairingly. "I don't want to be
a father, Erica. I keep telling myself it won't be so bad . . .
that maybe I'll learn to love it . . . but I don't want to have to
learn to love it. I don't want it."

He dropped his head on her lap and cried some more. She
stopped caressing his head. Suddenly she was stiff and angry.

"Erica, I'm so sorry," he pleaded. "I know you'll probably
never forgive me. And I'll support you both. There's no question about that. This isn't about financial responsibility. I'm
just a coward. You know, when you moved in here I just
thought we would go along until you wanted more and . . .
God, that sounds awful. . . ."

She pushed his head off her lap and stood up.

"I keep having this nightmare," he went on, "where I'm chasing my father down the street, running after him and screaming for him to come back. That's how he left us, you know. I don't know if I ever told you that—"

"No, but thanks for telling me now," she said, and she went into the bedroom and started packing.

At first she was angry with him for being such a schmuck, and angry with herself for having wasted all that time on such a schmuck, but when that finally wore off, once she was settled in at Tiala's, she began to feel relief. In the end, all she'd had to do was make the choice to leave him—which she had done, standing on the street with Mitchell that day. Once she'd decided, God backed her up, wouldn't let her renege. Because Paul was the one to end it, she couldn't second-guess herself; she couldn't change her mind or doubt herself the way she usually did. She would never have the burden of her own indecision.

It still felt like something had been severed. How do you tell when love is over? Is it when you stop thinking about the person entirely? When you stop reminiscing? That may never happen. She is willing to concede that Paul may have been the first real romance of her life—but what is a romance anyway? A gauzy, fleeting thing without substance, without longevity. A marriage can be ignited by romance, but not sustained by it.

Mitchell is like wrapping herself up in something worn-in and familiar. And yet he is constantly surprising her. It turns out he has a strong, melodic voice and wants to go back to school to become a cantor. He's been a Big Brother to a Honduran boy from the Bronx for the past five years (and what she loves most about that is, he never told her, not even to woo or impress her while they were first dating). Sure he's moody when his business isn't going well, or when the Mets lose. But what matters is, he gets her. He accepts everything about her. She is allowed to go to Starbucks and watch *Sex and the City* and read Oprah's magazine; she is never embarrassed about what interests her anymore. She doesn't have to persuade, pretend, cajole, or change for him. They are like-minded, in sync. She knows now that love should be simple. Not boring or easy, but simple. And that solidity and trust have more long-term value than awe.

"Can I have a moment with Erica?" Dorothy asks now.

Everyone shuffles out of the room, leaving Erica alone with her grandmother. They stand one behind the other, facing the mirror. Erica thinks she looks enormous. She thinks it will be amusing when she waddles down the aisle, but she doesn't care. This is how she wanted it. Once she made her decision, there was no point waiting.

Her dress is white crepe silk with an Empire waist so as to elegantly conceal her belly. Very simple. Lilly and Milton bought it for her. She'd wanted something off the rack, something casual and comfortable. But Lilly just had to see one of her girls get married in Vera Wang. It was her one and only holdout, even if it is Vera Wang Maternity.

"Such a beauty," Dorothy says to her. "It's all my genes, you know."

"Ah, for *that* you want credit!"

"I want credit for everything about you. I'm so proud of you."

Erica turns to face her grandmother, sheepishly touching her round belly. "You are?"

"You have to ask?"

The fact is, she's carrying a baby whose natural father is

living in New York. She's marrying another man altogether. And there's still the writing career that never panned out. It's hardly a perfect life so far.

"I know we're hard on you girls," Dorothy concedes. "But here's a little secret: it's only because we want you to be happy. We don't *tell* you that, mind you, but really it's all we want. And don't think we don't know it when you're not."

"So that's it?" Erica says suspiciously. "That's *all* you want for us?"

Dorothy shrugs. "It's better for us if you're happy with a successful Jewish man. There are some minimum requirements, of course."

"We're starting!" someone yells from downstairs. "It's time!"

Erica can hear the violins starting up.

Dorothy kisses her on the forehead and whispers, "You chose the right one."

*W*hen she gets downstairs, her whole family is huddled in the kitchen, standing by the archway that opens into the living room. Mitchell is already walking down the aisle between the chairs. Her family is quiet as they wait their turn before following him. First her parents, then Jessie and the best man, then Estelle and Tiala and the groomsmen, and finally Ilana with her bouquet of flowers.

Erica stands on her tiptoes and jostles to have a better look. She can see Mitchell, already reaching the *huppa,* with his parents keeping stride beside him. She watches as they leave him alone there and move to their seats. She feels calmer and more certain than she imagined she would. He turns slightly, searching for her in the distance. His hair is long again—the Scott Baio hair she first fell in love with. She can see his face now, beaming and excited. Some of the guests are waving at him, but he has seen her, and his eyes are fixed on her, as hers are on him.

Erica takes her first step toward him, toward all that awaits, and smiles to herself. *Thank you, God.*

Acknowledgments

I would like to thank my number one fans, Miguel, Marsheh, and Jack, for their valuable feedback and their unwavering support. Thank you to my wonderful agent, Beverley Slopen, and to my editor, Susan Folkins. Special thanks to Eliza Clark, whose suggestions and encouragement helped shape and bring this story to life. Thanks also to Marlene and to my "sisters," Sue and Rena. And finally, thank you to H.P. and Jessie Faith for bringing more joy into my life than I ever could have imagined.

You Made Me Love You is **Joanna Goodman**'s second novel. Her debut novel, *Belle of the Bayou,* was published in 1998 and received wide critical acclaim. That same year, her work was excerpted in Elisabeth Harvor's fiction anthology *A Room at the Heart of Things*. Joanna Goodman's stories have also appeared in *The Fiddlehead,* the *Ottawa Citizen, B & A Fiction, Event, The New Quarterly,* and *White Wall Review*. She lives in Toronto and is at work on a third novel.

you made me love you

joanna goodman

This Conversation Guide is intended to enrich the
individual reading experience, as well as encourage us
to explore these topics together—because books,
and life, are meant for sharing.

A CONVERSATION WITH JOANNA GOODMAN

Q. What inspired you to write this novel? How much of it came from your own family, love, and career experiences?

A. The premise for *You Made Me Love You*, which is essentially a story about three close-knit but very different sisters, was inspired by my own relationship with my two cousins, whom I grew up with. Although I'm an only child, my cousins were like sisters to me, and I wanted to explore that "sibling" dynamic in the novel. My other main inspiration was to write a laugh-out-loud funny book, and the most hilarious people I know are the members of my family. In fact, all the characters in the novel are exaggerated conglomerations of the people I know and love—their quirks and foibles, their careers and love relationships.

Q. The Zarr sisters have a complex relationship with their hometown of Toronto. Estelle and Erica are eager to escape the city for the States, while Jessie reluctantly builds a family there out of a sense of obligation. Why did you choose Toronto as the novel's main backdrop, and what does the city mean to you personally?

A. I chose Toronto as the primary setting for the novel because it's been my hometown for a decade and I'm comfortable using it as the characters' "home base." But because I wasn't born here and because I still have a special fondness for Montreal, the city where I was born and raised, I suppose I feel a certain ambiguity toward Toronto, much the way Erica and Estelle feel.

Q. Your male characters in the novel—Paul, Skieth, Josh, Allan, Milton, Mitchell, and Peri—are colorful and realistic. Which is your favorite, and what or who inspired him?

A. My favorite male character is Paul. He is definitely the most fictional character in the novel—not at all based on anyone I know. He is more of a tribute to all the pretentious, self-centered academics I have come across over the years.

Q. You Made Me Love You *has a unique voice, since it's told from several different perspectives in the present tense. Why did you decide to write the novel this way?*

A. It was definitely an experiment, but I liked the format and style right away. I felt it brought each of the main characters to life in a very real way, allowing the readers to get inside their heads, to *know* them, to experience life as they do. It also turned out to be an effective device for juxtaposing the three sisters in a more immediate and intimate way than a third-person narrative could have done. In retrospect, it also allowed *me,* during the writing process, to really get to know and understand them.

Q. The question of finding one's identity is an important theme in You Made Me Love You, *for both generations of Zarrs. Why did you decide to incorporate the stories of Milton, Lilly, and Dorothy into the novel?*

A. I incorporated Lilly, Milton and Dorothy into the novel because I wanted to give the Zarr sisters a context and a foundation. I think the novel is richer and more textured for their being in it. Also, it was very important for me to reflect how this theme of finding one's identity—either making the wrong choices to please others, or following one's own heart—is not generation specific. For the Zarrs, it is a legacy. Dorothy is an example of a woman who made her own choices and became a poet. Lilly on the other hand gave up her career and her passion to do the "right" thing and raise a family. Even Milton married the wrong woman. The Zarr sisters are born into that dynamic and, consequently, their lives are influenced by the decisions their parents made long ago.

Q. The title and the Judy Garland song that inspires it provide particularly poignant moments in the novel where characters connect with each other. What is the main senti- ment .behind the song, and how do these characters embody that feeling?

A. The song "You Made Me Love You" has so many relevant meanings in the book. The main sentiment behind it is how people can almost inadvertently come to love other people, as opposed to that romantic concept of love at first sight. The title of the song implies that love is something that can develop slowly over time, or creep up on us when we least expect it. For instance, Milton is obsessed with Gladys throughout his marriage, but what he comes to realize at the end of the book, after almost losing Lilly, is that he truly loves Lilly. Over the years, she has "made him love her."

The song had another meaning for the characters, as well, and that is that love is something that can be manipulated. Estelle manipulates Josh into loving her by posing as someone she is not. Paul manipulates Erica into loving him by being a mentor and father figure. Erica manipulates Mitchell into loving her by pretending to be available. I just loved the malleability of that song title and the way it applied to so many themes in the novel.

Q. Jessie, Estelle, and Erica all find themselves in relationships that smother their true selves, their true desires. Why did you decide to put all the sisters in such situations?

A. I don't think I originally set out to put the sisters into such thematically similar situations, but their stories just seemed to evolve that way. What I was attempting to do was explore the whole idea of approval seeking. I think a lot of us make our major life choices based on how we can attain the elusive approval of our parents or society or both. I also think our craving for approval can often override our sincerest desires and personal integrity, and that's exactly what happens to Jessie, Estelle, and Erica.

Q. Dorothy is the strongest character in the novel and the wisest. Can you describe how she came into being, and is she based on anyone you know in real life?

A. Dorothy is based on my grandmother Dorothy. Although my grandmother was not a poet, she was very independent and practical. (And she did smoke Matinee cigarettes in the tub!)

Q. Ethnic and religious identity play a strong role in the novel, even though the Zarrs are secular Jews. Can you elaborate on this and why you chose to tackle this subject?

A. One of my first ideas for Erica's character was for her to be a rabbinical student. In fact, a lot of the novel was written this way before I realized she had become a very serious character and I was getting away from my original vision of a laugh-out-loud novel. The overall feeling of the book was getting quite heavy, so I changed gears. However, I really liked the spiritual component she brought to the book, so I decided to keep that theme and explore Erica's spirituality from a different perspective.

Q. How did you become a novelist and are you working on another book now?

A. I became a novelist when I was four years old and my mother gave me some lined paper and a pencil and I wrote my first story about a puppy and a kitten. I've been writing ever since! I've just finished my third novel, which is scheduled for spring 2007 release in Canada.

QUESTIONS
FOR DISCUSSION

1. Jessie, Estelle, and Erica all feel that Lilly has unrealistic expectations and harsh criticism for their lifestyles, and each sister is jealous of the attention Lilly gives her siblings. Do you have similar feelings about your own parents? What has helped you resolve or understand them?

2. Each sister finds herself in a relationship that smothers or interferes with her true desires. Have you had similar relationships? How did you get out of them or change them so that you could find yourself?

3. Mitch tells Erica, "You made me love you." What does this mean? Do you agree? Have you ever set out to make someone love you?

4. Even though Josh seems like the perfect guy for Estelle, she ultimately decides not to marry him. What is the exact problem with Josh, and what does Peri have that Josh doesn't?

5. Discuss the role religion plays in the novel. Why is Erica so drawn to Mitch and Miriam's family and their

adherence to Jewish customs? Does her newfound spirituality have anything to do with her decision to leave Paul? How does her religion provide her with a stronger sense of self, and why don't Estelle and Jessie share her conversion?

6. Do you think that Milton's longtime affair with Gladys has an effect on the Zarr sisters' relationships with men? Which sister does the affair affect the most and why?

7. How do Milton and Lilly resolve their conflict about Gladys? Why does their relationship remain intact after Milton's affair, Gladys' death, and Lilly's stroke? Do you think they will be happy from now on?

8. Jessie is an obsessive-compulsive perfectionist with serious doubts about her desire to be a wife and mother. Why do you think she's so fixated on perfection, and why aren't Erica or Estelle like her in that way? Why do you think the imperfect womanizer Skieth sparks a transformation in Jessie? Do you know people who are perfectionists like her?

9. Who's your favorite character in the book? Your least favorite? Why do you like or dislike them?